FORGED

VALKYRIE ALLEGIANCE
BOOKS 1-3

USA TODAY BESTSELLING AUTHOR

A.J. FLOWERS

BOOK 1: VALKYRIE LANDING

FAILURE

*A*lone. I couldn't remember the last time I'd truly been alone. My mother's spaceship pressed in all around me with its merciless metal plates and groaning sighs as it orbited Muspelheim, the volcanic planet I called home.

One single diamond window gave me one last view of the red world as I awaited the biggest moment of my life. This little chamber seemed to suffocate me, the view outside a final goodbye to all of my sisters and the warmth of our world. My love for them gave me fresh resolve. I couldn't let them down.

I was a Valkyrie. Fire lived in my veins and sent the metallic sheen of my prison glowing red as my emotions spun out of control.

I wasn't supposed to have these emotions, but I did. The way my mother set me apart from the rest, I still hadn't decided if I was special or if I was flawed. My speckled wings brushed my shoulders and I pushed them back, making sure the tips didn't touch the ground out of reflex. A trusty spear at my right hand kept me grounded and I shamelessly leaned on it as my red world became a retreating dot. Dizziness swept over me. This was really happening.

The ship groaned, then rumbled and gave a high pitched trill as it burned the power of its core to send me to a new world where I'd prove the truth about myself.

For the first time, an icy chill swept over my bones and threatened to quench the flames in my heart. My wings turned to ash and trailed down my back. I held onto my spear as pain ripped a scream from my throat. My Immortal form burned away and delicate, mortal flesh took its place.

I couldn't keep my Valkyrie body where I was going.

It was time to reap my first soul.

My transition from Valkyrie to human was a lonely one, but when I woke, I had a new life, a new family, and new friends.

A new home.

Sam, my Valkyrie mentor and older sister, gave me a warm smile. "About time you snapped out of it. I was wondering if I was going to have to knock some sense into you."

I'd been staring out of the window, absorbing my new memories of a house on a cul-de-sac in Mattsfield Tennessee. This was where I'd grown up—or at least that's what everyone would believe. Fake memories spilled into me, part of Grimhildr's programming to help me immerse myself into the human world.

"When do I get to meet him?" I asked.

Sam scoffed behind me. I turned to find her perched on a chair, one foot on a stool as she painted her nails. For a moment, I remembered her as a Valkyrie and the visage of ebony wings flashed. The memory faded, clamped down by Grimhildr's programming to show me Sam, the nineteen-year-old human. She'd retained her lengthy beauty with long, muscular legs and a sense of effortless grace that would make all the girls at Mattsfield High envious. According to them, she'd just graduated and now was saving for college—meanwhile stealing all of their boyfriends. She blew on the fresh paint. "I'm glad you're eager, but you're not ready to meet him yet." She glanced at me, her green eyes betraying the embers that slept within. "You need to know what you're looking for, first. And I can't tell you. It doesn't work that way."

I frowned. Reaping my first soul was going to be difficult if I didn't even know who he was, but this was a special mission. Grimhildr's programming didn't subdue the memories that told me why I was here and what I was fighting for. Our world was in danger. A darkness clouded the skies of Muspelheim and stretched icy fingers throughout the universe. For the first time, I couldn't feel its oppressive weight. This planet hadn't endured the touch of Ragnarök... yet.

"You're going to have to sense him," Sam instructed as she fitted her toes into a foamy device designed to keep them separated. "This isn't going to be easy. Most Valkyrie have watched their charges for a couple of lifetimes before the reaping."

I knew this was a special case. We didn't have time for

me to sit around for fifty years watching a powerful soul we needed be fed on by the Norn. We needed to get powerful souls like that to ally with us, come to the Einherjar and join the fight against the dark armies that threatened to rain down chaos and death on my homeworld at any moment.

I straightened my spine, determined to make my mother proud. "There are two tasks in reaping a soul. One: Trust. Two: Secrets." I recited the simple instructions. I needed to find my charge, get him to trust me utterly and completely, uncover any dark secrets he'd been hiding, and then I could bring him to the Einherjar. Once he knew what we were up against, and what I was saving him from, he'd come with me. He'd have to.

Sam nodded in approval. "Great." She thrust the nail polish at me. "Now, start painting. Getting a man to trust you starts with looking our best."

I rolled my eyes but accepted the bottle and curled onto the floor. I took off my socks and examined my toes. The newly pink nails didn't look like they needed color, but I didn't question my sister. I unscrewed the top and carefully layered the paint across my nails.

THE POOL

Sam wouldn't tell me where we were going, but I was too mesmerized by my first trip outside to bug her about it.

Wind. Trees. Birds chirping and a yellow sun streaming warmth down as if reminding me that Muspelheim could live anywhere, even here.

Sam directed my attention to the driveway and my eyes went wide. She thrust me into a brand new Porsche and off we went.

Oh yeah, Valkyries make their appearance in style.

I ran my fingers over the expensive leather interior. Sam smiled. "Like it? I picked it out myself."

I nodded. "It's amazing." I gave her a raised brow. "Did Freya really give us such a high budget?"

Allies on Earth helped Valkyries settle into their temporary lives. They didn't want the Norn getting any more powerful than they already were. Brief flashes of the dark, horrendous things that were born of suffering made me shiver. It wasn't a small task, the darkness we fought against. Freya spared no expense in making our immersion into the human world comfortable and easy. Yet... I didn't remember other Valkyries getting a Porsche.

Sam bit her lip before replying. "Well, she gave us a budget, but she didn't really say how I had to allocate it. My memories came with me working at the local Diner, so that'll keep me busy while you're doing *your* job." She grinned. "It's worth it though, no?"

I gaped at her. "You spent *all* our money? As in, the budget for all of our food for the next couple of months? What're we going to eat?"

She laughed and pressed on the gas. The car smoothly accelerated and we flew down the highway. Sam was lucky she still had some of her powers that sensed other humans, or one of the local cops would have given us a ticket that would have made us go bankrupt. "I said I work at a Diner, all right? We have plenty to eat. Just stop by after school."

I groaned and eased into my seat. I grudgingly had to admit that it was pretty comfortable, but from my memories, the Diner food wasn't that great.

Trees sped by in a blur of green as I leaned against the door panel and marveled how everything felt so familiar... yet so different. Two lives battled in my head, and even though I was supposed to embrace my human life right now, I held onto my Valkyrie side with determination. I needed the reassurance to know why I was doing this.

The other Valkyries didn't have to struggle with emotion like I did. One glance at Sam showed me that she was quite content to help me track someone down to rip their soul out of their body. She flipped on the radio and drummed her fingers to the tune, already adjusted to her role as Sam the human who works at a Diner and has to take care of her baby sister.

My stomach churned with remorse, because no matter what I'd been raised to believe, I knew it was wrong to do what I needed to do. Sam sure didn't seem like she felt any remorse, and I didn't know if it was because she physically couldn't, or if because I was being overly sensitive and there wasn't anything to feel remorse about.

Now that I finally had my mentor alone, perhaps she'd teach me the answers to questions that always got brushed off during my training on Muspelheim. "You'll find out later. Focus on the present," had always been the response.

I bit my lip. "So, this soul I'm supposed to reap," I began and Sam tilted her head towards me, "what happens if I never find him? His soul, I mean."

Sam sighed, as if the question was irrelevant. "I suppose you do need to know the background. You know about the Norn, right?"

I nodded. How could I not know about my nightly nightmarish bedtime story? "Be a good girl, or you'll turn into a Norn." Then Freya had amplified the warning with wisps of shadow trailing around her fingers.

That significance hadn't been lost on me, even at a young age. We were all capable of darkness. Emotion seemed to be the culprit, which was probably why so many Valkyries opted to bury their emotions completely. I didn't seem capable of just turning them off like a switch. My emotions often controlled me and not the other way around.

"The Norn are Valkyries who have failed," I answered with the standard response. "They feed on suffering and torment through the souls locked into a contract of reincarnation."

"That's right," Sam said with approval. "Reincarnation is not a normal human trait. Souls come from Yggdrasil, the Tree of Life, and they must bring with them the joys and experiences of their life back to the tree once they're gone."

I'd never seen Yggdrasil, but it appeared in my dreams with its silver branches and crystalline fruit of souls that fell to the outer realms to give new life. It was beautiful.

Darkness wasn't from Yggdrasil. The Norn discovered it and then spread it like a plague. "Souls trapped by the Norn can't return to Yggdrasil," I said, for the first time coming to that horrifying realization. I blinked at Sam. "If I don't reap this soul, and it can't return to the Tree of Life, then what happens to it?" My heart sank, already knowing Sam's answer.

"The soul is destroyed," she said, her tone serious. "Souls are supposed to be Immortal, but the Norn pile suffering on it like bricks until it's crushed under the weight. It's absolute blasphemy."

The passion in Sam's voice surprised me. I'd never pegged her as a religious type, but when it came to Yggdrasil, most Valkyries spoke of it with a sense of awe.

"The Norn have disrupted a delicate balance, so it is our job to give that soul a new home. It can't return to Yggdrasil, so we'll give it the next best thing."

I nodded, understanding now why we had an artificial replica of Yggdrasil on Freya's spaceship, the Einherjar. It was the most beautiful ball of light that powered its core and I'd had the chance to see it once when Freya took me there to understand what I would be fighting for. The sensation there had been one of peace, and it made me feel better about what I was going to have to do.

I needed that fresh resolve, for my stomach dropped when I realized where we were. The trees parted to reveal stone pillars that signaled we'd arrived at Mattsfield High. There was a swim meet today and all of the students had come out to watch the school's hottest guys swimming shirtless.

Sam parked, and then narrowed her eyes when she saw Tyler wave. He'd been waiting for us.

Tyler. Oh my gods. How could I have forgotten Tyler?

A smile sprang across my face as I lurched out of the car and ran to him. Laughter bubbled up inside of me and he grinned as I slammed into him and wrapped my arms around his neck. "You're here!"

His low chuckle rumbled as he untangled me from him. I wasn't used to his human body, but he still had his mischievous grin. I'd know that smile anywhere. Tyler was my best friend and I never went anywhere without him. I just never imagined that he could follow me all the way to Earth.

He gave my hand an encouraging squeeze before stepping away. Sam got out of the car and propped her hands on her hips. Tyler gave her a salute. "Human bodyguard, on duty."

Sam rolled her eyes and then walked past us, fully expecting us to follow.

I fell into her shadow, feeling giddy with Tyler by my side. I pitched my voice low, not sure if Sam still had her Valkyrie hearing. "How did you get Freya to let you come here?" Sam's fingers twitched, and I grimaced.

Tyler slung a bag over his shoulder and flashed me that familiar, triumphant grin. "No one can resist my charm. Not even a goddess like your mother."

My eyes roamed his new body, taking in the similarities and differences. He still *felt* like Tyler, someone I could trust with my life and often had. Yet, now, a glimmer settled over him as if holding in the natural light of what he was... which wasn't human.

Unlike me, Tyler didn't seem to go through the trouble of shedding his Immortal skin and fitting into a new body. I didn't blame him. I flexed my fingers, my joints still aching from the transition. But that's how it had to be. I needed to be completely immersed in this life to get my new soul to trust me. If he sensed what I was, he'd think me a Norn... or worse, and then I'd doom him to a fate worse than death.

He grinned as he watched me appraise him. "Like the new bod, huh? Pretty sure most girls do." He lifted his shirt just far enough for me to see the sculpted abs fit for a Roman statue. In his natural form, he often covered himself with armor that he summoned naturally, Odin's gift to his warriors. It was rare that I saw anything more than his elbows.

A blush crept up my face and I forced my eyes to lock onto Sam's confident gait. Tyler might be my best friend, but I still had eyes. "Didn't need to see that," I complained, but my words were taut.

He openly laughed, the sound making me relax. This was the Tyler I knew, always cracking jokes and making me smile.

Cheers erupted and Sam glared at us over her shoulder.

Apparently, we hadn't been following fast enough. "Hurry up!" she hissed. "We're late!"

Tyler winked at me. "Your sister buys a Porsche and she still can't get here on time. Glad to see nothing's changed."

Sam flipped him off and then stalked her way down the steps to the pool.

Pungent chlorine hit me in the face like an invisible wall and I kept close to Tyler as we passed under the walkway and into a glossy white cemented area with a fenced-in pool. The stands writhed with high schoolers and their families. Everyone seemed so happy and cheered, ignoring our entrance as we found seats near the edge of the pool. Water splashed under my flip-flops as we settled and I grimaced as the slick cold migrated under my feet.

"I can see why no one wanted to sit here," I complained and Tyler slung an arm around my shoulders. The motion was so casual that I found myself relaxing and slipping into his embrace. I wanted to purr at the heat that emanated from his body. Even though he looked human on the surface, his appearance was just for show. My fingers slipped across the thin layer of his shirt and I could sense his true self like the comforting heat of the sun.

"Whoa, girl," he said, pitching his voice low. He wrapped his fingers around mine. "We're in the human's world now. I know you're just curious, but behavior like that is going to get you in trouble."

I blinked at him, not realizing I'd been so mesmerized by him. Tyler often had that effect, but this time it was different. He'd always been a light against the darkness that shadowed my heart and I would trust him with my life.

However, now that I was in a human body, I saw him differently.

Another blush crept up my face and I folded my hands neatly in my lap. "Sorry," I grumbled, and then turned my gaze to the pool. Valkyries were sensual creatures and it was encouraged to use our sexuality to bring our souls closer to us. It was just one of our many tools and now that I was here, my instincts were kicking in. "It's just the hormones," I said, trying to sound clinical, but and then gave him a snide glare. "You chose that body on purpose. You're a jerk."

Tyler leaned back, lacing his fingers behind his head, giving me a view of Sam completely ignoring us. Her face said "I'm on a mission" and none of Tyler's antics were going to distract her right now.

Trying to take her as an example, I did the same as a horn sounded. I made sure to pay attention to the swimmers as they got out of the pool to prepare for their first race.

That certainly was a bad idea.

It was as if the flames of Muspelheim gathered inside my stomach and curled until sweat broke out on my forehead. Water dripped from lean, muscular bodies and every movement had me wishing I could look anywhere else than the row of hunk-meat before me.

The girls in the stands hooted and cheered, seeming to have no problem feasting their eyes on the display.

"Get to your posts!" a teacher announced, and the crowd fell into a hushed silence.

I knew that one of those guys leaning and balancing on their fingers, ready to launch into the pool was a soul I was supposed to reap. A soul fit for a Valkyrie wouldn't be in the stands, watching. He'd be out there, fighting the weight of the Norn's curse any way he knew how.

The horn sounded again, and the swimmers glided into the pool, strong arms curling over the turbulent waves as they competed to reach the other side.

My skin tingled as my powers kicked in and I cursed under my breath.

Tyler must have felt it, for he wrapped his fingers around my wrist, trying to help me control the darkness. "What're you doing?" he hissed and his warmth traveled up my arm.

"It's the adrenaline," I shot back. I wasn't used to this body and the powers that threatened to control me were about to win that never-ending battle. Even Tyler's magic couldn't keep the darkness away for long.

I was a Frigg, a division of the Valkyrie who had control over time and space... or at least, that was what we were supposed to be able to do. My powers seemed to result in the jerky snaps of time that left me prisoner in moments that made my heart race. Once, I'd frozen time when Sam had stabbed me with a spear. That was not a fun moment to be trapped in.

The air shook as time threatened to collapse and I squeezed my eyes shut, trying to control it. The world itself seemed to tremble as a vibration ran through my bones and a sharp pain channeled up my spine. Heat sparked under my fingertips and...

Snap.

Too late.

Tyler couldn't follow me here, but Sam could. She launched to her feet and growled. "Val!"

I forced my eyes open and groaned. Water droplets hung in the air and swimmers froze mid-stroke in a race to the end of the pool. I turned, only to find the crowd turned into a ripple of frozen excitement.

"Sorry," I said, then peered into to the pool, looking for what could have caused my powers to ignite. My darkness only took over when there was something for it to react to. Suffering. Pain. While I'd been anxious, it shouldn't have been enough to trigger a full time-stop.

I peered into the slippery distortion of waves; I sensed the darkness somewhere there. I couldn't imagine what any of the swimmers could be experiencing to give me the kind of suffering that wrapped icy fingers around my heart, but then I spotted it.

I pointed at two silhouettes too far underwater to be involved in the race. "Sam," I whispered, then flinched as the airwaves distorted around my face. Sound couldn't travel when time was frozen and my innocent whisper would move when time unlatched from its lock like a spring let loose from a cannon. Good thing I hadn't shouted.

I pointed until Sam stepped to my side and leaned over the pool, water droplets brushing aside at her movements.

When time stilled, disturbing the space around us could prove dangerous. Sam was another Frigg, but she had power over her gifts and space distorted around her as she moved—unlike me. As I moved, time stretched and bowed with me, groaning as if in pain. Sam glanced at me and embers danced in her eyes as she worked to stay in the bubble of distorted space-time I'd accidentally created. She'd seen it too.

Now that the waters moved, shifted by my movements, I

could make out a boy at the bottom of the pool and another swimming to reach him. The rest of the swim team had their sights set on the end of the pool. I looked up and spotted the lifeguard who'd already noticed the submerged swimmer, teetering on the edge of her platform and muscles taut, ready to launch into the pool.

Sam grabbed my wrist and yanked me back to my seat. She pointed at me, the look on her face telling me to stay put while she fixed my mistake.

Shivering, I fought the pain as darkness threatened to close in around me. I couldn't stay in a space-time bubble for long and ice spidered over my skin.

I glanced at Tyler. He was still leaned back with a grin on his face. Space warped around him, his magic making him heavier than the typical human. I knew that he couldn't feel it, but I rested my hand on his thigh, drawing in the soft warmth of his magic to center myself.

Sam flicked her wrist, sending the time-bubble bursting and making my ears pop.

I winced as the world came back to life. Cheers sounded like a roar, sound enough to mask the disturbance of my stolen whisper. It wasn't lost on Tyler though and he jolted under my touch. His warm fingers wrapped around mine and his grin disappeared, replaced with a knowing frown. His fingers glowed, surging me with enough warmth to stop my teeth from chattering.

Tyler was my light against the darkness and my source of heat when my own embers failed. I hated the look in his eyes when he knew I'd lost myself in the tumult of my powers. Tyler would follow me anywhere, but when I used my powers as a Frigg, even he couldn't follow.

A different kind of horn sounded, one that shrieked with shrill panic. The cheers abruptly stopped and the swimmers paused until the once violent pool turned calm.

The lifeguard leapt from her post and when she splashed into the water, a teacher realized what was going on and shouted for everyone to get out of the pool.

The boys obeyed and splashed their way to the edges of the pool. We all peered over the edge and held our breaths until the lifeguard emerged, but she didn't have the boy. The swimmer I'd spotted had the lifeless form under a strong arm and he pulled him over the edge.

Pain thundered through my skull as Grimhildr's programming kicked in. Freya had several programmings running in the space-time net, and Grimhildr was one of the most frequently utilized. Powered by the Einherjar, she had memories that went back generations, enough so that she could recreate nearly any memory Freya deemed necessary.

It could also read memories, and Grimhildr showed me who this boy was through the eyes of those who knew him.

William Johnson, the best swimmer on the team and known for his heart-warming smile. The unconscious boy he dragged over the edge of the pool was Michael Donovan, one of his best friends throughout his childhood.

Will immediately began compressions while the lifeguard pinched Michael's nose, waiting for Will to pause before she pushed in a breath.

I couldn't help but rise from my seat. The entire place seemed to hold their breath, but I knew they couldn't see what I was seeing. A blue aura engulfed Michael and light billowed out of his body, his eyes, his nose, his fingertips, until the air rippled with power.

The power of death.

I swallowed hard, glancing at Sam to see what she'd do. I startled to realize that she wasn't watching the scene unfold, as if she'd already known what would happen. She was watching me and her eyes narrowed. I was supposed to be here for this.

I knew what Sam wanted me to learn, but it didn't make any of this easier. She wanted me to understand the difference between a Soul trapped in the Norn's curse... and a soul untouched by darkness.

Michael's soul unraveled as if it were a creature being born, struggling to break free of its confines. The flesh which bound it wouldn't hold it for long, not now that his heart had stopped beating. A soul was life and it needed flesh that was alive in turn.

As it detached from flesh and darkness from every scrap of suffering and pain it'd endured, it hovered, just for a moment, shedding the pain of this life as if it were just ash drifting to the ground. Then the last of its weight was gone, and it flung into the sky so fast that I couldn't follow the blue streak that disappeared from this world.

"A soul returns home," Tyler said low under his breath, sending a shiver up my spine as if he'd spoken an omen.

I should have been looking to the sky with Sam and Tyler, following the path that none of us could follow. As an Immortal, we could only dream of what reuniting Yggdrasil might be like.

Instead, I kept my eyes on the darkness left behind. It wasn't just the ash that dissolved into the ground, but a living tapestry of pain that lived in William. He leaned back on his heels with his palms up on his thighs in defeat. He looked to the sky, his chestnut eyes glassy with tears, and I recognized his expression. He thought that he'd failed. I found myself slipping away from Tyler and moving towards him, but I waited just out of reach as the weight of his suffering hit me like a wave.

When Will's eyes met mine, I knew that I'd found my soul.

The paramedics arrived in record time, but of course it was too late. What had been a happy event was now shrouded in a familiar darkness of grief. I knew grief too well. It was something I lived with every day. The darkness inside of me carried with it the burden of a thousand strangers. All Valkyries were born of the souls that allied with us, souls that carried the darkness of the Norn's curse to the end. We inherited that power, and while most of us could suppress it, or use it, I seemed to only be at its mercy.

I found myself drawn to the soul I knew I would eventually reap. He parted from the friends that had curled around him like a giant embrace. They left, awarding Will with some final pats on his back, encouraging him that he'd been brave.

Will smiled and thanked them, but I knew he didn't accept their praise, believing he'd been too slow. I could feel his suffering and self-hatred from here and I curled my fingers around my skirt to keep myself from reaching out to him and shaking him. He was so wrong. He hadn't even hesitated to save someone else. While the other swimmers were distracted with trying to win the race, he'd seen what was going on. He'd abandoned his place to dive to the bottom of the pool. He deserved so much more than the darkness weighing him down made him feel.

I swallowed before I forced my feet to move and put myself in front of him. I looked back over my shoulder to find Sam who gave me an encouraging nod. Tyler stood behind her, sticking two fingers up so that she had bunny ears. When I didn't laugh, he put up another finger and hooked the air so that she had horns. That one made me smile, especially when Sam turned and slapped him.

I turned back to Will, who now was paying attention to me. He frowned as if trying to place where he knew me from.

A blush crept up my face. I didn't know how long it would take for Grimhildr to feed Will enough memories for him to recognize me. Maybe it would help if I could attempt conversation, but I'd suddenly realized how... half-naked Will was.

My gaze drifted down over abs smooth, dried from the Saturday sun. Unlike Tyler, William had bronze skin from all his training in the pool. His muscles weren't thick like a warrior's, but graceful and lean in a way that made his strength beautiful.

He cleared his throat, having noticed that I was staring. "Hey, Val, everything okay?"

I shook my head. He remembered me, but everyone on Muspelheim called me Valerie, or Tyler's nickname for me "Aerie." I decided that I liked Will's version. "Uh, yeah," I said, finding my voice again. I rubbed the back of my neck. "I just wanted to say it was really brave what you did."

He gave me a warm smile, but I knew that it was for my benefit. Dark tendrils slithered across his skin and dove into his chest, feeding off of his suffering. I wanted to tell him not to beat himself up, but I couldn't—not yet. "Yeah," he said with a sigh. "Michael." His eyes darkened as if he was reliving the passing of his best friend's soul. "He's been hiding his condition for a while. I just... I never..."

"You did everything you could," I assured him.

It didn't seem like he believed me, but he nodded anyway. "Thanks, Val."

A paramedic came over and offered him a towel, even though he'd dried off long ago. Will accepted it and wrapped it around his shoulders. I watched him go with them, as well as the glimmer of black suffering that followed in his footsteps like an eerie shadow that shouldn't have existed on such a sunny day.

FIRST DAY

The death of a fellow classmate hit the student body hard. I didn't want to get out of Sam's Porsche as she pulled into a parking spot what seemed like a hundred miles from the school. "Think you could park any further away?"

She put the gear into park. "If you think I'm going to park this beauty anywhere *near* those kids and their reckless disregard for shapely steel, then you're insane."

I grinned. "Wow. I had no idea you were such a nerd." Before she could retort, I jumped out of the car and shouldered my backpack, which of course meant I had to face the high school and contemplate walking inside.

Black shadows practically slithered through the windows, like some sort of grimy beacon of suffering. I let out a breath. Who knew that a high school could be such a depressing place?

Sam bumped me on the shoulder. "Don't be afraid of it."

I gave her a raised brow. "You can see it?" I chewed on my bottom lip. "What is that stuff, anyway?"

Instead of answering me, she marched confidently towards the school, her leather boots leaving patterns in the wet asphalt. Even though she'd taken a human body, she still resembled one of the Valkyrie with her long legs and even the clothes she chose to wear. The close-fitted blouse tucked neatly into her jeans and long dangling earrings glimmered beneath her blonde curls. I hunched my shoulders, forcing myself to follow her and realized that I hadn't put nearly as much thought into my wardrobe. She wasn't the one making a first impression.

"It's what powers the Norn," she finally said, giving me the standard answer to explain the sticky blackness that was born of suffering.

"I know that." I tugged my backpack across my shoulders as we walked. "I mean, if all life came from Yggdrasil, then did it make the darkness too?" It didn't make any sense. If Yggdrasil was anything like the vision in my dreams, then it would be incapable of creating such sadness. The tree defied the laws of space-time and was as weightless as the souls it produced.

Sam glanced at me. "I don't think you're ready to learn what it is we fight against. But when you are ready, I'll be the first to tell you."

I sighed, hating that Sam's training seemed so much more... complete than mine. It felt like there were giant gaps in my training to prepare me for reaping my first soul. I guess that was just a challenge I was going to have to deal with. My people were under attack by those who used this darkness and found themselves corrupted by it. If I could save Will, then that was one less soul on their side... and one more on the side of life.

Clutching my necklace for strength, I forced myself to step into the clamoring halls filled with students. Even though grief and shock rippled through the air like a tangible wave, there was excitement in death. I recognized how each student reevaluated the precious limit to their lives, one of the strongest deterrents against the darkness. Mortals only had so much time and it was vital to bring those joys back to Yggdrasil. That innate drive sent everyone talking and hugging one another, trying to find their way back to happiness.

I felt Will before I saw him. His darkness blacked out the end of the hall as if I was about to walk into a nightmare. My palms went sweaty and I wiped them over my skirt.

Sam tugged me away from the darkness. "We'll stop by the office and make sure your classes are in order," she said, and relief swept over me. I didn't have to face Will... not yet.

After talking with a counselor and verifying that Grimhildr's programming was functioning correctly, I clutched the new card with my schedule. The teachers thought I'd just had a readjustment, but the truth was that I was a new student.

Sam gave me an encouraging pat on the back before heading out. "Where're you going?" I called after her.

She smirked over her shoulder. "The Diner. Meet me there after school!"

I narrowed my eyes. She was far too excited to work at the diner. It wasn't like Sam to enjoy any sort of work.

Shrugging off whatever Sam might be up to, I hurried to my first class. Swimming through the meandering blackness felt like I would drown. Even though girls smiled and waved as I walked by, they were the unhappiest of all.

I collapsed into my desk and wrapped my backpack to my front and clutched onto it as if it were a life jacket.

A warm touch on my shoulder made me jolt, then I realized that the darkness had parted. I looked up to find Tyler smiling down at me. "Hey," he said and settled into the desk next to mine. He inched closer so that he could keep our skin in contact. He slouched, stretching so that his leg hit up against mine.

My eyes fluttered closed as I greedily absorbed his sunlight and energy. It was a much needed reprieve against the weight of blackness that I certainly hadn't been prepared for.

Just when I was starting to feel somewhat normal, the bell rang and shortly after it felt as if my breath had cut off from my lungs. The temperature dropped until I shivered and I flung my eyes open, only to find Will in the doorway staring straight at me.

The moment only lasted for a second, but the hairs on my arms stood up as my Frigg powers threatened to activate.

Tyler slammed his hand on my desk, jolting me out of the mesmerizing connection between Valkyrie and soul. "Hey," he whispered, the word harsh, "get a grip. I can't pull you out of it like Sam can."

I bit my lip, because I knew he was right. I was better than this. My powers shouldn't control me.

The teacher—Mr. Jefferson—I remembered with a dizzying hum from Grimhildr's programming, began our daily lesson as his marker squeaked across the whiteboard.

I wasn't paying attention at all because I realized that someone had joined Will, also having pulled her desk closer as if to give him a light against the darkness.

Long, graceful legs that even rivaled a Valkyrie stretched out as she crossed her ankles and laughed, the sound a delightful chime against the hum of the classroom. She leaned forward and put a hand on Will's thigh. When he smiled and placed his hand on hers, unexpected jealousy ripped through me.

"Who is that?" I hissed. Grimhildr's programming was coming up short, because I had no idea who this was.

Tyler frowned as he appraised the girl. "I don't know, but it looks to me like you have competition."

I growled and set my textbook upright to block out my view of the sickening couple.

Since when did a soul, ripe with misery and in need of my help to be saved from this horrid life, have a girlfriend?

W hat felt like years later, I'd endured what passed as lunch on this world and wrapped up the final few classes of the day. Tyler had somehow managed to get in at least three of my classes, which saved me because Grimhildr's programming had placed me in every class with Will.

The human's relentless darkness made me feel like I could fall into the depths of sorrow with him and never come out. I never did work up the courage to speak with him; most of his classes he seemed too engrossed in whatever his girlfriend had to say, anyway. There was no way I was going to get him to open up to me if he already had a romantic interest. I had to get Sam to give me some instruction. Surely she'd know what to do.

Just when I thought the day was over, a classmate handed me a flyer. "Memorial in thirty minutes. Hope you can make it."

I clutched onto the printed paper and cringed.

When I found Sam out in the parking lot, I handed her the crumpled invitation. She smoothed it out over the steering wheel. "Well, of course you have to go," she said, winning a groan from me.

"But I'm going to suffocate if I have to endure any more of the darkness," I complained. Plus, Tyler had disappeared, leaving me to fend for myself. "I can't do this without Tyler."

She narrowed her eyes at me and shoved the flyer into my lap. "I told Tyler to get lost. You need to do this without his handicap." She revved the engine and the conversation seemed to be over.

I sighed and looked out over the parking lot with high schoolers getting into cars, mixed emotions painted across their faces. Guess we were all going to have to say goodbye.

PRETZELS AND PEANUTS

I was already exhausted, but I knew Sam was right. I had to go to the memorial service. Michael was loved by everyone and his sudden return to Yggdrasil wasn't a happy occasion to those left behind to fulfill their own missions. That meant that the focus was off me as much as it was going to be. Any new introduction came with the hum of Grimhildr's programming, and while most humans wouldn't realize what was happening, I knew I had to be careful around Will. This would be the best chance to catch Will off guard... assuming Sam could distract his girlfriend long enough.

The memorial was set up at Michael's favorite place. A field behind the pool where he'd died was where the kids had parties and where Michael had made half the cheerleading squad fall in love with him. It seemed an appropriate place to have one last party and say goodbye.

Watching Will from my seat at the back of the field, I wondered if he had any idea what had really happened. He kept looking at me as if he wanted to come talk to me, but then his girlfriend would say something and steal his attention again.

Penny, my "assigned" human friend, parted from the gaggle of cheerleaders and bounced to my side. She was not supposed to be her perky self at a memorial service, but Grimhildr's programming hummed so loud it felt like a drill in my ears. The poor human was getting the works and reverting to her natural state—which, unfortunately for me, was excessively perky.

Penny paused at my side and blinked at me until the humming finally stopped, then she bounced on her toes while she talked. "Hey, Val. I'm glad you could come."

I nodded. "Yeah." I looked out over the display of flowers, pictures of Michael with his friends, donations of teddy bears, and chocolates that dotted the lawn. "He's going to be missed."

My solemn mood finally seemed to get Penny to calm down. She sighed and curled her arm around mine as if we were the best of friends. I tried not to flinch, reminding myself that to her, we *were* best friends. "For real," she agreed.

Tyler returned with two cups of punch. He winced when Grimhildr mercilessly speared information about Penny into his brain. He handed his offering over. "You girls look thirsty."

I sipped my drink as Penny took hers and rambled on about cheer practice. "Michael would want us to carry on," she insisted and forced a smile. "Do you think you could come to our next practice, Tyler? We could use the moral support." She all but batted her eyelashes at him. Even brainwashed, all the girls loved Tyler.

"Penny," I hissed, "you're going to hit on Ty at a memorial service, really?"

"Hey now," Tyler said, his eyes dancing with mischief, "the girl is grieving. Give her a break."

I glowered at him. "She's not grieving. Grimhildr is struggling to hide what you are because you keep glowing through your skin and she's responding to it."

Tyler made a face, because his Immortal side was starting to shine through. He looked away from me and a flicker ran over his body until his *otherness* disappeared underneath mortal skin.

He frowned at Penny who'd gone rigid. "Don't go saying so much in front of a mortal. It's not good for her mind."

Penny flinched as a high pitched screech filled the space between us and I stuck my fingers in my ears. Grimhildr was working overtime today. "Sorry, sorry!"

Tyler gave me a brief kiss on the cheek. "You're just nervous. I get it."

I immediately turned beet red. "Jerk," I muttered.

Ignoring me, he pointed at Will. Sam had somehow lured his girlfriend away and now was my chance to talk to him.

"Excuse me," I muttered and left Tyler with Penny, the most flirtatious human on the planet. A part of me felt an unexpected protectiveness, wanting to tell him to stay away from poor brainwashed girls, but I knew that Penny was harmless, and I knew Tyler could be trusted. Freya wouldn't have allowed him to stay for so long on Muspelheim if he'd tried anything.

In spite of my mental reassurances, I found myself glancing one last time over my shoulder as my gut twisted.

It's just the hormones…

Marching over to Will, I couldn't help the sinking sensation that Sam would lose interest in helping me and his girlfriend would be back any minute. I twined my fingers over my skirt and tried to tell myself that I was doing the right thing. Will was going to spiral into the darkness without me, and just like Tyler had saved me from that horrible fate, I could do the same for him.

Sweat gathered in places I didn't even know I could sweat by the time Will noticed me. He raised a brow as the silence stretched into uncomfortable territory.

"I, uh, sorry," I muttered, suddenly forgetting how to string words together in a coherent sentence. My eyes kept dropping to the loose folds of his shirt, remembering what he'd looked like in his tight swimsuit. Tyler had been the only male I'd been around for much of my life. Even though I remembered watching the human world and being taught about the other gender, being faced with all the muscles and handsome cheekbones made my knees go weak.

Hormones…

Will got up from his blanket that stretched across the grass. Like most of the students that filled the background with comforting chatter, he'd been enjoying one of Michael's favorite summer treats. The pretzel balls were a fitting tribute and Will handed me his bag. "Have you had any yet?"

I stared at the offering and my stomach growled. Other than the mystery lunch, I hadn't had anything else to eat. I plucked one of the salty pieces and popped it into my mouth. My eyes went wide when I crunched it between my teeth and a creamy, nutty flavor filled my senses.

Will smiled. "Peanut butter. It was Michael's favorite snack after a game." Darkness licked around his eyes at the mention of his friend. His gaze swept over the students lazing on the grass. "He would have liked to have been here."

I'd abandoned my cup of punch, but Will offered me his and I took a sip, a blush heating my cheeks. "You shouldn't blame yourself," I found myself saying.

His eyes shot up to meet mine, part shock and part challenge. I knew that look. He wanted to beat himself up and no one else was supposed to have noticed. "What?" he asked.

Movement caught the corner of my eye and I realized that a very beautiful blonde was barreling down on us.

"Excuse me, can I help you?" Will's girlfriend propped her hands on her hips, clearly none too happy that I'd swooped in while she'd been distracted. I peered over her shoulder to find Sam shrugging as if to say, "Sorry, I tried."

"Jules," Will said, his tone chiding, "don't be rude."

So, the beast had a name.

She straightened and glowered at Will. "I'm not being rude. You're my cousin and I'm going to look out for you whether you like it or not." She glowered at me. "Val is bad news, and I'm not too proper to admit it. So stay away from Will, you hear me?"

My eyes went wide.

...cousins.

And somehow, as I backed away and murmured apologies, I got the sinking feeling that this Jules knew who—and what—I was.

A TERRIBLE IDEA

"Why have I never heard of this Jules person?" Sam asked, although I had a feeling that her question was rhetorical.

Having retreated to the diner, I pushed around a lopsided piece of meat on my plate. "Did you cook this?" I asked, trying to keep my lip from curling with disgust.

"Of course not," Sam snapped. "Joe did."

I glanced up, unable to see who Joe was. A dark silhouette moved beyond a tinted window, every now and then pushing plates under the shelf for Sam to deliver to the regulars who streamed in for dinner.

Good thing Sam worked here, or I had a feeling this Diner wouldn't be nearly as popular.

Tyler, however, didn't seem the least bit perturbed about the state of the meal. He dunked a generous portion of meat into a puddle of gravy before cramming it into his mouth. "Who cares," he said around his food, "at least Jules isn't his girlfriend." He gave me a wink.

I kicked him under the table. "Don't talk with food in your mouth."

Sam leaned over our table, pouring water into my glass even though it was already full. "I just don't get it. I know that resources are scarce right now, but for Grimhildr to miss an entire person is out of the question. We should know *something* about her."

I motioned her to stop before she overflowed the drink onto the entire table. "Look, Jules doesn't matter, right? I just need to figure out Will's secret." I didn't want to share my suspicion that Jules wasn't who she pretended to be. Grimhildr didn't malfunction. Ever.

Tyler shoved another bite into his mouth before replying, no doubt just to annoy me. "Aaaaand he has to trust you," he said, pointing his fork at me for emphasis.

I went to kick him again, but he moved out of the way, using his supernatural speed to avoid the blow. I glowered. "No cheating."

"She's got a point," Sam said, ignoring us as usual. "Val is powerful enough that she can lure him out when it's time, trust or not, but she needs to know his secret if she's going to stand a chance." She straightened and grinned at me. I didn't like it when she grinned.

"What?" I asked. "Why're you looking at me like that?"

"I've got an idea."

⚜

This was absolutely the worst idea in the world. No, in all the worlds in all the galaxies across the universe.

Darkness fell over Mattsfield like a blanket and I shivered, wishing I was under a real blanket of my own. Instead, I was out in the middle of the street about to break into Will's house.

Yep. Horrible idea.

I glanced over my shoulder, but Sam and Tyler had already gone. She'd dropped me off and told me to call when I learned Will's secret. Which translated to: get the job done or spend the rest of the night out in the street.

I palmed the cell phone in my pocket, not accustomed to the bulky technology. On Muspelheim, we could communicate over vast differences through the power of embers. When off world, though, we needed more practical technology. It made the most sense not to introduce new technology to humanity, but I still felt out of place with the bulky weight in my back pocket.

Brushing off my anxiety, I forced myself closer to the quiet home and yelped when blaring lights illuminated the yard. I dove into a nest of trees on the edge of the property, but no one came out to investigate.

Motion sensors, even at a residential location. Human technology sure had improved from what I remembered of them.

I should have had so much more training, but there were distinct gaps in my memory. Freya told me that it was the darkness infecting me and making me weaker. That's why I had to reap a powerful soul. Our planet was drifting too close to a rift, as well as living under the constant threat that our enemies would find us. The Einherjar and my Frigg sisters could move the entire planet and keep us safe until the shadows found us again...

but that kind of magnitude of power required souls, and a lot of them.

My sisters were all over the world right now, and while I was hiding behind leaves, they were doing their part to save our people. Valkyries were the last line of defense against Ragnarök, so doing our part went a long way to helping everyone, including this planet and the people who lived in these quiet houses in Mattsfield Tennessee.

Building my courage again, I delved into the warmth of my chest where my magic lived. My necklace reacted to my efforts and warmed on my collarbone, showing me the souls that slept beyond the layer of wood and metal.

Three souls. Will, and... his parents? No, none of the souls were together. One soul on the second floor shimmered as if otherworldly. It seemed to emanate an emerald light, and I wasn't quite sure what to make of that, but if I had to hazard a guess, I'd say that would be Jules—whatever she was.

I squinted, finding another soul in the next room sucking the light into the heavy weight of darkness. At first, I thought it was Will, but when I searched the ground level of the home, I found another soul wrapped in darkness.

Either Will had a brother trapped in the Norn's curse... or someone suffered with so much pain that they'd attracted half the shadows in Mattsfield and shared Will's pain.

To figure out which one was Will, I closed my eyes and inhaled, using my other senses. Wet pine needles under my feet, musty moss on the tree I hid behind... and the metallic scent of embers. My eyes flung open. I hadn't expected such a familiar scent to tinge my nostrils, but that was Will's soul

I scented, and he had the heart of a warrior. Flames burned underneath all the ice and sorrow and if I could help him break free of the weighty chains of blackness, he'd become one of the most powerful allies in Freya's fleet.

Straightening, I spotted the cracked window that let in the humid air. The floodlights guarding the home flickered off and I left my hiding spot, careful this time to skirt along the perimeter of the house. Once I reached the side of the house, I ran my fingers over the damp wood and peered inside.

The backs of my eyes glowed with embers, my Valkyrie side responding to the pounding of blood in my ears. I was used to training, but I wasn't used to this kind of tension. I couldn't imagine how I'd explain to Will what I was doing here.

Hey, yeah, uh, I'm trying to devour your nightmares like some kind of reverse-engineered dreamcatcher so I can learn your deepest darkest secrets and eventually rip your soul out of your body so that you can help me save the universe from being destroyed.

Yeah, that'd go over great.

Swallowing, I forced my fires to simmer to a low burn and my eyes adjusted to the cool darkness of Will's room. For a high school boy's room, I'd expected the floor to be littered with boxers and the walls decorated with scantily-clad women. I frowned when I saw quite the opposite: a pristine room to the point of being clinically clean, without a single piece of clothing to mar the beige carpet. The walls were bare and only a single shelf, perched over a desk, held up swimming trophies.

Only Will himself seemed out of place in the room, a

tangle of arms and legs with sheets wrapped so tightly around himself, he looked more like he'd battled with a sea monster and lost. He shivered and sweat glistened on his brow as he murmured. I should have been glad that he was trapped in the depths of his nightmares. Instead, a sting of guilt stabbed through my chest.

Reminding myself that the only way to help Will out of this was to learn his dark secrets, I pulled the window up, wincing when it squeaked, and pulled myself over the edge.

Once inside, I crept closer to Will's bed as quietly as I could. I didn't think it would have mattered if I'd been yelling. He clenched the sheets so hard that his knuckles went white.

A single touch. That's all I needed to slip into his mind, but my fingers trembled just inches from his face. What if I didn't like what I saw? Even worse... what if I fell in with him?

I gave myself a mental slap. Sam would be disgusted with me and Tyler would be flat out disappointed if I chickened out now. If I couldn't do my part, then they and all of my sisters would die. I couldn't let that happen.

My fingers grazed the perfect curve of his cheek... and then I fell.

I'd expected the shadows... but not the flames. Roaring heat singed at my skin and I flinched under the brutal pain. The air shimmered as blasts of fire-induced winds whipped around the endless sea of ash.

"Will?" I called.

The flames parted, revealing Will with his back to me as he stared at the edge of a lake that billowed with fire.

I forced myself to take an agonizing step towards him. Whatever dark secret ate away at him, could it have something to do with a Valkyrie? The flames licked at my skin, so hot that they could have been the fires of Muspelheim. I tried to summon my Valkyrie form, but of course, I was in Will's mind. I wasn't the one with the power here.

I gritted my teeth and put one foot in front of the other until I reached him. I reached out and my fingers grazed his loose shirt.

He turned, his chestnut eyes alight with embers as if he'd drawn up my power and now was using it against me.

"You," he whispered, and then the flames consumed me.

GRIMHILDR'S LOG: DAY ZERO

rimhildr's Log
Deleted Memory—Day Zero

As a Valkyrie, there are three unbreakable laws. Each law comes with swift and merciless punishment if broken. Having broken the first and most sacred, Freya towered over me as my knees ground into the perfect metal of her ship. I wasn't on Earth anymore where I'd forgotten the consequences of breaking laws that I was still bound to. I was on the Einherjar, the mothership that had ferried me back to Muspelheim, the fiery planet where I'd been born.

"You've broken the first law of the Valkyrie," she whispered. It didn't matter that Freya kept her voice sleek and quiet. Her words speared through me like the sharpest of blades. The hurt of my actions spread deep creases across her otherwise flawless face. "You know the punishment."

I swallowed hard. It wouldn't do to beg. She was going to take my memories because that was the law. It was *her* law, and no matter how much she loved me—especially because she loved me—I could not be spared.

Even though I knew the consequences were unavoidable, I couldn't imagine losing everything that had changed my life. William, my human, my soul. I was supposed to have reaped him and brought him into service of the gods. But I'd broken the first law of the Valkyrie. I'd fallen in love.

"Yes." My voice sounded pathetic as it wavered with the faintest of hopes that I could still see him again. Even if I wouldn't remember him, I craved another life together, no matter how short. "I do not deny the justice that must be served. But I do request one mercy."

Freya raised a perfectly white eyebrow. I was her youngest and most adored of the Valkyrie. Everyone knew it. That was exactly why she couldn't show me special treatment. "There is very little mercy I can allow—" she began.

"It is so I might be redeemed," I cut her off. I widened my eyes and pleaded with all of my heart and soul. "Give me another chance. William has been assigned to me. If enough of my memories are gone, I won't remember that I loved him. I will not fail you this time. Send me again."

Her fingers curled into fists at the proposal and the perfect aqua of her gaze flitted with concern. "I would have to wipe your memories farther than required by the punishment's decree. You watched William since you were initiated. For a true reset, those memories must be wiped as well."

I'd watched William for three entire lifetimes. He'd always died so young, as was typical of a Valkyrie's charge, but I'd fallen in love with him each and every time. When it was finally time to go to Earth and reap his soul, I'd been determined not to let my feelings get in the way of my duty.

It didn't matter. William and I were made for each other. I understood that now.

"I know," I whispered, my voice a scratchy sound. "I accept the consequences of this choice."

She narrowed her eyes. "I'll have to send Samantha and Tyr to make sure you don't fail us again. Your job is to reap his soul, nothing more." Her glance went to the long span of crystalline glass that separated us from the vacuum of space. Muspelheim, my home, gleamed like a ruby beacon. We were far enough away that I could spot the treat. Long, dark tendrils stretched as if wishing to devour the source of strength and might. If I failed again, that darkness could blot out my entire world, and then nothing would stop Ragnarök from bringing its dark prophecy to fruition.

"I understand," I said. Sam would revel in making sure I didn't fall astray again. As for Tyr—Tyler, when I'd been human—I'd been so cruel to him. Watching me reap Will's soul would be grim justice for my failures to him and to my sisters.

Freya sighed. "Very well."

She didn't look at me when she drew her spear and pressed a sequence of buttons. She faced it to me and spoke the words that would erase my entire life. It would be as if my past hundred years watching over Will had never happened at all.

I closed my eyes when Freya's weapon glowed and tingles of Grimhildr's merciless power slithered across my skin.

William. Please forgive me.

MATTSFIELD HIGH

After waking up on Will's bedroom floor feeling like I'd been sucker punched and then burned with a thousand hot-pokers, I'd found Will, his mother, and Jules staring down at me.

I'd failed. Hard.

Valkyries are supposed to be all-mighty forces of the universe, but I didn't feel very all-mighty as students sauntered past me in the school's courtyard and snickered behind their hands. Crumpling myself into as tiny a ball as possible, I gripped my knees to my chest and squeezed myself against a tree, hoping I could somehow just fall right through it and never come out again. The bark scratched painfully against my shoulder as I groaned. All I wanted to do was to go home. The fires of Muspelheim seemed a kinder burn than the scathing look Will had given me.

"There you are," Sam said when she finally found me.

I squeezed tighter into my little ball and sniffled. "Go away."

The autumn leaves crunched under her feet as she

kneeled and placed a soft hand on mine, unraveling my fingers and forcing me to look into her eyes. "It's your first time. Don't be so hard on yourself." She smiled. "That's why I'm here, right? When you fail, I'm here to pick you back up."

Anyone else would have been put at ease by her charms, but I knew Sam better than that. She always seemed particularly disingenuous when she reminded me why I sucked at this.

The lunch bell rang.

Great. More mystery food. I still hadn't decided if it was better than Joe's cooking at the Diner.

Fresh tears welled in my eyes as I imagined getting through the rest of the day. "I can't," I protested.

Sam tugged me to my feet. "The sooner you face him, the sooner we can put this behind us and get your mission back on track. C'mon."

How I wish I had Sam's confidence. But she'd done this for hundreds of years. She waltzed around pretending to be human as if this was actually her life. I, on the other hand, never felt more like an imposter in my own body than I did right now.

The way Will had looked at me had been one of utter betrayal. His gaze had flashed between a flicker of realization, horror, and then flat out disgust. Grimhildr's hum still burned my ears.

Running my hands over my flat abdomen that was part of this body constructed by Freya to house my warrior spirit, I tried to remind myself that I could still fix this. I was constructed by a goddess and even if I'd messed up, I wouldn't be here if she didn't think me worthy.

Sam offered me a sly smile. "I told them that you weren't feeling well, and with all the rumors going around my presence here isn't that odd. Why don't I mingle with some of the students and see if I can turn things around." She wiggled her fingers at me. "I call it Valkyrie voodoo."

I rolled my eyes. "I think I've had enough Valkyrie voodoo for a while. Thanks."

Sam sighed and linked arms with me. At over six feet tall, she jerked me awkwardly along with her lengthy gait. She was everything a Valkyrie was supposed to be. Tall. Elegant. Beautiful.

Heartless.

"When you've been around as long as I have, you learn to roll with the punches." She gave my arm a squeeze. "It gets easier."

It took every bit of willpower—and a hefty shove from Sam—to get myself into World History class. The pack of students watched me with a collective set of predatory eyes as I hurried to my desk. My gaze flew to the back row, but it was empty. I cringed. I couldn't believe he'd skip a quiz just to avoid me.

"Everyone close your books and pull out your pencils," Mr. Jefferson instructed. "You too, Miss Val," he said with a friendly smile as I eased into my seat and gave him a grimace.

I rummaged through my bag and spotted Penny already flirting with one of the quarterbacks, Liam. She ran her hand under his desk and squeezed the bulge of his thigh. I frowned and quickly looked away, heat running up the back of my neck. Seduction was a powerful weapon for a Valkyrie, and there was a reason Grimhildr had chosen

Penny for my human companion. My mother's creation likely thought I could use some practice in that arena.

"Miss White," Mr. Jefferson said with a scowl, calling Penny by her last name, "keep your hands to yourself."

The class snickered and Penny folded her hands neatly on her desk. "Apologies, Mr. Jefferson," she said, her voice a charming allure as she sent Mr. Jefferson a wink.

He ignored it and began rustling an envelope full of papers. "I'd like to begin, but it seems we're missing a student," he said. "Has anyone seen Will?"

Most teachers proudly threatened they wouldn't wait for tardy students, but Mr. Jefferson wasn't that type. He knew that Will had been close to Michael.

"Maybe his stalker killed him in his sleep," a voice offered from the back of the room.

All eyes flew to me and my face went scalding hot.

Before Mr. Jefferson could scold the unruly student, the door creaked open and Will appeared. His eyes immediately locked with mine and electricity zinged through the air. It didn't matter if I'd been caught standing over him while he slept, or that he thought I was a wacko for it. When his eyes met mine and that unspoken connection sparked through the air, my powers threatened to lurch out of control.

Electricity fled over my arms and I squeezed my eyes shut, wishing that Sam could have been there to stop me.

Too late.

Snap.

I opened my eyes. Everyone in the room had frozen, so had the birds outside, the clouds in the sky, and most importantly, Will's eyes looking into mine.

Something in Will's piercing gaze sent my DNA all out

of whack. I was a Valkyrie, capable of bending time and space, reaper of souls, evaluator of human warriors, and the most pathetic sixteen-year-old to have ever been birthed by Freya.

I squeezed my eyes shut again to break this human's hold on me and the roar of the classroom made my ears ring as time resumed its natural pace.

"Settle down!" Mr. Jefferson snapped.

When I opened my eyes, I found that Will was still studying me. He knew something was off, but hopefully, he couldn't tell what it was. Finally, his gaze broke from mine and he stormed to his desk as if exasperated I existed at all.

I relaxed when he opened his notebook, his attention sufficiently deterred, and I could breathe again.

Mr. Jefferson slid a piece of paper on my desk and I stared at it. There was no way I could process the scribblings trickling horizontally across the perfect parchment. Of course, I could read English; My first job as a Valkyrie had placed me in Tennessee, so it was technically the only language my brain had downloaded. I missed the Old Norse from my homeworld, leaving the English in front of me feeling sticky and foreign. It was just one more element that proved I was trying to be someone I wasn't.

With a sigh, I folded my arms and put my forehead on the desk. Maybe if I tried hard enough, the text would seep into my brain by osmosis.

"Miss Val?" Mr. Jefferson asked.

I groaned and eased from my desk as I forced myself to look up into his eyes. "I'm all right, Mr. Jefferson," I assured him and wrapped my fingers around the golden necklace that hung about my neck. The locket always seemed to give me a sense of warmth and strength when I was feeling empty.

The class simmered into cool uncertainty, half of them not having studied at all after staying up way too late at Michael's memorial party. While I couldn't claim to be grief-stricken, I'd not bothered to study all the same. Poor grades didn't matter, not if I did my job and got out when I was supposed to. Yet, looking back at the paper on my desk, a part of me wanted to pretend I actually was a student just about to look into college prospects. It sure did beat the weight of the end of the world I faced as a Valkyrie.

After I'd bombed my quiz, I waited impatiently for the rest of the class to finish, ignoring snickers and glances from my classmates as they turned over their papers one-by-one. Finally, the quizzes were collected and a boring lecture ensued, but the whispers never fully stopped. By the time the bell rang my ears were burning.

"Slow down," Penny said as I jerked my way to the front of the room. Just as I was about to jostle past Will as fast as I could, he surprised me by taking my wrist.

"Hey," he said gently, "we need to talk."

The students within earshot of his invitation gasped and fed the fresh gossip through the class like wildfire. My face flamed and I desperately wanted to dunk myself in the school pool.

Instead, I forced myself to peer up into Will's gentle eyes and nodded. "Okay, um, now?"

He moved through the doorway, still holding tight on my wrist, and I had no choice but to follow. Just as we rounded the corner, Sam flashed me a giddy smile. She'd been waiting outside my classroom—of course—and now she'd completely gotten the wrong idea.

Will didn't seem bothered by the whispers and stares and I envied his confidence. Then again, everyone loved him. It was hard not to when he was so freaking beautiful. It amazed me how he moved with such fluidity and grace, as if he'd grown up to be a dancer, and maybe that's why he was so good on the swim team. Images of him resurfaced. No shirt, lean muscles with water glazing over his skin—

"I'm going to give you one chance to explain yourself," Will said, jerking me out of my hormone-fueled fantasy and pulling me close to the lockers.

Desperately glad he was nothing like some of the Valkyrie on the Einherjar, I safely pushed the thoughts he couldn't read aside. "Explain myself?" I asked innocently.

He leaned against his locker and crossed his arms, glowering. The close proximity made me dizzy and I copied him, leaning against the lockers for support. "Everyone thinks you're some kind of maniac stalker," he said as he dropped his voice. "I know you're not, Val. You might be a lot of things, but you never do anything without a reason."

I frowned before fumbling with my backpack, straightening its curled strap that twisted painfully into my shoulder. Those didn't sound like Grimhildr observations. "Thanks, I think."

He leaned in closer, his chestnut eyes enrapturing me with all the mysteries that swirled behind his gaze. "I need to know what exactly you were doing in my bedroom last night?" He eyed me with annoyance mixed with curiosity. I had to give him some kudos. At least he was giving me a chance to explain.

Trying to think of a lie, I bit my lip before I blurted out something stupid. "I was, uh…" What could I say? I was following orders? My home planet was under threat and I needed powerful souls… that his was unfortunately being evaluated by a complete rookie?

"My sister—" I began.

He slumped and released a sigh. "I should have known."

"Should have known… what?" I asked.

He glowered at Sam who was now in deep conversation with Mr. Jefferson. "Sam put you up to it. You lost some bet or something, yeah?"

I blinked a few times before nodding dumbly. "Something like that."

He bounced off the lockers. "I'll fix this," he said. When I blinked at him, he added, "I've seen this before. You lost your parents, yeah? Sam's suddenly having to take care of you and she's putting all her grief at your feet." Shadows danced in his eyes. "I know what it's like to lose a parent— and to be on the receiving end of someone's grief."

I frowned. Grimhildr hadn't told me about his father, not that I'd thought much about it. The programming had trouble reading memories through darkness, and after what I'd seen at Will's house, darkness enshrouded it like an impenetrable shield.

I wanted to ask him about his father, but instead I bit my lip. If this was his big secret, then I needed to let him open up to me about it.

He continued, oblivious of my internal struggles. "Just hang tight for a few days and this'll all be turned around. You have my word." And then he walked off, leaving me staring and confused.

"Val!" Penny screeched before slamming into me.

I staggered with an *oomph* and steadied myself against the locker still warmed by Will's body heat.

"Since when do stalkers get one-on-one with their victims?" She winked. "Are you some kind of Houdini? What's your secret?"

Peeling Penny off my chest, I frowned. "It's all just a misunderstanding, okay? I'm not a stalker." I gave her a side-long glance. "And what's a houdeenee?"

She giggled, as if programmed to not comprehend my question, and linked arms with me as we made our way to our next class. I cringed, realizing I must have asked a question that would have jolted against her fake memories.

Unlike Penny, I was able to distinguish my fake memories from the real ones. They were flimsy and uncomfortable, kind of like a pebble in my shoe. I grimaced with pain as Grimhildr forced the unwanted knowledge of a magician named Houdini who got himself out of ridiculous situations into my brain. Dratted implants.

My next few classes were pure torture wondering what Will had in mind to "fix" my stalker reputation. As if I'd find the answers in the faces around me, I stared to the point of awkwardness. I didn't find anything useful, but I did get some weird looks. Not that weird looks directed my way were anything new.

Penny kept herself glued to my side, not seeming to mind that I'd become some kind of pariah. She escorted me to the parking lot when school finally ended and I kept out a sharp eye for a tall, lean swimmer that made my heart lose its rhythm.

"So, what *did* you do?" Penny pressed.

Wanting to ignore her, I hurried my gait toward Sam's car, but slowed when I saw she wasn't inside. She was probably still talking to Mr. Jefferson, and gods knew about what. "It's not important."

Penny giggled. "C'mon, Val. I'm your best friend! You can tell me."

Best friend? No. Penny was programmed to like me, and that fact grated on me just like her annoying voice.

Reaching the scorching vehicle, I used my jacket as a shield to lean myself against the sun-heated metal, careful that my zipper didn't scratch the expensive paint job. Sam had enough things to be mad at me about.

I stared Penny down, not feeling the least bit comforted by her perfect blonde curls and manicured nails. A girl like her would never actually be friends with someone like me. Just like everything else in this life, I was a fraud and everyone around me was programmed to help my mission.

I sighed. "Are you saying that if I tell you, then you're not going to instantly judge me and splatter gossip throughout the school?"

A hurt expression painted across her face and she gasped. "Val! How could you say that? I would never do anything to betray you."

I narrowed my eyes. There it was again, her indoctrination thinking first of her *loyalty* to me. Not the kind of loyalty won by true friendship, but a mind-numbing brainwashing performed by technology millions of years ahead of people like Penny.

Seeing real tears in her eyes cracked my armor. I might not be human, but I wasn't a monster. "All right, calm down," I said. Penny instantly brightened. "Will's special to me, and I'm worried about him."

Her smile faded and she squinted. "So… you thought you'd stand creepily over his bed while he slept?"

I snorted a laugh. "Well, when you put it like that, it does sound pretty creepy."

"Seriously, Val. I don't believe you're some axe murderer or something. I know you've got a good reason why you were at his place last night. What were you doing? You can tell me!"

I sighed. It was impossible to explain what I'd actually been doing without saying what I'd… actually been doing. "It's Sam's fault," I said, shamelessly using Will's conclusion. It wasn't really a lie. It *had* been Sam's idea that I analyze him when he was at his most vulnerable. When humans slept, their subconscious opened up and was easier for a Valkyrie to read, which meant past lives surfaced in their dreams. Surely I could find some hint of what kind of Norn had latched onto his destiny. I'd been coming up with nothing for weeks and I wasn't here indefinitely. Will was going to die, the true kind of death where his soul became so weighed down by darkness that it crushed him. Every reincarnation under the curse of the Norn could be his last —unless I figured out what dark secret was after him and helped him escape it. It was the kind of secret that followed a soul through lifetimes. This life wouldn't be any different. Will didn't have much time left, and that thought made my insides twist.

Penny's eyes widened, taking my nauseated expression as a reaction to Sam's shenanigans. "What'd she want you to do?" A smile lit her face and she giggled. "Oh! Did she dare you to kiss him? She did, didn't she?" Penny screeched with delight. "I can't believe you did it!"

"What? No," I screwed my face with horror, "I didn't kiss him."

Not that the idea sounded horrific…

Penny pinched me and gave me a wry smile. "You're so cool, Val. I'd never be brave enough to take on a dare like that."

I sighed and spotted Sam making her way to the car, her vibrant locks reflecting the sunlight as if her features were made of perfect metals. She would have looked like a nymph, if it weren't for the rage in her eyes that tinted the world around her red. For once, I was grateful to see her, even if she did look like she was on the warpath. Mr. Jefferson probably told her how awesome I did on my quiz. If I started to act out against the picture Grimhildr had painted for me—a vibrant student that would impress Will, someone who got good grades and always did the right thing—then I'd blow my cover.

She marched right up to me and stuck her nose in my face. "What's this business about you losing a bet?" My stomach dropped. Will had talked to her? She raised a finger with indignation. "A wager that you supposedly made with *me?*"

Penny giggled and bumped shoulders with Sam. Sam jolted as if she hadn't even noticed the human was there. "You're always up to no good, Sam," said Penny. "Bet you didn't think Val had the guts to do it!"

Sam rolled her eyes.

That's when Will exited the school and I sucked in a breath. I snapped my eyes shut before Will's gaze could hit mine. I didn't want to make time stop for a second time today, not when Sam was pissed off at me already.

Even though I couldn't see, I could still feel his eyes on me. The tingling on my skin zipped through me like lightning, telling me that Will was close and his senses were heightened. Sam told me it was the effect of being a Valkyrie when around an assigned charge, but it felt like something more than that. Will's soul made me feel things I wasn't supposed to feel.

First law of the Valkyrie, I reminded myself. I could seduce. I could enrapture. But I most certainly could not allow feelings that went beyond that.

Just hormones… right?

"You okay?" Penny asked as she gripped my arm.

I peeked my eyes open only to see Will halfway across the parking lot. His gaze swept past me like a kiss and turned hard when it landed on Sam. When he reached us, he matched her height and glowered, hovering a couple of inches too close for common courtesy. "I knew you were no good, Sam Frigg," he said coolly. "But to make such a wager with your little sister and let the whole school think she was a creeper? C'mon." He frowned and crossed his muscular arms. "You trying to live vicariously through her? If you wanted to come to my bedroom at night, all you had to do was ask." He gave her a smirk.

Sam flushed with anger. "You wish," she snapped.

Struck with an idea, I beamed and eased between Sam and Will. "Thanks, Will. I'm glad you know the truth, because now you can help me make Sam keep her side of the bargain!"

Sam's eyes narrowed and Will cocked his head. "Oh?" he

asked.

I wanted to rub my hands together and laugh maniacally, but I smiled sweetly instead. "Since you figured it all out, it kind of negates the bet. You see, Sam said I couldn't figure out your darkest secret. I'd hoped I'd find something in your room, but you don't keep a journal." My memory flashed back to his pristine room. He hadn't kept anything except his swimming trophies. "But if you tell me what it is, then she'll have to…" I momentarily coughed, trying to think of what kind of revenge I could get on my older sister.

"She'll have to what?" Penny asked, brightening with excitement.

I locked eyes with Sam and she didn't seem all too pleased, but she didn't stop me. If Will revealed something personal about himself, that'd only help our mission. Even she couldn't be so self-righteous not to take one for the team. Never mind if I enjoyed the heck out of it.

Shifting my gaze mischievously to Will, I leaned close to his ear and cupped my hands around my mouth. I ignored the zing of sheer thrill that ran down my neck being that close to him. "She'd have to give me her Porsche for the rest of the school year."

Sam scoffed with outrage when she heard the terms. Super-hearing sucked sometimes.

Will grinned, clearly pleased. "So, if I tell you my deepest, darkest secret," he said, drawing out the words, which was over-the-top sexy, "then you'll drive me to school in that?" He pointed to the Porsche Panamera, his grin turning fiendish.

I smiled and tried not to bat my eyes at him like some love-sick teenager. "You have yourself a deal."

Sam put on a show of acting all upset, scoffing and flicking her wrist so that her hair went flying over her shoulder. But I knew she wasn't really mad. She was probably even a little proud of me.

Will ogled the Porsche and went all hotrod-crazy. Before he got too excited, Sam gave him a nudge away from the car. "You have to reveal something personal," Sam reminded him, "or no deal."

Will's smile faded until it no longer reached his eyes. There was more than just a Norn plucking at the strings of his destiny. Something dark and hideous haunted him. "We'll have to go somewhere private for this."

Curious, but solemn, I held out my hand for Sam's keys.

She shook a finger and tsked. "No. The deal was you get the car *after* you learned Will's darkest secret."

I sighed and Will nodded to the far end of the parking lot. "It's okay, I'll drive."

Penny's eyes told me that she was absolutely *dying* to go with us, but she was smart enough to hold back. Her presence wouldn't help me learn Will's secrets. Maybe the real "non-brainwashed" Penny would have forced herself into Will's Jeep Cherokee, but instead she smiled, waved encouragingly, and waltzed to the group of popular cheerleaders where she seemed to be accepted into the gaggle to bum a ride.

My nerves made me a trembling wreck, but I managed to follow Will and gave one glance over my shoulder to see how Sam was taking this in. I expected her to be smiling, or showing some kind of indication that she was proud of me. I would even settle for one of her fake pouts, but instead what I saw was a different Sam. She stared at Will, looking at him like he was a juicy burger, and she wanted to stab him with a fork before she devoured his soul.

When she caught me looking, the cruelty in her eyes vanished. She squinted a smile and waved before climbing into the driver's seat.

*Shoving my hands under my legs, I ignored the soft burn of the leather seat as I eased into Will's Jeep. He pulled out of the school lot without a word and I kept my eyes focused on the grainy road ahead, desperately trying not to let Will know that I was more nervous than a cat in a spaceship. Why had Sam looked at him like that? Never mind her going creeper times one hundred. I knew that things were dire on Muspelheim, but there'd been more than just desperation or determination in that look. She'd seemed… hungry.

I didn't know squat about Will, other than the fact that he was a potential candidate for the Einherjar. Grimhildr fed me with memories of anyone new I came into contact with, but Will was a challenge. The darkness shrouding him made it impossible for the program to read him. Only a Valkyrie could uncover his secrets, and even then, it could prove dangerous.

I decided that part of my attraction to him was that he was so mysterious. Being a candidate meant that he'd been dedicated as a child to the old gods, his original lifetime landing him in Scandinavian territory. Humans weren't naturally reborn. They only got the one life. But when a soul got mixed up with the Norn, that's when a Valkyrie came in. He could be a powerful ally when Ragnarök eventually came, or he would be devoured by the curse of the Norn. It was my job to figure out what exactly had happened and get him to trust me enough to follow me into the afterlife, and into Freya's service.

"You okay?" Will's voice filled the empty cabin.

"Oh, yeah, sorry." I smiled and tucked a tuft of hair behind my ear. "Was just in my own world for a minute there." My own screwed up Immortal world.

He gripped the steering wheel and peered at me out of the corner of his eye. "You do that a lot."

Before I could reply, he turned onto a dirt road and the Jeep jolted.

"This isn't the way to your house," I said.

He grinned. "Remember the way to my house, do you? I thought you weren't the stalker type."

I blushed, but gave him a playful wink. "Had you fooled, didn't I?"

He laughed and eased off the gas. "If I'm going to tell you my darkest secret, then it's best if I show you where it happened." His smile dimmed.

I went silent and creased my lips, peering out the window and taking in the autumn shrubs and trees. Bright yellows and oranges engulfed the landscape, and out here the leaves had gone completely wild. I could barely even see the path anymore, but Will seemed to know exactly where to go. After climbing a few hills, a lake crested in the distance and Will only stopped when we reached a small dock with one lonely canoe. My back went rigid, my memories flashing back to when I'd been in his dreams with a lake engulfed in flames.

The engine sputtered into silence and we sat there for a moment staring at the glassy water that looked too perfect and serene for the ominous mood Will was in. With a glance at him, he gave me an encouraging nod and I opened the door to step outside. Cool, humid air played with my hair and leaves crunched underfoot. The bite of pine made me draw in a deep breath.

"This is a nice place," I said and wandered closer to the docks. Nothing at all like his nightmare.

"Yeah," he agreed, shoving his fingertips in his waistline as he followed. It was hard not to feel dizzy knowing we were alone in a romantic setting like this.

It was a chilly autumn day, but not exactly cold. Will's proximity affected me in a multitude of ways, and I wrapped my fingers around my elbows and shivered.

He eased off his jacket. "Here, wear this."

A part of me wanted to complain, joke that this was too much like a seventies movie, but I clamped my mouth shut and accepted the offering. Wrapping his jacket around my shoulders was a delicious pleasure, encasing me in Will's scent mixed with the flavor of burning embers that made my insides stir.

"So, what's the big bad secret that required us to come all the way out here?" I nudged him with my elbow. "You're making sure you earn time in the Porsche, huh?"

He smiled, but something about his expression lande me shut up. This wasn't a joke, and he really had something he wanted to share with me. There was more to this than just keeping a deal.

"Jules would kill me if she knew we were out here." He startled me by talking about the girl I knew so little about.

"Uh, yeah." Heat crept across my cheeks. "Was it because she saw me in your room? She seemed to hate me before that."

He shrugged. "She's just overprotective, that's all." He sighed and ran his fingers through his dark hair. Normally his locks looked black, but in the low light the tinges of chestnut filtered through. "She's been there for me ever since it happened," he said wistfully, "but now she's on overdrive since Michael died." Shadows licked around his eyes. "I'm used to pain. She doesn't seem to understand that."

I played with one of the buttons on the jacket around my shoulders. "What side of the family is she from? She doesn't really look like you." He had long chocolate curls that hung in his eyes and he brushed them away. The motion made me swallow. His chestnut eyes glittered with specks of gold as if he could absorb my powers of the Valkyrie, even now, while we were both awake.

"She's from my mother's side," he said with a shrug. "Scandinavian, I think."

I froze. Did that mean Jules knew about his curse?

I searched the glassy water again, seeing only drifting leaves and ripples betraying fish nipping from underneath the surface. It looked too peaceful for Will's life-changing event to have happened here.

"I used to come here as a kid with my dad," he said after a moment. "When he passed away, well, I wouldn't have been able to come back to this place. It was Jules who helped me see the beauty of nature again, even though something so terrible happened here." His gaze drifted to the docks and the lonely canoe. "My dad would have wanted me to keep coming here, but it was hard at first, without him. Jules helped me with that." He smiled. "Appreciate the forest and nature, and all that, like my dad used to."

He went silent and I followed as he wandered down the dusty path to the dock. He didn't stop until we reached the very edge and he teetered there as if he was tempted to jump in.

The part that really sucked about being a Valkyrie was that sometimes souls manifested an aura. But now, watching Will as his soul delved into his past, reliving his historical event, was absolutely enchanting. He was already a beautiful human, but seeing the power of his soul seeping through his skin made him otherworldly. The blue haze fluttered like northern lights, shifting to purple and green.

His gaze flicked to mine and a small smile quirked at the side of his mouth. "What?"

I hated to look away, but I forced myself to stare at my shoes. "Nothing."

"I've got you worried, huh?" he said when I'd gone quiet.

"Well, any secret that involves a lake, your dad, and your overprotective cousin does sound pretty ominous."

He laughed. "Well, I'll break the suspense. It's not a big deal really, but I haven't told anyone else, not even Jules."

I blinked at him. He hadn't told his deep, dark secret to Jules, the girl who'd uprooted her life to help him and his mother. Yet, he was going to tell me?

"It's just a stupid bet," I found myself saying. Sam would have killed me, but I couldn't push him into divulging secrets just because I'd manipulated him. "You don't have to tell me if you don't want to." I took a step closer. "We could make something up to keep Sam happy."

His hand wrapped around my shoulders and I froze. "This is why I like you, Val. You're sweet."

Blushing, I didn't move, but fluttered my eyes closed and memorized the way it felt to be held by him. It should have felt new and exciting. Instead, it only felt right... *familiar*.

He pulled away and the cool air rushed in to replace his brief embrace. "When I was a kid, my dad and I used to go night fishing." He pointed to the canoe. "We'd go in that little thing, all stocked up with a tiny cooler to hold fish and a separate bag of colas." His fingers twitched as if he wanted to grab for those distant memories and bring them back. "When my dad had asked me to go with him one night, I chose to play video games instead. I'll never forgive myself. If I'd been with him, he wouldn't have drowned."

I blinked a few times. Guilt was a powerful emotion, definitely one strong enough to trigger the Norn's curse. "What was your dad like?" I asked. I don't know why I asked, but I wanted him to keep talking. If I could lessen his guilt, perhaps there was a way I could help him.

He smiled, the handsome gesture making butterflies churn in my stomach. "He was my best friend. You'd never know it, but he was actually a government research scientist. Top secret stuff. He wanted me to go into it one day, but now he's gone and I wouldn't even know where to begin." His smile faded as quickly as it had appeared. "It's all my fault."

I shook my head. "Maybe not. Maybe it was just his time, and if you'd gone with him, you would have drowned too."

He frowned, but didn't argue. He turned back to the Jeep. "C'mon, let's get you home."

I wasn't sure what to make of Will's revelation, and it didn't really tell me when or how he was going to die. I chewed on my lip as I pondered the possibilities. Fate liked symmetry. Maybe he was going to drown in that lake, too? He was the star of the swim team, so that seemed highly unlikely. The fact that he'd lost his father to drowning gave me a whole new perspective of his lone shelf of swimming trophies.

Of course, Sam thought I'd made great progress and she drilled me for details. "What kind of scientist?" she pressed. "Did his dad make rocket fuel? Or maybe bioweapons?" She perked excitedly. "Oh! You know, there's an alternate timeline where the humans wipe out their race by a discovery meant to cure cancer, but it gave everyone incurable cancer instead. Maybe it had something to do with that."

I sighed and smothered my face with a pillow as I tried to block out Sam's musing out. Freya told me that I shouldn't be sad for reaping Will's soul. A Norn had already latched onto his destiny and if we didn't intervene, darkness would destroy him, but not before using him to further their dark agenda. "I don't know!" I said, my voice muffled.

Sam ripped the pillow out of my grasp. "Will you stop being such a baby? This is good news. We have something to work with here."

I glowered and sat up on my bed. Her bed was only inches away like we were some kind of toddlers. Stupid Valkyrie system didn't allow us to have separate rooms. I needed to be properly "guided and mentored." Pft. Sam was the worst mentor. She never told me anything.

"Spinning off guesses and alternate timelines doesn't really tell me how he's going to die," I insisted, then a pang hit my heart. "What if we're wrong? What if we can save him? What if he will become a scientist like his dad? What if he does something important? Who are we to say he has to die at all?"

Sam swung her legs over the side of the bed and made her way to the window and settled into her tiny desk filled with manicure supplies. She began vigorously filing a nail. "Your powers will tell you his future. The more you learn about him, the more you'll know when his time is coming." She paused and met my gaze. "Now that you know his secret, you'll be able to rip him free of it. You'll have to concentrate on his worst memory and break its hold on him."

I crossed my arms. "His dad drowned. That shouldn't be hard to do." I'd already seen the lake that tormented his nightmares. I could find my way back to that place... but did I really want to do that to Will?

She frowned, studied me for a moment, then turned her attention back to her nails. The soft filing grated across the silence. "I feel like you aren't taking this seriously. Sometimes humans have more power than we give them credit for, and they can mess with Valkyries. There's a price to pay when tampering with a powerful soul, and we already know Will triggered the scanners; that's why we're here. We just need to figure out what'll make him trust you so that he doesn't do anything…" Her voice drifted off. "So that we can get him back to the Einherjar," she amended.

I tilted my head, hoping my curiosity wasn't terribly obvious. "Are you worried that Will's… dangerous?" I grinned, playing it off as a tease.

Instead of laughing, she stared me down, full big-sis-serious mode. "Don't get on his bad side," she warned me. "You'd do better to take some notes from Penny and seduce him. Men will follow their lust all the way to the afterlife."

I growled. "That's so petty."

She shrugged. "We do what we have to."

I opened my mouth to argue with her, then thought better of it.

I watched while Sam finished sanding her nails to perfect square angles and was surprised as she shamelessly began to shed her clothes. "Sam!" I complained and covered my eyes. "I don't want to see that."

She chuckled. "Don't be so weird. If only you took your mission as seriously as your human propriety."

Not listening to her, I waited until she was completely clothed before I peeked through my fingers. She propped her hands on her hips and gave me a wry smile, looking far too adorable in lounge shorts and a baggy tee to be some all-mighty ancient Valkyrie.

"Whether my impulses are human or not, this is my life

now." I said. "You yourself told me that I have to immerse myself completely."

She pinched my cheek. "Sorry, Sis. I'm just messing with you." She gave me a genuine smile. "Once you reap your first soul, then you'll know everything about what it means to be a Valkyrie. It'll all make sense. Trust me, okay?"

Right. As if I could ever trust her. "What if Will isn't safe to reap?" I found myself asking.

Sam fingered her golden necklace, the object that gave her all this information she liked to hide from me. I gripped mine, only finding the familiar comforting warmth.

"When will my necklace talk to me like yours does?" I asked.

Sam shrugged. "When you've earned it, I guess."

Sam shrugged, the way she always did when she had information she refused to divulge. "According to the scanners, we have two more weeks to get Will to trust you. We're making progress, so don't worry."

My field of vision narrowed onto Sam's face and I balked. She purposefully ignored me, taking the brush from her bedside and gliding it through her already untangled silky hair. The straight, sleek strands filtered through the brush's prongs.

Rage surged in my chest and I snatched the brush away. "What do you mean two weeks?" I snapped.

She blinked at me, seeming surprised. "You didn't think we'd stay here forever, did you?"

She reached for the brush, but I growled and threw it across the room. "I can't believe you'd keep something like that from me."

She glared. "Seriously, get a grip."

When I crossed my arms and slammed myself into the mattress, Sam was wise enough to give me some space. She turned off the lights and got into bed, rolling over so that her back was to me.

I stared up at the ceiling and clenched my jaw. We'd only just gotten here and I'd hardly had any time at all to adjust. My life from the Einherjar and Muspelheim was becoming fuzzy and distant, my experiences there growing even fuzzier than my fake memories of my human life that I kept rejecting. Without my Valkyrie memories, I was losing my resolve.

Sam had said this was the way it was meant to be. The human memories were meant to be strong and dominating. They allowed us to seamlessly blend in during our assignment and it was our embers that kept our mission strong in our hearts. I gripped my necklace and drew strength from its warmth, but it didn't seem to help. Since the memories were extrapolated from those of the humans I'd be expected to interact with, they weren't entirely fake, just adjusted to include me in their lives, and allow me the knowledge I'd need to get the job done.

Nothing about this made me feel like I was on a job. This was my *life*. In two short weeks, I'd be expected to let this all go? And what then? What would happen to Will?

The potential answers to those questions terrified me and I found myself clinging to my retreating Valkyrie memories, thinking of when I'd trained with Tyler and felt so carefree.

My eyes finally eased closed at that comforting thought. Tomorrow was Saturday, which meant Sam would allow a training session with Tyler. Perhaps that's what I needed to center myself.

***

Sam was still passed out even when the sun was well beyond the horizon. I opted for a shower and got dressed, stealing some of her makeup—because let's face it, mortal beauty needed a little help compared to Valkyrie perfection. The sun seemed to bring out little brown spots sprinkled across my nose. A single flinch as Grimhildr supplied me with the name: freckles.

It was time to give Tyler a call. I pulled out the clunky device and frowned at it. Only two numbers had been loaded on it. Sam and Tyler. Of course Sam's contact was under "The Mean One" and Tyler's rested under it, displayed as "The Fun One." I rolled my eyes, not having to guess who'd set up my phone. I tapped his icon and pressed the device to my ear.

Tyler picked up after a single ring. "Hey! You found my contact info." I could almost hear him grinning on the other end. "Glad you decided to call the fun one."

I glanced at Sam who'd pulled a pillow over her tousled hair. She was definitely not a morning person. "Yeah," I said, pitching my voice low as I walked out of the room. "I could use a little fun right now."

"Say no more!" Tyler said. "I'll be right over."

While I waited, I meandered downstairs to see if there was any food in the kitchen. I opened the fridge to find some styrofoam Diner leftovers, but not much else. I sighed and took out the container and opened it, frowning at the mangle of meat and mashed potatoes. Not exactly breakfast, but I was hungry.

Grimhildr hummed, guiding my hands to the pantry to pull out plates that would safely heat the food in the microwave.

I sat at the counter and pushed the food around, debating if I'd train better on an empty stomach or dealing with the nausea that would come after eating the leftovers.

A knock at the door sounded, followed by a jingle of keys. It shouldn't have surprised me that Tyler had his own keys. He was an ally, but still, I straightened when he wandered into the kitchen.

"There you are," he said with a big smile that made him look like the best friend I'd always known. He was missing the inhuman glow and eerie crystal eyes that I'd grown accustomed to, but the way he held himself in his effortless way made me feel at ease. When he pulled a crumpled bag from around his back, my eyes went wide. "I brought you a proper breakfast," he said, eyeing my bowl. "Looks like I was just in time!"

I shoved my bowl away and ran to him, my mouth already watering as I smelled the smoked sausage and toasted biscuits. On Muspelheim we preferred smoked meats. The mole-like creatures named "Meers" were a particular delicacy and favorite of mine. Tyler laughed and handed over my portion. It wasn't Meer meat, but it would be close enough.

Salivating, I sank my teeth into the treat and actually groaned.

"Wow," he said, his features softening, "I sure do like to watch a girl enjoy her food."

Ignoring him, I scurried to the table and tried not to devour my food like some sort of animal, but I was starving. When I finally came up for breath, Tyler handed me a glass of orange juice. I gulped it down. "Thanks."

He nodded. "While you digest that, I'll tell you what I've learned." I perked up at that. He hadn't been at school all day. I'd just assumed he was keeping to his role as local loser. Grimhildr came from Freya's psyche and didn't seem to have any qualms about placing him in that category.

I took a napkin and wiped my face. "Yeah? Were you looking for the source of darkness?" Tyler was a Valiant, one of Odin's warriors, which made him particularly good at tracking dark things.

He nodded and leaned over the counter, his biceps fighting against his tight shirt. I'd never stopped to notice his physique before, but now I admired him as the perfect example of the male gender. He was a warrior, even in human form, and his lithe grace betrayed his ancient training in the way he moved. "The Norn keep their power hidden. They create new darkness by making Will suffer, but they need somewhere to put it, yeah? I think I found one of their tokens."

I straightened at that. "Oh?"

He smiled, and for some reason the motion sent my stomach fluttering. I clutched at it, wondering if this body disagreed with sausage. "Yeah, it's in a forest not far from here. I found a lake—"

I stopped listening as he went on. My gaze fell to my hands and I curled my fingers, hoping that Tyler couldn't see them tremble. I was starting to really hate that lake.

Tyler fell silent and came around the counter. He

squeezed my shoulder and gave me a worried look. "You doing okay? You're quiet."

I forced a smile. I didn't want him to know how hard it was for me to adjust to my human form. As a Valkyrie, I would need to be able to transform between the two on a regular basis. Tracking souls was nothing like tracking darkness. I needed to immerse myself in this life... but I wasn't ready, not quite yet.

"I was hoping we could do some training," I offered.

Tyler startled, then gave me a mischievous smile. "Training, huh? You sure?" He appraised my mortal form. "My body is just for show. Yours is real flesh and blood."

I nodded. "That's precisely why I need to train. You said the Norn have enough power that they're hiding it like buried treasure. I need to be ready to fight them if it comes down to it."

Tyler frowned, but nodded. "You're right." He motioned me outside. "C'mon. Let's do some warmups and then go from there."

I hadn't realized how suffocating the house was until a fresh cool breeze of autumn air hit my senses. I drew in a deep breath and felt my muscles uncurl.

Tyler settled into a fighting stance and an unexpected flash made me yelp and cover my eyes. When I peered through my fingers, I squinted at a blade that burned with white fire.

Tyler's idea of training wasn't for the weak.

"Let's practice summoning your spear," he offered and began pacing a slow circle around me. The fenced-in yard boasted a long string of trees, barricading us from prying eyes.

In my Valkyrie form, my spear was an extension of my body. Just like everything I did, it was born of the eternal flames of my heart—the core of a Valkyrie. But that very essence was suffocated in this mortal form. I couldn't simply spontaneously combust into flames in the middle of Mattsfield High.

With a sigh, I concentrated on the embers in my chest, my fingers curling around my necklace that radiated warmth. My memories seemed to retreat even further at my effort to grasp who I was and Grimhildr hummed with warning.

"You're going to have to fight it," Tyler instructed, sensing my hesitation. He lurched, thrusting a testing blow towards my face.

Out of reflex I dodged. Without my wings to give me balance, I quickly stumbled and collapsed hard to my knees. Tyler backed up and nodded at me to try again.

I picked up what he was doing. He waited until I didn't expect him, then he attacked, his blow just short of my fragile skin.

"You have to access your instincts," Tyler said. "Grimhildr can't touch that part of your brain, the part that is all heart." He grinned. "That's why you're on this mission and not Sam. Having a heart is kind of a prerequisite."

A laugh bubbled out of me, the sound just as unexpected as one of Tyler's blows. No matter what hardships I endured, he could always make light of the situation and make me laugh.

"Hey," Sam said, appearing at the doorway. She crossed her arms and glowered. "Don't fill Val's head with lies. I've got a heart, thank you very much."

Instead of a witty quip, Tyler launched at her, his sword flashing with blinding speed. A sharp *ping* rang through the air and I winced at the flash of sunlight on Sam's brutal spear. Embers splattered onto the grass, threatening to light up the ground. Sam growled and pulled away, sending her spear withering into a puff of ash. As it drifted in glittering pieces to the ground, squelching the ember's attempts at starting a fire, Sam smirked. "See? I can summon my weapon just fine."

Tyler rolled his eyes and dismissed his sword, his body losing its Immortal glow. He murmured to me, "That's because she's old."

I snickered as Sam threw her shoe at Tyler's face. He ducked, laughing when Sam growled and ran after him, getting a punch in to the gut. "Okay! I relent!"

The laughter died as quickly as it had risen when Sam drew me aside. "Why are you training?" she bit out. "Training is only supposed to be for Ragnarök."

I bit my lip before replying. "I just have a feeling that the Norn aren't going to let Will go. There's so much darkness." I left out the part where Tyler had mentioned that they'd accrued enough power to create tokens.

She blew out a breath. "Look, this is going to be hard to hear, but that's a good thing. It means that Will is going to make a great ally for us and help us save Muspelheim."

I frowned. There were no males on Muspelheim, and I'd always assumed that the reaped souls went to another planet, but the way Sam had been talking about Will was so... final. "Tell me what's going to happen to him," I said and gripped her arm. "The truth."

Embers flared in the backs of her eyes with warning, but

something in me must have convinced her it was time. "You're going to save him from complete destruction, but it doesn't mean he's going to go to Valhalla." The place where Immortals rested. It was second-best to returning to Yggdrasil.

I squeezed my grip harder, not able to tap into my Valkyrie strength like Sam could, but having enough raw determination to make her wince. "Then where will he go?"

She held up her necklace. "See for yourself."

Catching my breath, I hesitated. Touching another Valkyrie's pendant was a terrible invasion of privacy, even when offered. It held her power... as well as her memories.

She rolled her eyes. "By the gods, just do it." She grabbed my hand and pressed it to her chest.

The harsh metal burned under my touch. It was nothing like my own necklace that radiated heat and comfort. This came from Sam's experiences of a cruel life mercilessly reaping souls.

She showed me where they went. A replica on the Einherjar of Yggdrasil itself, but darkness dripped from its leaves and the roots tangled over the wire mesh of the ship's interior hull. The sickness dripped down into a vat to be recycled.

Souls harvested from the Norn's curse couldn't be saved from their own darkness, but that power could be converted and used. This was how new Valkyries were born, why we were both parts fire and darkness. Freya took life and remolded it into a new form, into her daughters that were the last line of defense against Ragnarök only because they knew it best.

If I let Will succumb to the Norn's curse, he'd be obliterated.

If I reaped him… he'd be used.

*S*torming off seemed like the best idea at the time and Sam had stopped Tyler from going after me. I needed to process what she'd just shown me.

Maybe Sam thought I'd come around, but that was her Valkyrie side full of merciless fires. She'd been molded by our goddess like a blade purged by flames. She only knew how to slice.

What if I knew how to save?

Will's curse was what kept his soul locked into reincarnation. If I could break him free of it, then maybe he could live out his life. Maybe there was a way to give him another option. It couldn't be so black and white. Be destroyed, or be a battery for the Valkyrie.

Taking Sam's car that I'd earned fair and square, I found myself driving down the dusty road that led to Will's old middle school. I don't know what I expected. When I arrived and saw familiar low-rise buildings and colorful posters, a welcomed wave of nostalgia hit me. My fabricated memories were so real, and I indulged in the brevity that they really belonged to me.

Yellow reflectors guided my way to the playground and I sighed with relief when I found that it was just as my memories had said it would be. Glittering rays brightened the clouds, revealing the sandy field with lonely monkey bars and swings. Without hesitation, I slipped past the benches favored by the teachers and made my way to the end of the playground. The climbing beams speared into the sky, and still looked tall, even though they'd seemed so much bigger in my memories of Will as a twelve-year-old child.

The biggest one wasn't meant to be climbed all the way to the top. The foothold spokes stopped halfway and an attached beam bent down in an L-shape with a neat row of rings. But if you knew how to climb a cylindrical beam, it wasn't hard to get to the top.

Wrapping my legs around the wood and gripping my nails into the sides, I shimmied my way up and heaved myself over the top. Sharp stings radiated under my fingernails and I was glad I didn't have a fetish for manicures like Sam or Penny. If I didn't have my practical short nails, I'd have never gotten to the top.

Settling myself on the peak and letting my legs dangle over the edge, I marveled at the landscape. The trees spanned out just like they had in my memories, giving the land a splash of foliage before receding into the lake's embrace. Now that I was here for real, the memories became stronger, filling me with emotions of searching and longing. My Valkyrie resolve was slipping away into another kind of mission… one where my human memories enveloped me like a blanket and told me that Will was worth saving.

I sat there for a long time before I realized that it must have been Will who'd sat here, searching the waters for his father on his canoe. Even at twelve, he'd feared what might happen.

I pinched my lips. Did he know a curse followed him? Could he feel it?

For the first time, it felt like I was actually getting somewhere, but revelations only seemed to come with more questions.

I made a battle plan before I descended. If I could uncover more of Will's story, then maybe I could figure out what to do next. I had to keep feeding Sam information. If I kept her on the hook long enough, she'd eventually slip up and give me enough information to figure it all out, right?

It felt like a leap, but it was a start. I'd need to learn more about Will. Good thing he'd already agreed to let me be his chauffeur for the rest of his life.

Sunday meant payday and Sam grumbled, but gave me a portion of her earnings for real food. I spent the better part of the day learning what passed for food in the human world. I picked up a cookbook too, and indulged my human side during the evening by making a hot meal.

Tyler had devoured my simple dish of creamy pasta, but I wasn't going to be too impressed by his enjoyment. He'd eat anything.

Sunday was a great day for recharging and refocusing, but Monday came with a sinking sense of dread. I needed to find a way to make the Norn reveal themselves… and I had a feeling that wasn't going to be easy.

Pulling the Porsche into Will's driveway felt surreal. I'd always watched him from afar, and now getting to have scheduled time with him, alone, was exactly what I needed.

The sun was well on its way into the clouds and birds chirped, making sure I knew I was disturbing an otherwise pleasant morning. I climbed the short steps to the front door and tried the doorbell. Rustling sounded from inside and Will's mom cracked the door open. "Hello? Can I help you?" she asked, her brows scrunching.

"Hello," I said and desperately wished I had Sam's charms. Will's mom probably knew my reputation as her son's creeper. "Is Will home?"

She eased the door open so that I could see beyond her shoulder and into the kitchen. An empty plate littered with crumbs was paired with a drained glass lined with orange juice froth.

"I'm sorry," she said, smiling politely. "Will already left with Jules."

I tried to keep my features steady, but my heart dropped to my feet. Jules? I'd almost forgotten about her.

"Oh," I said, trying not to show how disappointed I was. "Okay. Sorry to bother you."

"No trouble at all, dear," she said. After a quick glance over my shoulder, she must have noticed the Porsche, because her eyes darkened and she added, "I'll let him know you stopped by."

I gave her a small smile and said my goodbyes, trying not to sprint back to the Porsche. So, maybe she did know who I was.

The drive to Mattsfield High was only ten minutes, but it felt like ten hours. I replayed my conversation with Will's mom over and over again. It made no sense that she'd know what I was, but what if Jules had told her? If she'd been able to hide herself from Grimhildr's scan, then who's to say Will's mom hadn't been protected as well? Maybe she knew everything.

Deep in my thoughts, I'd almost forgotten that I was driving.

Red lights flashed and I screamed, slamming on the brakes.

Time slowed as my brain flashed to the present where I was about to slam into the stopped eight-wheeler in front of me.

In my thoughts, and inner conflict, I'd slipped on the gas and knew I was going far too fast. First the silly fears came, what Sam would do to me if I totaled her Porsche.

I pushed those thoughts aside, moving slow-motion into the inevitable crash that would do more than simply damage Sam's car. The eight-wheeler towered over me and cast me into its shadow. It was tall enough that a low-rise Porsche would slip right under its frame. The metal would be crushed like a panini, and what would happen to me then? I was still in a human body, and what would happen if I died? Would I return to the Einherjar? Or would I really die like a human and find myself in Valhalla with the other Immortal's who'd failed their missions?

Thinking about death terrified me. I didn't know if I even had a soul. I was Freya's daughter, and after what I'd seen through Sam's memories, that meant I was recycled fear and darkness and flame.

As panic swelled, my heart took over and filled my vision with Will's face, his brown eyes looking into mine and the memory of how his jacket enveloped me in his scent of soft embers. I closed my eyes, allowed myself to become immersed in the sensations should I die and never feel them again.

The blistering screech of my car's tires skidding against

the road faded into silence. I expected pain to come next, but when it didn't, I opened my eyes and found the eight-wheeler was gone.

Time resumed its normal pace and I eased the car off the side of the road, setting it to park. I got out and looked around as a sense of unease made me queasy. The road was completely empty, but after a moment, I heard an eight-wheeler coming.

I stared as the semi-truck eased to a stop. He was about to pull off to the side of the road when I heard a familiar, blistering screech.

A bright red Porsche barreled down the road, slowing down but inevitably on a path to crash right into the eight-wheeler.

Then it vanished.

*

The semi-truck driver must have heard the screech; he jerked the truck into drive and pulled off the side of the road. He got out and searched the road. "Did you hear that?" the lanky man asked, taking off his cap and scratching his balding head.

Desperately fighting past the shock, I tried to put on a blank face. "Hear what?" I asked, hoping my voice didn't shake.

He searched the road again, and when nothing appeared he turned his attention to me and the Porsche. "Are you having car troubles, Miss?" he asked, his gaze still flicking nervously back to the road.

"Uh," I looked back at the car and then to him. "No, I

actually needed to take a phone call," I lied. When he stared at me, I reached into the car and snatched my bag, rummaging until I found my phone and took it out to show it to him. "Can't be too careful!"

He offered me a grin. "Well, I suppose I'm glad you ain't like them other kids, yapping and texting and running me off the road." He rubbed the back of his neck and gave me a toothy grin. "But seems you managed to pull that off anyways!"

I chuckled and nodded my thanks. "Terribly sorry to interrupt you, Sir. Thanks for checking on me. I really appreciate it."

He gave me a polite wave. "Well, be careful now. Next time just turn your phone off until you get where yer goin'. Pullin' off on the side of the road in a small town like Mattsfield will just have people like me making sure yer all right."

One good thing about the Porsche was he'd assumed I wasn't from around here. Which, was partially true. "Absolutely. Won't happen again."

He smiled and climbed back into his rig. It rumbled to life and he pulled onto the road and drove into the horizon.

I stared at the phone in my hands, marveling that I was becoming a much better liar. But what had happened back there? Had I actually traveled through time? Sam already thought it was unsettling that a rookie like me could stop time without being a full-fledged Valkyrie, but to travel through it and into the past was something even she couldn't do, at least not on her own.

A part of me wanted to call her right now and tell her everything and ask her what it meant. But then I remembered the way she'd looked at Will, how her face flashed with hunger and cruelty that scared me to my bones. No, I couldn't tell her about this. I was on my own.

Even though it felt like so much had already happened to me today, I still got to school before Penny. My new memories told me that she would meet me and walk with me to class, but her normal waiting spot was empty. I walked up to the painted slabs that led to the school and made myself comfortable, taking my turn to wait for her for once.

Students filtered by and seemed to pay less attention to me than they had yesterday. I pulled my backpack into my lap and hugged it as I people-watched. My memories may have impacted my personality, but the last few days' experiences had begun to form who I really was. I had real memories of this place, and as I watched the students joke with each other and laugh, I could only describe it as home. The faint memories of heat blasting into my face when I stepped off the Einherjar felt farther away than ever. Even though I longed for it, I knew that I had a purpose here.

My heart caught when I saw the flash of Will's jacket. Jules kept stride with him and gave their friends pleasant smiles. The way she shifted one foot back when they stopped to talk told me how protective she still was of Will. Now that I knew what had happened to his father, she probably though Will would take Michael's drowning the hardest.

When Will briefly met my gaze, time didn't stop. I felt too drained to have that kind of reaction to him. Instead, sadness weighed in my heart, and I searched his face with the pathetic hope that he'd tell me what was going on. Recognition flashed in his eyes before he looked away.

Did he regret telling me his secret? It'd felt like he'd needed to confide in me, but now I knew something about him that he hadn't shared with anyone else—except for Jules. Watching him lean on her for strength sent fresh agitation through me. I glowered until her smile dimmed and she looked at me. I could have flinched away, but I didn't. She didn't know that I wanted to protect Will just as much as she did.

When she gave me the finger, I just about launched across the field to strangle her.

"What's with the face?" Penny's voice speared into my anger and deflated me like a balloon.

She bounced into my field of vision and her body broke the death grip that was Jules' stare.

I glared up at her and hugged my backpack tighter. "Will's cousin is getting on my nerves," I said.

She turned to look in the direction I'd been seething and sighed. "Oh. Yeah, she tends to do that." She turned back to me and gave my arm an encouraging tug. "Don't be a sour-puss! He's too attached to her. It's kind of creepy, anyway." She glanced at Liam and the other buff guys gathered in front of the school. Her eyes glittered. "Plenty of other fish in the sea."

I rolled my eyes. "Oh, is that so. I feel so much better." I let her drag me to my feet and I slung my bag over my shoulder. "Let's get to class."

She looped her arm in mine and bounced into a skip as we entered the school. The other students gave us polite smiles and waves, and I knew it was because of Penny. She was always so bubbly and pretty, making a "sour puss" like me gain some much-needed clout.

"I just thought that we had something special yesterday," I said. "He *did* share a pretty big secret with me."

Penny frowned. "Maybe that's why he's clinging to Jules. He reopened some old wounds talking about it with you."

I nodded in agreement. "Probably. But I don't see why he needs her. He's strong enough on his own."

She shrugged. "Boys. Strange creatures." A wry smile formed on her glossy lips. "What do you think of Liam? Looks like he's into you."

I rolled my eyes and purposefully avoided Liam's lewd stare. He slumped against the lockers with his other jock friends, giving me a once-over that was completely inappropriate. I'd worn one of Sam's tight-fitting sweaters to impress Will, but it was completely backfiring on me now that I was grabbing the attention of every hotdog on a stick in school.

"Gross." I tugged at the edge of the too-short sweater.

She giggled and untangled herself from me to get into her locker. "I'm not saying you should date Liam; just pop your cherry and get that sour puss face cleared up."

"Penny!" I hissed. "That's totally not my style." Not to

mention I'd probably literally burst into flames and kill us both.

She batted her eyelashes and folded her hands against her cheek. "Oh, I know. You're little Miss Fairy Tale. You and Will will get on a horse and ride off into the sunset and live happily ever after."

"Sleipnir," I corrected her without thinking. If Will and I would ride into the sunset on anything, it would be the fabled steed that Odin rode into battle. Of course, Sleipnir was actually a satellite that a cyborg turned god used to travel between planets, but a horse sounded so much cooler in war songs.

She blinked at me and her eyes glazed over as a hum surrounded us, Grimhildr jostling her brain so that she'd forget what I'd just said. When it passed, she was back to her normal self, and I ignored her as she proceeded to make kissy noises and teased me about Liam.

Homeroom was a welcome distraction. Government being the first class of the day was a bit of a drag—talk about boring, but I had a level of focus that made even Mrs. Larson proud. She went over the Electoral College and how it was developed as part of the constitution so that the presidential candidates would be forced to make a nation-wide campaign instead of focusing only on the highly populated cities. Mrs. Larson loved to talk about politics and lessons always seemed to drift into topics of how the government valued the underdog and even small towns like Mattsfield were important and had a voice in the way the country was run. Without systems like the Electoral College, no one would care what the people of Mattsfield thought. If only the universe was run that way, humans might be more than a cog in an ancient Norse machine. All that mattered was Asgard's vote.

When the bell rang, I gathered my things and kept myself glued to Penny's side. "So, what's up with Will?" Penny asked. When I gave her a raised brow, she shrugged. "You're clearly moping. Let's talk about it."

I snorted. "Beats me. Yesterday he was all chummy; today he's using Jules as a security blanket."

Penny elbowed me in the ribs. "If the other fish in the sea really aren't your thing, then you should fight. You going to let Jules get in your way like that? It's time Will cut the apron strings."

I frowned. Will blamed himself for his father's death and now that I knew, I could see the layers of his soul. Even now, his aura glimmered around him like a fuzzy backdrop, fluttering blues, greens, and purples through the air like tiny sparks of lightning. Absolutely mesmerizing. His soul was so powerful that even though I wanted to save him, my Valkyrie-side salivated at the raw source of power.

"Don't be so obvious," Penny said. "Drooling isn't going to win him over."

I glowered. "Then what's your bright idea?" I clapped my hands together and fake-pleaded. "Oh please, matchmaker, tell me how to win my betrothed!"

She chuckled. "If you're so determined, then you've got to play hard to get! If he told you a dark secret, that means he likes you. But now he's testing you, and you're tooootally falling for it. Stop drooling, and get yourself another man." She winked. "Trust me."

I sighed and shuffled into my next class with Penny close

on my heels. Any idea that Penny thought was good *had* to be bad.

Even if it was a bad idea, the thought of making Will jealous stuck with me throughout my morning classes. While I was stomaching his rejection decently, I didn't have any classes with him all morning. Now that lunch was over, I was going to have to face him, and being in the same room with him meant going back to how things used to be: me desperately trying to read him for information. Back to being a creeper.

Maybe Penny was right. I needed to find another guy.

Surveying my classmates for a potential temporary boyfriend, Liam seemed like too easy a pick. But Will wouldn't get jealous over a guy like that. I watched Liam flirt with one of the petite popular girls as she politely smiled. He tucked a curl of her hair behind her ear and she blushed. Liam was hot, but such a sleaze. Any girl who paid him a second of interest could call herself his girlfriend for the day. No, I wanted someone that'd really get Will bothered.

I was still searching for my potential love-victim as I head into lunch. Today was Taco Tuesday and I decided to let the line die down before getting my meal. I sat at my usual table and surveyed the crowd.

"Going on a hunger strike?" Tyler asked cheerfully, sitting next to me.

It shouldn't have surprised me that Tyler would *eventually* show up to school. As he stuffed his face with the grainy taco meat, I suppressed a smile. Should have known that free food would attract him.

I glanced at Will, then back at Tyler.

… That could work.

He squinted. "Why're you looking at me like that."

I nuzzled up to him and smiled. "*You* are going to be my boyfriend."

"Say what?"

I walked two fingers up his chest until I got to his face and playfully flicked his nose. "I need a fake boyfriend to get Will jealous." I nodded in Will's direction. He was still with Jules, but me snuggling with Tyler had definitely gotten his attention. He glanced at me from the corner of his eye, not seeming to be fully involved in the story Jules was telling to the fellow football players sitting across from them.

"Ooooh," Tyler said. "Okay, I can do that." He settled his arms around my shoulders and snuggled me close. "I've always wanted a fake girlfriend. This'll be more fun without the threat of eternal fires being plunged into my gut."

Penny walked up with her taco tray and did a double-take. "Uh, what's going on?" She looked half-disgusted and half-perplexed. Grimhildr had not been kind with Tyler's fabricated memories. She eased into her seat as shock settled onto her face. "The first time you actually take my romantic advice, you decide to do it with the school loser?" She jerked her chin at Tyler.

"Hey," Tyler protested. "I'll have you know, I'm a great faux-boyfriend." He peered down at me and smiled. "My lady is hungry and I'm going to go get her lunch now. How about that?" He gave me a peck on the cheek before launching himself out of his seat and made sure to blow me kisses on his way to the cafeteria line. Perhaps it was all a joke, but I couldn't help blushing. Tyler was a bit too into this masquerade.

Heat of a different kind sizzled across the room and I felt Will's eyes on me. When I met his gaze, I saw that he was openly staring now. The connection between us made my Frigg powers come to life, sending a ripple of electricity over my skin.

I wasn't the only one affected. Red embers sparked around him and the bite of burning metal wasn't just my imagination anymore. I'd actually pissed Will off.

Penny sighed. "Of all the guys. I mean, why? Why would you do this to me?"

Struggling, I turned my attention to her. "What's wrong with Tyler?"

Her silence answered my question and I sucked in a breath. "No way, you're into Tyler." I slapped the table. "Oh, come on. It's not like it's real. I'm just trying to get Will jealous. I don't have much time."

Penny stabbed her taco shell with her fork, sending it splintering into pieces. "That blush looked pretty real to me."

When I ignored her and stared at my hands, she sighed and looked at Will again. "Maybe you're onto something." She leaned closer and lowered her voice to a whisper. "He looks pretty intense."

I didn't look back at Will, but I could feel the sizzling heat burning low in the room. He wasn't just intense; his soul was aflame. If I looked at him now, time would freeze and I'd be stuck in this moment that was making butterflies do backflips in my stomach.

"It's hard to tell," I lied.

She snorted. "Well, he's nice and riled up." She shoved a bite of taco meat into her mouth, then pointed her spork at me. "When you're done with Tyler, you make sure to give him to me." She glanced at him as she chewed. "For some reason, he's gotten hotter."

I didn't have to look to know that he'd started to glow. Grimhildr's hum added its plethora to the symphony of tension in the cafeteria.

GRIMHILDR'S LOG: DAY ZERO

Grimhildr's Log
Deleted Memory—Day Zero

Trembling, I relinquished my human memories. They had no place in my brain anymore, not after what I'd done.

"I can't save you from this," Tyler insisted. His tone had gone shrill with panic—not a trait I was used to from him.

While I knelt on the harsh metal of Einherjar's plates, my mortal skin peeled away, revealing the Valkyrie form hidden underneath.

I accepted the pain that scathed its way over my dying nerves. I dragged my fingernails over my thighs, encouraging the skin to split and shred. I didn't deserve this body anymore.

"I want her to take these memories," I bit out through

clenched teeth. "I don't want this life anymore." Not now that he wasn't in it...

Tyler crouched and gripped my chin hard. He knew it'd cause me pain and I flinched, but I swallowed my screams and glowered at him. His crystal eyes glittered with fresh rage that I knew was just misdirected feelings he held for me. He'd been the first to remind me of the First Law of the Valkyrie. Now, I'd broken it with a human. I should have reaped him. Instead, I'd saved him the only way I knew how. He'd be reborn, still trapped in the Norn's curse... but at least he wouldn't be Freya's slave.

"You need to understand what this means," he growled. His warning tones rumbling through his chest. "The laws exist for a reason."

I flinched away. "Don't stand there and be so high and mighty. You don't care that I broke the First Law of the Valkyrie." I leaned in close and lowered my voice. "You're just upset I didn't break it with you."

Will continued to stare at me and Tyler did a great job playing attentive fake-boyfriend. He carried my books, opened doors for me—which was entertaining when he had an armful of my stuff—and made sure to give me a kiss on the cheek before going to his own classes.

When I found Tyler lingering outside the doorway before the bell rang in my last class, I was surprised how seriously he was taking this. It couldn't be just his loyalty to help me in my mission.

A nagging hum tingled in the back of my mind and I scratched the back of my neck. It felt like there was something there, a deep-seated memory just hidden under the surface that I couldn't quite make out. Tyler's reaction was important, but I couldn't grasp why. I sighed. I really wasn't used to this mortal body yet.

As he drew me in for a hug and peeled my bag off my shoulder, he smiled politely at the other girls giving him shy looks. Grimhildr's programming might have painted him as a loser, but it couldn't cover the fact that he was hotter than Muspelheim's core.

"You're enjoying this a bit too much," I said as we walked to the parking lot.

He grinned. "I've already gotten two phone numbers today." He balanced my books on his knee and held up his fingers. "*Two!*"

I laughed. "Right, like you're going to call them."

He shrugged. "It's not about the follow-through." He winked at me. "I'm all loyalty, baby. Don't you worry."

When I was about to respond, a wave of heat tingled up my spine.

"Hey, Val," Will said from behind me and I whirled around. He towered and the aura around him shimmered with red and blue, swirling and mixing together until it drifted over me like a fog.

I swayed on my feet, dazed by the effect his soul had on me. My Frigg powers threatened to rise up like a storm and I shoved them back down again. At least some training with Tyler seemed to have helped me get a grip on my Valkyrie side. "Hey, Will. Uh, what's up?"

He glared over my head at Tyler. "Since when are you two a thing?"

I frowned. "I guess since you ditched me for your cousin." I peered past his shoulder. "Where is Jules, anyway?"

He stared me down until I thought he wouldn't reply. "Look," he said finally. "I told you something I shouldn't have, and Jules is just helping me get through everything."

"You mean since you couldn't save someone else from drowning?" I blurted and Will winced.

Tyler pinched my arm. "Val."

"Not now, Tyler," I hissed.

Tyler shrugged. "I can tell this is a private moment. I'll drop your things off at the Porsche." He gave me air kisses. "Bye, darling. See you tomorrow."

Will's eyes narrowed as Tyler waltzed off. "Is that guy serious?"

"You're avoiding the question."

He sighed. "Look, you've figured me out, okay? I have savior issues, but they're justified, don't you think?" The aura around him fluttered and turned a soft blue. I couldn't help but be mesmerized.

"What?" he asked as I shamelessly stared.

"I…" My voice drifted off. Was it just me or was his soul becoming exponentially more powerful? Heat and energy wafted off of him, draping over me like a weight. I locked my knees to keep from toppling over.

As if by instinct, he reached to steady me, but when his fingers grazed my skin, lightning zapped through my body and I jolted at the impact of his touch.

Snap.

Ah crap. Not again.

The world around me warped, as if struggling against the space-time bubble I'd trapped it in.

What I didn't expect was for Will's aura to move.

It flung itself wildly, as if trying to rip itself through space-time to find me. It fought against the twining black fingers that speared in and out of his body.

My eyes went wide. When I froze time, I could actually see Will fighting the Norn's curse.

I flinched and time detached from my hold.

Will snatched his hand away. "Holy…" His eyes went wide and he stared at me. "What was that?"

"You mean, you felt it?"

He huffed a short laugh. "Uh, yeah? What the heck was that?"

The air around him was now fluttering with all the colors. Reds, blues, even greens and oranges. I couldn't help but reach out and hover my fingers over his skin. The aura reacted to my touch, sputtering and writhing around my fingers.

He didn't move, didn't even breathe. I couldn't tell if he was confused, fascinated, or terrified.

"Will?" Jules' shrill voice pierced the moment. She hurried to his side, clung to his arm and glared at me. "What's going on here? I thought I told you that girl was toxic?"

"Jules, not now," Will murmured and shoved his hands in his pockets.

She huffed and tugged him away. Something inside me growled when he allowed it. "You said there was nothing between you two. If that's true, then you've got nothing to say to her, right?"

Even though Jules was a tiny thing, she stared at him, determined and patient.

Fight sparked in Will's eyes, sending blue flames licking the air, but then the colors thinned and he gave me an empty smile. For some reason, he didn't seem to be able to stand up to Jules. "See ya around, Val."

Jules glowered, glaring at me until I wanted to punch her in the face. Instead of giving me a reason to, she led him to his Jeep.

Rooted to the ground, I watched them drive away. Just as they rounded the bend, I caught Will's brown eyes in his rearview mirror. But he kept his gaze focused on the road in front of him and didn't even flinch in my direction. Hurt burst in my chest like a blossom, filling me with the aroma of rejection.

THE GODS AREN'T PLEASED

"The Tyler-Kling plan is soooo not working," Penny drawled, hanging herself halfway off my bed.

I chuckled and aimlessly doodled on my math homework, taking full advantage of the offered distraction to gaze longingly out the window instead of facing Penny. "'Tyler-Kling?' What does that even mean?" I asked.

She giggled. "He's so clingy with you, but it just sounds dirty, doesn't it? Tyler-Kling definitely has a ring to it. It's got all the girls gossiping." She righted herself and rolled back her shoulders, putting on a show as she mimicked. "Bet Sam's had a taste of the Tyler-Kling."

"Ew!" I shouted and threw my good eraser at her. She squealed and blocked it. "Don't be disgusting."

"Well, wouldn't blame you if you did take your little faux relationship to the next level. I know I would." She laced her fingers under her chin and sighed. "I'd just never noticed how dreamy he is."

I rolled my eyes and attempted to erase my poor excuse for a math equation. The nub on the end of my pencil squeaked and protested at the effort.

Penny sighed and returned the eraser I'd thrown. "I get it. You're into Will. I'm sorry I wasn't more supportive before." Her face went thoughtful. "There's definitely something between you two. I've never seen a guy try so hard to avoid someone."

I grimaced. "Pretty sure being avoided isn't a good thing."

"No, seriously," she protested. "Don't you remember in third grade when boys would pull your hair and then run away? It's the same idea. Guys try to be all mean and distant, but that just means they're really into you."

"If he's so into me, then why is he letting Jules push him around?" I winced when I heard the bitterness in my voice.

She pulled up a stool and took my hand, forcing me to look at her. "He's running the only way he knows how." She gave me a soft smile. "You've got to stop playing games with him. Do something that'll make him want to come out of his slump."

I sighed. "And why should I do that? What makes me better for him than somebody else?"

Confusion flickered across her features. She couldn't answer a question like that. It would require her to question what was different about me compared to other girls, and that would inevitably lead her to some Valkyrie-related conclusions.

I sighed. "This is so frustrating."

She smiled weakly, looking relieved as the hum in the air eased off. "I know."

"No," I snapped. "It's frustrating that you can't just be my friend, a *real* friend. You can't listen to my *real* problems without your brain constantly reprogramming itself."

Penny tried to say something, but her face jerked with a twitch.

"What do you think you're doing?" Sam's stern voice speared into me.

A bag hung off her arm. Great. More Diner leftovers.

"If you need someone to talk to about *personal* problems," Sam continued. "Then you've got me. All right?" She turned her attention to Penny. "Don't break the poor thing."

"H-hey, Sam," Penny finally managed to say. Sweat beaded on her forehead and she swiped it away. "I, uh, I'm not feeling so well." She wobbled to her feet and gave me an apologetic smile. "Raincheck on studying?"

"Yeah," I murmured, guilt stinging in my chest. I gave her a weak smile. "See you tomorrow."

She said goodbye and bolted from the room. Guilt continued its purge over me and Sam only made things worse. "What were you thinking?" she chided. "Humans aren't here to play with. They're tools, and if you play with tools, you'll break them."

Chewing on my eraser, I contemplated her words. "What if having Penny on our side helped us? I mean, *really* on our side?"

She snorted. "We can't allow a human to know who we are, much less why we're here."

If that was true, then I wondered if Will's mother knew what we were.

"Why not?" I asked.

Sam's eyes narrowed. "Didn't you see what happened? It'd probably kill her."

I straightened. Up until now, I'd thought that Sam was the thumb holding me down. "You mean, you can't just, you know..." I rolled my wrists to indicate whatever Valkyrie-voodoo that'd done to Penny. "Undo her programming?"

"No, I can't undo her 'programming.' Our mother, *Freya*, sent us on a mission. Everything was already prepped for us when we got here, and I got a fresh set of memories just like you. Except, I have much more experience dealing with them, which is why I'm the perfect Valkyrie to help you reap your first soul."

I frowned. "I'm sure there are plenty of Valkyries who've been around the block." My words came out crisp and short, and I crossed my arms not caring that this was the first time I really stood up to Sam. She might have been my mentor, but she was just one of many ruthless Valkyries that had tried to beat me into a weapon.

She chuckled, but it was a derisive sound. "I'm here to help you, Val. You can hate me or love me; I don't really care. But you're here for a purpose, and it's my job to help you do it."

I glowered. She wasn't here to "help." She was here to babysit. As I stared at her and her icy blue eyes bored into mine, the air tinged with red. I hissed in a breath from the shock of seeing my sister's aura. *Maybe we did have souls.*

"What?" she snapped.

I froze. I hadn't even known for sure if we even had souls, but I was fairly certain I wasn't supposed to see my sister's. If she knew, she'd send me back to the Einherjar for sure.

"You've, uh, is that new lip gloss?" I tried not to grimace from the utterly lame cover-up. But, to my surprise, Sam absently brushed a finger across her lips and looked thoughtful. "Yeah," she said. "Figured I'd try something new." Her gaze flickered an emotion I didn't recognize. "Just making sure I blend in."

I grinned. She liked this life too.

Knowing that Sam enjoyed being human didn't mean that it was safe to share soul-altering secrets with her. Luckily, I didn't need Sam's cooperation to get answers. Will already seemed to bend the rules of what a Valkyrie should expect as far as her first charge and I was determined to figure out what all this meant and how I could use it to save him.

Déjà vu slammed into me when I pulled into Will's driveway for the second time. The sun barely breached the horizon and sent warm rays scattering through the windshield.

Except, I wasn't here to pick Will up for school. I'd survived a whole week of that nonsense. Today was Saturday and Will was probably still asleep. I cocked my head to the side and listened to the promising silence. Good.

I'd gotten into Will's room once before without anyone noticing—at least until his nightmares had flattened me on my behind. It felt like I'd been sucked in and my brain was still mush trying to remember it. Nightmares or not, this time I was prepared.

I snuck across the lawn and approached his window, which was surprisingly still open. I didn't know if he was just forgetful, or if that was supposed to be some kind of invitation.

Opting for the best-case scenario, I peered inside. Will sprawled atop his sheets and his chest rose and fell with the deepest sleep imaginable and I chuckled. He was totally not a morning person.

I didn't want to scare the poor guy to death, but there wasn't a way around it, so I eased all the way inside and shut the window hard enough to wake him up.

"What the—" he blurted and flopped onto the floor.

I sprung my hands up in surrender. "Just me."

He grabbed his chest and heaved a long breath. "Oh, just you, my stalker. Why didn't you say so?"

I gave him a wry smile. "I wouldn't be here if it wasn't important."

He narrowed his eyes, but I could tell he was curious. "What's up?" he asked.

I approached his bed, a blush creeping up my neck as I realized he was in his boxers. "You, uh, want to put on some pants?"

He grinned. "Aw, look at you. A prude stalker."

I pulled up a chair and averted my gaze while he tugged on some sweats. His aura sprang to life when I focused on him again, the bright greens and blues writhing within one another like northern lights.

"So," he said and plopped back onto the edge of the bed. "What's so important that you need to sneak in my room at the crack of dawn?" I opened my mouth to answer, but he shot up a finger in warning. "It'd *better* be important, or

Jules is going to have my head on a platter if she catches you here again."

I bit my lip, finding it interesting that he was more worried about Jules than his own mother.

"It is," I promised, but then shut my mouth when I realized I wasn't quite sure where to start. I knew it in my bones that he wouldn't be brainwashed like all the rest. Even an untrained Valkyrie such as myself could feel the intoxicating power wafting off his skin. His soul was powerful, enough that he could handle an Immortal's reality and resist the scanners from retraining his brain when I told him the truth.

He leaned forward and the air tingled with his impatience. "Well? Spit it out."

I swallowed. "Right." I straightened. "You see, I'm a Valkyrie."

He stared and I waited to see how he'd react. Any other human would have gone into a seizure as my mother's compulsion rewired their brain, but he just stared at me like I was a nut. Good.

"Okay. Not sure what that means," he said slowly.

I held out my hand. He just needed to touch my skin and he'd feel our connection again. "You're a powerful soul and I'm supposed to evaluate if you're suitable to be recruited for the Einherjar."

His eyes narrowed. "You mean, like, Ragnarök?"

I flinched at the term. "Sure." I offered him a hesitant smile. "I've read some of the lore you've compiled on us. It's not particularly accurate, but at least it's proof that my mother's brainwashing doesn't always stick."

He eased to his feet. "Uh, okay. I think you should go. You—"

He moved to push me out of his room, likely thinking I was ripe for a white jumpsuit and padded walls, but when his fingers wrapped around mine the air exploded with vibrant colors. Lightning zinged through my skin and made my teeth clack. Time slipped out of its eternal wheel, flinging the room into the warped frozen glaze of a space-time bubble.

What I hadn't expected was for Will to follow.

He jerked away, and then his eyes wandered. I realized he could see the blazing colors. "What the heck is that?" he asked. He peered over my shoulder, then rushed to the window. "The heck… is that?"

Trees froze in mid-sway, a bird with outstretched wings caught the light just about to launch into take-off, and a car exuded a stilled line of smog into the air.

"I told you. I'm a Valkyrie."

He whirled, his eyes wide with fresh panic. I didn't want to frighten him, but he had to know the truth.

His fingers wrapped around my arms, the contact breaking my fragile hold on the space-time bubble he'd somehow invaded. I knew that he didn't have Frigg powers. That was impossible, but somehow, our connection was strong enough that'd he'd followed me.

I helped him collapse to the bed. "You're a powerful soul, Will. I need you to understand what I'm telling you."

He stared at me for a long time, looking as if he wanted to touch my skin again. His fingers curled into his palms.

"You can't tell anyone what I am," I blurted when the silence pressed in like a vice.

He flicked his eyes warily at me. "Why not?"

"Because, they, uh…" my words drifted. How could I explain Grimhildr? Or even worse… the backup safeguard: Thor.

"Are there more of you?" he asked.

I nodded. "Yes. But, it's difficult for others to understand, maybe even dangerous. They must not have a soul as powerful as yours to resist the programming."

His eyes narrowed. "And what does that mean?"

I dismissed his confusion with a wave of my hand. "That's not important. What matters is that we figure out how to protect you from your curse."

He shot to his feet. "What curse?"

Shakily, I rose to my feet as well. Still, he towered over me. Red had begun to invade the colors weaving around his face and even his eyes took on a crimson hue. A draining sensation spilled from my core, and I realized that he was feeding on my power.

"Listen," I said. "I know this is a lot to take in, but you're going to have to trust me."

"I barely know you," he countered. "You tell me something crazy, that you're straight out of Norse mythology, and then you do… that." He pointed to the swirling colors in the air that had begun to clump and writhe together like a living thing.

I hadn't the faintest idea what the colors meant, but I swished my hands through the cloud and was relieved when it dispersed. "It's new," I admitted. "I'm not used to the aura, either."

"So," he said as he eased back onto the bed, and the red

in his aura faded, leaving a calmer turquoise hue to frame his face, "we have an effect on each other."

A blush found its way up my neck. It didn't take much for this body to scream my emotions just like Will's aura. "I guess so," I admitted, my blush even hotter now that he could see exactly how much he affected me. Aside from the flutter of my emotions across my face, he stared at the sprawling of red and blues that wafted over my skin. It was as if I hadn't had a soul before, but now that I was with Will, he'd awakened something in me.

He offered his palm. "Come closer."

I stared at his fingers, not sure that I would like the jolt of electricity zapping through me the moment we touched, but I found my feet bringing me to him anyway. This time before I touched him, our auras collided and merged, and then I slipped my fingers in his.

Memories snapped in my mind and my gaze shot up to his. He felt it too. There was something more between us, something older. We weren't strangers, after all.

There were no words to describe the blossom of feelings he awakened in me. I allowed him to ease me onto the bed and he curled his arm around me protectively. His lips dangerously close to mine parted as his gaze went hooded. "Who are you?" he whispered.

My tongue flashed across my lips. "I don't remember," I admitted. But the memories were beating against a wall in the back of my mind, and if I let myself get just a little bit closer, if I let him kiss me, maybe I could tear it down.

Grimhildr's Log
Deleted Memory—Day Negative Two

I couldn't allow him to kiss me. If I did, I knew it'd open up a door I'd kept securely shut in my heart.

We were close to the ocean and I dug my toes into the sand. The sun warmed my face, reminding me of Tyler's power. Guilt swarmed through me, as if he was watching us even now.

"What's with the sullen look?" my human asked, curling his finger under my chin until I rolled my head across the towel to look at him.

I didn't care that sand had gotten in my hair as the wind lazily sent particles flying around us. My human was here and we had one last day together before the Norn's Curse ripped us apart.

I blinked away the sting of tears. "I don't want to lose you."

He sat up, forcing me to rise with him. His arm wrapped around me and tugged me in close. "I know what's coming for me, baby. But you have to know that no matter what happens, I wouldn't have changed a thing."

I pulled away from him and my fingers pressed against his hard chest. "How can you say that?" I asked. My voice cracked as pain whispered through me. He didn't know what he was saying. He didn't know what I was going to have to do.

His fingers glided over my cheek and his thumb ran over

my bottom lip, making my breath hitch. He was staring at my mouth now and a new warmth curled in my chest.

He leaned closer until his lips hovered over mine. "We live in the now," he reminded me, his favorite phrase when he'd learned that he was going to die. "Do you want to live with me?"

His aura sprang to life and caressed me like a thousand tiny kisses. I should reject him. I should shut down this other part of myself that intertwined with another soul, but I couldn't. I was a breath from opening that door that held a part of who I was, and I wanted to see what was on the other side.

I found myself closing that minuscule distance between us. My mouth opened for his and then his kiss wiped any cares from my mind. Our auras collided and merged until it felt as if he could explore every inch of me and it'd never be enough.

I knew what this meant. It was too late. I'd fallen in love.

❦

Present Day: Will's House

A crash sounded from outside as a flash blinded us. Will and I ran to the window as another lightning bolt hit a tree. Bark split and terrible screeches sounded as the tree skid across roof tiles and slammed to the ground. Both Will and I froze as we listened to the building howls of the wind and spotted a tornado touch down just down the street.

As if on cue, the tornado sirens sounded and Will's

mother cried from upstairs. "Will!" she shouted, her voice still thick with sleep. "Get to the storm room!"

Cursing, Will grabbed my wrist. "Come on," he urged.

I resisted. "Your mom can't know I was here," I said, knowing that I wasn't making a lot of sense.

Grimhildr had a failsafe. When all else failed, Thor was set free.

Thor retaliated against a mortal knowing the truth. Will's soul was too strong to be programmed by Freya, leaving Thor at the helm to do his worst. This was all my fault. I wasn't going to drag Will's mother into this mess.

Will tugged me again. "There's a *tornado*. Who cares if my mom knows you're here." His eyes widened as the storm approached. "We've got to get to the basement. Come on!"

Just when I was about to give in, headlights swerved through the bedroom and I turned to see Jules pulling into the driveway. I staggered. No wonder I hadn't gotten caught. She hadn't been home.

I didn't have time to process what was happening. Even as a tornado screamed down pavement and sent debris flying through the air, Jules beat on the door and Will cursed. "I'm letting her in. You," he said, shaking a finger at me, "get into the basement immediately."

There was no room for argument from his tone, and even though I nodded my agreement, I turned and faced the window while he gathered Jules and brought her to the basement with his mother. He called for me, but I knew this tornado wasn't natural. This was a warning.

When Will tried to come and get me and his mother and Jules screamed for him, I did something I didn't know I was capable of. I gathered the power of my aura and pushed at him, *hard.*

He blinked with incomprehension and his eyes unfocused. The colors I'd seen snapped and dissipated as if they'd never existed at all. Whatever I'd done, it had worked. He turned, retreating to the basement and left me alone.

I shivered, because I had a bad feeling that I'd just lost what little connection with locked away memories I'd found.

With Will safe, I faced the danger that threatened his house. Even as the wall of black encircled the property, I balled my fists at my sides and stood my ground. I was still a Valkyrie. I was going to act like one.

More tornados landed and ripped through the dirt at my defiance. Wind ripped through the window and wound around my face. I pushed back, determined not to allow whatever this was anywhere near Will. At my push of power, the storm died down and an angry wind prowled the streets. I didn't move until the ominous sensation lifted and fled north. That was where Sam and I lived.

I left the home and ignored the frightened murmur of Will's mother and Jules. He consoled them, already having forgotten that I'd paid him a visit. Whatever I'd done to him would keep him safe, for now. Yet, the sting in my chest felt like I'd slammed a door closed… one that was meant to be open.

I didn't have time to ponder the strange sensation. The evidence of the catastrophe that nearly befell my human displayed itself with trees twisting with each other all around the property, the tornado having eaten its way around the house without ever touching it. The gods weren't pleased, which meant I was onto something.

Now it was after Sam and I had to get to her before it made matters even worse. I still wasn't sure which side she was on.

EIR: THE VALKYRIE OF MERCY

I pressed my foot to the pedal and sped the Porsche down the empty streets. All of Mattsfield retreated to their storm rooms. They'd stay there for a while since there was enough of a howl in the air to keep everyone inside. When I reached my home, the tornados had vanished, but threatening low clouds bobbed with rain and I scurried inside before the bottom fell out.

Sam growled when I entered the kitchen. "Oh, look who decided to come home," she snapped as she stabbed a knife through an orange. She always seemed to eat fruit when she was upset. Juices bled all over the kitchen counter and Sam jabbed the blade through again, seeming to gain satisfaction from the fruit-massacre. "You went to Will's, didn't you? What did you tell him? Thor isn't activated lightly."

My fingers curled into fists. Because of me, all of Mattsfield was in danger of a reset. How selfish could I be?

I drew in a shaky breath, held it, then let it out. "I need to tell you something."

Sam pointed the knife at me and gave me an incredulous

glare. "Oh, *now* you're ready to tell me something. Well let me tell *you* something. I'll make sure to phrase it in Earth teenager lingo so you're not confused. We're screwed, okay? Royally and utterly screwed."

Wind ripped around our house. Even if the tornados had stopped, the threat wasn't over. My shoulders hunched. "I know I messed up, okay? I went to Will's and told him what I was." Her eyes went wide and I leaned forward. "It worked. Will trusts me now. I can protect him from—"

Sam scoffed. "Protect him? We aren't here to *protect* him. We're Valkyries. We're supposed to claim his soul before the Norn take what's left of him."

Blood drained from my face. "Are you that cruel?"

She tossed her knife in the sink and grabbed a slice of orange, shoving it into her mouth and wiping the juices on her sleeve. This wasn't the dainty popular girl of Mattsfield. This was the true soul that hid underneath her human mask. "Will is going to die no matter what we do. Humans aren't meant to reincarnate. When they do, their souls become vital sources of power for the gods and either the Norns are going to get him, twisting fate like they love to do, or we can take him to Freya where he'll actually do some good."

This was the first time Sam had spoken so much of what we really did as Valkyries. I believed her when she said that Norns twisted fate. After seeing the darkness following Will like an ugly cloud, I had no doubt that I had to do everything I could to keep his soul away from them. But was being a battery for the Einherjar really any better?

I hugged myself and suppressed a shiver. "What if he

doesn't have to die?" I insisted. "If I can figure out how the Norns intend to kill him, then I should be able to save him."

I expected rage, but Sam gave me a sympathetic smile instead. "You're amazing, Val. Even when your memories are wiped beyond repair, you still wind up at the same conclusions." She dropped the remains of her orange in the trash and wiped down her hands with a paper towel. "I think we need some reinforcements. If all of Mattsfield undergoes a reset from Thor, you'll never get a chance to reap Will. It's time to give our exiled sister a call."

No longer able to suppress the emotions wrecking havoc through my body, I trembled. My fingernails dug crescent-shaped lines into my palms and even though I knew I couldn't trust her, she had answers. Will was already on the clock and now we had to do something to stop Thor from wiping out every memory in Mattsfield. "Have I activated Thor before?" I asked. I'd had the nagging feeling that William and I had met before. Memories were starting to come back to me and I wasn't going to play dumb with Sam anymore. If events were replaying themselves, I needed to get ahead of the game. "You have to tell me what to do differently this time. If I've failed to save Will before—"

Sam's smile twitched. "Stop, Val. I was hoping I wouldn't have to do this, but you need to know why trying to save Will is a bad idea." She tugged me to the door. "Come on. It's time to meet Elaina."

I had the feeling that Elaina was Sam's plan B in the event I wasn't willing to cooperate. "There's nothing this woman can say that'll make me let Will die," I told her. "We're wasting time."

Sam pulled off the highway and ventured onto a dirt road that led into underbrush. She ignored me until I was certain she was driving us into the wilderness. Trees branched out enough for me to spot a house that looked older than Sam and I put together. Moss covered it and vines strangled the long pillars that kept it upright.

"Here we are," Sam said and pulled into a dusty driveway next to a rusted pick-up truck. She jumped out and I followed her with a sigh.

"Sam, seriously. Why are we here?"

She gave me a tempered glare. "You might be able to mess with time, but you can't see the future, not yet." She knocked on the door, the sound a wet thud against molded wood. "But when you see Elaina, you don't need to be an oracle to understand what's going to happen to you if you continue down this path."

The door creaked open and I sucked in a gasp as a woman answered the door. She didn't have a manufactured human body like Sam and I. A majestic mane of hair unfurled over her shoulders and eyes of volcanic red glowed with the promise of Muspelheim, the birthplace of Valkyries and the origin of our immortality. She smiled and waved us inside. "I was wondering how long it would take you to stop by. Please, come in."

When she turned, the jagged skin beneath her tank-top

revealed the remains of two serrated stubs on each shoulder blade. She'd once had wings… but they'd been sawed off.

*laina poured us tea while we took our seats in the humble living room. I'd expected a rundown place like this to have an equally distasteful interior, but the furniture gleamed with fresh fabrics and an aroma of scented candles kissed the air. "My Valkyrie name is Eir. It means mercy," she explained as she handed us our cups. She smiled. "Although I prefer to go by Elaina these days." Sam sipped at the porcelain edge as if she came and had tea with an ancient in-the-flesh Valkyrie all the time.

Elaina moved to her own seat with such grace that I didn't notice the tea in my hands until the burn registered through my palms. I hissed and set the cup clattering on the table. "How is it that you don't have a human body?" I asked. "And what happened to your wings?"

Sam clicked her tongue at me. "Val, don't be rude."

"It's all right," Elaina said. She smiled, but the light of it didn't reach her eyes. Sadness followed her like a Norn's curse. "It's my punishment. Valkyries are awarded mortal flesh to accomplish their duty. But I failed to reap my soul. Now I am bound to my natural state until I may redeem myself at Ragnarök, but not before my wings were taken to ensure I'd never find my way back home."

I glanced at Sam before I asked my next question. "You failed to reap your assigned soul? What happened to him?"

She sighed and Sam gave her a wide-eyed stare. "Well, go on, Elaina."

Pain passed over Elaina's face. "I take care of him now. I was able to break the Norn's curse, but there was a side effect I hadn't anticipated."

Elation and fear rolled in my stomach at her admission. "So, the Norn's curse can be broken?" I didn't care if there were side effects. Nothing could be worse than ceasing to exist at all—except maybe what Freya had planned for him if I didn't find another way.

Elaina nodded. "It's better if you see for yourself." She stood and the folds of her gown shifted with her as if an invisible wind followed wherever she went. I caught a glimmer of a dagger shoved into a strap at her thigh and swallowed. Even if she seemed nice, she was a full-fledged warrior of the Valkyrie. I kept my senses on full alert as I followed her into the darkened hallway.

We rounded a corner and she eased a door open, revealing a dark silhouette facing the window. Storm clouds overhead blocked out the sun, leaving only ominous drifting rays to filter into the room.

"He hasn't moved from his bed in years. When you activated Thor, I had to place him in front of the window to get him to stop screaming." She shivered. "What memories he has left haunt him, even now."

With my heart in my throat, I forced my way into the room. I glanced at Elaina, but she gave me an encouraging nod. I approached the man who could have been old enough to be my grandfather. Leathery folds of skin drooped at his chin and glassy eyes stared out into the distance. If I hadn't been a Valkyrie, I would have thought him incapable of knowing I was there. But his aura roared to life at my presence and his body betrayed an indecipherable twitch. Elaina gripped my shoulder and eased me away.

After retreating to the living room, I shakily dropped to the sofa again and cupped the tea in my hands. Sam rested a hand on my thigh and gave me a sympathetic nod. "It's okay, Val. That doesn't have to be Will."

My gaze flicked to the Valkyrie who eased into her chair with unmatched grace. She took her cup and blew steam over the edge.

"Tell me everything," I demanded. There had to be something I was missing.

Darkness licked at her eyes, reminding me that even Valkyries held the vile magic within their bodies—including me. "That man in there is what's left of the love of my life. I made the mistake of breaking the first law of the Valkyrie." I flinched at the flat admission. I couldn't tell if she regretted her grievance or accepted that there was nothing she could do about it now. Her fiery gaze met mine and I had no doubt that no matter her feelings on the matter, rage was all she had left. "I broke Henry from the Norn's curse, but in doing so I also broke his mind. He's trapped in a cycle of reincarnation. Without the curse to link him to the gods, he cannot be salvaged for the Einherjar or recruited into Odin's ranks."

My eyes widened. "I thought all souls went to the Einherjar?" What was this about being recruited into Odin's ranks? I perched on the edge of my seat. "You mean he could become one of the Valiant?" He could be like Tyler…

Sam hissed. "You're not supposed to tell her everything, Eir. Just get to the important bits."

Elaina waved away Sam's outrage. "It's so rare for a soul

to qualify for Odin's army, and it's not worth the price, anyway. It's why I wouldn't consider it for Henry." She sighed. "Not that it matters. The life where the curse was broken was his only chance. We lived together, were even happy for a time. When he died from old age, I sought him out again." She fumbled her hands together and her gaze went distant. "I didn't know all his next lives would be like this. When his memories catch up to him, he goes insane. Now he's locked into his new destiny. One I chose for him and I have to live with every day."

Frowning, I bit my lip from asking more questions. I knew where Elaina lived now. I could always come back when Sam wasn't around and get answers she didn't want me to know. For now, Sam seemed content for me to learn how terrible life was for Henry because Elaina had broken his curse. I leaned in, ready to learn from Elaina's past mistakes. "So, you said there were side effects when you broke the Norn's curse. What do you mean 'when his memories catch up to him?' Is remembering a bad thing?"

She leaned back in her chair. "Without the curse to take him at a young age, he lives a long life." She frowned. "But his mind can't handle the memories that come rushing back on his seventeenth birthday. That's when the curse normally would have taken him. Everything comes flooding back until he drowns. His past lives. His deaths. His rebirth." Her lashes hooded the ruby glitter of her eyes. "His love for me."

A shiver ran through me. If memories were the problem, perhaps I could fix that. Will and I had already been barred from remembering our past together. "How did you break his curse?" That was the next step. Without breaking the curse, I would lose Will for sure.

Elaina rushed to her feet and jabbed a finger at the hallway. "Did you not see what I've done to him? Why do you ask me how to break the Norn's fate? Can't you see, I freed him from one curse only to trap him in another?"

Rising, I jerked my chin up with defiance. "You said it yourself. There was another way. You could have given Henry to Odin. What would have happened to him then?"

She scoffed. "Unruly child. Immortal life under Odin is no better than death. I wouldn't wish it on anyone, and you wouldn't be able to handle the cost."

I narrowed my gaze. "Why are you so sure?" I glanced at Sam, waiting for her to stick up for Tyler. He was happy, wasn't he?

Sam glowered and raised her cup to her lips and took a long sip.

Fury burned in Elaina and I knew that I was close to crossing a line. "Because, little Valkyrie, I served Odin's wife, and she is no better."

So many revelations in one day made my head spin. It was possible to save Will, but in doing so I would doom him to an even worse fate—according to Elaina, anyway. There had to be a way around this. I gripped the edges of the damp wood as my feet dangled over the dock and sent ripples unfurling across the glassy lake.

I'd come to the place where Will had revealed his dark

secret. The Norn's curse seemed to emanate here. They'd already taken one life. How many souls did the old hags need? I hated the feeling of inevitability that sucked the life out of the air, and with Thor's winds still howling through the skies, I felt like every force in the cosmos was trying to work against me. Even the answers I'd gotten from Elaina, the ancient Valkyrie who'd actually achieved what I was trying to do, warned me against my course of action.

"Damn it!" I yelled and hurled a rock into the water. It skipped three times before sinking into the abyss.

"Having a bad day?" a familiar, masculine voice asked.

I whirled to find Will towering over me, his trusty jacket draped over his arm and a sexy smirk plastered on his face. "Figured I'd find you here." I blinked with surprise as he settled himself at my side and handed me the jacket. "You really should wear warmer clothes."

I hadn't realized that I'd been shivering, but I snatched up his jacket and wrapped it around me. Instantly my trembling muscles eased as the musk of Will's scent of familiar embers wrapped around me. "What're you doing here?" I asked. I wasn't sure how well my powers worked on him. If he couldn't remember me revealing myself as a Valkyrie, perhaps Thor's reset could be kept at bay. But if his memories hadn't drawn him here, what had?

"Well, I'm not sure what you did, but after the storm eased off I realized that I'd left you all alone in my room with freaking tornados touching down." He shook his head and dark locks fell across his face. I resisted the urge to run my fingers through his hair and sweep the strands away. His gaze fell on me, his expression pensive and his chestnut eyes glittering with wonder. "Ever since I met you, I feel like I've known you forever. Why is that, Valerie Frigg?"

My name on his tongue sent fresh shivers down my spine. Even though I'd been given a fake human life, my name was my own. Frigg represented my division among the most precious of Freya's ranks, and Valerie is what my mother had named me. It was in homage to the Valkyrie, the promise that one day I'd grow to represent everything the warrior race was supposed to be.

I clenched my fists at the life that my mother had planned out for me. She envisioned me leading us all to glory, which included reaping souls and stepping on anyone who happened to be in the way. Being a Valkyrie didn't have to be about death. It was about justice, and while I was still on Earth, I'd do right by my charge. *That* is what it meant to be a Valkyrie.

I glanced at Will and drew in a shaky breath. I had to be careful how I phrased my words or else risk sending Thor into full-fledged activation. As if in reminder, thunder rumbled across the horizon. "Why do you think I'm familiar?" I whispered. "When you look at me, what do you see?"

He narrowed his eyes, his gaze going over the fleeting betrayal of my aura that wanted to merge with his. But ever since I'd pushed him away, the connection between us had dimmed. We weren't ready to remember our connection, not yet. "I don't know," he said. "It's more of a feeling, really. Like I've found something I hadn't realized I'd lost."

Heat crept over my cheeks, but this time I welcomed the physical reaction to his words. I couldn't tell him how he made me feel, but my body could. He smiled at my blush.

I leaned in closer until my heart fluttered with the nearness of him. It felt forbidden... and amazing. "Focus on that feeling," I told him.

His gaze fell to my lips and a familiar zing flitted through my chest. His chestnut eyes cleared of confusion, now burning with stoked embers of desire. Maybe he couldn't remember what I meant to him, but he couldn't deny the feeling that I awakened in him. If I had broken the first law of the Valkyrie with him before, then it meant there was something epic between us that couldn't be erased. "Something tells me I'm not supposed to get this close to you," he whispered, his breath hot on my face. He smirked. "My mom would freak."

"Do you always do what your mother tells you?"

He laughed, and I took that as an invitation. Wanting him to know what he awakened in me, I pressed my lips to his and electricity zapped between us. Instead of pulling away, Will leaned into the pain, pushing past the invisible force that wanted to tear us apart.

I ran my fingers through his hair and his hands wound down my back, pressing me close to his chest. His heat enveloped me and fire ignited in my soul. If I'd ever doubted that I owned a soul, I had no question about it now. It raged with passion and even if I couldn't remember, Will and I were star-crossed lovers destined to be together.

Just as Will deepened the kiss and thunder raged on the horizon, a warning that if we went any further the gods themselves would be enraged, a blistering screech ripped us apart.

I blinked up to see Jules towering over us with fists shaking at her sides. "What the hell is going on?" she demanded. "You into creepers now?" She looked out over the lake. "You come to *this* place and make out with *her*?"

Will stammered apologies as he jerked to his feet. "Jules, sorry. You're right. I don't know what got into me."

The humiliation of being Will's immediate regret made me want to slip into the lake and disappear forever, but then I realized there wasn't another car pulled next to my Porsche or Will's Jeep. How did Jules get here?

Before I had a chance to ask, Jules grabbed Will's wrist and dragged him away. "You're going to take me home." She glanced over her shoulder and glared. "Stay away from my cousin if you know what's good for you."

I bit my lip. Now I had no doubt that there was something off about Jules. An invisible force draped over Will and made the fire in his gaze dull to quiet embers. Only someone with Immortal gifts could do that... but what was she?

Will didn't look at me again, but when he pulled the Jeep onto the dirt road, a blue aura flicked to life. The part of him that loved me was still in there. Love between a mortal and a Valkyrie was forbidden, being the first of only three laws among Freya's daughters. The gods would put obstacles in our path to keep us apart. Perhaps Jules was one of them.

A VISIT TO MUSPELHEIM

I waited at the dock still clutching onto Will's jacket. Tears welled in my eyes and confusion pounded into my chest. What was I doing? Will might feel something for me, but what if any history we had was locked away in a life I couldn't remember? If I'd really broken the first law of the Valkyrie, the punishment was a memory wipe. The fact that I'd remembered anything at all, even hints and glimmers, meant that the feelings had been strong. But that didn't mean Will and I were meant to be together.

Sighing, I made myself get up and jump in the Porsche. It didn't matter if I felt conflicted. All that mattered was making sure Thor wasn't activated, resetting all of Mattsfield and guaranteeing that any memories I'd awakened in Will would surely be wiped for good. Even if I couldn't get him to love me again, I could at least figure out enough to save him.

When I got home, Sam didn't berate me or comment on

the oversized jacket that I clung to myself. Instead she silently took me in her arms and gave me a long embrace.

"You have so much heart in you," she said, her words a soft rebuke. "You really are Freya's lovechild."

I pulled away. "What do you mean?"

She gave me a sidelong smile. "You don't really believe that Freya gets pregnant and carries us all to term, do you? A goddess of war doesn't have time for that." She sighed and curled into the sheets as if she were a regular teenage girl dreaming about what life could be like. "We're all incubated from Yggdrasil's replica. Most of us, anyway." Her fiery gaze found mine, the Immortal ruby red shining through her mortal green. "I think the reason you have so much heart is because you were born in love. Freya is cruel to expect you to be any different than what you were created to be."

Curling up beside her, I kept Will's jacket tight around my shoulders. "Tell me more."

"You remember Odin, right?"

The name invoked images of an ancient cyborg warlord garbed in glowing gold armor. He traveled the cosmos on his fortress of a ship, the Mojinir. He'd gifted Muspelheim to Freya as a part of their alliance against those who'd exiled them from Asgard. A hum flitted over my senses, and I realized I couldn't remember who had exiled them. "They're allies," I said. "But I can't remember much more than that."

She nodded. "You're fighting Grimhildr's programming. I didn't think you would be strong enough to overcome it, but Freya should have known better. If you're really her lovechild with Odin, then you're not just a Valkyrie; you're a goddess yourself."

Sam calling me a goddess made me burst out with

laughter. "A goddess?" I said, choking on the word. "I certainly don't feel like one."

Sam grinned. "I didn't say you were a very good one."

If I was truly the daughter of not only Freya, but Odin as well, it would explain why I didn't feel like a Valkyrie. This wasn't what I was meant to be.

When Sam closed her eyes and thunder rumbled in the distance, I wondered what it meant that she would tell me that now. What did she gain? Even though I wasn't a purebred Valkyrie, Sam was, and she never did anything that wasn't part of a bigger plan to achieve her mission.

All this time I'd thought that Sam's mission was to help me reap Will's soul. Maybe there was another reason she was here. I had a sinking feeling it had something to do with the possible event of my failure.

❧

J awoke to the smell of coffee and citrus. Sam was at the fruit again, which meant that something was bothering her. When I got downstairs, she shoved a mug in my hand. Her aura blazed with ruby reds as if she were about to go on the warpath.

"What's going on?" I asked as I sucked down the much-needed caffeine. All night my memories had tried to resurface and tell me everything I longed to know about my past. There was something that had happened between Will and me—something horrible. If only I could remember what it was, I could prevent it from happening again. The Norn loved to repeat events, as did all the gods. Each deity settled into a routine, the Norn most of all, falling into a rut of repetition and gaining pleasure when they could recreate their greatest achievements. That was, in essence, the pull of the Norn's curse. Tragic death of the same soul repeated every generation gave the Norn their power. Death released energy, especially a tragic death by a soul trapped in a cycle of reincarnation. It was a cycle I needed to break.

"Freya has called for us," Sam snapped. She lifted her necklace and it glowed. I'd almost missed it with the radiance of her aura overwhelming the air.

I leaned in and examined it. "What's that mean?" I asked.

"It means we're screwed," she said as she ripped into an orange. "Freya wants to know why Thor's been activated."

I relaxed. "Is that all? We can explain it was just a misunderstanding."

Sam rolled her eyes. "Yeah, because the goddess of war is always merciful."

My stomach churned too much to bother eating breakfast, but I nibbled on a piece of toast anyway. Nothing was worse than coffee on an empty stomach.

After a quick breakfast, I followed Sam outside. When I went to climb into the Porsche, Sam stopped me. "Won't be needing that," she said and pointed to the sky.

I looked up, for the first time noticing the red beam shooting down onto us. Sam lifted her necklace and closed her eyes.

I did the same and suppressed a scream when my flesh disintegrated and my soul transported to another plane of existence.

$\mathcal{M}$y mortal body couldn't follow me to the plane where Freya resided. Pain ripped through me as my soul detached from my Earthly form. I didn't even want to think of what was happening to my body as I scaled the heights of the ruby beam, catapulting into space and flashing far beyond Earth in a blink of an eye.

Freya waited patiently as my soul gasped for breath at her feet. The cool metal felt so real under my skin, and when I turned over my hands I saw the silky gleam of my Valkyrie body.

I looked up to Freya and took in her glory. She lived in a place outside of time and space, as did all of Muspelheim. She appeared as the goddess she was known to be as she sat on her throne, a gleaming spear alive with fire in her grip. Her ruby gaze matched the fury in her blade. The warrior's leathers garbed her body, boasting that Freya would always be ready for battle. But I knew that my mother was more than just a goddess of war. She was also the goddess of love, beauty, and passion. Those were traits she'd suppressed after being driven out of Asgard. I tucked that refreshed memory away, realizing that she had more to worry about than an unruly daughter. There was more to Freya than the cold warrior who sat on her throne.

"Welcome home, my daughters." Her words boomed throughout the chamber.

Sam straightened and I sucked in a breath at her transformation. This was what my older sister really looked like. As much as I'd been wrapping myself in my human life, I'd nearly forgotten. A headdress garnished her hair with long feathers matching the very real appendages at her back. Her wings flowed with her breath, making her look like a living statue.

The rustle of feathers sounded before Sam spoke. "We heard your call, Mother," Sam said, her words taut with expectation. "I assume you would like to know why Thor has been activated."

Freya nodded, her fiery gaze flicking to me. "I sent you to Earth with Val so that you might keep her on track. Has she deviated?"

I resisted the urge to shrink into myself. "It's not Sam's fault," I insisted. No matter the question of Sam's loyalties, I wasn't going to let her take the blame for something I did. "Will's soul is powerful. He can be so much more to us if you allow me to break the Norn's curse." Tyler had helped me, helped us. Surely she could see that if he would be allowed into Odin's ranks, he'd be an even greater ally.

Freya raised a brow. "A Norn's curse cannot be broken." She shifted her spear to her other hand and it blazed with warning. "Let the Norn have their sacrifice. It is our job to pick up the pieces." I knew what she meant by that. Let Will's flesh die, then rip his soul from it and take what was left.

I growled with an inner-rage that was the Valkyrie in me. "You want me to take the Norn's scraps? We're better than that."

If I had tried to plead with the goddess of war that I believed in love, that I was living proof she still believed in it too, I would have lost her.

The flames of her aura peaked. "Go on," she said.

Sam glanced at me, her gaze a warning that I had better

be careful with my next words. Freya was not known for her mercy. The fact that I was on a mission to Earth after having failed her once tested the limits of what mercy I might be awarded again. "Deactivate Thor," I asked, amazed that my voice wasn't shaking. "The only way I'm going to break the Norn's curse is if Will works with me. That requires him knowing what I am and why I'm in his life. You can't expect a soul like his to break free of its twisted fate if left in the dark."

Freya's eyes narrowed. "Let's say you do break the Norn's curse. What then? He'll be useless in this life. In the next, the moment his soul remembers his past lives he'll break." She glanced at Sam. "Has she met Henry?"

Sam nodded. "The moment I sensed she was getting too close to Will I made sure to introduce her to Eir and Henry."

I bit my lip. So, I'd been right. Elaina had been a deliberate Plan B in the event I wasn't working with the Valkyrie program. The second I started to show any feelings for Will, Sam had marched me right on over to Elaina's house.

My fingernails bit crescents into my palms. "It's no coincidence that Elaina lives in that shack right down the street, is it?"

Freya sighed. "No, my daughter. I might have been weak enough to give you another chance on Earth with your soul, but I know you are of my blood. Which means you're stubborn and driven. If I have to show you an exiled Valkyrie and the unfortunate result of her 'love,' then that is what I must do." She straightened. "There is nothing I wouldn't do for you, my daughter. I took precautions this time." She glanced at Sam. "But I cannot save you if you don't wish to be saved."

I approached the throne and the heat of Freya's power radiated with warning. Sweat licked at my neck as I sucked in the heavy, heated air. I flinched when my wings caught the warm draft and fanned out. This body knew what it was like to live as a Valkyrie, but my soul craved to be back on Earth with Will.

"I will find a way," I promised. "All I ask is that you deactivate Thor. If you reset all of Mattsfield, I'll lose any progress I've gained. I won't stand a chance to break the Norn's curse." I spread my fingers in surrender. "I won't even be able to reap Will's soul. If he doesn't trust me, he won't come with me to the Einherjar, and I will not force him."

Freya offered me a slow nod. "You bring up a valid point, my daughter. Even if you don't have your memories, you're wise beyond your years. A soul trapped in the Norn's curse this long will be strong. He should have been reaped before this point, but now we must be careful." She rose from her throne and flames licked at her sides. She spread magnificent wings that took my breath away. "Very well. I will deactivate Thor." She ran a thumb over her spear and a mechanical click sounded. My shoulders relaxed. "Even if you do break the Norn's curse, my daughter, Will must die, and his soul must be reaped, or else he will suffer Henry's fate." She stabbed the butt of her spear into the pristine marble tiles. The strike echoed throughout the chamber and rang in my ears. "Do you understand?"

I nodded. "Yes, Mother."

I bit my lip as Sam took my hand and the ruby gleam tugged us back towards our mortal bodies. My wings disintegrated, sending ash down my back as pain ripped through my spine.

There was another option neither Sam or Freya had mentioned, but Elaina had let slip. Odin was another player in the game of souls, and if he really was my father, perhaps he'd help me save Will once and for all.

DAMN THE GODS AND THEIR GAMES

*E*ven though Freya had deactivated Thor, the storm clouds persisted, sending thunder and rain to punish all of Mattsfield for the sole actions of a Valkyrie who'd angered the gods. I'd hoped to see Will again, but school was canceled today.

I watched the radar on the weather station showing a localized system swirling around the town. Forecasters babbled excitedly about their theories of what was going on with Mattsfield. I nearly turned off the screen until aerial shots grabbed my attention.

"Is that Will's house?" Sam asked absently as she leaned over my shoulder. She yawned and draped herself over me like a cat. Both of us were exhausted after our out-of-body experience. An entire day had passed and I'd woken up on the lawn with my nerves on fire and the craving to sleep for a thousand years too strong to ignore.

I suppressed my own yawn and covered my mouth. When the shot zoomed in, my eyes widened. It was definitely Will's house. "Do you see that?" I asked, pointing to the screen.

She leaned closer and squinted. "Wow. Thor wasn't joking around." She snickered. "He even left you an omen. He usually only likes to do that with crop circles."

The trees twisted and debris perfectly settled around Will's home to paint the picture of a serpent eating its own tail.

Jormungand.

I dug through my blistered memories as the name surfaced. "Do you think it's from the Norn's curse?" I asked. A serpent eating its own tail represented Jormungand, Thor's alter-ego at the apex of Ragnarök. The program meant to serve the Valkyries would eventually malfunction and would poison the sky, raining terror on the world. Even Thor feared its inevitable end.

"I wouldn't worry about it," Sam said with a shrug. "Thor likes to be dramatic. He thinks he's so powerful that his malfunction will destroy the world." She winked. "That's only if Ragnarök is triggered, which isn't going to happen. Only a Valkyrie can trigger Ragnarök and I'm pretty sure none of us want to see the end of the world."

I swallowed and stared at the screen. "Hope not," I murmured. I had enough problems to worry about trying to save Will. The end of the world was far beyond me.

Sam stretched. "I'm going to head out to the Diner." She glanced at the TV. "You coming, or you going to beat yourself up over activating Thor all day?" She gave me a sympathetic smile. "I'm proud of you, though. You talked Freya down and got her to give you another chance." She brushed her hair back into a ponytail, wrapping the band from her wrist around her hair. "I guess it pays to be a favorite."

Ignoring her attempts to rile me up, I waved her away. "You should get some rest. It's my fault Freya summoned us."

She shook her head. "Your job is to reap Will." She turned. "Mine is to make sure you have food…" She gave me a sly grin over her shoulder. "and perhaps to flirt a little bit with the local chefs."

I absently waved. "Have fun." I propped a book up and squinted at the text. English had gotten easier to read, but it was just for show. The last thing I wanted to do was test my nightmares after my visit with Freya.

She glowered. "Aren't you tired?"

I allowed the yawn to overtake me. "Yeah," I said around the exhaustion that pressed in on me. "But I don't want to sleep. You go ahead. I'll see you later."

She shrugged. "Suit yourself."

I waited until Sam's footsteps glided down the stairs and the car revved. When she was gone, I slammed the book down.

The walk to Elaina's was probably only twenty minutes.

Time for some answers.

*

I found Elaina on the front porch staring out into the forest. Her gaze had been on the skies as if keeping an eye on Thor and his threat. When I approached, she glanced at my necklace. That's when I noticed the scar on her collarbone where her own necklace should have been.

"You want to tell me about that?" I asked and ran my fingers over my collarbone. "What happened to it?"

She sighed and patted the seat next to her. "Sit." Her tone took on an ancient accent that bespoke of Muspelheim and our shared history. "I'll tell you all about it. But first..." her gaze went to the skies again, "you must tell me how you stilled Thor's hand."

I grinned. "All I had to do was remind Freya of her competition. She's just as keen on the Norn taking souls as she is of me breaking any of her sacred laws."

Elaina hummed thoughtfully, her fingers going to her scar. "I wish I'd had such insight when I'd tried to save Henry. I destroyed my necklace so that his soul couldn't come with me to the Einherjar." She frowned. "But without anywhere to go, he was reborn, and now he's trapped in a curse of my own making."

"You'd mentioned that there was another way," I reminded her. "You said that Odin recruits souls." I tilted my head to the side. "So why didn't Henry qualify?"

She scoffed. "Silly child. There's a price to pay for immortality, and usually it's one of equal value to the reward." She raised her cup and let it fall to the harsh cement. It shattered and I flinched. "Now my cup is broken beyond repair. How am I to drink tea again?"

I pondered her question thoughtfully. Ancient souls like Elaina liked to talk in riddles. "You could get a new cup," I offered.

She nodded. "Precisely." Her gaze met mine with

renewed fervor. "A life for a life. That is how immortality works."

I swallowed the lump in my throat. All Valkyries were immortal. It had never occurred to me that immortality was an earned trait. "The Einherjar," I began, "it has a replica of Yggdrasil." That's where reaped souls went.

Elaina nodded. "The last thing I wanted was for Henry to find himself picked apart in that place. Freya's invention salvages souls and uses that energy to create her daughters —Immortals, no less."

Blood drained from my face and my fingertips went cold. "So, any soul that is reaped and sent to the Einherjar… is destroyed?"

She shrugged. "It's not true destruction, not in the way the Norn do it. But it's death, in a way, no less. That is why I could not reap Henry. I could never destroy the love of my life." Her eyes brimmed with tears. "But I fear the endless life I've given him wasn't worth the price. Seventeen short years. He only just starts to learn about himself before I lose him all over again."

As if Henry had heard her, he cried out. The guttural sound swept through me and sent the hairs on my arms on end.

Elaina wiped away her tears. "I must tend to him. He's been a mess since Thor threatened the skies. I hope it dissipates soon."

"Wait," I begged with an upraised hand. "And what about Odin? Does he devour souls too?"

Elaina shook her head. "No, sweet child. What he does to those souls is a hundred times worse. They qualify for Odin's ranks by sacrificing an Immortal. It's why Freya and

Odin have such an unsteady alliance. For every soldier Odin gains, Freya loses a daughter." She rested a hand on my face and wiped away my tears. "If you want to doom Will to live an eternity without you, then that is your choice. In the end, one of you will die." Her hand dropped. "I suggest you embrace what it means to be a Valkyrie. We serve Freya, bring her souls, and in return are awarded with sisters to give us comfort amidst the sins we must commit. One day, Ragnarök will come, and the dead will rise again. That is our only comfort."

A thunderbolt struck with ominous timing, sending Henry into a fresh wave of panic. Elaina hurried into the house and I curled into myself before shuffling my way back home.

"Damn the gods and their games," I hissed and kicked a rock down the street. As I stormed down the dusty road, desperate to get away from Elaina's home, I vowed that I'd find a way to save Will... even if it killed me.

A PLACE ON THE LAKE

considered going home and trying to read Sam's mind while she slept. Although that plan hadn't worked so well for me the last time I'd tried to read an unconscious mind. Jules had found me leering over Will's sleeping body when I'd tried reading him. Who knows what would happen if I tried the same thing with Sam. I doubted she knew much about Odin anyway.

"So, to Will's it is," I said aloud and turned left down Eavestreet. I'd arrive at Will's place in another twenty minutes, but a sinking feeling told me to stop. With no one else on the road, still petrified by the officials that told everyone to stay inside, I listened.

Then I heard it. A distant, eerie cry.

A silhouette formed and ghost-like figure drifted across the road. "The hell?"

The creature drifted towards me and I rubbed my eyes. When I opened them again, I realized whatever I was seeing was very real.

"Who's there?" I demanded.

The creature solidified into a woman and black wisps curled around her arms and ankles. Smoke covered her body, clothing her in a sticky web and glimmered as she moved. Her eyes, black as pitch and a sinking deep void, sucked me in and made my blood run cold. "Stay away from our prize," the creature hissed.

By the gods… it was a Norn.

Her words slithered over me like an intrusion and I resisted the urge to slap away the tingles of a thousand spiders skittering across my skin.

A shiver ran down my spine. "Will doesn't belong to you," I insisted. Even though terror made my feet feel like they were surrounded by cement blocks, I forced a step closer to her. I reminded myself that I was the love child of Freya and Odin and a goddess in my own right. Not even a Norn could stand in my way. "You have no right to him. Release the curse you've placed on him and I will show you mercy."

The Norn grinned, revealing black, rotted teeth that clashed with her flawless, youthful face. "Stupid Valkyrie. Reincarnation comes with a price. It's the closest humanity can get to immortality. We don't choose the souls that give us power. They choose us." She spread her fingers. "Test him for yourself, if you don't believe me." Her eyes glittered. "If you can make it to him before I do, that is." With a blistering screech, she catapulted into the air and smoke swirled in a new tornado as it careened down the street.

I cursed and ran after her, my muscles burning with the effort. "Damn it," I hissed. Why'd Freya have to give me an unconditioned mortal body that preferred a couch to a sprint?

The harder I ran, the more I realized it wasn't just me being out of shape. My lungs constricted and I crashed to my knees as I struggled for breath. I grabbed my throat and my necklace went white-hot with rage. The Norn was sucking oxygen right out of the air. The trees jostled as her tornado went by, well out of range and en route to Will's house with no-one to stop her.

I tried to gulp in fresh breaths, but my vision dotted with black stars as I crumbled to the street and gravel tore at my palms. Was I going to die? Had the Norn already won?

Just when I was about to go under, a masculine form towered over me.

Tyler, wide-eyed and gorgeous, blinked down at me. His blue-eyed stare was the last thing I saw before I blacked out.

When I came to, I jostled in the comfort of crisp sheets and a tender touch on my arm. "Hey, glad you're awake."

I blinked at Tyler, almost not recognizing him in his human form. His shirt clung to him, drenched in sweat. Twigs stuck out of his hair as if he'd run through an entire forest to get to me. "How did I get here?" I asked, then clutched at my throat. My words came out scratchy as if I'd been strangled. I lifted my necklace and examined the charred edges that rimmed the sides of the amulet. I ran my thumb across it and cleaned away the dirt, revealing the immortal metal still intact underneath the tarnish.

"I brought you here," he said as he handed me a glass of water. "You should drink something."

My tongue stuck to the roof of my mouth and I realized that he was right. I grabbed the glass and gulped down its contents.

When I finished and let out the breath I'd been holding, he took back the glass with a sidelong smile. "The Norn are pretty rude. I'm glad she wasn't actually trying to kill you. That would have made my life pretty boring."

I curled the blanket up to my chin and stared Tyler down. He stood and offered me a hand. "If you're up for it, I'd like to show you something."

Swallowing, I numbly slipped my fingers into his and allowed him to pull me from the bed. My jeans plastered to my legs as if I'd been sweating and I tugged at the fabric.

I'd thought he'd taken me home, but he'd taken me somewhere else. I blinked at him, realizing that he had his own place.

He took me outside and showed me the edges of a lake. In the distance I spotted the dock where I'd shared my first kiss with…

"Will," I gasped his name. Had the Norn gotten to him?

Tyler rested a hand on my shoulder. "Don't worry about him. He'll be okay, for now. We still have time."

Shivering, I narrowed my eyes. "Where are we? I don't remember there being a house on the other side of the lake." When he didn't reply, I turned around and my jaw fell open. I pointed a shaking finger at a row of trees where a house should have been. "I'm not going crazy, am I?"

Tyler came up from behind me and I froze. There was something off about him, like he'd been holding back all this time and I was about to see what it was that he hid behind his mask of jokes and laughter.

Sunlight curled around his fingers as he slipped his arms over mine.

"Ty," I whispered, "you're glowing."

Before I could pull away, he reached around and stroked my cheek with such affection that I jerked with surprise. I whirled to face him, only to find that pain washed over his features. "Val. William isn't the only love you've forgotten." His gaze went over the lake again. "Freya permitted our relationship. She knew that you had too much passion in you to be a heartless warrior she forces all her daughters to be."

I blinked at him. He'd always been my best friend, but those gaps in my memory where Will had been taken out... what if parts of it had included Tyler?

"But you're one of Odin's warriors. Don't you have some decree of loyalty, or something?" I searched his face in the hope that something would trigger my memory. Yet, no matter how much I tried, I couldn't remember anything that would explain the raw tension between us.

He curled his fingers through my hair. It should have been invasive, but his touch was oddly comforting. "What if I told you only you had my loyalty?" He grinned, the motion charming and sent unwanted shivers down my spine. He'd never looked at me like that before, not that I could remember.

My fingers trailed up his chest and caressed his face. His Immortality shined through his skin like light trying to escape a cage.

"You like me without the glamour, huh?" he asked. I

watched in amazement as the dullness of his humanity fell like ash, as if his mask were a Valkyrie's wings disintegrating into the dust of Muspelheim. What was left was nothing short of a god worthy of marble statues and ballads and boy-bands. "I've been waiting to remind you what we had, but I'd hoped it would be after I kissed you."

I shook my head and broke free of his magnetizing spell. "Kiss me?" I blurted, feeling both incredulous and perplexed that all Tyler could think about was kissing me. My gaze flew to the docks and the air around us chilled. Whatever Tyler was, he affected the temperature, the clouds, and even though he didn't have an aura, he emanated an undeniable glimmer of gold that made his golden locks look like a crown and his ice-blue eyes a powerful weapon that could see right through to my soul.

"How can a mortal come between us?" he asked, his voice a low, husky whisper. "Please, Aerie, try to remember me."

The nickname jolted awareness through me with such clarity that my eyes squeezed shut at the pain. Memories forced themselves open in my mind like rusted clams relinquishing long-held pearls. I'd hated the name Valerie. My mother wanted me to represent all of the Valkyrie, but then he'd called me Aerie, a promise that with him, I could live in freedom in the skies. I recalled spreading my wings and flying with him for hours, releasing the burden of war for the precious moments that he could take me away from it all.

He hadn't just been my best friend. He'd been the foundation for my capability of love.

"Your name isn't Tyler," I whispered. "It's Tyr."

His lips were on mine before I had a chance to react. Memories of a life before Earth filled me with desperate need. I knew it was wrong to want this, to want to feel Tyler's touch on mine, his sunlight on my face. He was a reprieve against the darkness that beat against the wall of my soul… but he wasn't mortal. He wasn't capable of being what I needed him to be.

Tyler growled when I pulled away. "Why are you loyal to him? You're remembering."

I bit my lip before replying, the skin still plump from his kiss. "Yes," I whispered. "I remember that I loved you. I also remember what it felt like when you betrayed me."

He glowered. "I never betrayed you, Aerie. I was saving you from a choice you'd regret."

"By letting Will die?" I screeched. Tyler had been there, ever the helpful sentinel. I should have known that Odin wouldn't have left his secret daughter unprotected. Even now I was monitored.

"You're the one who activated Thor," I hissed and slammed my palms against his chest. As a warrior of Odin, he was easily five times stronger than me, but he backed away nonetheless. "Have you been following me? Stalking me when I was with Will?"

His crystal eyes darkened as he frowned. "Do you think it was easy for me to watch you fall for him again?" He swiped away my answer before I could speak it. "No, I don't want to hear your excuses. You're the one who failed me, but I made a vow to protect you, and that's exactly what I intend to do."

I shivered, unable to digest that Tyler was really my unwanted guardian angel. No matter how hot he was, calling Thor on me was not acceptable. "Why?" I asked as my voice broke. I wasn't angry with him, not when the memories of what he'd given me before I'd come to Earth were unfurling in my mind. He'd always been hopeful and smiling, never too tired to take a ride with me in the skies. My wings had been strong and graceful, and his power over the wind vibrant enough to lift us both into the clouds for as long as I needed. I'd never been permitted to leave Muspelheim, but Freya's allies were never far away. Any chance he got, Tyler made sure to come and visit me and wipe my tears away with a joke or a kiss. Our relationship had never moved beyond that, for it wasn't a physical relationship I'd needed. He'd filled a void of loneliness that was a place meant for Will. A place meant for the kind of love that broke the laws of the Valkyrie.

"Why do I keep to my vows?" he asked. "You insult me, Valkyrie."

I glowered. He knew that I hated to be called that. "Enough," I said and pulled myself together as I faced the lake. "A Norn has her clutches into Will. I don't have time to argue with you."

Tyler growled. "I'd say he'll be well into the second stages of the curse. You've pissed off a Norn something fierce. They usually leave their charges alone until it's time to feed, but now she's going to toy with him. Whether you intend to reap him or not, the Norn gaining more power is not going to be in our favor."

"What's that mean?" I snapped.

He waved his hand and the house reappeared. He stepped inside and waited for me to follow. "It means that we need reinforcements."

"How many immortals *are* there in Mattsfield?" I asked, my voice hitting a dangerously high pitch.

Tyler winced and stuck a finger in his ear. "Let's use our inside voices, shall we?"

Settling into a sofa that looked more like it was suited for a roman veranda than a lake-side shack, I let out a shaky sigh. "Mr. Jefferson," I repeated the name with the whole new meaning it now had behind it. Tyler had just told me that our World History teacher was a Surtr, one of the Jotun who'd allied themselves with Freya and *very*... very old.

There were more Immortals than just the soldiers of Odin and the daughters of Freya; there was a whole slew of Norse mythos that my human memories were doing a good job of burying. I needed my human brain to learn things my Valkyrie side wanted me to forget. Good thing one of them happened to be a teacher.

Tyler grinned. "There're a few Immortals who've come to spectate this second chance that Freya has given you. It's better if you don't worry about them. But the few who are actually here to help you are allies you need to make use of." He patted his chest. "Me, of course. I'm the most valuable ally you have." I rolled my eyes, but let him continue. "Sam is your mentor, but more of a babysitter that tattles everything to Freya. I wouldn't tell her too much if you're going off-script."

"Yeah, I got that much already." I shrugged. Even though it bothered me that I couldn't trust Sam, it felt nice to actually be able to talk about it. "I've been confiding with Sam just enough to get some information out of her, but hopefully with you on my side I won't need to anymore."

A handsome smirk lit his face, then a shadow fell over his gaze. "What about Elaina? You've met her yet?"

I narrowed my eyes and pushed myself deeper into the sofa. "Yeah, but she's not much help. She wants me to let Will die."

He gave me a raised brow. "She's you, just older and dumb enough to break a Norn's curse without a backup plan."

"She's not me," I snapped, then realized what he'd just implied. "You think it's possible to break the Norn's curse without turning Will into a vegetable like Henry?"

"If anyone can figure that out, it's you. You're bent on helping Will, and I know better than to try and talk you out of it." He frowned. "That didn't work out too well for me the last time. He grabbed his keys from the counter. "We should go talk to Jefferson. He's a lot older than you and I put together. I bet he has some ideas."

Reluctantly, I peeled myself away from the couch. "Then why hasn't he been helping already?"

Tyler shrugged. "That's not a Jotun's way. He still has his alliance with Freya. He can't act out on his own, but if you initiate the conversation, he'll be free from his promises."

"What promises?"

He held the door open and waited for me to go through. "The promise not to interfere with a Valkyrie's mission unless called upon. He's been waiting for you to see through his mirage and approach him." He gave me a cocky grin. "Good thing I'm here. Otherwise you'd have floundered without me."

I rolled my eyes. "Yes, yes. I would be forever lost without you, all-mighty Tyr. You are my prince in shining armor."

Crawling into Tyler's truck, I expected him to flash another charming smile. I didn't even ask how he'd acquired the vehicle, much less a magically-shielded house. Instead, I watched as he settled behind the wheel, his mood turning somber. "I'm not doing this for the human," he said, looking straight ahead over the dash. He cranked the car and jerked the transmission into drive. "Jefferson isn't the only one bound by vows."

❧

I pondered Tyler's words all the way to the school. "Thought it was closed today," I said.

He broke the long silence to grunt at me. "It's cute that you think Jefferson ever leaves a place of knowledge." His arrogant grin was back. "That old Jotun doesn't know how to get his face out of a history book, especially mortal ones. He finds them cute, like fiction stories."

I chewed my lip as we pulled into the parking lot. "Uh," I said, tugging on Tyler's sleeve that fluttered with a mysterious, unseen wind. Golden motes continued to dust over his cheekbones when I asked, "Don't you think you should fix your glamour?"

He blinked at me with surprise, then burst out in the most adorable laughter that I couldn't help but smile. "Gods, Aerie. I'm so used to being myself around you, I almost forgot." I blinked and the golden aura faded, the majestic perfection of Tyr, the Immortal in service to Odin, vanished as if it had all been a dream. All that was left behind was my hot human friend. "Better?"

I grinned and pinched his cheek. "Much."

Rolling his eyes, he walked with me to the school doors. Usually Mattsfield kept itself locked, but Tyler waved his hand and smirked as the lock unlatched. "You're not the only one with a little magic. Feels good to stretch my wings."

I resisted the urge to peer around his shoulder and see if he actually had grown wings. During our flights before I'd been assigned to Earth, I would soar with him, my own freckled feathers dull compared to his golden appendages of battle-worn glory. Odin's soldiers didn't usually get wings, but Tyr had been a special soul who'd won more than his share of Immortal powers along the way. Even though my memories didn't share how he'd been awarded such gifts, I had a feeling that there was a ruthless ambition beneath Tyler's charms. Power, of all things, did not come without a price.

Pattering down the dark halls, I followed Tyler to Mr. Jefferson's classroom. We found him at his desk bent over a stack of papers. He jerked his head up at our entrance. "Tyler?" he asked, then his gaze fell on me as I peered around Tyler's broad frame. "Miss Val? What are you doing here?"

Tyler snapped his fingers. "She knows. Drop the act."

Mr. Jefferson relaxed and dropped his pen to the desk. "Finally. I was getting worried she'd repeat history." He frowned. "The Norn would have gained far too much satisfaction by that. Old hags."

A smirk tugged at my lips. "So, uh, you're a Sir…" my words drifted off as I rubbed the back of my neck.

Mr. Jefferson stood and flames flickered behind his eyes. A cold sweat broke out over my skin to see him so casually prove that he wasn't human. "Surtr," he said and extended a hand in greeting as if we were meeting for the first time. "I'm one of the natives of Muspelheim where you were born. I've watched over you since you were but a child. You might not remember me. Heard Freya did a number on your memories and now you're human to boot—but that's all right. We can start anew." He smiled and even though smoke drifted around his eyes, I wasn't afraid. He was right. I didn't remember him, but I didn't need memories. I focused on the way he made me feel, which was comforted and safe, like I'd found an old friend. My instincts hadn't failed me yet.

Taking his hand, I shook it and introduced myself with a laugh. "Still Valerie Frigg, confused and hopeless sixteen-year-old human."

He took his pen again and stabbed it in the air. "Part-human," he reminded me. "There's a Valkyrie in there, somewhere. We'll make sure she comes out again when you're good and ready."

Easing into one of the desks, I tried to pretend this was just like any other day at school; except my teacher was an immortal elemental that had known me since my infant days on another planet. Sure, completely normal. "So," I began, my voice already cracking, "you know anything about the Norn's curse on Will?"

Mr. Jefferson glanced at Tyler and they shared a moment of understanding. Ty motioned for Mr. Jefferson to continue. "Will's going to die in approximately thirteen days," Jefferson said in a flat tone. "Since you've angered the Norn, there's likely to be some amount of tragedy to build up to the event. They can only claim so much power from suffering at one time, but it won't stop them from trying anyway, especially when a Norn has been angered."

I glowered. "What did I do to *anger* it?"

Jefferson leaned over his papers. "Her," he corrected. "It always amazes me how similar races seem to despise each other the most."

I glanced at Tyler and he shrugged. "Apparently Norn are just really, really old Valkyries." He grinned. "Don't worry. You have thousands of years before you have to worry about becoming one of the old hags."

Rolling my eyes, I leaned on my elbows. "What a comfort. Thank you." I tilted my head. "So, what kind of tragedy are we talking about?"

Mr. Jefferson scribbled on the paper, and I realized he was grading quiz scores. I leaned closer. He couldn't possibly fail me now that he understood I had more important things on my mind than studying. "You really should listen to the lectures," Mr. Jefferson complained, ignoring my question. He frowned at the quiz and pushed it at me. "You always scored highest in class."

Getting out of the desk to snatch up my quiz, I crumpled it before I even looked at the score. "You mean *Valkyrie* class? Hate to inform you, but World History is the least important thing I've got going on right now and quite different than what I learned on Muspelheim."

Mr. Jefferson gave me a toothy grin. "Don't dismiss human mythology, Miss Val. It makes for good bedtime stories."

r. Jefferson and I talked until my stomach started to growl. He offered me a chocolate bar. I gave him a raised brow and he shrugged. "I like some of the human inventions," he admitted. "Sugar, I find, is a good boost when you're donning a fleshy form."

That made my other brow go up. "And you don't normally have a 'fleshy form?'" His devilish grin made me snap up the chocolate bar and add, "Never mind. I don't want to know."

"It's best if you savor it," he suggested.

With a sigh, I peeled away the plastic and placed the bar on my tongue, letting the chocolate melt. I couldn't understand how there was such a big world out there with Immortals and rules I didn't understand—couldn't even remember. Just when I was starting to figure everything out, my human side worked against me, stripping away memories that could help me fight injustice.

"Why do you look so pensive, Valkyrie?"

I took a bite of the chocolate, stubbornly chewing. "Because my own mother took away my memories and I have to ask a sugar-addicted Surtr for information about what's going on." I waved the chocolate bar with defiance. "Why would she do that? Just because of some stupid rule? So what? She fell in love, too, didn't she? I don't see anyone wiping her memories."

The Surtr shifted uncomfortably in his desk as he grabbed a pen, hovered it over the ungraded papers, then put it down again. "I'm allied to your mother," he began.

I clicked my tongue. "I don't care. Just because you're allies doesn't mean you have to stand for her hypocrisy."

He shook his head. "You're wrong, Valkyrie. She's no hypocrite. She'll pay the price for her love." His gaze flared with deep-seated embers. "That price is having to punish you. It eats her up from the inside to try and force you to be something you're not. You're anything but heartless."

I hissed. "Then why does she punish me? Why can't she just give me back my memories?"

Mr. Jefferson folded his hands, his demeanor becoming more human as if he were my professor once again. "I've come to learn many things about Freya, as well as her daughters." He unfurled his fingers, revealing molten veins that glowed red on his bronze skin. "I'm a Surtr, which means that I'm a native of your birthplace: Muspelheim." He clenched his fists and the air sizzled with heat. "It's also the graveyard of lost Valkyries, and the price of their past sins weighs on my kind more than you will ever know. Freya wishes to protect you from that fate, for she feels that pain as if it were her own."

I stiffened. "What?" I leaned in my chair. "What about Valhalla? Why aren't they there?"

He took a long sip of water, sending steam wafting across the glass by the time he set it down. "Valkyries are attuned to fire in that even death can't truly hold them. They're not destined for Valhalla. That's a paradise for Odin's warriors and privileged Immortals free of such weighty sorrow." He lifted a wooden pencil. I flinched as it burst into flames. He crushed it, then showed me the remains of glimmering embers across his palm. "You can't be destroyed, only transformed. Sins must be paid, and if they are not, that is how Ragnarök comes. Ragnarök means death to pay the price, then rebirth to bring the world back anew."

I frowned. "What's that have to do with me?" I gripped the sides of my chair. "Do you plan on killing me? I'll give you a run for your money, old man."

He grinned. "I pity any who put an attempt on your life. You aren't one to accept anything easily, much less death." His mood grew somber as the pile of embers flashed, leaving behind the same pencil that he'd burned. He twirled it around his fingers.

"Neat magic trick," I said, trying not to sound too impressed.

"It's not magic," he insisted, placing the pencil down. "It's understanding how matter works; how energy transforms. Your mother understands that better than anyone. She knows that if she doesn't uphold the three laws of the Valkyrie, the cycle of death and rebirth will consume us all."

"Ragnarök," I repeated the term. "So, you're telling me that making out with Will is going to bring about the end of the world? Why does loving him mean death and destruction?"

He chuckled, then turned somber. "You may not remember this, but I do. When you lost Will during his last life, your heart fractured into a thousand tiny pieces. There is no wound cut deeper than by love's loss. It's not love that Freya fears. It's love lost."

"But Elaina does it," I protested. I'd never seen someone so in love and miserable. "She hasn't brought about Ragnarök."

"No," he agreed, "but she gave up on Henry long ago. She is not the spark that could trigger Ragnarök." His chair creaked as he stood. Suddenly it felt as if he were a mountain, his eyes a storm that brewed over me with ominous premonition. "Should you break the first two laws of the Valkyrie, you would be in grave danger of breaking the third. Your mother knows what you're capable of, and that is because she has loved and lost." His eyes darkened. "Look where she lives now."

Muspelheim, I realized, had not always been a planet of volcanoes and flame...

BAD OMEN

There wasn't much I was able to get out of Mr. Jefferson until I was keen on stabbing him in the eye with a mechanical pencil. Tyler had finally returned, only briefly commenting on the tension in the room and yanking open some windows. He pretended to be annoyed, but his smirk said that he was getting far too much enjoyment from the situation. Mr. Jefferson sure did love to hear himself talk.

Only when the sun began to set did Mr. Jefferson finally get to something useful.

"Oh dear," he said as he absently looked out the window. "I hadn't noticed the omen." He scratched the back of his head. Flashes of red zapped through his fingers as he momentarily lost control of his glamour. "Illness, of all things. You must have really gotten under that Norn's skin."

I jerked to my feet and a blanket of graded quiz papers fell to the floor. The rest of the class had done surprisingly well. It shouldn't have surprised me that a Surtr made a good storyteller. "What illness?" I asked.

Tyler joined the Surtr at the window and shielded his eyes. "I don't see anything."

Mr. Jefferson pointed to a low-hanging cloud. "I would have thought that lingering evidence of Thor's impending activation, but that's too dark and too localized to be a storm cloud. Look." He hurried to the next window and pressed his nose to the glass, sending a shimmering wave of heat puffing an invisible layer of soot against the surface. Tyler wiped it away and narrowed his eyes.

I joined him and peered over his shoulder, but all I could see was one lone storm cloud hovering over an eastern part of the city.

My blood ran cold when I realized what I was looking at.

That's where Will lived.

***

"You can't go in there," Tyler said.

Upon my insistence, Tyler had reluctantly brought me to Will's place. We sat in the car parked two houses down as we stared at the singular swirling grey cloud that beat at Will's rooftop.

"Isn't someone going to notice that?" I asked as I leaned closer to the dash and peered into the sky.

Tyler shrugged. "We're probably the only ones who can see it." When I glanced at him, he gave me a sympathetic smile. "The Norn wants to get under your skin just as badly as you're under hers. If she's giving Will a new symptom of his curse, she's going to make sure you can see its omen."

I crossed my arms and expelled a breath. "I don't get it.

All I'm trying to do is the right thing. Why do they have to sink their claws into him like this?" Rage prickled over my chest and ran down to my legs until every inch of me urged with the need to run into that house and rip the Norn's curse apart with my bare hands. "Mr. Jefferson said this was an omen for… illness?"

Tyler nodded. "Haven't seen a Norn's curse take this form for quite some time. It's an insult to a soul like Will's." He straightened. "He has a warrior spirit. He will die fighting for his life. Illness is a different kind of battle that even makes a warrior feel helpless and humiliated." The way his eyes flashed with knowing made me wonder if he'd battled such sickness before.

Growling, I ripped open the truck's door. "Then I'm going to help him."

Tyler called after me as I stomped down the street. "Don't think that's a good idea!"

I didn't care what anyone said. I wasn't going to let a Norn do anything to Will. Not take his soul. Not put a stupid cloud over his house. And most certainly I wasn't going to let a Norn make Will deathly ill.

When I reached the front door I went to knock, but my fist fell through air as the door yanked open. I'd expected Will's mom, but it was Jules who glowered at me. "What're you doing here?" she snapped. "I think you've done enough damage already."

"I'm here to see Will," I said, my voice cold as ice. "I can't explain it to you, Jules. Something bad is happening to him and he needs me right now."

Her jaw clenched before she spoke. "All Will needs is for

you to get out of his life. He caught a cold sitting on the docks with you." Her gaze fell to the jacket wrapped around my waist. "If you hadn't been trying to seduce him, he would have worn proper clothing in the middle of a forest late at night." She jabbed a finger in my face. "Actually, he wouldn't have been out there at all. This is your fault. Now get out of my sight before I call his mother down and let her lay into you like you deserve."

If Jules hadn't had a good point, I would have snapped right back at her. Maybe the Norn's curse helped illness along, but what if they couldn't create illness from nothing? What if I'd opened that door, just like Jules said?

Tears pricking my eyes, I retreated from the front patio and shuffled down the street. Tyler pulled up and gave me a solemn look. "Hey," he said, "don't be so hard on yourself. Why don't we go get something to eat?"

I waved him away. "It's okay. I'd just like to be alone for a while."

Tyler glanced down the empty street. "You sure you don't want a ride home or something?"

I shook my head. "No. I'm fine."

Perhaps it was the crushing defeat he sensed, or something else that made Tyler get that protective look, but he pulled over and jumped out of the truck. I blinked and he was at my side. "You don't look fine."

I didn't like how close he was, or maybe I did. Confusion swarmed over me as he tucked a hand around my waist as if it belonged there. I hesitated, then pulled away. "Tyler, look, I know we have this history, but my memories are still suppressed." I met his gaze. It was impossible to read him when he looked like this. His chest was a hard, impenetrable wall and he wasn't going to move until he knew I was okay. Instead I gave him the best smile I could manage. "Really. I'm fine. I just want to be alone."

He stared down at me for a moment that stretched out. My heart thundered in my ears until he finally pulled away. "Fine," he relented. "If you need me, all you have to do is say my name."

He got into his truck and then he was gone.

Finally alone, I let out the breath I'd been holding. Will's house sat on a cul-de-sac and looked out over an inviting forest. I marched to it and found myself a dry spot to sit on while I pondered what to do next. The ominous cloud continued to swirl over Will's home, mocking me every moment it unleashed a Norn's wrath on a human who didn't deserve it.

Then I remembered something Mr. Jefferson had said. Will might be human, but I wasn't. No matter how much I felt like a sixteen-year-old Mattsfield High student, there was a Valkyrie's soul within this borrowed flesh. I fluttered my eyes closed and focused on that inner fire that came from Muspelheim's volcanic centre. I might not have been conceived like most Valkyries, but that just made me more special. Freya and Odin were my parents, which meant that there was untapped power within me, if I only knew how to reach it.

Part of my punishment for breaking the first law of the Valkyrie was a nasty side-effect, I realized. The suppression of my memories also changed who I was. Exasperated, I opened my eyes, unable to access the core of greatness that should have been within me. It was locked away in a tight ball of chains that couldn't be penetrated, not without the right tools.

Even though I couldn't access my core, the effort heightened my senses. Distant whispers sounded on the wind and I knew it was Norn communication I was picking up on. I didn't know how I knew that other than the crawling dread that turned my stomach at the sound of slithering words I couldn't understand. Old Norse had been my first language, but now it was buried along with a past that was growing harder to access.

My vision blurred and panic gripped my chest, but then when my sight snapped back to normal, I realized I'd done it on purpose. I tried again, this time with a target in mind and the blurry distance across the cul-de-sac came into focus—straight into Will's bedroom.

Jules sat on the edge of his bed and dabbed at his forehead with a washcloth. Will groaned and shivered, his face pale and his lips cracked and dry. He had more than a cold by the looks of it. It'd only been one day but already he looked as if he'd lost weight. His cheeks sank in until his cheekbones stood out with sharp points. His chestnut eyes glazed over with foggy residue as if a layer of dark magic draped over him like a shroud.

My fingers dug into the dirt. The Norn's curse had its grip on him all right, and Jules hadn't let on how bad Will really was. Maybe she just wanted to get rid of me...or maybe there was something I was missing.

Will's mother came into the bedroom and handed Jules a glass of water. Instead of trying to get Will to drink, Jules gulped down the whole thing herself. Before my rage cata-pulted me out of my hiding spot, I realized that the voices I'd been hearing weren't just the Norn. Will's mother's mouth moved and my eyes went wide.

She was speaking Old Norse.

*E*ven though I wanted to, I couldn't just barge into Will's home with the possibility that both Will's mom and Jules were Immortals. I didn't know anything about them. Who they were, what they wanted with Will, and what they'd do if they knew they'd been found out.

I didn't think Mr. Jefferson would be much help. If I wanted to know the history of Muspelheim, he might be a good place to start, but information on what kind of Immortals Jules and Will's mom might be didn't seem something that would be his forte.

Tyler, on the other hand, had deliberately said that there were other Immortals in Mattsfield. If he knew about this, I was going to kill him.

Super hearing and sight weren't the only Valkyrie talents I'd tapped into. I ran, my feet feeling as light as the wind as I sped down the empty sidewalk towards the forest where Will and I had shared our first kiss—and where Tyler had watched it happen.

My peripheral vision blurred as I went faster and faster, until I realized that I was reaching inhuman speeds. A gleeful smile erupted across my face. If I could unlock the Valkyrie inside of me even while I was in human form, perhaps I'd be strong enough to save Will from a Norn's fate.

I catapulted across the road and through the trees that led to the lake. I slapped leaves as I ran by, delighting and laughing with my newfound strength. When I reached the dock, however, only a circle of swaying trees applauded my achievement with their low creaks, as if they had distant, low laughter to mock me.

Tyler's house should be hidden on the other side. I cupped my mouth and called for him three times, but there was no answer. Putting my hands on my hips, I frowned.

Either Tyler wasn't here, which meant he was up to no good, or he was ignoring me. I didn't much like either of those options.

*Defeated, I made my way back to my house. My hair stuck to my face and sweat dampened my back as every muscle in me screamed that I'd overdone it. I might have a Valkyrie soul inside of this body, but my packaging was still couch-potato quality.

Gasping for breath when I finally reached my front door, I shoved my hand in my pocket, but my keys were missing. Cursing, I knocked. Must have lost my keys somewhere in the forest when I'd gone all supersonic. "Sam?" I shouted. "Lost my keys. Let me in."

A scuffle sounded as Sam ran down the stairs, the heavy thud of her steps far too loud for her one-hundred-and-ten-pound body. She was pissed.

She ripped the door open and scowled. "Where have you been? You're pretty sneaky to leave me like that when I go to take a nap. I woke up and you were gone."

I wasn't sure how to explain this one. Yeah, so, a Norn materialized and tried to eat me. She did some voodoo and turned into a tornado, so I had to run after her. Then I lost consciousness and woke up with Tyler gone super-sexy human-turned-god and then I awakened my Valkyrie powers and ran around really fast for a while, but now I'm back... "It's a long story," I said instead.

She rolled her eyes. "I'm sure it is. Get inside before someone sees you. Your hair is a mess."

Frowning, I ran my fingers through my frizzed ends and stepped inside.

I wasn't sure who'd been in charge of doling out the bodies when we'd been placed on Earth, but now it occurred to me that while this body was attractive, it did come with some major flaws that made me feel more mortal than Valkyrie. As I watched Sam make her way to the kitchen, no doubt to massacre some more fruit, she at least held some resemblance to our Immortal origins. Where Sam towered over me and boasted flawless, tanned skin and metallic hair, I was exactly the opposite. As a five-foot-two brunette with a set of increasingly glaring freckles, I realized that perhaps I'd made an enemy of whichever Immortal had been in charge of giving me this body.

As Sam settled at the bar and poured herself some soda, I decided to make an attempt to get some answers. "I was checking on Will," I said, making sure to keep my lies steeped in truth, "but I ran into some trouble."

She took a sip. "Clearly." She narrowed her eyes. "I got back from the diner an hour ago and expected you to be here." She raised her brows. "You should be focusing on reaping Will. If he's too strong for you to reap, then letting the Norn beat him down isn't necessarily a bad thing."

I growled. "Do you hear yourself? The Norn are not our allies. They don't want us to get stronger. Even if reaping Will was an option, allowing them to gain strength is a bad idea." I made a fist. "Plus, I've started remembering." I bit my lip. "Things about Will… and about Immortals."

Sam straightened at that. I knew that if I was going to get anything out of her, I had to give her something to take back to Freya. If Tyler was right, then Sam was more than just my babysitter. She was my mother's spy. "What do you mean, you're remembering?" she asked.

I shrugged and grabbed my glass. Soda fizzed as I poured and I realized how thirsty I was. I took a long gulp before responding. "Enough to know that there are more Immortals here than just us and Eliana." I glanced at Sam. I had her full attention. "Mr. Jefferson. I feel like I remember him. He's an Immortal too, isn't he?"

Sam shook her head. "Un-freaking-believable." She'd downed half a glass of soda and then refilled it. She took a long sip before speaking again. "I hate being a teenager. I could use a real drink."

I smirked. "What, do you drink ale or something?"

She rolled her eyes. "Not quite, but that'd be a start." She clicked her tongue. "You know those mortal stories about

Valkyries serving Odin's soldiers ale? Hilarious. Valkyries can beat those pansies at a drinking game any day. And we certainly wouldn't be the ones serving them. They'd be serving us." She laughed. "They follow us around like puppies as it is. It's pathetic."

I chuckled at the idea. It felt good to laugh. It also delighted me that Sam had slipped up enough to reveal that she was familiar with Odin's soldiers.

Soldiers like Tyler. Maybe he wasn't the only one to pay a visit to Muspelheim. Maybe… she knew a way for Will to become one without someone having to die.

"So who else is an Immortal around here?" I asked. "Do you think Jules or Will's mom could be ones? I don't get such good vibes from them."

Sam raised a brow. "You mean the overprotective cousin who keeps you away from Will? Can't imagine why you wouldn't like her." She took another sip of her drink. "As for Will's mom, you hardly know the woman. It's probably just your mortal memories getting in the way." She grinned. "Girls never like the mom. That's typical."

I watched Sam as she plucked out her phone and surfed the web. She was starting to look like a teen more and more each day. But I wasn't going to be fooled. If what Tyler had said was true, then Sam would go tattle to Freya the second I left her alone.

Even though I was exhausted, I only pretended to sleep. I wanted to go take a shower after my sweaty escapade, but I couldn't risk Sam slipping out without me.

My struggle against sleep was rewarded as night swept its blanket over Mattsfield and Sam snuck out the front door. With no car, there could only be one place she was going.

Although we'd been beamed up to speak with Freya in person, I had a feeling that Sam had some other means to communicate with our mother when needed. My suspicions were confirmed when I followed her out behind the house and she paused in front of an ancient tree. She lifted her necklace and placed her fingers onto the bark. Embers came to life at her touch and a red aura gleamed in the darkness like a beacon. Just like the Norn's omen, I doubted that what I was seeing would be within the human's spectrum of sight.

The tree's core disintegrated as if it were being burnt from the inside, yet it stood tall and massive as if untouched by the devastation. In the crevice formed a circle of fire, and in the center appeared Freya's face.

She was just as I remembered her from our previous visit, but now her features were marred by the lines of bark and I realized that the tree was actually unharmed. This was a mirage that worked between the space-time plane, a feature of our necklaces that gave us our power. I clutched my own necklace that burned in reaction to Sam's activity.

Freya greeted Sam and the ground trembled. "What news do you bring, my daughter?"

Sam straightened, clearly proud to have the title of Freya's daughter. Unlike me, she had no father. Freya had birthed her with a thousand others without the help of a man—at least, not in the traditional sense. Freya used the broken souls reaped by her daughters. A terrifying cycle of "saving" souls from the Norn was starting to have a whole new meaning.

"Valerie is starting to remember things," Sam began, immediately outing me to our mother. "What should I do?"

Freya frowned, but a ruby glimmer in her eyes sparkled. "Out of those disciplined with Grimhildr, none have recaptured their memories."

I sucked in a breath. Grimhildr was a program imbued into Freya's mystical spear. It cast a beam of forgetfulness programmed by Freya herself with a sequence of buttons. My mother had such power at her fingertips. I shuddered to think of what else her spear could do, or the fact that she'd actually used its destructive power on me.

"She remembered the Surtr, and she's starting to suspect Jules and the mother." Sam clenched her fists. "I don't know how much longer I can keep her in the dark. If she loses her trust in me—"

"We need that mortal's soul," Freya snapped, her tone turning dangerous. "Valerie's weakness is her capacity to trust too quickly, to love too strongly." Freya leaned closer to the shimmering edge of bark. "Show her an ounce of kindness and she will follow you to Hel and back. If you fail me now, all could be lost." She retreated from the screen and her gaze snapped to a place off the screen as a boom of metal on metal sounded in the distance. "Baldr's forces have found my decoy satellites. It's only a matter of time before he finds the Einherjar." Her face twisted with a snarl. "We don't have enough power. William is our last chance to fight

Baldr. If Valerie does not have the strength to do what must be done… then you must take her place."

Flames engulfed the tree, sending Sam covering her face and falling to the ground as heat wafted over the yard. In a brilliant flash the connection ended, leaving the tree swaying with the wind.

Only one sound remained to break the sudden stillness.

Sam's muffled sobs.

⋎

I ran back into the house before Sam could see me and dove under the sheets. It took her a full thirty minutes to collect herself and come inside. When she did, I squeezed my eyes shut and held my breath. Her presence lingered at my back as she appraised me.

When she retreated to the bathroom and closed the door, I expelled a lungful of air.

By the gods. Sam might be a Valkyrie, but I'd failed to see past the armor she wore every day. She wasn't heartless. Quite the opposite. All she wanted was for Freya to be proud of her. Freya—her mother and only parent. And whoever Baldr was, it sounded like he had my mother and her entire fleet in his crosshairs. If someone was really after the Einherjar, I couldn't just sit by and do nothing. That spaceship was the core of the Valkyries. Flesh was molded there, both of the mortal and immortal nature. Travel through galaxies, as well as the space-time plane, centered around the thousands of years of technology housed in the elite ship. I couldn't let anyone destroy it. No matter how I felt about my mother, I couldn't let the Einherjar fall into someone else's hands. I couldn't imagine what someone like a Norn, or a power-hungry elitist, would do with a ship like that. I didn't know who Baldr was, or I couldn't remember, but I had no doubt that if he claimed the Einherjar, humanity itself would be in danger.

There was only one slight problem. No way in "Hel" was I going to give up Will's soul to save a bunch of Immortals who'd had plenty of their share of lifetimes, even if Earth's future was in jeopardy.

Conflicted, I forced myself into a fitful sleep and drove to school the next day, eager to confront Tyler. It wasn't easy to get him alone, but at least Jules was still out of school to watch over Will. No matter what she was, I'd seen the way she'd looked at him. She cared, at least enough that she wanted to keep him alive. He would be safe with her, for now.

"Hey, *Tyr*," I said with a smirk, catching him at his locker.

He flattened his eyebrows. "We don't use our real names in public," he reminded me. He grabbed his books and shoved them into his bag.

He slung his pack over his shoulder and turned to leave. I gripped his arm hard enough to make him stop. "Hey. I've been trying to talk to you for twenty-four hours. Are you avoiding me?"

He shrugged me off. "It was a mistake to reveal our past. I was weak. Won't happen again."

Blinking, I gaped at him as he rushed into his next class before I could follow. Students snickered and Penny must have sensed my distress, for she broke from the herd of popular girls and clung to my arm. "Aw, what's with the frowny face? You and Tyler have a fight?" Then she made kissy noises. "Did he take the fake-boyfriend role too seriously and now he's all jealous?" She stood on her tiptoes and caught a glimpse of Tyler sitting at his desk. "I'll admit, though, for some reason he's gotten a lot cuter. Has he been working out?"

Yanking her back to eye-level, I shushed her. "You know what? I think I'm strong enough to overcome your programming now. Come on. Let's go somewhere I can focus."

Blinking at me with that dumb doll-like expression that her programming forced whenever I said something weird, she tottered after me. "Focus studies? Uh, okay, sure."

When we rounded the hall and the bell rang, I cursed "Hold on, I've got to do something first."

She nodded like a bobble-head while I slipped into Mr. Jefferson's class. He stared at me with his dry-erase marker poised on a pristine board. "Miss Val," he said, "while I know you love my class, I'm afraid you've already partaken in World History for today."

I curled my hands in front of myself with my "oh aren't I so innocent" face. "Sorry, Mr. Jefferson, it seems that I've lost the two hall-passes you gave me to pick up some research papers from the library. Could you redo them?" When he stared at me with incomprehension, I added, "And I'll be sure to get that permission slip signed by my mother after I'm done with my research project."

Swallowing, he grasped my meaning. When this was all over, I could either sing his praises, or demand his ruin.

With a glance at the classroom, Mr. Jefferson sighed and pulled out his pack of hall-passes. He wrote out two and ripped them off, handing them to me with a stern frown. "You be sure to tell your mother I said hello."

I nodded and smiled as I took my prize. "Of course."

When I emerged and took Penny's wrist, I flashed the hall-passes that were good for the rest of the day. Her eyes went wide. "How did you get those?"

I winked. "I'll explain everything. Now come on. Let's get to the library."

NEW ALLIES

Up until now, I'd only had Immortals for allies—if I could even call them allies. Sam ran to mommy every time I slipped up. Tyler may or may not be on my side, depending on his mood. Elaina was so crushed by her own faults that she couldn't see the possibilities of what I was trying to do. Mr. Jefferson was so terrified of Freya that I could manipulate him to do anything—while he thought I was still on official Valkyrie business. No telling how long that'd last.

Immortals were unreliable, I decided. It hadn't occurred to me to try and make a mortal one.

Taking Penny to the back of the library, I sat her down and wasn't surprised when she obeyed. Her programming was strong, but I was stronger.

I focused until I sensed the light hum that surrounded her. Once I found it, I flexed my fingers and reached into my core where the Valkyrie part of me lived. Grimhildr was the AI that had suppressed my memory—and thus my powers. I knew what she felt like now. Every day I reclaimed more of who I was and I could do the same for Penny.

The magic—no, the intelligent software—that suppressed my memories was a hammer compared to the soft thumb that Grimhildr kept on Penny's mind. She'd been a normal, albeit prissy, girl before the gods had interfered with her life. Without even knowing it, her thoughts and motivations had been overridden with the constant worry about what I was up to and how she could help me. I didn't completely undo that compulsion, or else she'd run screaming into the next town and I'd be back at square one. I investigated each layer before I unwound just the ones that blocked her comprehension of Old Norse lore and left her altered motivations intact. I needed her to know the truth about me without having a seizure, but I also needed her to want to help me.

I tugged on her mind until I felt the light snap against my senses that was the loosening of Grimhildr's grip, then I backed off. Enough of her programming was left intact that she hopefully wouldn't flip out when I told her the truth.

Fluttering my eyes open, I found her staring at me. "Val?" she asked, her voice rising in a hesitant question.

I took her cold fingers in mine and rubbed her hands. "Yes, I'm here. How're you feeling?"

She scrunched her brows together. "Fine, I think." She tilted her head. "You look...different. Did you cut your hair?"

I grinned. "When you look at me, what do you see?" I couldn't tell her I was a Valkyrie outright, but I could reveal my inner soul. Grimhildr was Freya's creation, and I could control it enough to manipulate her programming. But if I moved too fast, I'd unleash the other AI that messed with memories. Thor was Odin's creation, and didn't unwind memories or create new ones. It outright destroyed.

She leaned closer and narrowed her eyes. "This is going to sound weird, but you're not human… are you?"

I slammed my hand over her mouth. "Shh! We're not supposed to say that out loud." I wasn't sure how sensitive Thor might be, or who might be listening. I searched our corner of the library, but there weren't any spies peering between the shelves, at least that I could see.

When I released her, she smiled. "I should be freaking out, but for some reason I feel relieved." She squeezed my hands. "I mean, Sam is more my crowd. It never did make sense why I always hung out with you instead."

"Gee, thanks," I said. I resisted the urge to tweak her programming again.

She laughed. "Oh come on, don't be offended. But I get it now! You have the coolest secret, Val." Her eyes went wide. "So, what's the mission? I get to know it now, right? I'll be so useful, you'll see."

I debated undoing the compulsion that made her want to help me because I realized that Penny was going to get annoying, and fast. Only the knowledge that I had just twelve days left before Will died kept my questionable ethics in check. That part of her programming I'd leave intact.

I bit my lip before replying. "I need you to do something for me."

Penny brightened. "Name it."

⚔

I might have been banned from Will's house, but a Norn and her allied Immortals wouldn't attack Penny. After some careful tweaking of her programming, I was able to get her to work for me rather than for Freya.

She tottered to Will's front door with a gift basket and a pack of make-up homework in hand and rang the doorbell. When Jules answered, she flashed a frown, then covered it up with an appropriate smile.

Jules opened the door wider. "Oh, Penny, you're so sweet. Please, come in."

Teetering in my hiding place between two trees, I waited until I picked up murmurs of Penny greeting both Jules and Will's mother in the living room. That was just far enough for me to get into Will's bedroom without being noticed—depending on what kind of Immortals I was dealing with. Only one way to find out.

I slammed into my Valkyrie core and sped to Will's window with supernatural speed. Dizziness washed over me at the effort as my mortal flesh protested and I steadied myself on the sill before yanking on the window, but it was locked. Will never locked it since Jules usually snuck in this way. She must have latched it closed knowing I'd have the same idea.

Squeezing my eyes shut, I concentrated on the latch on the other side. I couldn't make it move, but I could make it burn.

The scent of melting metal tinged my nose and I tugged on the window again. It creaked open under protect and embers fell to the floor. I cursed and jumped inside, stomping the emerging flames from the carpet.

Will remained motionless in his bed, looking even worse than he had yesterday. I tiptoed to his side and pressed the back of my hand to his forehead. I'd expected him to be warm to the touch. Sweat glistened on his skin as if he were with fever, but I yanked my hand back when I felt the icy tautness of his skin.

I peered closer and lifted his eyelid. A foggy layer settled over his unfocused pupil. I pressed two fingers to his neck and held my breath. There was still a pulse, albeit a weak one.

Penny's raised voice broke me from my inspection. "I'm sure Will needs his rest," she said, loud enough for me to hear. "I can go over the make-up work with you one more time?" she offered.

I didn't have much time. Whatever new curse the Norn had placed on Will, it lived in ice. If there was anything I knew what to do, it was how to plant an ember and burn my enemies with fire from within. I leaned over Will and hesitated. This could help him, or it could kill him, but as footsteps came closer, I decided there was no other choice.

I parted Will's lips and placed mine over his, exhaling the essence of a Valkyrie into his lungs. He breathed it in, and twitched under my care, his mouth moving with mine.

A kiss of life. A Valkyrie's secret gift and my specialty.

Just as the doorknob twisted, I blurred out of the room and didn't stop until I was safe in my hiding place again. When I turned, Will was sitting up on his bed with the fogginess in his eyes cleared. I smiled, because Jules and his mother blinked with confusion. Whatever the Norn had done to him wasn't stronger than our passion. Maybe there was still a chance.

"That was incredible!" Penny exclaimed the next day in school. No doubt our timetable had sped up, but at least the first step of our plan was complete. We'd broken the Norn's illness, and next up would be the curse itself. I still had to worry about how to protect Will from the repercussions of reincarnation, but I had an idea for that too.

I straightened and smiled, having finally gotten a good night's sleep. This was the first time I felt like I was in control, like I had a handle on what was going on and what I was going to do about it. "Yeah," I agreed. "You did a pretty good job, too!"

Penny beamed at my praise and settled her lunch tray, taking an apple and biting into it. She sighed with content.

Shoving a spoonful of mashed potatoes in my mouth, I watched Sam and Tyler powwow on the other side of the lunchroom. They completely ignored me as they hunched over their untouched plates and whispered. They didn't know that I'd altered Penny's programming, so for once I had the upper hand. "What do you think they're talking about?" I mused. Sam had somehow gotten a job as a lunch chaperone. Whoever had let her in here no doubt had some Grimhildr programming humming in their ears.

Penny glanced at the pair. "No idea," she said. "Since when are those two buddies?"

I sighed. "Tyler's been acting really weird. He let me in

on some 'secrets,' if you know what I mean, and I thought we were cool. But now he's totally avoiding me." I frowned. "He told me to stay away from Sam, but now he's acting like her best friend."

Penny shrugged. "Maybe the No—"

Before she could finish the word that might trigger Thor, I yanked the apple out of her hand and shoved it into her mouth. "We don't use that word, remember? Let's make up a word for her if we're going to talk about this." Even though Freya had deactivated Thor, I wasn't going to be careless enough to trigger it again.

Penny glowered and took another bite of the apple, answering me after she swallowed. "Okay, fine. Let's call it Nancy." She drew in a deep breath. "So, Nancy, then, let's say she got to Tyler somehow. That's possible, right?"

I slowly nodded as I considered that possibility. "So why is Tyler all buddy-buddy with Sam?"

Penny leaned on her elbows as excitement built in her eyes. "From what you've said about your mom, your, uh, *family*, doesn't actually want to work against Nancy." She grinned, pleased with her theory. "So, what if, Nancy and your mom are working together?"

Chills ran up my spine. It had never occurred to me that Freya and the Norn would be working together, but that made too much sense to ignore. If my mother wanted Will's soul, and the Norn wanted Will's sacrifice, what better way to achieve both of those than to team up?

On cue, the double-doors to the lunchroom burst open, sending the students into silence. I turned to find Will leaning on Jules. He was still pale, but an unmistakable fight glimmered in his eyes. He was going to be okay.

The students clapped and the swim team jumped to their feet to greet Will. He parted from Jules' support to accept hearty slaps on his back from the swim team and football team alike. While Jules fussed at the guys to be careful with him, he smiled ear-to-ear. That joy faded when his gaze landed on me.

"Uh oh," Penny whispered, "he doesn't look too happy to see you."

Will averted his gaze, smiling again and resuming the laughter with his friends. Jules, however, gave me a triumphant look. Whatever magic she'd worked on Will, she'd turned him against me—for now.

NORN'S TWIST OF FATE

Tyler wasn't the only one who was avoiding me. Getting Sam alone was surprisingly difficult and all I wanted to do was just bypass all the manipulating and scheming and march over to Will's place and demand answers. I might have overcome his illness, but Jules still had her claws in him. Trying to talk to him until I figured out what kind of Immortal I was dealing with would certainly result in failure.

I reminded myself that I was making progress. Penny had done a great job as a distraction and was proving to be even more valuable in helping me unravel the Nordic mysteries that were hard at work in Mattsfield. She could look at the whole thing with some clarity and distance I just didn't have because she lived on the outside. But distance would only get me so far. If I wanted to get real answers, I needed to find out what Sam was hiding from me.

My Valkyrie sister came home late at night and tossed her keys on the table.

Sam startled when I came out of the shadows. "Goddess, Val. Don't scare me like that."

My eyes fell to her change of clothes. She'd been wearing a flowing white blouse this morning. Now she wore a man's shirt spotted with water droplets. Where my hair would have frizzed out of control when exposed to any sort of liquid, hers sprung into attractive curls. "Where have you *been?*" I asked, my mind spinning with unwanted images of Sam swimming in the lake with my supernatural ex-boyfriend. I could do the math. After I'd rejected Tyler, he'd gone straight to chumming it up with my sister. Now Sam comes home with the evidence all over her. "Were you with Tyler all night?"

She grinned. "Sucky feeling, isn't it? Wondering where I am. Speculating what I might be up to. How's it feel getting a dose of your own medicine?"

I took a threatening step towards her. "This isn't the same. I'm trying to figure out how to save Will's life when you're hooking up with my best friend. Plus I try to be a good person. You just like to make it a habit of stabbing me in the back."

She straightened. "That's pretty harsh, coming from you."

Rage engulfed me until I felt as if flames licked at my fingertips. "So, you don't deny it?"

She rolled her eyes. "Come on, Val. Like I'd hook up with Tyler." She climbed the stairs and I stormed after her. "I was with Joe."

I blanked, then remembered the mystery guy at the diner. I frowned. "Since when are you allowed to hook up with guys? Doesn't that break the *rules?*"

She laughed. "Please. Seduction isn't the same as love. It's called fun." After grabbing a towel and rubbing the remaining droplets from her hair, she seemed to relax. "Look, truce, okay? I'm trying to help you, believe it or not. Tyler told me he found a Norn's token, so I figured I'd have a look-see at that lake he's been protecting. That's where the Norn's curse is anchored, you know." She shrugged. "No reason I should be walking around at night on my own. Joe was my protector."

Human distraction, she meant.

Hackles lowering, I eased onto the edge of the bed and stared at my hands. "I want to trust you, Sam. I really do. But you want me to deliver Will's soul to our mother. I can't do that."

She sighed. "What if there was a way we both could get what we wanted?"

I glanced up at her. "And how do you propose we do that?"

She settled onto the bed and wrapped an arm around me. No matter how tough I thought I was, I craved Sam's approval and empathy. She felt like a sister to me and I hated to admit that her betrayal stung. "Do you remember anything about Baldr?"

The name sent an unwanted tremor down my spine and sweat broke out across the back of my neck. "No memories," I said, "just a bad feeling. Who is he? What's he got to do with Will?" Even if I didn't trust Sam, I wasn't going to turn down information.

"Who he is isn't important, it's *what* he is. An Immortal with a need for vengeance so strong that it'll turn the universe inside out if we don't find a way to stop him."

I swallowed. Whether or not I trusted Sam, I knew that statement to be true. "And his connection to Will?"

Sam leaned in, her voice turning conspiratorial. "Freya's army is only as powerful as the number of Valkyries she commands. In order to create new Valkyries, she needs the strongest power in the cosmos—the power of souls."

I tilted my head. "Unless you're proposing replacing Will's soul with something of equal value, I'm not interested."

Sam bounced with excitement, reminding me of a teenage girl. "That's precisely what I'm proposing. It struck me when I was looking for the Norn's anchor in the lake. Guess what. *I found it.*"

I blinked. "And what did you find, exactly?"

She leaned in close and whispered in my ear. "Why don't you come see for yourself?"

Sam promised me that we'd go to the lake right after school. Suffering through another day was absolute torture, especially with Will and Tyler both still avoiding me. Sam reminded me that my humanity was the only way I was getting close enough to Will to get him to trust me. She wanted me to reap him, but I needed his trust to do something far more terrifying. He had to trust me to help him walk into an afterlife that even Immortals said was impossible. That undeniable logic was the only reason my butt was in this chair.

"How do you go from two guys chasing you, to both of

them avoiding you like the plague?" Penny asked as she shook her head.

"Don't ask me," I said, muffling my words as I stuck my nose deeper into my textbook.

We were in World History class, which Penny hadn't been in until she'd applied for an adjustment of her schedule. She shouldn't have been allowed to change classes in the middle of the school year, but Mr. Jefferson seemed inclined to indulge her and had pushed the change through. Whether I liked it or not, she had become my constant companion and faithful sidekick.

Mr. Jefferson knew I'd done something to Penny, and I just hoped he wouldn't tell on me to Sam. Since he couldn't do much else, he crammed history down our throats and only when he started getting into the history of a Norse nature did I pay attention.

He placed his marker on the board, squeaking a long line across it to underscore the title he'd written.

The Norn: a dangerous deity of Fate.

"How many of you are familiar with Norse mythology?" he began.

The students shifted uncomfortably in their seats, especially Will. I glanced at him out of the corner of my eye and he pretended to be engrossed in his textbook.

Sun shed unabashed rays through the window, betraying dusty motes in the classroom. I'd have expected Thor to go on full-alert at the slightest mention of the truth, but a classroom with the purpose to teach history seemed to be a caveat to its programming. Perhaps Mr. Jefferson was an ally after all.

"You mean, like Thor and Loki?" asked Liam with a grin.

He flexed a bicep. "Ladies always like a man with some muscle."

The students snickered and Mr. Jefferson waved them down. "History is told by the victors, and in this case, the Western world has made their own interpretation of ancient history. Not all depictions are correct, but the closest I've seen in my... research, is the description of one of the lesser known deities. The Norn, weavers of Fate." He glanced at me, warning and danger a storm in his eyes. "They don't like to be messed with, especially when you're sniffing too close to their source of power."

As if to augment that statement, a loud thud jolted me out of my focus. I looked at the window to find a dark splatter, then another shadow approached.

Birds.

At first only a few hit the window, then the sky blacked out as an entire swarm beat themselves against the glass, sending cracks streaking across the surface. Students jerked to their feet and girls screamed.

"It's the Norn!" Liam shouted, his tone joking, but his eyes wide with fear.

To my surprise, Will appeared at my side and took my hand. He glanced at me before he guided me through the classroom which was distracted by the bird-suicide phenomenon.

Once in the halls, the thudding finally relented and the students roared to life, shouts and confusion leaving the classroom in chaos.

Will's eyes burned with the embers he'd stolen from me. If I hadn't known any better, I'd say that the fire in him was growing. "Was that your doing?" he asked me.

I ground my teeth together before responding. "Yeah, Will. I have magical powers and I sent the entire Mattsfield population of birds to their deaths." I shook my head. "Of course not. Why would you think that?"

He frowned. "Jules told me you're a witch."

I snorted on a laugh. "A… witch." I splayed out my palms in defeat. "Yeah, you got me. I'm totally a spooky witch."

"I'm serious, Val. If you're not a witch, then what are you? Why do I feel like we've met before, when I know you've never been to Mattsfield before a few days ago? Before Jules opened my eyes, I had all these manufactured memories of you and I growing up together." He squeezed my wrist until it hurt. "But we didn't grow up together, did we?"

Okay, that was new information. "Did Jules help you remember that?"

"This isn't about Jules," he snapped.

"Wait a second. You're going to call me a witch, but Jules is the one feeding you all these lies and she's off the hook? What about her? Did she tell you what *she* is?"

He released me and clenched his fists. "Unlike you, Jules has been honest with me from the start. I've always known what she is."

My mouth dropped open. "You're telling me you know what she is?"

He growled. "Stop pretending. You know exactly what she is and that's why you hate her. You're a witch who's made a deal with the devil and she's an angel sent to stop you before you do any more damage. I fell for you once, but it's not going to happen again."

I couldn't help it. I burst out laughing. "She told you that she was an *angel.* Oh, Will, that's hilarious." If anyone was an angel around here, it'd be the one with wings.

He slammed his palms against the wall, shutting me up fast. He leaned in, trapping me when his arms. "You think ruining my life is all fun and games, don't you? Well, let me tell you something. After I kissed you, I got sick. I learned from that mistake. It won't happen again."

A growl emanated in the back of my throat. "You got sick because of your curse, Will, not because of me. I'm trying to free you from it." I leaned in until my nose grazed his, proving to him that I wasn't afraid of his threats. If he thought what we had could be wiped out by a stupid lie, he had another thing coming. "And I will save you, with or without your help."

The bell rang and students filtered out of the classroom, still too wrapped up in what had happened to notice Will and me at each other's throats. Will's brows scrunched together and doubt glimmered behind his eyes. "I'm cursed, all right," he hissed. "Cursed to fall for you when I know that you'll be my downfall."

The admission and truth in that statement hit me like a blow.

He'd loved me once and paid the price with his life. Perhaps he was right. Perhaps my love was just as much of a curse as a Norn's Fate and we were both fooling ourselves.

THE UNIVERSE ON MY SHOULDERS

Ten more days, I reminded myself. I had to keep it together for ten more days, because after that, I had more than just a Norn to face. Freya would be expecting a soul and if she didn't get one, the universe itself was in danger.

"You look like the entire world is on your shoulders," Tyler said with a smirk. After Sam brought me to the lake, Tyler seemed to be on good behavior. Being nice to me was in his favor right now, at least as long as Sam and I had a truce.

"Try the entire universe," I complained and shuffled through the weeds that lined the bank. "I hate swimming," I reminded him. In my fake-memories, I'd been to all of Will's swim meets, but I never got into a pool. Even Grimhildr couldn't rewrite memories to the extent of my hatred for water.

"Of course you do," he said with a good-natured smile. He'd dropped his human glamour and radiated with handsome glory. I regretted not insisting that Penny join us.

Without a mortal around to keep Tyler in check, he wanted to make sure I knew what I was missing. His eyes glittered like crystals and even though it was the middle of the night, the soft golden glow he naturally emanated kissed me with the familiar warmth of the sun. "You were born on a rock of molten fire. I'd be repulsed if you liked water."

"Maybe that's precisely why I *should* like water. Plus, growing up without something should make me crave it, right? I had to grow up without oceans," I found a shallow entry into the water and slipped my bare feet into it, "or lakes." My lip curled with disgust. "Except, it feels all slimy and cold and gross. Kind of hard to like it."

Tyler snickered. "Leave it to a Norn to hide the source of her power in the muck."

I frowned, because even though Sam hadn't explained what exactly waited for me at the bottom of the lake, I knew what it was. There'd already been a sacrifice here, something that would feed a Norn's power with continual suffering every time Will came to visit it. "It wasn't just the Norn's curse that drowned Will's father," I said. "They needed something more to keep the loop going, didn't they?" Sam had said that reincarnation wasn't natural. Even though the Norn got their power from sacrifice, they needed to feed some of it back into the soul to keep it weighed down enough that it couldn't return to Yggdrasil and was forced to be reborn.

"If the sacrifice is strong enough, a human can stay in a state of perpetual reincarnation like Henry. He's likely got a last life somewhere waiting for him, the poor bastard is probably looking forward to it. But Will, as much as I hate to admit it, carries a lot of power. Too much power for the

Norn to handle without something extra to give them an edge."

I kicked up a splash of water. "Okay, so they sacrifice his dad, what for? Are they preparing for something?"

He tilted his head to the side. "They were preparing for you, I'd imagine."

My fingernails pricked painful crescents along my palms. Everyone seemed to know more about me than I knew about myself. "I'm fighting Grimhildr's suppression of my memories, but I'm not fast enough. We only have ten days left. Everyone thinks I have this grand plan, but trust me, I'm just winging it."

Tyler snickered. "Valkyries are very good at 'winging' it."

I rolled my eyes. "Very funny."

"No," he said, openly laughing at me now, "that's a good one. I'm writing that one down."

I wanted to be mad at him, but it was so hard when he smiled like that, his cheeks pinching into dimples that made him look so joyful and innocent. "You're dumb," I murmured. "You think you're so funny. Bet you don't even know what's at the bottom of this lake."

He straightened. "I bet it's something really gross, like an eyeball." He grinned. "They like squishy stuff."

I rolled my eyes. "Now you're just being ridiculous." I had no idea what object a Norn might imbue with their power for safekeeping, but an eyeball didn't make any sense. "An eyeball would be biological matter and would rot, especially at the bottom of a lake."

He pointed to the water. "Okay, smarty pants. Why don't you dive to the bottom and fish it out?" He leaned toward me, his grin an open challenge. "Prove me wrong, Aerie."

I glanced at Sam who lingered on the docks. It felt so weird to see her there where I'd made some of my very own memories with Will. I didn't have many, and as much as I hoped I'd make more, I wasn't naive. It was quite possible that all of this would be a giant waste of time and I would fail miserably, but that wouldn't stop me from trying.

"Did Sam try to get it before?" I asked. "When she came home last night, she was soaking wet."

Tyler shrugged and turned from me before I could see his face. "Sure, she tried. But she didn't want to touch it. You're Will's assigned Valkyrie. If anyone is going to mess with the Norn that cursed him, it should be you."

I pinched my lips together. Brushing aside my apprehension, I sucked in a deep breath and jumped into the lake.

Even though I knew I was an immortal Valkyrie, holding my breath underwater for a prolonged period of time terrified me. This was still a human body that needed oxygen to function, and even though I had mystical powers, I couldn't recall anything that would help me dive to the bottom of a lake.

I kicked as hard as I could into the darkened depths with the sole waterproof flashlight that Tyler had so graciously given me. The beam was powerful, but barely managed to cut through the murky waters a few feet. The lake wasn't supposed to be that deep, so even though my lungs were already starting to complain, I kept going.

The bottom of the lake glittered with gold, which wasn't what I'd been expecting. The flashlight beams bounced off the precious dust and it kicked up as I reached the sandy muck.

I didn't have much time to find my treasure, but I knew that the source of the Norn's power was down here, somewhere.

I swept the flashlight back and forth, only finding more of the glimmering dust. Bubbles escaped my nose as my body fought the urge to suck in a breath. Yep, out of time.

Launching myself from the floor, I winced as the shards of gold dug into my feet. I kicked, each motion costing me precious oxygen to fuel my body. My lungs burned and I followed the bubbles that rushed to the surface. When I had no air left to expel, the urge to breathe in was so great that I kicked as hard as I could before I gave in.

I broke through the surface and sucked in the most delicious mouthful of air in my life. I sank back into the water and splashed, coughing and sputtering as I fought my way to the shore.

"Well?" Tyler asked.

Sure, I nearly died, no big deal. "Glad you're so concerned," I croaked out. "I didn't have enough time. The lake is too deep for me to get a good look around." I tossed the flashlight onto the bed of weeds. "Plus, this thing doesn't give me enough light."

"Hey," Tyler protested, picking up the beam that shot a ray effortlessly through the forest. "I paid a lot of money for this trinket. Humanity might be eons behind us in technology, but they're getting better."

I frowned. "Well, it certainly didn't work that well underwater."

He sighed. "Okay, fine, I'll help." He pointed the beam at

my face and I slammed my eyes shut as black discs danced across my vision. "But you owe me one."

"Don't point that at me," I complained and slapped the beam away.

"You think that's bright?" he asked with a mischievous smile. He brought the flashlight close to his face and whispered in Old Norse I could no longer understand. An unexpected pang hit my heart that I'd lost so much of who I was that I couldn't even understand my native tongue.

After Tyler was done, the beam blasted renewed light that lit up the forest like a beacon.

"Hey!" Sam shouted from the dock as she jumped to her feet. "All of Mattsfield is going to see that thing! Put it out!"

Tyler tossed me the light and I dunked it under the water and pointed down. The beam crushed through the darkness and obliterated the Norn's protective power I hadn't realized was even there. "It's not just the water," I said with amazement. "The Norn is trying to hide her power."

Tyler grinned. "You're welcome."

*It took three more tries, but with Tyler's augmented flashlight, I finally found the source of the Norn's power.

Of course, it was a freaking eyeball. Gross.

If it weren't for my burning lungs, I would have hesitated to snatch it up, but I didn't have time to be squeamish. I also had no interest in attempting to drown myself swimming back down to the bottom of the lake for the fifth time.

When I surfaced, I resisted the urge to throw the object as hard as I could into the forest.

Tyler buckled over and laughed. "Oh, gods, it *is* an eyeball. I was joking!"

"Shut up and give me something to put it in already! This is disgusting."

Still heaving with laughter, Tyler managed to give me a towel that had been intended for drying off. I gladly sacrificed the luxury to have a place to wrap up the source of the Norn's power that I'd worked so hard to get. It didn't mean I wanted to touch it.

Marching inside Tyler's mystical lake home, my feet slapped against the wood and water went everywhere as I tossed the towel onto the dining table and unraveled the prize.

"Hey, I eat there," Tyler complained. "And you're going to warp all of my wood. You should dry off first."

Rolling my eyes, I ignored him and peered at the eyeball. It had felt real down at the bottom of the lake, but now that it was out of the water, it turned marbled and glossy like an ancient relic.

"What's that?" Sam asked as she followed us inside. She sucked in a breath when she saw what had our attention. "You found it."

I didn't have to ask what Sam had been doing while I'd been sucking down lake water trying to reclaim this thing. The tension between her and Tyler gave off a hum in the room. Something had happened between them and whatever it was, it was over.

She inched away from Tyler and closer to the marbled eye. "I couldn't find it when I was down there."

"Yeah," I huffed, "it took a few tries."

"No," she said, shaking her head. "I mean, I couldn't see *anything*. The Norn cloaked the source of her power." Her gaze flashed to me and I thought I saw something that looked suspiciously like admiration. "You shouldn't have been able to get through it."

"Thanks for the vote of confidence," I murmured.

"I've tried too," Tyler admitted, his body heat a distinct reminder of his closeness at my back. "Never been able to get close enough to it to see what it was, even with my light."

I frowned and snatched up the eyeball before backing away from them. The marbled skin burned with an icy cold power against my palm, but I squeezed my fingers around it. "If both of you tried and failed, why didn't you tell me? What if it's dangerous?"

Sam pointed at Tyler. "It was his idea."

Tyler smirked. "Don't look at us like that. You retrieved it. It's yours. I'm not going to take it from you."

Yeah, right, I thought. They both were just using me and I wasn't going to be too naive to see it. "It doesn't leave my sight," I instructed. "Both of you keep your distance from me from now on until I figure this all out."

Sam gave me a raised brow. "You plan on breaking the Norn's curse without our help? Because if you don't trust us, that's the result: we can't help you."

"And why would you help me?" I asked. "What's in it for you?"

Sam sighed. "I told you. You don't need to reap Will's soul if you have the source of the Norn's power." Her gaze fell to my closed fist. "But right now it's bound to him. We have to break the curse on Will before its power can be used somewhere else."

I shivered, both with the wet cold seeping into my bones and the realization that Sam and I were tentative allies, but only because our goals currently aligned. Even if she was on my side, that could change in an instant. "And after we break the curse, what happens to Will then? I won't have him becoming like Michael."

She shrugged. "It makes no difference to me. If you want to waste your energy trying to save him, go ahead." She took a threatening step closer to me and her eyes narrowed with warning. "But let me tell you this." Her fingers wrapped around mine and pressed my fist to my chest, the cold power of the Norn a haunting feeling in my grasp. "If you don't get this back to Freya with enough power to fuel the Einherjar, it won't matter if you've saved Will from the curse. He won't have a life to get back to, not on Earth. Not elsewhere in the universe. It'll all be over."

I searched her gaze for any hint of a lie, but only found fierce confidence.

"Great," I murmured. "Back to having the entire universe on my shoulders."

EYEBALL

*A*fter convincing me that we were all allies, albeit tentatively, I agreed to stay the night in Tyler's lake house. Apparently it was neutral ground where the power of the gods could not be used, promptly demonstrated when Tyler tried to cut me with his blade.

"What the hell was that for?" I shrieked as he stabbed the blade at my face. Had we been outside of the mystical walls that awarded a truce, it would have skewered me right through my skull. Instead, the blade rang harmlessly against my cheek and fell to the floor. I rubbed the spot that tingled with the blow.

"I wanted you to trust me," he explained.

I glared. "Yeah, by attacking me with a freaking Odin blade."

The silver glint of the metal rimmed with delicate blue flames and glowed with a golden aura reminiscent of Tyler's presence. When he picked it up by the hilt, it vanished into dust as if I'd imagined it.

"Can you always conjure that thing so easily?" I asked, my voice two parts horrified and one part envy.

He nodded, then glanced at Sam who looked like she was about to summon a weapon of her own just to skewer some sense into us.

"Enough fooling around," she snapped. "Let's get some rest. We only have a few days left before it's showtime. The Norn is going to notice we took her eye and she's going to come looking for it." She yawned and slapped a hand in front of her face. No matter how scary she could be, I forgot that she was just as much in a human body as I was.

Tyler waved me down a hall. "Your room is this way."

Pinching my lips together, I followed him and kept looking to see if there was any hint of his magical blade. I knew that our world was part magic and part technology, and at some point the two forces became one. But a blade couldn't just disappear into thin air, could it?

"I'm sure you're tired of sharing a room with Sam, but that was kind of her idea to keep an eye on you," Tyler said as he leaned into a doorway.

He flipped on the lights and revealed a Victorian-style room with a glass box. I approached it and ran a finger over the edge. It was nearly as cold as the marbled eye in my palm.

"It's to hold the Norn's power," he explained. "I figured it'd come in handy."

"Where did you get this?" I asked, my suspicions rumbling in the pit of my stomach. I clenched onto the Norn's eye even harder until my bones protested. "If you think you can trick me into handing it over to you—"

He rested a warm hand on my shoulder. I flinched, but

then relaxed. He had that look again, the one that sprinkled sparks in my memory of a time when I would have trusted Tyler with anything, including my life. "I don't expect you to trust me," he said, his voice low and hinting with longing of a past neither of us could reach. "But if you give me a chance, I'll do everything I can to earn your trust again." His fingers slid up and tucked a curled strand of hair behind my ear. My hair's attempt at drying was becoming an unruly mane that'd be a nightmare to untangle. But at Tyler's touch, none of that seemed to matter. The way he looked at me was with such reverence and adoration. I found myself wondering what life had been like when he'd been more than just a friend and fellow soldier that tried to stab me with swords.

"Fine," I breathed and reluctantly pulled away from him. I yanked the top of the glass case open and dropped the eye inside. A moment of relief hit me when the icy cold power left my possession and bounced on an invisible barrier as it settled into the box. I lowered the lid and peered at it roll over itself until it appeared as if it was looking at me. Frowning, I draped the towel over it. "That thing is so creepy." I glanced at Tyler. "Do you think the Norn can see through it?"

He laughed. "Could you still see out of an eyeball that you'd ripped out of your head?"

"Well, no, but my eye wouldn't turn into an icy ball of marble."

I expected him to laugh at me again, but instead he frowned. "Icy, huh?" He ran the back of his hand over my forehead as if testing my temperature. "How're you feeling?"

I flinched away. "Fine, why?"

He flashed with golden warmth and gave me an empathetic smile. "I haven't had the best experiences with Norns. Sometimes they get under your skin...literally." He clapped his hands together. "All right. We have a long week ahead of us. You'll be safe here, but we're not going to break the Norn's curse by hiding. So once we recharge, we're going after the crazy old hag full force."

I wanted to tell him that I didn't need to rest, but exhaustion gripped its claws into me and made my arms feel like weights hanging at my sides. Plus, I kind of liked how he'd said "we." Even though Tyler's true allegiance was still a question mark, at least we were allies, for now.

Nightmares pounced on me the moment my mind slipped under the thin layer of sleep. Will's soul glowed with a white fire that signaled like a beacon to a destination that was too far to reach. Even in my subconscious I believed Will already lost, but stupidly I ran towards him anyway.

The screams came next. Bloodcurdling Norn cries that threatened to flay the skin off my bones. Embers brushed against my face as I fought the frigid cold that threatened to stop my heart. Darkness swirled around me in threatening tufts that licked and hissed at my feet.

"Will!" I screamed, hoping that he could hear me and meet me halfway. Will had been reborn four times. That was unheard of for a soul and each life he grew even stronger. I sensed him burning in the distance like a piece of the sun, in some ways like Tyler's power, and in others a warmth that comforted rather than burned. Even if I didn't know the secrets of how a soul was recruited into Odin's army, I had a feeling that Will was close to qualifying. There was just one, vital ingredient missing. If only I could remember…

When I awoke, the screams of my nightmares still grating across my nerves, I realized that the sounds hadn't stopped. I jerked upright and sheets fell from my chest. Tyler had tucked me in, but now I sensed I was alone—except for the darkness clawing at my window.

I hauled myself out of bed and approached the oily sheen of glass that separated me from the outside. Darkness swirled as if the Norn had ripped out of my nightmares and now tried to get inside my wakened mind. She beat herself against the window and shrieked again, the sound jagged nails across my skin.

I grimaced but forced myself closer to get a good look at my enemy. This was the creature that held Will captive. This was a vile creature that wanted Will's soul because she didn't have her own.

I knew what she wanted when I peered through the glass. A face materialized, sunken in cheeks and one wild eye rolling in its socket before it fixated on me. I couldn't miss the other groove that filled with shadow where another frantic eye should have been.

You have something of mine, the Norn hissed.

The hairs on the back of my neck stood on end in warning. The only thing that separated me from this ancient echo of a spirit was the thin sheet of glass, but pressing my fingers up against it I felt the warmth of Tyler's power. Ice teased on the outside gutters, but melted the moment it seeped too close.

"And you have something of mine," I shot back.

The Norn hissed and slammed against the glass, shrieking with pain as her face melted. She rolled into a ball of shadow and reformed herself, glowering with pure rage.

That's right, she said. *Perhaps I'll go toy with him until you give me back my eye, you thief.*

In a swirl of shadow the Norn was gone, leaving me shaking. I curled my fingers into fists to still the tremors running through my body.

I whirled on the glass box and yanked it off the desk, cupping it into the curve of my arm.

It was probably the worst decision I'd ever made, but I wasn't about to let a Norn mess with Will again. She'd already made him sick. She planned on killing him. If I'd made her mad enough, maybe she'd alter the schedule.

Biting my lip, I used my free hand to yank the window open and I catapulted myself outside.

THE NORN

 anding on the damp mossy ground that encircled the lake, I paused and waited to see if the Norn would come back for me, but she'd already gone. When I would face her again, I only hoped that the possession of her eyeball would be enough to protect me from her wrath. Tyler had more than enough secrets he was hiding from me, and I had a feeling that no one besides him could get into the magicked case he'd prepared for the source of the Norn's power—not even me. That would be something I could use to my advantage.

I couldn't risk the sound of a car starting waking up Tyler or Sam. Their slumbering minds filtered through the night like a comforting wave and I grinned. My Valkyrie senses were growing stronger every day.

Delving into the inner core of heat that fueled my gifts, I ran through the forest with super speed, my bare feet a feather over the ground as I glided across pine needles and followed the icy presence that was heading straight for Will's house.

I didn't expect to be faster than the Norn, but I sensed her making a detour, giving me a chance to get ahead. Perhaps she wasn't alone, and even if she didn't know I'd been right behind her, she'd find out soon.

Dizziness washed over me when I slowed as I reached Will's house. Trees still twisted in the yard, a reminder of all the powers that were working against me. I gritted my teeth, just as stubborn as I'd been in my dreams to face impossible odds if it meant there was a chance at saving Will.

When I peered through the window, I spotted him fitfully fighting nightmares of his own. A glittering sheen of sweat dampened his forehead and made the silky locks I loved stick to his face.

I knocked on the glass. "Will," I hissed, keeping my voice low enough so as not to alert his mom. When that wasn't enough to wake him, I beat my fist until the window shook under my blows. "Will!"

He jerked awake, but so had someone else. A crash sounded from upstairs and a shiver ran down my spine. If the Norn wasn't about to stop me from getting Will to safety, his mother might.

He blinked at me as the nightmares still glimmered in the backs of his eyes. "Val?" he asked, his voice a mixture of bewilderment and horror. His features hardened into a frown as he yanked open the window. "How many times do I have to tell you not—" His words cut off when an icy chill swept through the streets and sank into my bones. My teeth chattered and I clutched the glass box with the Norn's eye to my chest, even as it began to vibrate.

"I don't have time to explain," I hissed. "Just, get your

keys." He frowned. "I know, but I promise you, if you don't come with me right now, we're both in trouble." I held out my free hand. "Please, trust me, just this once."

Maybe it was the desperate pleading in my voice, or a past that still linked us even through all that had happened, but Will relented, snatching up his keys and then placing his hand in mine.

It was just in time. The Norn's screech blistered through my ears and I yanked Will as hard as I could out of his room. We both collapsed to the ground, the grass poking into my sides.

The blood drained from Will's face as he looked over my shoulder. I turned to find multiple shadows rolling over themselves like a storm cloud with legs. Chills ran through my body. "We have to get out of here."

Will yanked me to my feet and dragged us towards his Jeep. "I have to get my mother—"

"No," I snapped. "They're not after her." I couldn't tell him that I had my suspicions about her anyway. She could be a Norn herself, for all I knew. "She'll be safer if we draw them away."

Will nodded at my logic and rammed the key into the ignition. "You asked me to trust you, and I am." He slammed the transmission into reverse. "But if anything happens to my mother, I'm holding you accountable."

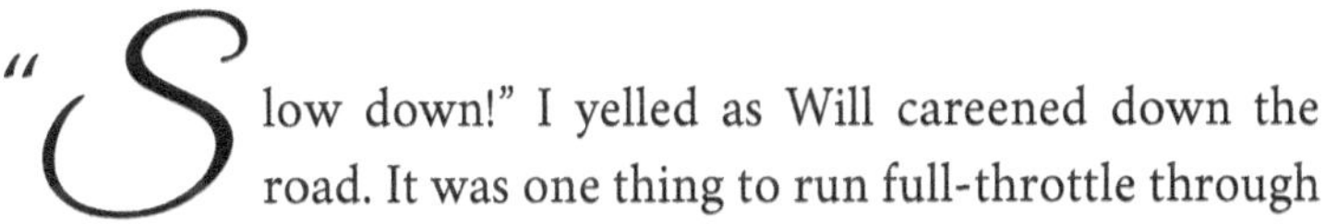

"Slow down!" I yelled as Will careened down the road. It was one thing to run full-throttle through the woods. It was entirely another to be at the mercy of a teenager behind the wheel of a car.

Will glanced at the rearview mirror and I didn't dare turn around to see what made his eyes go wide. The Norn screeched and sent terrible sounds splitting across metal as she chased us down the road. I didn't know how long the Jeep could keep a breath ahead of her supernatural speed. Shadows licked around the wheels and beat against the windows as Will slammed his foot on the gas pedal, putting us a few inches away from the shadows, but the trees blurred with dangerous warning that one false move would send us to our deaths.

"What are they?" Will yelled over the screeching that tunneled like a tornado made of metal shards behind us.

I shook my head. "You wouldn't believe me if I told you." I glanced at the sky and it was already roiling with clouds. I decided to try it anyway. "Does the word 'Norn' mean anything to you?" I reached over and squeezed his hand that was white-knuckled against the wheel. Electricity jumped between us the moment I touched his skin. There was a connection we couldn't deny and Will glanced at me with brows drawn in concern.

"No, but I'm sure it's not good." His jaw bulged. "Do you care to tell me where we're going?" he asked, his voice containing an uncharacteristic tremor.

He was right. We couldn't go full-speed all the way out of town. Luckily, I had a destination in mind.

I pointed to the exit that would take us back towards the lonely dock where a single canoe floated and the memory of his lost father haunted. "There," I said.

Will turned the corner, the wheel shrieking and adding

its own cry to the bellowing that followed us. "The lake's a dead end," he said. The edge of his voice tightened with warning, but his eyes were alert and ready. He had a warrior's spirit and he was ready to fight, even when something strange and impossible licked at our heels. It was no wonder that he'd gotten the attention of the Norse gods.

"There's a house," I said and pointed into the darkness that lingered behind the foggy layer of the lake. "You'll have to park and we'll make a run for it."

Will slammed on the brakes as we reached the lake and shadow billowed around us, laughter sounding triumphant as if we were trapped.

"I don't see anything!" he cried.

I yanked open the door. "Just keep on trusting me. We're almost there."

When my feet met the soft mossy bed that surrounded the lake, I found myself face-to-face with one of the hags. I knew it was the one that had her claws in Will's soul by the way she reeked of the darkness that suffocated him. She gave me a toothy grin, her sunken-in face both malicious and terrifying. When she lifted a fist, she twisted it and Will screamed in pain behind me.

This was it. I produced the glass case with the Norn's eyeball. Her expression changed from vicious glee to panic when she saw it. She jerked back in surprise, then stretched out her spindly fingers, blindly groping for it.

Just like I'd been aching to do ever since I'd found it, I reached back and hurled the case as hard as I could into the forest. A bit of Valkyrie power went behind that toss, and soon the glow of the Norn's power disappeared into shadow, causing her and her sisters to go screeching after it.

"Hurry!" I shouted and grabbed Will's hand. I yanked him along the edge of the lake and ran towards the hinting shimmer in the distance that was Tyler's house.

I'd been right. Whatever that thing was, the Norn's power was more important to them than Will's soul—at least for now.

I prayed, to the old gods and the new, that I'd be able to get us inside before they reclaimed it and came back for him.

❦

*D*istant screeches echoed around a protective barrier the moment I stumbled over invisible wooden planks that surrounded Tyler's home. His house sprang into view as if someone had turned on a light and Will gripped my arm in surprise.

"Don't freak out," I whispered, but Will was taking this better than I would have expected.

He recovered from the reveal of the magicked mirage and turned to stare into the darkness of the woods with wide eyes. No matter what weirdness I threw at him right now, none of it would compare to the Norn. "They were after me, weren't they?" he asked, his voice holding a low tremor that I wasn't sure was fear or rage. He eyed me with suspicion. "What did you throw into the woods?"

I took Will's hand and squeezed. I didn't even know where to start, and I couldn't guarantee that this would play out in our favor. I'd given the Norn my only bargaining chip, but if my suspicions were correct, the Norn would need us to get into that glass box. Tyler would have made sure that no one could get into that thing.

"Come on," I said, tugging him towards the door. I tested the latch, expecting it to be locked, but it swung open at my touch. Tyler glowered down at me as if I was a delinquent coming home after a night of partying.

Tyler's eyes darted to Will, then back to me. A growl rumbled in the back of his throat. "What do you think you're doing, bringing him here?"

Shoving past him, I yanked Will inside, only to face another disapproving face as Sam crossed her arms and glowered. "Do you think I was going to just leave him to the Norn?" I said to both of them. "They'd already hit him with illness. They were there, just slinking around his house. No telling what they were planning on doing to him next." I shot a finger at the doorway as shadows billowed out of the woods and screeches grew into a frantic pitch. Hints of sunken-in faces painted the darkness as they swarmed closer, stopping when they hit the invisible wall of Tyler's defenses. "Just look at those things," I shrieked, pulling Will closer to me out of reflex. He allowed it, but every muscle in him was taut and ready to bolt. I had no doubt that Will had felt these dark spirits hovering over him like a bad feeling that wouldn't go away. I glowered at Tyler. "You had a safe house all this time. I should be asking you why you haven't been protecting Will?" I untangled my fingers from Will's and stalked to Tyler who slammed the door, blocking out the metallic stench of the Norn. I stabbed him in the chest with a finger. "Is this about jealousy? Because if so, that's really petty."

I expected Tyler to get angry, but he just looked tired

and hurt. His sad eyes scorned me more than words ever could have.

To my surprise, it was Sam who slapped my finger away. "There's so much you don't understand." She opened her mouth as if to say more, then gave Will a wary glance. He hadn't moved from where I left him and had been listening intently to our conversation. Sam seemed to accept that it was time to let the mortal in on what was going on. "You've brought the target here, which changes everything. The Norn know we were coming after his soul. But now that we've taken him hostage, they're going to come at us, and they're going to come at us hard."

Will finally broke his silence. "My *soul?*" he asked incredulously. "Are you going to talk about claiming my soul like I'm not even standing here?"

Sam straightened. "Like it or not, your soul is up for grabs."

Stunned, Will fell into silence again. I rushed to his side. "Sam!" I cried. "Nobody is getting anywhere near his soul."

Tyler scoffed. "You gave the Norn their source of power. It might have distracted them long enough to get Will here without them ripping you apart, but the second you step off these grounds, they'll come at you full-force." I didn't like how his tone had changed. He talked as if I'd crossed a line, and now the Norn were my problem.

"What's done is done," I said. They couldn't argue with that. "I don't care what you think." Tyler's longing was a whisper of a dream that had been squashed. Sam's camaraderie was a shaky facade that didn't work when I wasn't playing by the rules. "You guys can stand there and judge me all you like, but it doesn't change that Will is here now and the Norn are out there. The next step is to get their claws out of him."

"You want to break the curse," Sam stated.

Will coughed. "Now I'm cursed?" He wobbled on his feet and I guided him to a sofa.

"Don't just stand there," I snapped at Tyler. "Get him some water or something."

Rolling his eyes, Tyler disappeared down the hall mumbling complaints about "pathetic humans."

"He'll grow on you," I promised Will.

He gave me a weak smile. "Right. Your boyfriend is actually some supernatural servant of the gods. Great."

Sam snorted, then shrugged at my glare. "At least he's funny, and he's not wrong."

Tyler reappeared and handed a glass to Will. "So, you brought him here. What's next in your grand plan?"

"Elaina," I said and glanced at Sam. "She can help us break the curse. She's done it before."

Will gulped down his glass and exhaled a long breath. "Stop saying I'm cursed. I'm not—"

Tyler rolled his eyes. "Come on, man. You're definitely cursed." He started counting on his fingers. "First, your dad mysteriously drowns in a lake he's visited all his life. You really think he forgot how to swim? He had more trophies than you did."

Will shot to his feet. "Don't you talk about my dad." Anger simmered behind his eyes. "How did you know about his trophies?"

Tyler kept his finger pointed. "We've watched you, Will. Val might not remember, but we've watched you all your life. Your father was a target, primed to give the Norn enough power to keep your soul locked into reincarnation. This sacrifice is going to give them a huge boost, just like your father did."

Will growled and shoved into Tyler's face. "You're telling me the Norn *killed* my father?"

Tyler wasn't fazed by Will's aggression. Instead he leaned in. I'd never realized how similar they looked in the way their cheekbones cut hard angles across handsome features. Tyler however had an edge, letting his mortal mirage slip until he looked like a Roman god. His skin emanated with a faint glow and his hair turned a metallic shade of blonde. "There was a storm that night, right?" He glanced out a window at the low-hanging clouds that betrayed the Norn that waited for us to leave our sanctuary. "Do these storms remind you of that night?"

Will was somehow keeping it together. "What do you know about it?"

Tyler grinned. "I know that it was the start of your curse in this life. So, what was next? Oh yeah." He unfurled a second finger and gave me a pointed look. "You were brain-washed into thinking that Valerie had always been a part of your life, when in reality you've only known her for a couple of weeks." When I cleared my throat, he sighed and added. "Okay, in this life, anyway."

Will glanced at me, then back at Tyler and Sam. Sam stuck a finger in the air and added her commentary to the building reasons that no one could deny Will was cursed. "Then tornados encircled your house. Would you call that normal?"

Tyler indicated a third finger for Sam's observation, then a fourth. "Getting sick. Then a flock of birds hurled themselves at the windows of your classroom, didn't they? That's just the start of the bad omens the Norn are sending your way," another finger, "and the eyeless wonder of the big bad Norn herself chasing you down the lake?"

By now, Tyler had run out of fingers. "All right, all right," Will said in defeat. "I just… I need some time to wrap my mind around this."

Will wasn't the only one. Enraged screeches swarmed around Tyler's home, making me feel more trapped than I'd ever been before. Even though I'd brought him to a safe place, it was just a cage. We couldn't stay here forever. He was still cursed, and if I kept him here, it would still claim him. I couldn't imagine Will dying, nor did I want to imagine how the curse would bring itself to fruition. One glance at Tyler's clenched fists gave me a hundred possibilities of how Will could die.

"Don't look at me like that," Tyler whispered. "I'm not going to hurt your mortal."

"Not yet," Sam said, confirming my fears, "but the Norn's curse is going to start working on all of us now that Will is trapped here." She produced a cell phone and began dialing. I almost forgot that modern technology would still work.

"Who are you calling?" I asked.

She placed the phone to her ear. "Elaina."

DEATH IS DEATH

Sam tapped her foot while the phone rang. When Elaina answered, she put it on speaker and set the phone on the table. We all leaned in to listen.

"Why are you calling me?" Elaina snapped. She'd always seemed put together, if not a bit lonely and defeated. But now, the rage in her voice sang clear through the garbled connection. "Don't think I haven't noticed Norn careening through the woods. There's only one thing they'd be chasing."

Sam glanced at me when she spoke, choosing to use my words. "What's done is done," she said. "We're trapped at Tyler's, at least until we figure out how to neutralize the Norn. In order to do that, we'll have to break the curse." Sam tilted her head. "If you help us, we can help you."

Silence.

It hadn't occurred to me that there might be something we could do for Elaina, but when she spoke again, I had a sinking feeling of what her request might be. "It's too late for Henry, at least in this life. I'm so tired of watching him suffer day after day." She strangled her words with a sob. "He could be happy, though, if I were stronger."

"That's okay," Sam said, her voice coaxing and cool. "We can help."

Another sniffle sounded. "Fine," she said, her voice almost indiscernible behind the faint hum of the connection that seemed to fight to break through Tyler's invisible shield. "I'll help you, but first, you must help me."

***

"No way," I said. "There's no way we're going to kill somebody. That's murder."

Will gripped my wrist, surprisingly keeping it together for all that he'd been subjected to already. I reminded myself that he was stronger than I gave him credit for. This was his fourth lifetime, and somewhere in there, he already knew who I was and what my world was like. He'd been a part of it in my last life, enough to warrant the full force of Freya's punishment. "You heard what she said. He's suffering, and it's not murder when he's going to be reincarnated. He's coming back."

I balked. "I can't believe you're saying that." I clenched my fists to keep my hands from slapping him. "Death is still death."

There was power in sacrifice. None of us had missed Sam's ulterior motive. With Henry's death, we could garner power, and with power, we could fight the Norn and their curse... but at what price?

Sam cleared her throat, reminding me that this was a group decision and I'd better get with the program. "We have to figure out a way to distract the Norn long enough for Tyler to get over there unnoticed."

I shook my head. "I can't believe you're even talking about this." I glanced at Tyler. "Are you accustomed to killing poor old men in their wheelchairs? Does that give you kicks?"

Tyler didn't flinch, but the air simmered with warning. "Aerie, I'd like to talk to you alone."

Will gave me a raised brow at the nickname, but shrugged when Tyler stalked out of the room. "Go on," Will said. "I'd like to ask Sam a few questions, anyway."

Leaving Will and Sam alone together seemed like a terrible idea, but I had to talk Tyler out of this absurd plan. "Fine," I snapped, "but don't even think about going anywhere."

He glanced at the window that still swirled with warning shadows. "Don't worry."

I found Tyler sitting at the kitchen bar, his long legs propped up on the edge of a barstool and his elbows grating against the counter as he palmed a fist. "Everything I do is for you," he said through clenched teeth.

I took a chair and pondered that blatant admission that he cared about me more than he should. Tyler had just admitted that he was willing to kill for me, albeit I didn't see how murdering Henry was something to be proud of. "It's just so barbaric," I said, my voice low and unable to hide the terror that swarmed in my stomach. When his brilliant eyes met mine, unabashedly Immortal, I sucked in a breath. "You don't seem capable of murder."

Tyler let out a cold, humorless laugh. "You clearly don't remember me, Aerie."

The nickname never failed to send a shiver down my spine. It wasn't one of fear, but one of deep knowledge of a life that I might have forgotten, but still existed in my heart. Tyler and I had history, whether I remembered it or not. "Then tell me," I said, my fingers gliding across the table and finding his of their own accord. It seemed right to touch him, to connect with him and try to understand the bond we had. No matter what I felt for Will, Tyler was still my friend. Now that I'd brought Will to his house, I was in his debt. I matched his gaze and wished I could let him in my mind to see how sorry I was for the way that everything had turned out. I wasn't blind. I could see the evidence of deeper feelings he wanted me to share. "Do you think that if you do this for me, I'll eventually regain my memories? That I'll feel something for you again?"

He pondered my question, then slowly nodded. "You've already started to reclaim memories that Thor should have made inaccessible to you. But," he squeezed my fingers and gave me a weak smile, a glimmer of radiance lighting up his face, "I know who you really are, even if you can't say the same for me. I don't know if you'll remember what you feel for me, but if I don't help you now, I'll regret it for the rest of my life." He chuckled. "And life for an Immortal, well, regrets linger for a long time."

I realized then that I had no idea how old Tyler actually was. If I'd been alive long enough to have witnessed Will's first life, then I was at least a hundred years old. "Holy shit," I murmured and reclaimed my hand in my lap.

"What is it?" he asked.

I tried not to hyperventilate. Will and I were technically

the same age, both in flesh and in spirit, but it didn't change the facts. "I'm old."

He barked a laugh. "Just figured that out, did you?"

I slapped him on the shoulder. "It's not funny!"

He grinned, my anger simmering into nothingness as fast as it had arrived. "Thanks, Aerie."

"For what?"

He shrugged. "For this. For making me feel... normal." He shook his head. "Believe it or not, I didn't get to see you for about twenty years. You were so wrapped up in your assignment during Will's last life, which left me with my own duties." He shook his head. "When Freya ordered me to..." He frowned. "When I had to see that look on your face, I felt like I'd lost you forever."

It was odd for me to picture Tyler being serious, but I'd never seen him more serene than he was right now. He was always laughing.

"What kind of duties?" I found myself asking. "When you weren't with me, that is. What kind of duties did Odin ask of you?" I bit my lip when he raised a brow. Yes, I was shamelessly digging for information to understand what Will might have to face should he become one of Odin's warriors.

He frowned. "It's better if you remember for yourself."

After the silence stretched between us, I found the strength to pull myself away from the questions of the past and focus on the present. I glanced at Tyler, straining to see through the god-like angles of his face and see the soft heart that was hidden underneath. "So, what'd you want to talk to me about that we had to be alone?"

He blew out a long breath. "I'll be straight with you,

Aerie. I don't want to save Will. I want you to reap his soul and send him off to the Einherjar and be done with it."

I crossed my arms. "But you're going to help me break the curse, right?"

He nodded. "Sure, but you don't understand. We can't just break the curse, or else he'll wind up like Henry."

"Yeeees," I drawled out, "I know. That's why I need Elaina's help."

He narrowed his eyes. "Why do you think she wants me to kill Henry?"

I flinched, but tried to think about it from his perspective. "Because he'll be reborn and she can see him again before he goes mad." Henry would be normal again, might even fall for her before the scheduled date he is supposed to die. When he lived on, all his memories would come rampaging back, turning him mad. I wasn't going to allow Will to be trapped in such an existence.

"There's more to it," he pressed, leaning closer. "The Norn's curse is a vital part of their survival. They need sacrifice in order to maintain their immortality. If we break the curse, then that doesn't mean the soul is free from their influence. That's not how their power works. Breaking the curse is one thing, but breaking the cycle of reincarnation is impossible. The soul will hit the afterlife and loop back into the world on a never-ending spiral. It takes magic to do that."

"Because reincarnation isn't natural," I added.

Tyler nodded. "That's right. And a soul already locked into reincarnation will continue to draw from the Norn and their power. It becomes the exact opposite of what they're trying to accomplish. A death which isn't on their terms isn't a sacrifice. It's just… death."

My eyes widened. "So if Henry dies, his soul will automatically reincarnate, and that will put a strain on the Norn."

Tyler grinned. "Exactly. It's Elaina's one and only weapon against them."

I wobbled on the stool, suddenly wishing it had a back to support my weight. "Do the Norn know that she's here with Henry?"

He bobbed his head to the side. "She's become adept at evading them. They tend to leave her alone since she allows Henry to live a full life." A shadow crossed his gaze. "Taking his life means she'll have to wait for him to be reborn. She'll have to find him again and go through the bittersweet years of him falling for her again. She has to gather enough magic to maintain a mirage to enter into the human world, which isn't easy for her."

I twined my fingers nervously. "And does Henry remember her?"

Tyler nodded. "Yes, on some level. But when he regains his memories, when he *truly* remembers her, that's when he loses his mind." He gripped my shoulder. "I don't want that for you, Aeric. If we break the curse without a Plan B, that's Will's future, as well as yours."

Tyler left out the part where Freya would force me into my Valkyrie form and rip off my wings, leaving me stranded on Earth to find Will over and over again, going through the same horror as Elaina.

"It's not going to be like that. Because I'm going to find

out how to make Will an immortal." I just needed another immortal to sacrifice that deserved it...

*S*aying it out loud was even more ridiculous than hearing it in my thoughts. *Turning* someone into an Immortal wasn't on the list of Valkyrie skills. But Elaina had said there'd been one more option to save Will from a fate like Henry's, and it had to do with Odin.

Good thing he was my father.

I waited until nighttime to test out my connection with Odin. If my necklace was capable of bringing me to Muspelheim, then I had another object of bringing me to the Mojinir.

I only had one other supernatural object, and that was my weapon. I wasn't sure what I expected when I closed my eyes and unlocked that part of my mind that was forever bonded to my spear. A Valkyrie's weapon was a part of her soul, and no matter what Grihildr had done to me, it couldn't deny my connection to it.

My body spasmed the moment the connection jolted into place. I envisioned the long, smooth staff of my blade and clutched onto it for dear life. My soul spiraled out of control, ripping from my flesh and catapulting through time and space. A distant memory expected it to take me to Asgard where Odin ruled, but when my feet clanked against harsh metal of a drifting spaceship, I knew something was terribly wrong.

Exiled. The word rang harsh in my mind.

Odin stood with his back to me as he gazed out of a

crystal-clear window that gave a perfect view of glittering stars and the endless void of space. A long, vibrant robe rippled around his broad frame, occasionally revealing the cyborg's mechanical left arm.

At first I thought that he hadn't sensed me, so I stayed perfectly still and held my breath. What was I going to say to him? Hello, uh, sir, Odin... no, mighty Odin, uh—

"What brings you to the Mojinir?" Odin asked, his voice booming as he turned and regarded me with an amused smile. "I told Freya that Thor wouldn't keep you from me for long."

I balked at him as I continued to clutch my spear. The hilt teetered on the thin metal of the hallway and I felt as if I could sink through the floorboards, finding myself drifting aimlessly in space.

Odin frowned, his puffy beard smoothing at the motion as if it were his customary facial expression. "You still fight Thor's influence."

It was more a statement than a question, but I nodded anyway, still clinging to my spear as if I could fly away at any moment. "I need to know how you create Immortals. Is it possible without sacrificing a Valkyrie?"

He moved to me and wrapped his fingers around mine, grounding me to my blade and sending my shoulders unhinging from my ears as I finally felt stabilized. "You've barely come into your gifts long enough to know how to contact me, much less stay on my ship as it moves through space. You endanger yourself, Daughter."

I shivered at the casual way a god called me his daughter. Everything Sam had told me was true. "Then tell me what I must know and I'll be on my way."

If he was offended by my brusque behavior, Odin didn't show it. He kept his fingers wrapped around mine, feeding me with the warmth and power I needed to stay on his ship. "I made the offer to recruit that mortal of yours in his last life." He leaned closer and the heat of his power singed my cheekbones. "You refused me. Told me the cost was too great."

In spite of the heat unfurling from this ship and the god who commanded it, a chill ran through my bones. Why would I have denied the one thing that could save Will? "I made a mistake," I insisted. "I will break the Norn's curse before it comes to fruition. When I do, I need to know that his soul has someplace to go. I can't doom him to a loop of never-ending madness."

Odin hummed with thoughtful agreement. "Yes. That hasn't ended well for Eir and her mate." He sighed. "I'm afraid there's no mighty secret of how to make an Immortal. It's something that naturally comes from warriors strong enough to claim it for themselves. I only recruit those who have already converted to our race. The Norn make the first step in prepping the soul for the transition, but those who break free of their own accord, they are the ones who will live forever."

I frowned. "Then why did Elaina... Eir, tell me Henry could have been recruited into your ranks? Why did she act like that was a bad thing?"

I was so tired of the secrets. Odin knew exactly why Elaina would rather have allowed the love of her life to endure such a horrible fate rather than serve as one of Odin's soldiers. I didn't believe him for a minute that he played no part in the creation of an Immortal.

I thought he wasn't going to answer me, but then he knelt to one knee and searched my eyes. I leaned onto the hilt of my spear, my body feeling so heavy on this ship. I had my Valkyrie form and my wings curled over my shoulders, brushing Odin's face. "Your sisters are the only sacrifice that can ascend a soul. Immortality of any sort must first start with death. The kind of death required to turn a mortal into an Immortal is not for the weak-hearted or even the compassionate." He brushed a sweaty strand of hair from my face. "The death to bring you into this world was almost too much to bear."

I froze. It'd never occurred to me that my own immortality had come at a price. "Who?" I asked, my voice a bleak whisper.

He continued to brush strands of hair from my face. That's when I realized he was much more machine than I remembered him. He should have only had a robot hand and an eye-patch, but half of his body whined with a metallic groan. "A part of both of us died, but you were worth it."

Tears pricked my eyes. What had died in my mother to give me life?

"Freya was right, my daughter. You are more her child than you'll ever be mine. You're something we've both lost. You are love, and for that, I will always be a stranger to you."

Before I could respond, he lifted his grip and my spirit slipped through the cold workings of the ship. I launched into space, reeling back towards my body, but not before I got a good look at the Mojinir. It formed a long blunt head like a hammer, the end of it glowing with gold that held enough power to decimate worlds.

A DARK DEED

hen I woke, I rubbed against the tender wound along the sides of my cheek where I'd bit myself. It'd been no dream that had tormented my sleep. I'd actually traveled through time and space and met with Odin—and now I knew the truth.

I stormed into the living room, finding Will, Sam, and Tyler already up and eating breakfast. I blinked at the steaming bowl of oatmeal, garnished with a side of eggs and bacon. Ty handed me a plate. "What?" he asked. "Just because I'm an Immortal doesn't mean I don't know how to cook."

I ate my share in silence, glancing at Will more than once.

"You okay?" he asked, inching closer to me and handing me a glass of orange juice.

I finished it off in three gulps. "We're going to kill somebody, and you're going to be Norn bait. So no, of course I'm not okay."

He sighed. "Look, if there's another way, I'm all ears. I

know I'm new to this, but I don't feel like it's all that new. Maybe that's why I'm not freaking out." He rubbed the back of his neck. "It's like there're memories just out of reach. It starts with a feeling, but the moment I think I have a grip on it, it slips away again."

That was the Norn's curse. The moment he remembered his past lives, he'd go insane—unless he was Immortal.

I rested my hand on his, not caring that Tyler clattered the dishes noisily into the sink and glowered at our contact. I could almost hear his thoughts from here. *This is my house.*

Tyler was just going to have to deal with it.

I squeezed Will's hand. "It's okay. Once we break the Norn's curse, you're going to remember everything." I smiled. "We both will."

***

Sending Will off into the woods as Norn bait was not my idea, but I wasn't about to leave him to do it alone—much less under Sam's supposed protection.

Sam rolled her eyes when I stood my ground. "You should really go with Tyler. Elaina is going to need to get back here. Tyler will be drained after he helps Henry move on to the afterlife."

I crossed my arms. "Why? Is suffocating an old man with a pillow so taxing?"

Sam gave me a dangerous glare. She stabbed a finger in my face. "You don't know what Tyler is doing for you. He's not a Valkyrie. He's not meant to help a soul move on."

"Then why don't you do it?"

She shivered. "No way do I want to be anywhere near

that soul when it plunges under."

I raised a brow, but that was all she was going to give me. "Okay, fine. We'll both protect Will." She shoved me at the doorway. Will gave me a sympathetic smile. "The Norn are going to come after him the second he crosses the threshold. We'll need to take turns boosting his speed."

The burning core of my power had never been stronger. Muspelheim's flames licked at the insides of my soul. Odin was right. I was my mother's daughter and it was her power that made me strong. "I'm ready."

We'd waited for dusk to make our run. Tyler waited at the back of the house where he'd slip through the shadows unnoticed while we distracted the Norn. They weren't really after us, and the fact that we were all Immortals meant that we were very hard to kill. Will, on the other hand, was their target and I wouldn't put it past them to take his sacrifice where they could get it, even if it was early.

"Go!" Sam shouted and Will catapulted off the doorstep.

Shrieks sounded the moment he left the protective barrier of Tyler's home. It took every ounce of willpower to stay my ground and let Sam take the lead. She was older and stronger than me and would be Will's best chance to get ahead. She ran up behind him and placed her hand in his, jolting them both with a vibrant red power that shot through them like lightning.

For a split second, I saw Sam for what she really was. Majestic black wings unfurled at her back as she lifted from the ground, seeming to fly rather than run as she glided into super-speed movements. Her wings weren't spotted and flawed like mine, once again reminding me that Sam was everything a Valkyrie was supposed to be.

Shaking off the feelings of inferiority, I delved into my core and released the heat that rested there. My weight lifted as my own invisible wings carried me across the grass, sending me following a safe distance from the pair.

The shadows unfurled from the forests and lapped over the mirror sheen of the lake, coming at Will and Sam from both sides. I sucked in a breath, hoping that they wouldn't find themselves trapped.

I checked the gathering of trees, finding a distant pair of headlights trailing away. Tyler had gotten out.

We had to keep the Norn distracted for a bit longer, but just as I feared, they were coming in from three sides, and if I didn't do something, Will and Sam would have nowhere to go.

"Turn back!" I shouted, but my voice wouldn't carry past the murky weight of the Norn.

Sam seemed to sense the plan, because she jerked to a halt with a nauseated looking Will at her side. Her wild eyes found mine and she mouthed something I couldn't make out until it was too late.

Behind you...

M y first thought when I struggled my way out of unconsciousness was about Will. I should have been more concerned about myself seeing as three of them loomed over me. We'd expected the Norn would go after Will when we'd sent him out here as bait. We were wrong—they were after me.

One of them sneered at me. "The little Valkyrie graces us with her lucidity."

Trapped on the forest floor, I fought against unseen slimy vines that constricted about my ankles. Shadows swirled around my wrists and only the flame of the Valkyrie power inside my chest fought to keep me warm. My entire body wanted to go silent and still at the invasion of the Norn's power. *I'm Freya's daughter,* I reminded myself, *daughter to a goddess.*

"Where's Will?" I snapped, finding my strength once the embers in my heart thawed the lethargy attempting to drape over me.

The Norn squirmed under my brusque question. The one whose eye I had stolen slithered closer and gave me a close-up view of her misshapen face. "We'll claim him when the time comes." She grinned and the sight of her rotted teeth made my stomach churn. "He thinks he's safe in that house of Odin's spawn, but nothing can stop our curse from coming to fruition."

I forced heat through my limbs and managed to sit fully upright. The Norn shifted away as if out of instinct not to touch me. She clutched something to the caved in remains of her chest. I squinted, making out the faint glow of Tyler's box. I smirked, pleased to see that I'd separated the Norn from the core of their power.

"I can't get into that box," I said, pointing to the glow the Norn tried to hide from me. "You can gross me out with her slimy shadows and your lake-monster breath all you want, but it won't change that I didn't place the bind that holds your eye captive." I leaned in and a maddening grin overtook my face. It frightened me that a part of me was pleased by the horror on their faces. "If you hate Odin so much, then you can hate him a little more. It's his power that has trapped your precious commodity."

One of the lankier Norn with stretched sinew along her forearms snatched up the box and shook it as if it were a Christmas present. The Norn with a missing eye, and clear owner of the object, shrieked as if the movement caused her pain. "Sister! Don't do that!"

The Norn ignored her and squeezed, creating the faintest of hairline fractures along the box's edge. She tried to continue, the lanky bits of her arms nearly snapping at the effort before the Norn with one eye reclaimed the treasure. She clutched it to her chest and shivered and growled like a street cat. "Beast. Breaking an Odin's lock will only destroy our power. Don't be a fool!"

The third Norn, having let this argument play out, took her turn to speak. She had no legs, the bits that used to be knees having rotted off, so she clawed her way across the dirt until she could latch her grip onto my ankle. Her nails bit painfully into my skin as she bore her teeth. "We're not supposed to look like this, pretty Valkyrie." She stabbed a finger at me in accusation. "It's because of *you* that we are reduced to ghoulish monsters. That soul you deny us is supposed to rejuvenate our youth." She snarled, the stretched lines of her jaw wrapping over gleaming, white bone. "The last lifetime surprised us. We didn't think you'd have the strength to do it." Her foggy, white eyes rolled into the back of her head. "You're going to do it again, aren't you?"

Even though I wanted to assure myself that this *thing* talking to me was nothing but a nightmare, I couldn't shake that she'd struck a vital memory buried deep in my psyche. No matter how much I fought Thor's programming, I wasn't going to regain that one anytime soon. "Tell me what happened last time," I found myself asking with a shaky breath.

The Norn grinned, and just when I thought she might tell me what I wanted to know, they all shivered and lurched with renewed shadows, their grotesque forms decaying even further before my eyes, revealing shards of bone and streaks of sinewy flesh peeling across cannibalized muscular layers. They screeched and I threw my hands over my ears, but nothing could block out the bloodcurdling screams that ripped through my body.

Forcing myself to my feet and backing away from the writhing remains of the Norn as they hurled themselves deeper into the forest, I knew what this meant. Tyler had succeeded in his mission.

I didn't have time to consider how I felt about Tyler killing another human being, even if it was a mercy. All I could do was run and get back to the house to make sure that Tyler returned, to make sure that Will was okay.

Ancient whispers followed me on the wind as I spread invisible wings and pushed myself towards Tyler's home. The edges of the house hit the moonlit sky as I spotted the weakness in Tyler's magicked camouflage. I gulped in breaths of the murky air as my feet glided over the mossy ridge that lined the lake. Icy reminders of Norn licking at my ankles as my Valkyrie power seemed to wink out of existence and my toes sank into the muck. I gritted my teeth and pressed on, the edges of Tyler's home within reach.

As the final screeching cries of the Norn ripped through

me like shards, I dove through the veil and landed on damp floorboards of a patio. I righted myself, frantically whirling on my heels and searching the roiling darkness. Surely Will wasn't still out there.

Relief slammed into me when Will rested a hand on my shoulder, letting his fingers drop when I turned, startled to find him alive and safe. I'd been so busy looking for him in the shadows, I didn't think to look for him in the light. The natural glow of Tyler's home illuminated Will's form. He smiled. "You're okay."

I laughed. "I'm okay? You're the one I was worried… about…" My words slurred and my eyelids fluttered as dizziness swept over me. An icy sensation rippled up my leg where the Norn had sank her claws into me and when I slumped over Will's shoulder, I knew she'd done something.

"Val?" Will asked, his voice rising in concern. I fought against the chill that settled into my bones. It sank deeper towards my core, as if seeking out the embers of my Valkyrie power.

Will tugged me inside and settled me onto the couch as I began to shake with uncontrollable shivers. Tyler was already there with a concerned-looking Sam hovering behind him. For a moment I jolted out of my shock, finding myself searching his hands for bloodstains and seeing none. The evidence of what he'd done could only be found in his eyes as a darkness that chilled me more than the Norn's power ever could.

Sam moved to push around Tyler and comfort me, but he shot up a hand in warning. "Don't," Tyler instructed. Sam narrowed her eyes at him, but backed away. "You'll just infect yourself. Let me handle her. You can go get the salve."

Sam swallowed hard, then nodded and glanced at me before hurrying out of the room.

Tyler likewise warned Will away, even though I had no doubt he was already saturated with the chill of the Norn. I didn't want him apart from me right now, but I bit my lip against sounding pathetic and calling out for him. The way he looked at me with such worry and longing in his eyes made me want to wrap my arms around him and never let go. It was a familiar emotion that threatened to yank me back into memories that were locked up tight. I wondered if it was the same stranglehold for him, and just as infuriating. Something precious had been taken from both of us, and I would do whatever it took to get it back.

When Sam reappeared with a vial filled with sloshing, golden liquid, she handed to Tyler with a grimace. He guided me to the sofa to sit down and I didn't protest when he uncorked the vial and lifted it to my lips. The silky smooth substance went down easy like honey mixed with milk. My eyelids fluttered closed as warmth centered in my chest and drove the icy fingers out of my heart.

When I opened my eyes again, everyone was watching me with a sense of horror mixed with fascination. A blush crept over my face. "What?"

Tyler was the first to shake off the peculiar reaction. "How're you feeling?"

I managed a nod. "Better, I think."

He eased onto the chair across from me and leaned on

his knees until we were eye-to-eye. His proximity felt too easy, as if we were the closest of allies.

I glanced at Will as guilt settled into my stomach. He'd looked away as if Tyler and I had something special and he was just interrupting. I tugged on his sleeve to bring him back to me and his shoulders relaxed at my invitation.

Tyler ignored the gesture and curled his fingers around my own that still held what was left in the vial. "If the Norn touch you again, you fight them. Don't let them get close, but if they do, drink what's in that vial." He narrowed his eyes. "It's not enough for three of them. I'll have to make more."

"What's in it?" I asked.

He smirked. "You don't want to know."

Will squeezed my shoulder. "So, is it done?"

A moment of silence fell over the room and I wanted to curl into a ball and hide. Tyler had killed someone, and I was just going to sit here and say it was okay. No, even worse, I *needed* Tyler to be a killer. He'd done something I'd have never been able to do.

Tyler frowned, but inclined his head. "Yes." His gaze lingered on the hallway and I hadn't noticed that Elaina had been standing there watching us. Her fingers wrapped over her arms as she seemed to attempt to suppress the uncontrollable shivers that shook her body.

I bit my lip as a pang of guilt hit me even harder. How selfish could I be? Here I was, worrying about myself, my relationship with Tyler and Will, yet Elaina had just lost the love of her life... again.

I tried to think of something to say, but my tongue went dry and stuck to the roof of my mouth. I wanted to be stronger than this, to demand that she keep up her end of the bargain, but the pain in her eyes made my stomach clench.

"Come join us, Elaina," Sam said with the smoothest voice I'd ever heard from her. Sam wasn't known for being gentle, but today, she coaxed a broken Valkyrie and treated her like the sister she was.

It was all the encouragement Elaina needed. She burst into tears and ran into Sam's arms, burying her face into her shoulder. Sam enveloped her with warmth and smoothed her hair. "It's all right," she whispered. "You did the right thing. You're going to see Henry again and he'll fall in love with you just as he always has. You don't have to watch him suffer anymore."

My stomach tied into permanent knots as I watched Elaina's face twist with agony. I couldn't imagine what she was going through. She'd just lost the love of her life and she'd have to wait at least sixteen years to see him again as she remembered him. Even when she did find him, he wouldn't know who she was. By the time he fell in love with her and all the pretenses were gone, he'd go mad with the true memories of past lives his soul couldn't handle.

I glanced up at Will who still held a warm, protective grip on my shoulder. Echoes of Elaina's pain rang in my own heart, for hadn't Will and I loved one another in his past life? Desperation beat at my chest, wanting him to remember me just as much as I wanted to remember him. But when I looked back at Elaina and took in the full measure of her uncontrollable sobs as Sam held her upright, I wondered for the first time if it was worth the risk to attempt to break the Norn's curse.

A DARK DEAL

It took three days, but Elaina finally told me what I needed to know in order to break the Norn's curse. Of all things, there was a physical contract made between a human parent and the Norn during Will's first life, exchanging his series of sacrifices for something of significant value in return. I couldn't imagine the kind of parent that would curse their own child, or what could possibly be worth such a horrific sin.

In order to retrieve the contract, we first had to figure out who had it. I'd always been suspicious of Will's mom, especially when I'd caught her speaking Old Norse to Jules. If she wasn't the culprit, she'd know who was.

Against my better judgment, we resumed normal life and met up at the high school before we tackled our plan to check out Will's house. His mother never left, not even to buy groceries. She had one of the high schoolers deliver food on a weekly basis.

Passing through the halls and wishing I could make time pass faster, I kept an eye out for Jules. She hadn't called, or at least Will hadn't told me if she'd tried to reach him. When I cornered him and asked what happened to her, I was only met with a blank stare. "Who?"

"Come on," I insisted and clutched my books to my chest. "Don't joke around. She's your cousin, remember? Overbearing and protective?"

When Will brushed me off and went to class, I stared after him and realized he was serious. He had no idea who Jules was.

"Why do you look like you've seen a ghost?" Penny asked, scampering to my side so she could rest her chin on my shoulder. "Everyone has been acting so weird. It's not just the tornados. The air itself feels different, doesn't it?"

I'd almost forgotten about Penny and I glanced at her. "You still remember me?"

She laughed. "Silly, what kind of question is that?" She eased up closer to me and dropped her voice. "I've been *dying* to know what you've been up to. Is it Immortal stuff? Can I help?"

I gave her a weak smile. "Maybe. Tell me about Jules. Do you remember her?"

The laughter fell from her face like a mask. "Yeah. She hasn't been doing so well." She wiggled her fingers at me. "Did you do some voodoo magic on her?"

I wrinkled my nose. "What? No. Why?"

"Because Jules is messed up. She's freaking out." She pointed and I followed her finger, startling when I focused and realized I was looking at Jules. I shook off a cold layer of fogginess that tasted like the metallic oppression of Grimhildr... but this was something else.

Jules huddled in the corner between lockers while

students passed her by. If she tried to walk out, they'd plow right over her as if they couldn't even see the terrified blonde ducking out of their way. When she spotted me watching, she bit her lip.

"You going to fix whatever you did to her?" Penny asked. "Because I'm sure it's all fun and games to you, but just look at her. She's like a kicked puppy. Maybe it's time to let up."

"This isn't me," I hissed. At least—I hoped it wasn't.

I pushed past the mortal and cornered Jules. Penny trailed behind me, lingering at my shoulder as she bounced on her toes with excitement. Her programming to be my friend still was holding strong.

"What do you want?" Jules snapped. Her gaze darted and she swiped away fresh tears. "Why does no one remember me?"

I frowned. Whoever or whatever Jules was, I hadn't expected her to start crying when things got tough. "My guess is you pissed off my mother."

Penny made a sound but I elbowed her in the ribs. Jules blinked at me. "Excuse me?"

I crossed my arms and put my weight on my hip. "What'd you do? My mother doesn't use Thor lightly." I could taste the sour, lingering essence of it permeating the entire school. Everyone had gotten their memories zapped.

Penny wobbled on her feet as a fresh hum swept through the halls. I cursed. I'd been protecting her from my mother's programming, but Thor wasn't nearly as easy to overpower as Grimhildr.

I'm not sure how I expected Jules to react, but erupting in outrage with a protective hand to steady a woozy Penny wasn't it. "Why are you talking so blatantly in front of a mortal? Are you trying to get her brains scrambled?"

I wanted to say, so you admit you're not mortal? But I resisted and focused on Penny whose eyes had rolled back in her head. I pushed the warmth of my Valkyrie strength into her, untangling the stranglehold Thor had on her mind. It constricted like a viper and hissed at my efforts before releasing the mortal.

"I knew you were a Valkyrie," Jules snapped. "I just had no idea you were as heartless as the rest of them." She steadied Penny and then whispered something in her ear. The mortal smiled and tottered off to class as if nothing amiss had happened at all. Jules set her glare on me. "I've been protecting Will from Sam. I didn't think you'd come all the way back from that fire pit you call a home just to reap him." She gripped my wrists, shooting pain up my arms at her impressive strength. "You're supposed to be one of the good ones, but I know what your mother did to you." She growled. "She has to be stopped."

I untangled myself from her grip. "Will you stop going on like a crazy person? I'm not going to reap Will's soul, okay? I figured out how to break the Norn's curse." I straightened. "I was hoping you could help me."

Her eyes went wide at my proposal. "Break the curse? Are you mad? Even if he survives it, he'll go insane." She leaned in, her voice lowering to a dangerous whisper. "*Forever.*"

I narrowed my eyes. "How do you know so much? What kind of Immortal are you?" Even among the inhuman, I didn't imagine knowledge of breaking the Norn's curse to be commonplace, much less the outcome. Whatever Jules was, she wasn't a Valkyrie, wasn't a Norn, and she certainly wasn't working for Odin. None of her traits lined up with what I'd learned of the various races.

"It doesn't matter what I am," she insisted. "What matters is that all my work is trashed. Your mother—"

I cut her off, suddenly feeling defensive of the Immortal who'd given me a second chance. "If my mother erased everyone's memories of you, it's because she deemed you a threat. So if you know what's good for you, you'll scamper back from wherever you came from."

Jules gave me a humorless laugh. "If your mother erased everyone's memories of me, it's because I was getting too close to helping you." She gripped my arm as if to prevent me from running. "I've been gathering information on Will's mother all this time. She's a horrid woman. She knows everything that's going on and I was so close to uncovering what had happened to his father." She glanced down the now empty hall, the bell having rung over ten minutes ago. Yet when a teacher paraded past the lockers, he didn't even see us. The hum of Thor's power rang strong around Jules like forcefield intended to keep her hidden even from the most prying eyes—allowing me to hide as well.

I eased closer to Jules and lowered my voice. "Tell me what you've learned so far."

She brightened at my invitation to discuss Will and his past. "There's a contract, which if you know how to break the Norn's curse, I'm sure you're looking for it too." She gripped my wrist until my fingers went numb. "It's in that house, somewhere. Will's mother has magicked it. If we have the right power, we should be able to uncover it."

I frowned. "What power would that be?" Tyler's golden vial burned against my thigh where I'd jammed it in my pocket as if it were made of pure sunlight. What better to fight the shadowed power of the Norn than with the golden light of Odin?

"There's more," Jules pressed. "The curse that bound Will didn't just happen by accident. His family dedicated him when he was a child in his first life, binding the contract into place." She leaned in until our noses touched. "Will's mother is one hundred and fifty years old."

I staggered at that revelation. "Excuse me?"

"She's becoming a Norn." Jules' voice had become frantic, each word a jagged slice of fear settling into my chest. "If she sacrifices her son enough times, the others will have the power to make her Immortal. But if we break that cycle, all that power goes to waste. The Norn *need* a ruthless woman like that. Everyone has suffered after being cut off from Asgard."

I gripped onto Jules to keep from falling over. "Why have you gotten so close to Will? What's he to you?"

She smiled, but the glimmer of joy didn't reach her eyes. "It's bitter-sweet, really. I met Will when his father died. The forest is my home. When I experienced such tragedy, I couldn't help but feel the need to help him." Her gaze went distant as she hugged herself and breathed a short laugh. "Will has such an affect on me. Maybe it's because he's close to becoming an Immortal himself, but when he's happy, so am I. Whatever happened to him in that forest impacted me.

For the first time in centuries I cared enough to give myself a mortal form." Her eyes sparkled as she shared her joy with me. "I danced and sang again after so much time being silent." Her smile faded. "But now the Norn have spread their dark sickness through my woods like a plague, infecting everything. Their shadowy fingers claw at my trees and bring Will's beautiful soul down with it." She shivered. "It's the most invasive feeling. I can't let them win."

I started to put together what Jules was. There was only one such creature that would be impacted like that by a powerful soul. "You're a Huldra." A forest creature known for beauty and seduction, heavily influenced by beautiful souls. They more often destroyed the things they loved rather than helping them, but it didn't mean Jules was evil. She just loved too strongly—and hated too fearfully.

She gave me a weak smile. "It's nice to see that Thor didn't take everything from you."

I frowned. "How do you know about me?"

She laughed behind her hand. "Seriously? I can't remember the last time a Valkyrie broke one of Freya's three laws. They're fairly straightforward."

Rolling my eyes, I separated myself from the Huldra. Without realizing it, I'd allowed her seductive scent to draw me in and listen to her story. With everyone else forgetting who she was, all her attention was focused on me. I had to be more careful. "If you really want to help, then get me past Will's mother."

She pouted, but nodded.

Finally, I had a new ally.

I debated telling Will about Jules when he jumped in his Jeep. I still hadn't told him that his own mother was turning into a Norn, but I didn't even know where to begin with that.

"Are you sure you should go home?" I asked as I curled my fingers over the edge of his window.

He cranked the car and patted my fingers. "I'll be all right." He glanced at the cloudless sky. "Thor's quiet. All's well in the world."

"It's not Thor," I said, grinding my teeth before forcing myself to tell him something I knew would hurt him. "It's your mother."

He narrowed his eyes. "What about my mother?"

"She's…" My tongue went dry.

He sighed. "Look. She's not human, right? Is that what you were going to say?"

I blinked at him. "What?"

"That's not new to me. She's been super weird all my life. Known things that would require a century of sitting on Wikipedia. I've heard her talk a weird language when she thought I was too young to remember. I put it together. There's something off about her." He shrugged. "And when I met you, it just kind of made sense."

"Then, why are you going home? Maybe she's dangerous."

I expected him to snap at me for insulting his mother, but instead he just nodded. "Maybe, but if I'm really going to die in a few days, I have to at least say goodbye."

Those words hit me like a stone. I'd been so focused on breaking Will's curse that I hadn't even realized what that meant. Even when I did, he couldn't stay alive. A Valkyrie reaped a mortal's soul, giving reprieve to one trapped by the Norn's curse.

"Maybe there's another option," I offered, my words drifting off.

He patted my fingers again and yanked the shift into reverse. "I'll see you soon, okay?"

Watching him drive off left me with a gutted feeling. Will was going to die, and for the first time, I felt like there was nothing I could do about it.

⚜

Sam gave me a ride to Tyler's house. We no longer used our own home and I found myself missing our shared room. It'd felt like we'd actually been sisters. Instead, we were heading to a magicked house on the lake. I pretended that we were just going to spend a few nights at a friend's house, but I knew that I was fooling myself. Tyler wanted to be much more than friends.

Sam smirked at me as she straightened her elbows and lazily drove us down the road. Her delicate bangles clinked against each other. "You look like a dumped high-schooler. Isn't that Penny's job?"

I smiled. Even though I'd broken the worst of Grimhildr's hold on the mortal, she'd remained my friend. I told myself that was her programming, but what if it wasn't? What if she genuinely liked me? "Don't pick on Penny," I said. "She's not so bad."

I expected a smart comeback, but Sam gave me a wistful laugh instead. "We're getting too comfortable here, aren't we?"

Sam wore her customary "popular girl's" outfit, complete with skimpy shorts that clung to her thighs and a puffy blouse that floated around her like a cloud, complementing the golden sheen of her hair. She glanced at me, her crystal blue eyes full of mischief and excitement I'd expect to see in a bright-eyed teen. If I didn't know any better, I'd say that Sam was just another Mattsfield grad and my big sister. But, if I squinted hard enough and touched those hot embers inside my chest, the glimmer of her Valkyrie spirit came through. Majestic wings folded against the confines of the car and feathered adornments made a tiara about her head. We weren't human. We weren't regular teenagers. No matter how much either of us wanted it, this was all just pretend.

I turned to face the lake as it broke through the foggy layer that seemed like a permanent fixture since I'd antagonized the Norn. I sucked in a breath when Tyler's house came into view. "Where's the mirage?" I asked, my voice tinged with concern.

The slanted roof reflected sunlight against rusty tiles. The chipped paint along wooden slats made it seem like a normal lake house, yet it was the magic that wrapped around it with hinting whispers that glimmered like motes against dusty sunlight that gave away its supernatural origins.

Sam slammed the car into park. "Something's draining Tyler's power." She yanked open the door. "Come on."

Stepping onto the patio, I stopped and tried to sense the

protective barrier that was supposed to keep out mortals—and Immortals—unwelcome in Tyler's home. A glance over the cheerful forest could have fooled me this was any other crisp day in fall, perfect for reading a book against a tree and huddling against the bite in the air. I shivered, because that nip of cold on my nose wasn't just the seasons.

Pushing through the doorway and following Sam into the living room, I froze when I spotted Tyler. He bent over a glass bowl, dagger in hand, and ran a blade across his forearm. There should have been red blood, but a gleaming golden stream ran over his skin and dripped into the container.

Sam gave an exasperated sigh. "For gods' sakes, Tyler. Do you have to do that now? You've opened up your entire home to invasion. If the Norn decided to strike, where would we hide?"

His gaze flickered towards us as he pressed a cloth to his wound. "I already subdued the Norn by taking out Michael," he pointed out as he took an eyedropper and collected the upper layer of the golden blood. He took a vial and filled it to the top, corking it and setting it onto the table. The remnants in the bowl hardened before turning into ash.

Rising bile left a sour taste in my mouth. Tyler had given me a vial like that before. Had I drunk his blood?

Tyler's familiar smirk returned as the color returned to his skin. He peeled the cloth away, the wound closing before my eyes. "It seems the only 'invaders' here are you two."

Sam rolled her eyes and gathered up another towel, throwing it at his face. "Clean yourself up. You're still an idiot for draining yourself at a time like this."

He pushed the vial towards me. "Can't be too careful."

I swallowed and took it. "Thank you," I whispered.

"The Norn haven't thrown everything at us, yet," Tyler continued, adjusting on the couch and dabbing away the blood that had hardened on his skin. It came away like soot, reminding me of when I'd transferred from my Valkyrie state to my human one. "The Norn are weakened, but if Aerie actually breaks Will's curse, they're not going to have anything to lose." His eyes found mine, full of stubborn focus. "They're going to throw their very tattered souls at us."

I straightened, defensive of Tyler's disapproval. "Are you suggesting I don't try to save Will? Because that's not an option."

He glowered, but Elaina entered the room and cut him off before he could retort. "Valerie," she said, her words soft. She gave me a warm smile. "I think Tyler, Sam, and I need to speak alone."

⸙

*B*eing kicked out of a clear Immortal pow-wow didn't feel so great. I tried eavesdropping from the outside window, but Sam yanked it open and told me to make myself scarce before she tossed me her keys.

"Having permission makes stealing your car a lot less fun," I complained.

Sam glowered at me before closing the window. When I retreated a few steps, the house went back into camouflage and blended with the rest of the forest.

Sighing, I jumped in the car, but not before rolling down my window and commenting on the Huldra I knew was a better eavesdropper than I. "Come on, Jules. While these fools talk about how to stop us, let's go save Will."

One of the trees moved and its limbs bent until I spotted an unmistakable smile.

CONTRACT

Spending the night at my old home, I let Jules take Sam's old spot and we talked deep into the night. A single phone call to Will and our plan was solid.

Will's mother had the contract somewhere in her house, but it would take the power of an Immortal to find it. Jules had tried searching herself, and even though she'd sensed its dark power, she couldn't get her hands on it. Perhaps she was too close to the mortal world to break whatever veil Will's mother had placed over the ancient document. I wasn't sure if my power would be much better, but it was worth a try. Plus, I had a secret weapon.

Tyler was Odin's charge, which meant that his blood was warmth and sunlight. What better power to fight the Norn and any secrets they might want to hide behind shadow. If Valkyrie fire wouldn't reveal what I sought, the vial in my pocket just might.

Another painful day through school passed with agonizing slowness. All I wanted to do was barge into Will's home and demand the contract from his mother, but we were going to do things the smart way. I wasn't going to lose Will again.

Store-bought cookies in hand, Jules and I stood side-by-side to the entrance of Will's home. Mrs. Johnson answered the door and gave us a raised brow. "Jules you didn't have to ring the bell..." she said, letting her words drift off into a snide silence.

Jules gave me a nudge as she giggled. "Oh, it was all just a misunderstanding, Aunt Leanne. Valerie made these cookies herself! She heard Will was feeling sick again. Nothing a little sugar can't fix."

Mrs. Johnson didn't seem amused that Jules had invited me, but swung the door open. "Fine, come in."

Playing sick was already doing wonders for throwing his mother off our trail. She probably thought the Norn were messing with him again. When I asked Jules if Mrs. Johnson knew what I was, she shook her head, waiting until we were left alone in the living room while Mrs. Johnson prepared the cookies with some milk. "She thinks I'm the Valkyrie," she whispered, tucking her chin against her chest and leaning close. "She knows that Will's been targeted, being that you tried to take his soul last time..."

I grimaced. "Good thing I have a new body and she can't recognize me." I leaned closer. "Right?"

Jules laughed. "Yeah, don't worry. She's not Immortal yet. She's just really good-looking for her age."

Being reminded that Will's mother was over a hundred and fifty years old, I tilted my head as she poured the milk. "So, does that mean she gives birth to him every time he dies?"

Jules nodded. "Yeah. Pretty creepy, huh? It's part of the curse. The second he dies, *boom*, pregnant again." She tilted her head. "She does need some male help, but she's never had trouble with that."

I shook my head in amazement. Breaking the Norn's curse would break his magicked birth as well. If I didn't save him and he became another Henry, he could be reborn to anyone, anywhere.

"What are you two girls whispering on about?" Mrs. Johnson asked with far too much cheerfulness as she balanced a tray of cookies and milk. It looked so much more appetizing than the bowl I'd found to dump them in. She made the faux homemade cookies look scrumptious with her garnish of lace napkins and crystal glass filled with milk.

"Oh, just the latest gossip," Jules said. "Did you hear that Tyler apparently has a lake home hidden in the woods? Inheritance, I'm told."

Mrs. Johnson stiffened and gave Jules a hesitant smile. "No, can't say I've heard of that one. Must be a lucky boy."

Following her down the hall and into Will's room, I wondered if it was a good idea to put the woman on edge like that, but Jules seemed to be in her prime element. She continued to poke Mrs. Johnson with slips of the truth to let her suspect that I knew who she was, and what she'd done to her son.

Finally, after Jules had commented that it was strange tornados had seemed to skim around the sides of the house and it must be a bad omen, Mrs. Johnson finally stood up, flushed, and gave us a quick excuse before she fled the room.

"Finally," Will breathed as he sat up. "Thought she'd never leave."

I glowered. "She could come back. You're supposed to be deathly ill."

Will rolled his eyes and tugged the pajamas that choked around his neck. "She's really smothering me. It's almost like she feels guilty."

"She should feel guilty!" Jules whisper-shouted. "She's killed you three times!"

Will frowned. "There has to be something we're missing. My mother wouldn't kill me."

Sighing, I got to my feet. "I'm going to go look for the contract. You two stall her if she comes back and asks where I am."

"I should go with you," Will offered.

I pressed against his hard chest and flatted him on the bed. "No. You'll just get in my way. Stay here."

He grinned, grabbing my wrist and kept my fingers pressed against him. His body flexed under my touch. "But I missed you."

Jules rolled her eyes. "Gross. Just let her go."

Will frowned, but released me and I peeked through the crack of the door before pushing it open and tiptoeing down the hall.

I tried to do what Jules had taught me. She said that I could sense Norn's power if I focused. When I felt the embers inside my chest, I was focusing on my Valkyrie magic, but I could do that with any of the elements. Valkyries were fire. Odin's soldiers, the Valiant, were light. The Norn were darkness.

It was hard to describe darkness as a feeling, but that's what it was when I focused on it. Icy cold fingers that endlessly searched through an endless void.

Mrs. Johnson might be well on her way to becoming an Immortal, but she made a terrible sneak. I spotted her scurrying outside, no doubt trying to summon the Norn and confirm the suspicions that Jules had placed in her head. If they responded to her, they'd tell her that I was the Valkyrie.

It was a risky ploy on Jules' part. Lucky for us, the Norn didn't care to inform Mrs. Johnson of the ongoings of the Immortal world—or they didn't want her to know. I hurried through the house, stopping to sense where I felt the cold sensation of darkness the most and followed it.

Coming to a dusty office, I realized that this was where Will's father had worked. I wondered if he thought Will was actually his child or if he knew about his wife's unnatural past.

A deep walnut desk stood out, looking well loved by the polished sheen against the rest of the drab room. Tattered drapes collected dust and I coughed when I pulled them open to let light in.

One of the drawers of the desk seemed to hiss at the light, the wood going darker than it should.

"Gotcha," I whispered and leaned down to take a look. I ran my fingers over the creases of the wood and stopped when a chill swept across my skin. There was a definite layer of magic around this drawer. I wrapped my fingers around the handle and tugged, but it wouldn't budge.

Producing the golden vial Tyler had given me, I popped off the cork. The honey-sweet scent hit my nose and I tried to remind myself that this was blood and disgusting, but my senses told me otherwise. I poured half of the contents over the handle and darkness popped under the golden wave. Before the liquid could reach the floor, it converted into ash, dispelling the Norn's magic in the process with an audible tear as if I'd shredded a piece of paper.

It was like fire, I realized, and I was the conduit to convert Tyler's energy and the Norn's. Energy was never destroyed, only changed. A slab of wood would become ash when burned, just like Tyler's blood when exposed to binding darkness.

I yanked open the drawer and was rewarded by an ancient document with hand drawn runes and swirls. I pulled it out, wishing that I could read the Old Norse. My memories were returning, but that part of me that was truly Valkyrie was still blocked.

It didn't matter what it said. This was what bound Will to the Norn. Just when I was about to raise the vial and pour the remains over the contract, a desperate shriek split into my skull.

"Don't do that!" Mrs. Johnson cried as she dove for me.

Placing my thumb over the vial, I jumped back, allowing Mrs. Johnson to land painfully on the floor.

"You don't understand!" she cried as she reached for me. "I have a deal with the gods. Will wasn't even supposed to exist. He was a miscarriage." Tears pricked her eyes, but she forgot that I could see past the mask and to the swirling snarl of darkness underneath her skin. No matter her history or reason for making a deal with the Norn, she fully intended on killing her son.

When she saw my resolve, she snarled, her jaw unhinging as shadows whipped around her face.

I ran, diving into my core and accessing the Valkyrie power that would get me out of here alive.

The only hint that the Norn were on my tail was the whisper of ice at my back. I tried to screech time to a halt, but I'd seemed to have lost that power ever since I'd pushed Will away. I didn't stop running until I reached Tyler's house.

I'd hoped that Will would meet up with me, but it hadn't occurred to me that his mother would be strong enough to hold him captive.

"The Norn have him," Jules said when she appeared in the doorway.

I jumped to my feet. "What? I thought you were going to get him away?" I stormed up to her. "You're a Huldra. Aren't you supposed to be persuasive?"

"You need to spend some more time with Mr. Jefferson," Sam chided. "Huldra aren't persuasive. They seduce and corrupt." She glowered at Jules. "Looks like she's succeeded in one of those."

Jules rolled her eyes. "Oh come on. You Immortals meet one bad Huldra and think we're all the same. I'm just trying to help." She pushed her lower lip out in a pout. "I care about Will. I wouldn't let anything bad happen to him."

Crossing my arms, I decided that I wasn't going to trust this Huldra until Will was safe and sound with his soul intact. "Is that so?" I asked. "So where is he?"

Jules reclined on the sofa. "Listen. Will is slated to die tonight. We need to prepare because they're going to have to bring him to this lake to do it. The curse is still active, so they're going to try." Her gaze dipped to the contract I held in a death grip. "Don't destroy that thing yet. We need it."

I didn't like leaving Jules in charge. "This has to go off without a hitch," I said, sticking my finger in her face. "If I don't break the curse, then Will dies and I don't know if he's coming back this time. If I do break the curse and he survives, then he'll be like Henry, doomed to madness. There's an extra step Will needs to take. He needs to become a Valiant."

Sam appeared in the hallway and leaned against the wall. She crossed her arms and sighed. "Yes, and to do that, there needs to be a sacrifice."

I frowned. I didn't like what I was about to say, but there was no other way around it. "Will still has to die. He's been sacrificed so many times that there's power that'll otherwise go to waste. It'll be enough to award him a place in Odin's ranks."

Her lips quirked up in a half-smile. "We'll see about that."

I clenched onto the icy contract, wishing I could shred it into pieces right now. "You have a better idea?"

She shrugged and picked up the fractured glass that held the Norn's power. She turned it over as she examined it. "All I care about is getting this back to Freya. You do what you have to do with Will, and then we'll be called home." She set it down. "Let's get this done."

I pinched my lips together. "I thought you were on my side, Sam."

"I am," she said. "I could go to Freya right now and offer

this in exchange for Will's soul, but she'd just make me come right back and get both. We can't let her know what we have until this has already played out with Will. I'm doing you that favor."

"Fine." I approached the window. "Come midnight, we go to the lake and save Will's soul."

ASCENSION

Shadows curled over the waters until I couldn't see the glassy reflective sheen of the moon. I looked up to the sky, expecting the dotting of clouds, but frowned when a blanket blocked out the stars.

"They're here," Tyler said and straightened, blazing sword in hand. He nodded to Sam.

A spear appeared in her grip in a rush of flames. I blinked and looked down at my own hands, but only the icy contract wrinkled in one and the golden vial burned in the other.

Even Jules was here, ready to fight. Streaks of green vines wound over her skin and she smiled, impossibly beautiful, as she let her Immortality slip through. The forest breathed with her, moving and creaking with ancient moans as roots moved and shook the ground.

We had our small army, but it felt insignificant when the Norn came. They arrived in a rush of shadow, all three Norn having merged into one horrifying entity. Will's body floated on a stretcher of black mist. The shadows licked at his face and left sticky streaks across his forehead. I sucked in a breath, wondering if they would choke him to death right in front of me, but Will's mother appeared, her hand on his as she frowned.

"You can't stop what's inevitable," she said. Her gaze fell to the contract in my grip. "If you destroy that, you destroy my son."

I growled and uncorked the vial and held it over the contract. "Release him, or I destroy this right now. What you're doing to him is nothing less."

Her eyes went soft with sadness. She slipped her hand off of her son as she glided towards me, stopping until she was just out of reach. "I am doing this *for* my son. When I am Immortal, I can ensure he'll have a permanent place in this world. He'll never have to suffer the mortal fate of being forgotten." She smiled. "He'll always be known as long as I am alive. He will have statues and songs that will endlessly boast his name."

I growled. "Come on, you can do better than that. You're selfish. You want to live forever and pretend it's okay to sacrifice your son's soul to do it. He *won't* live forever. He'll die and his very soul will be used for the fodder of your creation. You're disgusting." I let the vial slip and the contract burst into flames. Its icy chill snapped and magic broke down around me like a pulsating wave.

She hadn't expected me to do it. Will's mom didn't know that I had another plan to keep Will from going mad. She crashed to her knees, sobs erupting as she twisted to see what would become of her son. "Do it now!" she cried. "Before the curse unbinds completely!"

Still locked in sleep, his eyebrows furrowed as the

shadows lurched away from him and lowered him to the mossy ground.

The Norn towered over him, their giant mass turning into a head with serrated teeth. It opened its jaw wide to bite through Will's neck and latched on like a viper. Will's eyes snapped open, finding mine in an instant.

I knew what I had to do. Instinct kicked in and my Valkyrie core exploded, sending my wings manifesting into existence. The tear through my mortal skin set my teeth on edge as my inner spirit burst through, but my flesh didn't matter right now. There was only one way I was going to save Will and it was by not holding back.

Tyler was at my side in an instant, his gleaming sword at the ready. "Get ready to fight," he said.

My spear manifested, hot and flaming in my grip. It felt good to be back. "I'll take care of the old hags," I promised.

He glanced at me. "They're not the ones you have to worry about."

Before I had a chance to ask what he meant, golden brilliance shot through Will's body and his eyes glazed over. Two long swords gleamed in his grip.

"Where did those come from?" I shrieked, and panic gripped me when he pointed them at my face.

"He's in Odin's trance," Tyler said and blocked Will's first blow, sending sparks flying as their blades met. Will growled at the obstacle. "He's not himself until an Immortal dies. It's how the Valiant are born. Either he kills you, or you kill him. That's how it works."

I wavered on my feet as black stars sprinkled my vision. Was this why my mind refused to resurface the memories I had of Will's past life? Did I... kill him?

Refusing to believe that passing thought, I readied my spear. "Will!" I shouted. "I don't want to fight you!" This wasn't how it was supposed to happen.

The white eyes that stared back at me didn't house any part of Will that I recognized. He roared and came at me again, and this time Tyler let him. "Jules and I will take care of the Norn," Tyler shouted over the crash of metal as I blocked Will's blow. "If you can't take care of Will, then Sam will have to."

I glanced at her, but she hadn't come to help. "Don't you dare!" I told her. There had to be another way.

The Norn shrieked when Jules strapped them down with her vines. She danced and twirled, kicking up autumn leaves that bobbed with her laughter. Tyler jabbed his gleaming sword into one of the hag's eyes. The mass disintegrated into three and Tyler laughed when he saw that he'd missed his target. "Was hoping to get your other eye, old hag."

The Norn who was responsible for Will's curse growled at him, her remaining eye still swirling in her head. Her sister clung to her, the bloodied patch above her cheekbone a mangled mass. "You die today, errand boy."

Tyler smirked. "Try me."

Will came at me again, his double blades gleaming and moving so fast that he sliced a line across my cheek. I screamed and fell back to the mossy ground. All of my Valkyrie power was nothing against Will. I couldn't fight the love of my life.

I looked up at him, accepting that perhaps this was how it was supposed to end. If Will killed me, he would earn his place among the Valiant. He wouldn't have to die. He wouldn't have to take any chances that he could ascend into Immortality. I'd been foolish all this time to believe that we could make it out of this together.

When he raised his swords, bloodlust a vibrant curse in his eyes, I smiled. "Do what you must."

His face twisted as if he was fighting the compulsion, but no one could fight the gods. I knew that better than anyone.

I closed my eyes, waiting for the blow to come.

"No!"

A scream. Sam's scream.

I flung my eyes open as sparks flew from the clash of Sam's spear against Will's swords. Her training made her one of the most formidable Valkyries in Muspelheim, but she'd been in her human body for too long, and Will's soul was far too powerful. He roared with renewed fervor and slammed against her again and again.

She fought back and I moved to help her, but she pushed me out of the way. "This is my kill!" she shouted. The fury in her eyes twisted my heart. I'd failed to reap my soul and she was going to finish the job. She was going to make Freya proud.

When she turned, she parried once, but missed Will's blow that came in low and sliced her across the stomach. She lurched and I cried out, but it was too late. Will roared, raised his swords as blood flung from one, and buried them deep in her chest.

I couldn't blink or breathe. There was no way this was actually happening.

Sam collapsed to her knees, the shock and disbelief vibrant in her eyes before her light faded. Her wings twitched before turning to ash and rolling down her back. She gurgled something that sounded like an apology before collapsing to her knees and dying before my eyes.

Then Will threw his head back, and ascended.

*W*ill still hadn't forgiven himself for killing my sister, but she'd been the sacrifice necessary to turn a mortal into one of the Valiant, a soldier that was worthy of Odin's power.

Grief had mixed with rage at Sam's needless death. I should have been the one to die.

"How are we going to get you back into a mortal body?" I complained. Tyler had never explained how the mirage trick worked, or if it was even possible on someone so newly turned. And we couldn't rightly ask, not when he'd disappeared without a trace. I did, however, find a note stuffed into my favorite jacket. It was Tyler's humor to place something private between us inside the one object that Will had given me. It was like he wanted to remind me that no matter what became of Will, Tyler had been my first relationship, and when I "came to my senses," he'd be back.

It'd taken me three days to build up the courage to read it. There wasn't much to it, just that he'd taken the Norn's eye to Freya and we had to lay low for a little while. He was sorry about Sam. For now, he was negotiating with Freya and Odin on my behalf, given that Will belonged to Odin now. He'd be coming back to claim him and start his training as one of the Valiant. I didn't like the sound of that.

At the end of the note, though, he told me to take this time to choose my future. He claimed that Will was no longer the mortal I'd fallen in love with.

I don't know why I kept that note. Maybe I was afraid he was right. Every time I looked at the perfect sculpture that was Will's new face, all I saw was what I'd done to him. He wasn't human anymore, and now he was a part of my world, but I saw when he looked back at me was a mirror of regret and sadness. Because of me, his mother had died with the Norn. Because of me, Will had killed Sam. Jules had disappeared without a trace, going back into her forest and haunting us with her whispers. So much blood spilt on the roots of her trees must have made her go insane.

"Hey," he said, rubbing his thumb across my cheek. I hadn't even realized that I'd started crying again. It was like my eyes leaked now, all the time, the only outlet for the river dam of guilt trapped in my soul. "You need to stop beating yourself up."

"Just look at you," I said, my voice hoarse from all the spent and unspent tears. My fingers fell down the ridge of his collarbone, tracing over his sculpted chest. He'd always been fit, but Will was a swimmer and meant to be lean and graceful. Now he was a god among men.

Tyler had left us his home, and so we'd spent the majority of it huddled inside like it was some kind of bunker at the end of the world. Yet the days and nights outside had passed without incident. The Norn were dead,

Sam was gone, and Tyler's note burned in my pocket as if it were a vial of his blood.

Will answered me just as he always did, not with words, but with a passionate kiss pressed against my mouth. He enveloped me in an embrace so tight that I couldn't breathe. When he let me go and I gasped for breath and he smiled, sending beams of sunlight over me until I was infected by his happiness. It was a brief moment of reprieve, but it was all just a band-aid for the suffering neither of us could let go.

"We still don't have our memories," I complained and rested against his chest. He held me, just as confident as he'd always been.

"We don't need them," he said. "We'll make new ones."

I closed my eyes and inhaled the sweet musk of him. My parents were Freya and Odin, god and goddess of war. Both of them had laid a claim to Will's soul, and I had no doubt that either of them had any intention of giving him up. When they came for him, they'd have a fight on their hands.

"We've broken the first law of the Valkyrie... again," I said and forced myself to look up into his gorgeous face. "We need to prepare for what comes next."

He brushed away a lock of my hair. "You've already served punishment for that. Do you think your mother will try to wipe your memories again?" He smiled. "I'm an Immortal now. I'm sure she can make an exception."

I bit my lip. "There's no way my mother will let this stand." I clenched my fingers into the delicate folds of his shirt.

I'd already broken the first law of the Valkyrie. What was one more...

BOOK 2: VALKYRIE REBELLION

Second Law of the Valkyrie… Don't Question the Gods

REBORN

Two days. We'd been here for two whole days and the world still kept turning.

Will tugged me away from the window. "Come on. You have to eat something."

I placed a hand on my stomach that hadn't had any food in it since Sam's sacrifice. I wouldn't call it death or anything so meaningless. She'd sacrificed herself for me, whether she knew it or not, and that's what I would call it.

"I'm not hungry," I insisted. I felt swollen with the guilt and grief that threatened to take me under.

Will took my chin in his hands and forced me to look at him, but he didn't know how much worse that made it. He wasn't human anymore. That night had changed everything. I wanted to see soft chestnut eyes looking back into mine, but instead my fingers wound up into metallic blonde hair as I gazed into the eerie crystal of one of the Valiant.

"Please," he begged, lines marring his perfect face with pain, "tell me what I can do to take that look off your face."

How could I tell him that it was his face that caused me

pain? Every time I looked at him, I saw my failure. "You should hate me," I told him.

His brows scrunched together. "What? Why would I hate you?"

I ran my fingers over his cheekbone, arched and perfect, but not the Will I remembered. "This is all my fault. I did this to you. Odin's going to come for you and—"

Will surprised me by pressing a kiss to my lips. I knew that he wanted to tell me I was wrong, but words couldn't change what I knew to be true.

The love that swept through me unhinged the darkness that clung to my insides and melted me until I was wrapped in his arms, returning his kisses with fervent need of my own.

Heat blazed across my collarbone, interrupting the moment of passion as I cried out and gripped my locket.

"What is it?" Will asked, his voice breathless. His gaze fell to the piece of jewelry that glowed like a burning ember. "Oh," he said, frowning, "I think your mother doesn't approve."

Growling, I forced myself to untangle from Will's arms and turn aside. "I'll talk to her."

She'd been trying to call me ever since Sam's death, but what was I going to say to her? She'd want me to come home, but would she even begin to understand the importance of my duty to Will? I couldn't leave him alone. It was my responsibility to make sure he was protected until Tyler came back.

I left the house before Will could stop me. He'd try to tell me that Freya could be ignored, but I needed her now. I was losing myself in guilt and in the effect Will had on me. I was losing control, and I knew once that happened, I would be a greater danger to Will than anything I was trying to protect him from.

Once I was safely on the brush of weeds along the edge of the lake, I gripped the locket that had cooled and closed my eyes. "Okay, Mother. I'm here."

Lightning flashed and my spirit transported to the Einherjar.

I could still feel my body on Earth, but when I opened my eyes, I was in my Valkyrie form as my mother remembered me. Wings brushed my shoulders and my hair pinned taut at my brow with a feathered headdress. I'd once been an admirable Valkyrie and my mother rose from her throne, relief on her face.

She set her spear to lean against her throne and descended the short steps to greet me with open arms. "Daughter," she breathed, "I'm so glad you're all right."

I'd expected a warrior goddess looking down the ridge of her nose, but this woman who wrapped her arms around me wasn't the leader of the Valkyries.

This was my mother.

I found my hands trailing up her back, stopping at the hint of downy wings that threatened to spring across her shoulder blades every time she embraced her love for me. "You called me," I said. My collarbone still burned with the rage with which she'd called, yet now she was all softness and concern.

She held me at arm's length. "Yes, dear, I thought you dead. I finally felt you, just now." Her smile faded and a flash of concern crested her gaze. "What were you doing?"

I bit my lip before replying. "I was with William. He's become one of the Valiant."

Her eyebrows rose. "Oh," was all she said before returning to her throne.

I shifted my weight, tugging at the lightweight boots that wrapped around my calves. How did my sisters fight in these things?

"You're fighting Grimhildr's programming," my mother said, her words chiding. "When I sensed a new Valiant in the universe, you must understand, I—" Her words cut off and her jaw flexed.

Realization swept fresh guilt through me. The only way a Valiant was born was by killing an Immortal—an Immortal like a Valkyrie that was trying to reap his soul for the Einherjar.

"It was Sam," I said, the words coming out of me as the scalding admission it was. "She died because of me."

I expected fresh rage, new punishments, or something to show that my mother agreed with me, but her face softened. "I'm so sorry. She was close to you. That must have been difficult."

I frowned. "You're not upset?" She should be. She should rip the wings from my back and bury me in the lava pools of Muspelheim. Because of me, one of her most loyal and perfect Valkyries was dead.

She shook her head. "No, dear. If she died protecting you, then she accomplished her mission the only way she could. I'm proud of her." She raised her chin. "And even though you had me worried, I'm proud of you as well. Hiding from me is not an act taken lightly. It takes a great sense of self to do that." She tapped her spear. "That boy must be special to you. After what he did to become a Valiant, you still protect him."

"He had to survive," I snapped. I wasn't going to blame Will for what happened. He wouldn't have been put in that position if it hadn't been for me.

Freya went silent and for the first time, I realized how quiet it was in her chamber. Usually I heard something from the outside world. My sisters training or the soft rumble of a planet that never slept. I raised a brow. "Is something going on?"

The movement of her fingers was so slight, I would have missed it if I hadn't known Freya to use her spear in the most unexpected of moments. A single button lit up under her touch and the room darkened. "Go back to your Valiant, my daughter. The next time I call you, don't answer until you're ready to leave him."

"Where did you go?" Will asked.

His touch graced my cheek and I groaned, the thunder in my head feeling like a thousand tiny explosions behind my eyes.

I opened my eyes to find the sky heavy with dusk and Will peering over me with brows drawn in concern. His warmth radiated over me, reminding me that he wasn't human anymore. I couldn't just pass out in the middle of the woods and leave him alone.

"I'm sorry," I began, but a snapped twig across the lake brought me fully awake. I sat up and peered through the foggy distance. Beams of flashlights scoured the forest and dogs barked, their pitch excited as if they'd just found a scent.

I cursed and gripped Will by the arm. We should be running, but disorientation rooted me to the ground.

I'd wandered farther from the lake house than I'd realized when my mother had called. She'd found me because my guard had been lowered, my mind mush around Will. But why had she called me *now?*

The shouts in the distance told me we were about to be discovered, and that was my mother's plan to get me home.

If the humans found Will in his current state, she'd be allowed to intervene in the world of men. The ancient ways of the Norse Gods cannot be shared among the populace. Only the blessed few who dedicate themselves to loyalty and discovery of the truth are allowed a glimpse into our world. Grimhildr's programming made no qualms about giving up that information.

When a flashlight streaked across our feet, my heart slammed double time and I finally allowed Will to drag me towards the lake house. He'd been trying to get me to move this whole time, but regaining any part of my memories made time seem to slow.

Time.

Heat flashed in the backs of my eyes and I shot a hand behind us, sending the leaves and the air freezing as we ran.

The only downside my mother hadn't thought of by allowing me to reclaim any part of who I was meant I had greater control over my abilities. Right now, the heat of her power burned in my necklace and I used it to fuel my control over space and time. I knew that I couldn't do this often, nor could I hold it up for long, but all we needed was to get back to the house. The magic that cloaked it from humankind would do the rest.

The second my feet slammed against the floorboards the air behind me popped. I turned, finding men with reflective orange jackets running, only to stop at the lake house. To them, it would only look like a dense forest.

The dogs ran in circles, having lost our scent and doubled back towards the lake. Their noses grazed the ground as they traced where we'd been, barking when they found the place I'd fallen during my talk with my mother.

Will and I stood silently on the porch of the lake house until they left. We held each other as strongly as we held our breaths, seeming to be frozen in time ourselves until the humans finally gave up and left.

"Must have drowned," one said.

"We'll dig it later," another agreed, his tone disappointed, but weary. They were ready to get this search over with. If they'd been looking for us for two days, I didn't blame them. Let them think us dead.

The forest hummed with its nightly song after the humans had left. A forest was never silent, and I hadn't appreciated that until now. Soft, sleepy calls echoed from creatures rousing from the heat of the day. Jules would have wound her own magic through the leaves, giving nature a melody that truly made the forest beautiful, but the creatures of the night recreated her song as best they could. Crickets chirped, their pitch in tune with the groan of ancient oaks whose roots dug so deep, I felt like I could feel the Earth for myself.

"They'll be back," Will said, breaking the trance the forest had put me in.

I shook my head and ran my fingers through my hair. My mother's magic had done a number on me. I supposed having your spirit ripped out of your body would do that. "Yeah," I agreed. "Best stay indoors for a couple of days."

Any tension between us had dissipated, replaced with edginess and worry. Will took my arm and supported me as we walked inside. "You should get some rest," he said.

I shook my head. I didn't want to fall asleep. There were only so many nightmares I could take. "The couch," I said. "Let's just sit for a while."

Will hesitated, then nodded.

After settling me onto the sofa, Will disappeared into the kitchen and emerged with two steaming cups of tea. I gratefully took one and blew steam over the edge.

He sat adjacent from me on a chair that complained under his weight. I glanced at the other sofa he'd tried sitting in, now a blackened mess. The light he emitted eventually singed cotton. We'd discovered a couple of iron chairs that hadn't seemed to fit in the lake house, until I realized that perhaps Tyler liked to enjoy his natural form on occasion without destroying all his furniture.

Will turned his cup around in his hands. Only ceramic could handle his touch. "What'd your mother say?"

I set my cup down on the table. "She thought I was dead."

He stiffened. "So she knows I'm a Valiant." The unspoken words scrawled over his face with a shadow of guilt that mirrored my own. His thoughts hit me like a stone to the gut. *She knows I killed.*

"Don't worry about her," I said. My confidence grew

when I saw Will like this. Guilt could tear me apart, but I wasn't going to allow it to drag Will under. I might deserve its icy claws, but he certainly didn't. "She knows I'm trying to help you. She has an alliance with Odin, so she'll tolerate it." When he didn't look at me, I reached out and rested a hand on his arm. His muscles bulged under my touch, but he didn't pull away. The heat of what he was now scalded my fingers, but I could take it. I was a Valkyrie. I was born of flames. "You are a good person, Will. That's why you're a Valiant."

He glanced at me and a wistful smirk lit his face. "So, you think all Valiant are good people, huh? Guess I better get to know Tyler a little better."

I laughed. "Trust me. He's good, somewhere deep down beyond that bravado of his."

Will's muscles relaxed and he laughed. The sound was music to my ears and in that moment, I could almost believe everything would be okay.

Except there was a lingering stench of humans outside our walls. They expected bodies to be in that lakebed when they came back.

My smile faded. Where were we going to find bodies?

I'm not usually a morning person, but come sunrise I was up and ready to get my terrible idea over with.

I went to the front door and opened it, inhaling the fresh dewy scent of morning. The trees brushed against one another with a smooth breeze and it would have been a beautiful day, had I not needed to conjure the dead bodies of the Norn.

Will yawned, startling me as I yelped and leaned against the doorway for support. "Will," I said, "don't scare me like that.

He laughed and rubbed his eyes. "You're about as sneaky as an elephant. What're you doing?"

I sighed. "I wasn't trying to be sneaky. I'm just looking to see if it's safe to go out."

He walked to my side and peered over my shoulder. I stiffened as the sunlight scent of him overrode the calm morning breeze and filled me with another kind of hunger. He was so intoxicating, especially when he was like this. As much as his Immortal body filled me with guilt, it was also familiar to something deep within me. A Valkyrie and a Valiant just seemed to fit together. Maybe that's why I'd been interested in Tyler.

"I don't see anyone," he said, then gave me a handsome smile. "You weren't thinking of going skinny dipping, were you?"

I hit him on the shoulder. "No, perv." My laughter diminished and I sighed. "You're going to think this is super creepy, but we need the humans to stop looking for us. If we give them some bodies, maybe they'll go away."

He gave me a raised brow. "Bodies?"

I nodded. "The Norn dissipated a lot of dark energy into the forest when they died. I could use it to create husks of ourselves. It's the perfect decoy. Then, once you get control over your gifts, maybe we can get out of here without feeling like we have targets on our backs." I squeezed his arm. "They aren't going to be looking for us if they think we're dead."

Will considered my plan as his crystal eyes swirled with light. He was worse in the morning with the effect, as if the sun itself gave him a fresh dose of power. "How do you know you can even do that?"

I tugged him outside. I couldn't tell him that Grimhildr's programming seemed to be feeding me memories that should have been buried. Valkyries learned a lot of tricks, and one of them was how to make humans believe we were dead so we could abandon our posts without messing with more brain cells. It prevented the possibility that someone would be missed, causing an even bigger problem. That's how conspiracy theories were born… and rightly so.

It didn't matter that Immortals like Freya played God. What mattered was how I could use it to my advantage. I'd sensed the darkness before, but I hadn't realized what it was.

Will reached out a broad arm to stop me. His power hummed like a live wire and I forced myself to listen. I'd been so focused on the dark energy that I'd completely blocked out my surroundings.

"Something's watching us," he whispered.

The hairs on the back of my neck stood on end, then I felt silly. If a human was out there, then he or she would take one look at Will and run screaming—or just think they'd gone insane. If it was a supernatural creature, then we'd just take them out. Here I was, a Valkyrie that had survived three Norn and a Valiant gone mad. With Will at my side, we could take on anything.

"Who cares," I said, and pushed his arm out of the way.

Will growled, but shuffled after me. His footfalls seemed to shake the forest. If there was someone out there, Will was going to make sure they knew what he was.

"Will you stop it?" I hissed when we reached the source of the darkness. Puddles of black glistened underneath overgrown brush. "You're starting to inherit some of Tyler's bravado."

Will glared at me. "Let's just get this over with."

Ignoring him, I knelt and dug my fingers into the darkness where the Norn had been slain. The second I grazed the suffering and cruelty that was a Norn's essence, I wanted to yank away, but I forced myself to push deeper into the soil and close my eyes. I drew in that darkness.

Something inside me stirred in recognition.

I realized there were a multitude of things I could do with this kind of latent power. There wasn't much here, which I found strange. A sacrifice of the magnitude of three Norn and a Valkyrie should have left more of an impact.

Heat burned at my back, reminding me that Will stood over me, watchful and vigilant in making sure nothing came down on us while I worked. Perhaps he was so strong because he'd absorbed a portion of this power into himself. It took a Valkyrie's sacrifice to create a Valiant.

I didn't like that thought, and what was stranger was I couldn't sense any darkness in Will. He was all light and good, and his presence would have been comforting had it not been for the raw tension of his nerves as he surveyed the forest.

"I can't concentrate," I complained. "Can you turn down the heat a little bit?"

Will grunted, but backed away until a cool breeze drifted between us.

The icy chill of dark magic wound about my fingertips and struggled up my arm. A part of me wanted to use this to pry Grimhildr's claws out of my brain, but I would regain my memories in time. Right now I needed to make sure Will could have some sort of life to come back to when he was ready… not one where he was hunted.

I focused on my mortal flesh, as well as all those the humans would be looking for. Tyler's sharp angles and Will's lean swimmer's body. When I got to Sam, a tear ran down my cheek, freezing solid mid-way.

When I opened my eyes, it was done. Crude, naked forms half-buried in the soot could have been us. The blood drained from my face to see how accurately I'd recreated bodies.

I was my mother's daughter.

When I turned to look at Will, I found him watching me with growing scrutiny. If he'd had his mortal face, perhaps I could have read his expression, but as a Valiant, he might as well have been a statue.

"What?" I asked.

He broke from his stare as if he'd forgotten I knelt at his feet, struggling to draw my frozen fingers from the ground. He looked back at the bodies. Roots wound around them and covered their skin. Only the crest of shoulders and faces could be seen over the eerie, dark soil. "Nothing," he said after a long moment. "I just… kind of wonder how accurate you got the bits under the dirt."

A blush ran up my chest and engulfed my face. I hadn't even thought of that. I turned and dismissed his comment.

"Think of them as Ken dolls," I said, plucking that human metaphor from my programming. "But, just to be sure, I'll take myself and Sam to the lake. You get the other two, okay?"

He glanced at me. "What about Jules?"

I shook my head. "Everyone forgot about her, remember? She wasn't supposed to exist in the first place."

Will turned while I made short work of digging up myself and then Sam. I wasn't strong enough to carry both bodies to the lake in my mortal form, so I slung my doppelgänger over my shoulder and dragged it across the forest. Once I reached the lakebed, I turned back, groaning at the path I'd have to cover. Maybe this would look like some kind of murder, but at least I couldn't be a suspect. I was supposed to be dead.

I ran inside the lake house and grabbed one of Tyler's old jackets. Filling it with stones, I tied it around fake-me's waist and pushed it off the dock into the lake.

After I took Sam, I gathered more jackets filled with rocks while Will got the other two.

He chuckled when he took one of the jackets from my hand. "Hey," he said, his voice husky and full of humor, "at least you were generous when you thought of me."

My face had just calmed down and broke out in a sweat again. "I don't need to know that," I said, my voice pitching into a shriek. "It's morphing magic, okay? It works off of DNA. We all were here in these woods long enough for me to find some samples." The logic was sound, but I knew a component of rebuilding a body came from my own mind. Will didn't have to know that.

He chuckled and walked back into the woods, this time

whistling. Whoever he'd sensed watching us must have given up, or gone after the police. Either way, it could work into our plans. I'd rather the police be out there chasing some phantom that didn't exist than Will and me.

The final splash sounded, which indicated Will had thrown Tyler's conjured body into the water. Droplets hit the backs of my legs and I frowned. I was well beyond the docks. "How hard did you throw him in?" I asked. "If you blasted the body I just made, this isn't going to work."

Faint heat lingered underneath his metallic cheeks and he stormed past me. "Let's just say I wasn't the only one you were generous with."

By the time we got back to the lake house and enjoyed a lunch of leftover pizza, I pondered what we were going to eat if we had to stay here much longer.

Before I could rummage through the pantry and see if Tyler had prepared for the worst, the sound of dogs made goosebumps spread across my skin.

I ran to the window and gripped on the ledge. My breath fogged the glass and I forced myself to back away.

"It working?" Will asked.

The men had brought long nets and poles. A grumbling engine sounded as they lowered a trailer with a boat. They were serious.

It wasn't long before they found the first body. My work at recreating flesh didn't include the ability to make it decay, so our timeline wouldn't exactly line up, but it would have to do.

No one seemed to care that I'd gotten the details wrong as they shouted and covered the body with a blanket. Wide eyes filled with horror and shock made me almost regret what I'd done. If it hadn't been for Will's arm wrapping around me and pulling me into his chest, I could have been lost in the sadness that wafted over the woods.

"Hey," he whispered, his tone gentle. He brushed away a tear from my cheek. "You did the right thing. They won't look for us anymore."

I wiped my eyes with the back of my hand and settled closer to him. "I know," I said. It still didn't make it any easier. Only a Norn caused pain—and that's exactly what I'd just done.

After the humans had gone, a couple of news crews came over the next few days. The magic that shrouded the lake house held strong and they turned back the moment they got too close to the perimeter.

With the threat gone, all that was left was for Will to learn how to appear as his human self, but that was going to take time. Days turned into weeks and I wondered if we'd ever get away from the lake house that was starting to feel more like a prison.

I found myself outside again, staring into the murky depths of the lake as I stood on the edge of the docks. The humans had plucked the bodies I'd made, but it felt like death left its stink on these waters and it'd never come out.

This was where I came to wallow in my guilt—something I was pretty good at by now.

A familiar burn radiated across my chest. My mother was trying to contact me again.

My necklace, an object that usually brought me comfort and warmth, hummed with the softness of a dentist's drill in my head. I cringed, but resisted. Freya thought she could make me answer her calls. She was wrong.

Another kind of warmth wrapped around my midsection as Will encased me in his arms. He rested his chin on my shoulder as we looked out over the lake. This place still gave me mixed feelings. There was Will, of course, and our first kiss. That memory still gave me butterflies. This place was also where tragedy had begun with the death of his father, then the loss of his own mortal life. Sam. Jules. Will's mother. All victims of that wonderful and terrible night when Will ascended as one of *us*.

Will's breath puffed against my neck. I tried to shy away from him, not in the mood for tenderness. His teeth nipped at my earlobe as punishment. "Your mother put you in a bad mood again?" he asked, recognizing the heat that flickered across my chest.

I turned and wrapped my arms around his neck. We fit together like two halves of a whole. And even though I knew that I loved Will, and that he loved me, I worried about letting him get too close. This interlude between the mortal world and Immortal one was just purgatory. It was all going to come crashing down on our heads and I felt helpless to protect him. I'd only made things worse by getting Sam killed, along with his mother. I was beginning to think that Elaina had been right. I'd saved him from the

Norn's curse only to award him with one of my own making.

Will brushed away my hair and tucked the strands behind my ear. "Now, I'm no mind reader, but I'd say your thoughts are going a mile a minute. Tell me what I can do to help."

I opened my mouth to speak, but there wasn't a thing he could do. Nothing, except for leaving me to prevent this from getting any worse.

Yet, he couldn't leave, not while he looked like a god. His skin glowed with an inhuman hue as if he'd swallowed the sun and it rested in his chest. His skin was marbled like a statue come to life and his eyes held a spectrum of crystal that glittered at me with the most mesmerizing gaze. I found myself staring at him in wonder, then hating myself because he couldn't live in this world while he looked like this. When Odin came to claim him, he'd have no choice but to leave his world behind. I needed to fix him.

I looked away from the gaze that threatened to drag me under. "Tyler should return soon." And then everything would be okay. He'd teach Will how to glamour himself a mortal appearance, then I'd help him get his life back. He wouldn't have to give up everything just because he'd been dedicated to the gods lifetimes ago.

Will frowned and grabbed my chin, forcing me to look at him. "I don't need Tyler," he insisted, just as he always did. He'd become childish and annoyingly confident since inheriting his Immortal body. He grinned and gave me a quick kiss before I could pull away. "Stop it," I said, but I couldn't help the laughter that bubbled up.

"I've been practicing," he said. "Look." His face shimmered and my world dimmed as his inherent light swept under the surface of his skin. An old scar across his cheek sliced anew and a freckle marred his chin. The familiar visage made my stomach lurch and I reached out to touch him, but the moment my fingers grazed his cheek the mirage wavered.

"That's very good," I said, forcing the words through the agony that ripped through me. I'd done this to him. Sweat broke out across his brow at the effort of just trying to pretend to be who he was... who he used to be. "Don't strain yourself. Once Tyler comes back, he can teach you how to use your powers naturally so it doesn't cost you so much." Then he'd have a choice when Odin came for him. He could stay.

He tried to hide it, but I caught the way his chest fluttered and he gulped in breaths of air at the effort it cost him to maintain the façade.

The mirage finally faded and Will gazed down at me with otherworldly eyes filled with crystal, light, and mystery. I hardly recognized him in his Immortal form even though we'd been trapped on the lake for weeks. What sent a shiver up my spine was the sensation that there was the familiar power that rested in him now and even though I didn't have my memories, I knew it was forbidden to love him, mortal or Immortal. A Valkyrie was not supposed to love. That kind of passion created a bond, and when that bond hardened into something deeper, I was afraid of what came next. There was a reason my mother upheld the laws of the Valkyrie above all else. Perhaps Tyler had a reason for why he should be my mate. If I had to be with someone, it should be someone I cared for, but not someone I loved. That was too selfless, too dangerous.

Yet, I knew I was capable of loving Tyler. Perhaps that's why I'd left him, only to fall into the arms of another.

"You're doing it again," Will complained.

I flinched under the sharp edge of his tone. "No I'm not." I turned, easing myself onto the dock and drifted my toes across the cool water.

Will sat with me and crossed his legs. He didn't much care for the lake, not that I could blame him. "It's not fair that you look at me like I'm some kind of stranger." He locked me in that magnetizing gaze. "I don't have anyone else to tell me it's going to be okay. You have to do that for me. When you don't, I feel like I'm falling."

I knew I shouldn't touch him, but my hand was already on his, squeezing his fingers. "I'll never let you fall," I said. "I'm a Valkyrie, remember? I can fly and catch you no matter where you are."

He smiled and just for a moment, I felt like I was allowed to be happy.

The moment was short lived. Just when I was starting to let go of all my seemingly irrational fears, bubbles formed under my feet and the temperature of the water plummeted. Ice spidered around the bank and I yanked myself free of the lake before the water's surface crusted over.

We'd had an uneventful couple of weeks, just long enough to absorb everything that had happened. We were due for something supernatural to break the calm. Whatever had been watching us decided it was time to reveal itself...

My breath puffed clouds in front of my face and a sheet

of ice broke over the lake, only the center remaining unfrozen as bubbles violently raged from the underwater storm.

I locked my jaw and took Will's hand, ready to face whatever deity had decided to call on us now.

Will sucked in a breath when a form rose from the waters… his mother.

I snarled, because if Will was in danger of becoming something I didn't recognize, his mother had become something far worse. "Stay back!" I warned.

"Mom?" Will asked, oblivious to the horror that had just risen from the lake. He pushed me aside, his brute strength toppling me over as if I were nothing.

The woman had him in her trap. Shadows wrapped around her like a corpse covered in dark velvet. The waters had rotted her flesh. I could spot the milky bones beneath her skin, but she pushed a mirage to make herself appear more human. She's the one that had taken all the dark magic I'd sensed and left only slivers behind. She'd been at the bottom of the lake feasting on the lingering essence of the Norn. It was a miracle she hadn't devoured the bodies we'd tossed in.

Two silver eyes gleamed underneath a mask of darkness and she'd kept her sweet "Mrs. Johnson" smile. She used it to full effect, forcing the shadows to part as she opened her arms. She drifted to us and kept Will locked in her gaze. "Son," she whispered as her lips stretched into a grin. Her words shouldn't have been audible, but the hiss of sound bounced off of the frozen lake and shoved into my brain. A familiar cold clawed into my chest.

"She's a Norn!" I cried, but Will was past listening.

"I saw an opportunity," she admitted, "but I am no Norn. I was already close to becoming an Immortal without their help." She grinned. "Will's father had been a fruitful experiment. When you killed the Norn, you gave me the last push I needed to unlock immortality."

Will flinched, but didn't move.

"I come to you with an offer," she purred, talking to Will. Her gaze flicked to me ever briefly, locking me in an icy prison of fear. "Your Valkyrie might yet live, if you cooperate with my master."

Will's fingers twitched again. This wasn't the first time an Immortal tried messing with his mind. The Norn's curse had wiped his memories, and then I'd tried to push him away as well. That was nothing compared to the bloodlust of the Valiant he'd found himself in when I'd broken the Norn's curse, resulting in Sam's death. Now, his mother was trying to control him, but Will snarled and twisted free, ripping the shadows off his face that clawed around his eyes. "Who is this creature making you do such terrible things? Tell me. I'll rip him apart and set you free."

She frowned that he'd so easily purged himself of her newfound powers, but pride hinted at the edges of her gaze. "Baldr." The name resonated through me like a bad omen. "He's made a bid against Freya and Odin." Her shadows screeched at the names as if enraged. "It's time to choose a side." She extended a hand. "Baldr could do great things with a Valiant."

"Don't listen to her!" I begged and gripped Will's arm. "Snap out of it!"

I would have thought my words ineffective except for the hairline fracture of gold that split across his skin. The icy bite in the air hissed as warmth emanated from Will, the scalding heat of his body sending me reeling back with a yelp. Will turned on his mother and growled as the shadows screeched and wilted before turning to ash. "You sacrificed me," he snarled, his words taut with accusation and hurt. "But that wasn't enough for you. You had to take my life, again and again, as well as Dad's. And now that I might be useful to you, you ask me to join your side?" He scoffed. "When I ascended, I gained knowledge of a world I can't even begin to understand." He straightened. "That night, a part of me died, just like you wanted." He flicked his wrist and a golden sword thrust into his grip, steaming against the cool air. "Get out of here before I send you back into the lake to join my father."

His mother frowned and glanced at the sword. "You're coming into your gifts quickly, my son." She glowered at me, seeming to need someone to blame. "The Valkyrie clouds your judgment. When she betrays you, I'll be here, ready to welcome you back." She eased into the water. "Blood is stronger than ash."

OLD FLAMES

After Will and I were absolutely sure his mother wasn't going to make another appearance, we made ourselves go inside and lock the doors—not that a couple of locks would keep out whatever Will's mother had become, but it made me feel better.

Will sighed and went to the kitchen to start up our evening meal of ramen. When we'd finally raided the pantry, we'd found Tyler's version of preparing for the end of the world. He'd stored away enough junk food to feed a fraternity for years, and I was growing sick of starch and salt. I just didn't know what else to do. Even though the police had found our bodies, it didn't mean I could just waltz into town. The lake house was the only place where we could hide from the humans. Now, though, I almost wished that we'd been found. At least we could have a decent meal.

Just when Will handed me my bowl and I forked a mouthful of ramen into my face, Tyler decided to finally make his appearance. His return to humanity was just as glorious as his departure had been; sudden and not without a sarcastic comment.

"Honeymoon over!" he said far too cheerfully as he sauntered into the room with a glowing sword balanced on his shoulder. He scrutinized my dinner before smirking. "Romantic."

I sent my bowl clattering to the table and jabbed a finger in his face. "Where have you been? You can't just abandon us like that. We've been sitting around just waiting to get attacked or worse."

Will's hand rested on my shoulder and once again, it felt like *he* was the one comforting *me.* I hadn't just lost my mother and turned into a new species.

Tyler narrowed his gaze and light glimmered through the crystal of his Immortal eyes. After a few weeks of adjusting to Will's appearance, Tyler didn't catch me off guard as much as he would have otherwise. "While you've been here..." He waved to Will, "canoodling with your toy and noodles," he jabbed a thumb at his chest, "I've been negotiating with Odin and Freya for your lives." At my blank stare, he added, "You're welcome."

"I didn't ask you to do that," I said, putting my hands on my hips. "And I don't believe for a second that you've been gone just playing the hero." I leaned in. "I think that there's something in this for you. I think that you came for Will. You are my father's soldier, after all."

It was brief, but Tyler lost control of his powers long enough for brilliant rays of light to shine through his skin and eyes. I shielded my gaze, not expecting that kind of power to be contained inside of him. "Can you turn down the lights?" I complained.

He shuddered and composed himself, the brilliance dimming enough that I wasn't going to get a splitting headache just trying to have a conversation with him.

Will cupped my elbow and led me to the couch, giving me a wink. "Let me handle this," he whispered, then faced Tyler and gave him a big smile followed by a bear hug. Tyler staggered under the unexpected embrace. "So you're back," Will said. "Val's just sensitive. You did leave for a while, but why don't you tell us what you've been up to?" Will made himself comfortable on the iron chair adjacent to the couch and leisurely rested a hand on my knee. Tyler tensed at the blatant display that Will believed I belonged to him. I shivered, not sure if I liked this possessive side of him.

Tyler eased onto the adjacent sofa and teetered on the edge, looking more uncomfortable than if he'd just remained standing. "I'm not going to lie to you," Tyler said to me, as if Will didn't even exist. "Your father sent me for the mortal. He knew that Will's death would crush you, so he tasked me with making sure Will ascended." His jaw flexed. "Why do you think he'd send me, hmm? Out of anyone an Immortal like Odin could have chosen?"

I stopped and tried to think of how many soldiers my father had acquired over the millennia of humanity. For every mortal that was assigned to a Valkyrie, only a small percentage of the humans trapped in a Norn's curse survived. Kill or be killed didn't seem to be the mentality for a long line of the galaxy's do-gooders, but maybe that's why Tyler had a point. The Valiant were ruthless, but Tyler and I had a bond. He wouldn't do anything that'd hurt me.

I glanced at Will. His fingers clenched hard around my thigh. "It's because you care for her," he said.

I fumbled for my necklace. Even though my mother tormented me through it, I had nothing else to anchor me when my feet felt like they were getting swept out from under me. Two Immortals were sitting here, trying to tell me who cared about me the most.

Tyler gave Will a nod of approval. "That's right. I damn well care for Aerie. If Odin says she's going to be sent to the pits of Muspelheim if I don't help some mortal ascend, then guess what? I'll rip out the eyes of a hundred Norn if I have to make that happen."

I flinched. "That eye we found at the bottom of the lake…"

He lifted his chin. "That's right. I'd already stolen it from the Norn. Problem is I needed you to have it without knowing it was me."

If Will hadn't been holding me down, I would have launched to my feet. "I could have drowned in that lake! Do you know how many times I had to dive for that thing?"

Tyler leaned back in the sofa and folded his arms over his chest. "I do what I have to do, Aerie. Just like I'm not the begging type, but I went and begged your mother to let you off the hook." He glowered at Will's hand still on my leg. "You two are clearly on your way to breaking the first law of the Valkyrie again. Freya would be within her rights to enact punishment. She's been too lenient already."

I growled. "She wants to wipe my memories again? Go on. Let her try. I'll just get stronger and eventually that stupid spear of hers won't have any effect on me."

Instead of a rebuke, Tyler smirked. "Such rebellion. It's almost like you're a real teenager."

Will must have heard enough. He pulled me onto his lap

and enveloped me in his warmth. Pressing a kiss to my hair, he whispered, "It's all right, Val. He's just trying to get under your skin."

"It's working," I hissed.

"I get it," Tyler snapped. "You two are a thing now. That's what I'm trying to warn you about."

I squirmed off Will's lap. Will got up and Tyler jumped to his feet, quick to rise to any challenge Will might offer. "I think you've upset her enough for one evening," Will snarled.

"Why don't you and I talk alone?"

"No way," I shouted and latched onto Tyler's arm. "He's not leaving my sight."

Tyler bristled. "I didn't intend to stay long. I've come to collect Will and then you can do whatever you like. Go take a vacation. Whatever."

That statement sent stars sprinkling behind my eyes. The hell he'd come to "collect" Will.

"What happens if I don't go with you?" Will asked.

Tyler straightened and his fingers curled into fists as if he wanted to knock Will out and just get it all over with. "You're an Immortal now. You can't just pretend like you don't owe anyone for that gift. Odin is the one who made you and Odin is the one you answer to. If you don't come with me, breaking the first law of the Valkyrie will be the least of your problems." His gaze found mine, making my stomach churn with the raw emotion that stormed in his eyes. "Breaking the second law comes with a much harsher punishment."

"You'll have to forgive me," Will snapped, shoving himself between Tyler and me. "I'm not familiar with the laws of the Valkyrie, or anything else about this Immortal business. You see, no one's been around to teach us. My girlfriend here had all her memories wiped, if you forgot. So please forgive us if we don't know what the hell you're talking about."

Tyler snarled. "You think this is a game? Breaking the second law of the Valkyrie means defying the gods. Even questioning them calls for the punishment of death or exile." He tilted his head and I didn't like the dangerous edge to his voice. "Remember Elaina? Haven't seen her around, have you? That's because her exile to earth comes with the torment of Michael's rebirth over and over again. She follows him into his own madness every life he lives. The only reason she's not dead for her blatant rebellion is because this life was deemed a worse fate."

I sucked in a breath. I'd assumed that Elaina had gone looking for Michael's new birth family. She said that she would be drawn to him and would find him again. Yet, I couldn't deny what Tyler was saying. Elaina suffered deeper than anyone I'd ever known.

"So, what are you saying?" I asked, my teeth chattering with fear and rage. "If Will doesn't go with you, you'll kill us both? I find that hard to believe. After everything we've been through, you must have something else up your sleeve." The Tyler I knew wouldn't destroy me like this. He was stalling because he wanted something. I just had to figure out what it was.

Tyler ran his fingers through the silky strands of his hair. I hadn't seen the gauntlets before, but the more I angered him, the more his golden armor layered over his skin and solidified. The leathers stretched as he flexed his fists. He looked as if he'd launch at me at any moment and rip Will and me apart. I squeezed Will's hand.

As if in response to my apprehension, Will gazed down at me and everything I needed to know rested in his eyes. I'd been beating myself up the entire time we'd been trapped at the lake. I hadn't been able to forgive myself for all the terrible things that had happened. But somewhere along the way, Will had filled an empty place in my soul. The way he looked at me now said that I did the same for him. We couldn't be parted. There was no argument about that.

"We stick together," Will said, echoing my thoughts. He faced Tyler. "You're just going to have to go back and bargain some more. Say we fought you, and that if Odin wants me, he'll have to accept his daughter coming along as well." His fingers squeezed mine. "That shouldn't be such a big deal, right? Freya can survive without one of her Valkyries for a little while."

"You don't understand how this works," Tyler said through gritted teeth. "Your circumstances are unique. You shouldn't even have the mental capacity to argue with me right now. Odin *owns* you. It's only because of Aerie that you have any capability of thinking for yourself." He flicked his wrist and his sword appeared. Golden dust drifted from the dangerous edge of the blade. "If you choose to be stubborn about this, I'll rescind that benefit myself."

Tyler had just revealed something that he shouldn't have. I reeled Will behind me before that golden dust could get anywhere near him. Will hadn't been the only one getting in-tune with their Immortal side. Flames ignited in my soul and I called forth my own weapon, a Valkyrie spear that sang in the air and stopped inches away from Tyler's throat. "You'll do no such thing," I said.

Tyler didn't seem like he had any inclination of standing down. The smirk that sprang across his face at my challenge only served to enrage me more.

Luckily, a knock sounded at the door, breaking the building tension.

Jules in her full Huldra glory stood with blooms budding in her hair and vines winding around her head like a crown. She smiled as if none of us had blades at each other's necks. "Well, hello. Are you having a reunion without me?"

When I found my voice, I asked Jules where the hell she'd been. She was one of the few Immortals who could have helped us. She still passed as human and no one was looking for her. Thanks to my mother, everyone had forgotten that she existed at all. It was unfortunate, but that meant that she could have freely walked around town and gotten us waffles and sandwiches. My mouth watered just thinking about the possibilities.

Jules ignored me and drifted to Tyler. She caressed his face as if he were a breakable porcelain sculpture. "I can't believe I missed it," she whispered as her eyes glittered with wonder. "All this time, I thought that it was Will's sorrow that awakened me... but it was yours, wasn't it?" Tyler stiffened, but didn't flinch away as Jules continued to brush away the golden strands of his hair. I frowned because she was no longer Will's overprotective cousin. She seemed softer, more ethereal. "It was *your* heart I felt breaking," she continued, her words smooth and relaxing. "It was you I'd been drawn to all this time, but then I got so caught up with Will and the Valkyries, I didn't even notice that it was you I was meant to heal all this time. I'm so sorry."

Jules was definitely different. Her hips swayed when she moved, making her look like a graceful dancer. The living blooms in her hair were a part of her, opening and breathing. She seemed sensual and divine. She was a Huldra, and this was definitely what I'd imagined a forest nymph to look like. When she'd tried to help Will, she'd turned into what he'd needed. His own mother had turned against him, whether he'd avidly known it or not. Jules had filled that motherly, protective void for him.

But now... she was filling a void in Tyler's heart—and it was a seductive one.

Tyler glanced at me when he spoke. "Yes, it was my pain that awakened you." The admission made my eyes go wide. He finally shrugged her away as if he gained confidence with his words. "I was glad you misplaced my pain for Will's. He needed you more than I did. Plus, it kept Will's mother distracted and..." he smirked, "for a time, kept a particular Valkyrie from getting into the mortal's pants."

"I'm not in anybody's pants," I snapped. Will and I had something special, but we hadn't taken that physical step. To do that, I had to allow Will completely into my heart. I couldn't do that to him. No matter my feelings, my world would destroy him. I'd already broken him, turned him into something he wasn't supposed to be. Now Odin called him to battle on the frontlines—not quite the future I imagined for someone I loved. I wanted him to find a way to be mortal, or at least to *feel* mortal, and live the life that I had taken from him. I wanted him to be happy, and I had no doubt my world would make him miserable.

Tyler gave me a raised brow. "Seriously? Three weeks alone in a lake house with nothing to do and you guys aren't doing it?" He smirked, clearly amused, but I sensed the layer of relief that fell from his shoulders like a cloak. "What's wrong, Will? You scared of Valkyries?"

"This has nothing to do with you," I reminded him. This was about Will and me. Tyler and I had been close in another life, and perhaps I'd loved him once. But I was different now. Even if I still sensed a connection that lingered between us, Will had every right to claim me. Even if I couldn't be with him, he'd taken my heart anyway.

"It has everything to do with me," Tyler hissed.

Anger spurred inside of me and I wanted to blame Tyler for everything, but I couldn't use him like that.

Tyler grabbed my arm and tugged me away from Will, leaning in close until the heat of his skin burned against mine. He whispered, "You can use me all you like."

My eyes went wide. Some Valkyries had the ability to read minds... since when could Tyler snatch my thoughts out of the air like that?

Unsettled, I jerked away. Jules pouted, not needing to read minds to understand what Tyler might have said to me. "Jules," I said, directing my attention to the Huldra, "you said that it was Tyler's sorrow that awakened you?" That was an important fact that I didn't want to miss. Tyler was just trying to distract me with revealing he could read my thoughts—or he'd just been a really good guesser. The fact was, it took immense grief to awaken a spirit of nature like the Huldra and give her a mortal body. Her mission would be to resolve that pain and bring peace to her forest again. I could have understood Will's grief when he'd lost his father and putting that kind of emotion into the forest. But if it'd been Tyler... something big had happened. Something that would have been wiped from my memories like everything else.

Jules batted her eyelashes at Tyler, clearly enraptured with him even though she'd never noticed him before Will's ascension. "I can't remember what sorrow awakened me, only that enough pain filled my trees and roots to give me flesh. I am a Huldra. I am called to mend broken hearts." Tiny vines twirled intricate patterns along the shifting crown atop her head. Her voice lowered with ominous wonder. "That sorrow feeds me even now."

I didn't want to consider what that might mean. If I felt a connection to both Will and Tyler, was I fooling myself into believing that Will was the one I was meant to be with? What if my memories of Tyler were just as lacking and we'd had something more? What if Tyler suffered even now, having to see Will and me together?

Deciding to focus on the present, I counted the broken pieces of my heart like currency. Each shard that cut me was the harsh pain of love that I felt for Will. Even if I'd had something with Tyler, that past was gone along with my memories. If they resurfaced, I'd deal with it then, but for now, Will was my primary concern. Tyler wasn't here as a scorned lover. He was here to take Will away from me and there was no way I was going to allow that to happen.

"You were gone a while," I pointed out to Tyler. "You claim you were negotiating for our lives. So tell me, why does my father need Will so badly? If you can explain what he needs, perhaps there's something else we can offer." We'd already exchanged Will's soul for the power of the Norn. I didn't imagine it would be easy, but if Odin held claim over Will, perhaps there was something else we could exchange in return.

Jules' eyes went wide. "Odin is your father? That's impossible."

Tyler waved her away before leaning close to me and addressing me with a chiding tone. "I wouldn't go spouting around that you're Odin's daughter. Freya and Odin procreating breaks a whole new set of rules. History is still playing itself out for the punishment of that venture." He pinched my chin and electricity zinged through me at his touch. Had Tyler always affected me this way? "Don't be selfish," he said. "This isn't about you. Baldr has done more than taken Asgard for himself. He's coming after the Immortals that have been exiled, which means your parents. He knows that Odin and Freya have been building their armies and he wants to nip that problem in the bud." I shivered and he released me with a frown. "Baldr has already targeted Muspelheim," he continued. "Odin is keeping him at bay, but he needs more capable soldiers on the frontlines."

Tyler glanced at Will, who no doubt looked the part with his glowing skin and armored leathers that appeared without his conscious effort. His fingers twitched and I knew he was resisting the urge to summon his sword which would only enforce Tyler's proposal that he join in on the violence.

"Do you know why this sounds like a war that isn't mine to fight?" Will asked, his voice a deep rumbling growl that made me proud. "You just said a whole lot of names I've never heard of before. Baldr? Asgard? Muspelheim? I don't know if you've noticed, but I'm from Earth. Why should I care about places I've never been to and people I've never met?"

Tyler hissed, his temper loosening as light flared across his skin like lightning. "Do you think you ascended by the will of your own strength? It is Odin who gave you this body when you should have died and your soul dissipated into the cosmos. You have magic that doesn't belong to you —it belongs to Odin. Without proper guidance, it'll consume you, but it doesn't have to." He extended a hand. "Come with me and let me teach you. We absorb the Norn's darkness to create a balance Odin's blistering light of Immortality." He glanced at me. "She can't help you do that. Only I can."

I wobbled on my feet. Didn't Tyler know there was darkness inside of me? Maybe he did, and he knew that I could never let it free.

"I've seen what darkness does," Will countered. "My mother succumbed to it. If that's how I'm supposed to survive, then I choose death."

I whirled to face him. "What?" I couldn't imagine him choosing any route that would destroy everything I've been trying to prevent. Will was supposed to *live.*

"Stop being stubborn," Tyler said and flexed his open fingers. "Come with me and be grateful I'm willing to help you."

"Grateful?" I spat and slapped his hand away. "It's because of Immortals like us that any of this happened in the first place. If you think I care about Muspelheim, you're wrong. Freya took that away when she took my memories."

Tyler appraised me with the authority of one of Odin's top lieutenants. "You don't need to care. If Baldr gets his way, it's only a matter of time before he descends upon the outer territories such as Earth." He took a step closer so that I could feel the heat of his magic that fueled an Immortal body that had seen far too much hardship. "Freya needs her Frigg daughters—all of them. You have control over space and time. With your help, Freya could move Muspelheim somewhere Baldr will never find it. With the Valkyrie stronghold safe, he couldn't complete his conquest and your precious Earth would stay safe." His finger traced over my locket, sending a hum of power through my body that responded to his magic. "You're the strongest Frigg, Aerie. Sam was the second, but now she's gone and your mother needs you more than she will ever admit. The least you could do is take Sam's place and be by your mother's side to see this thing through." He stepped away from me and raised his chin at Will. "And you, newborn Valiant, need to learn, and fast. Baldr has a terrifying army that is infiltrating exiled ships and planets as we speak. We need to fight him off. If we can keep Baldr's forces distracted and away from Muspelheim, then Freya might have enough time to move her people into hiding." His light dimmed. "However, if Baldr defeats Freya, he will take the core of her power and no one can stand in his way then. The universe will be brought to its knees."

Tyler was trying to paint a picture that would make us buckle out of fear. My fingers curled into fists, not appreciating the tactic. "I very much doubt I will make the difference in relocating an entire planet. My mother is a goddess, right? She can do that without me. And Odin, well, he doesn't need another Valiant. He has plenty of soldiers from the sound of it." I took Will's hand and squeezed, standing with him in a united front. "Will's right. You're telling us about a war that doesn't concern us. When and *if* Baldr ever comes after Earth, then I will fight him, but I'm not going to fight someone else's war. My mother wiped my memories, and that was her choice. My father wants to use me and those I care about, and I don't mean to let him take advantage of us. If Will and I join this fight, untrained and conflicted as we are, we will die. I'm not going to be a martyr for an Immortal's cause."

Rage glowed through Tyler with fresh brilliance as if he were about to go supernova. "I can't believe you," he spat. "After everything I've done to keep you alive and keep your mind in one piece, you decide to be stupid and stubborn. If you defy the gods, they'll come after you and I won't be able to protect you anymore."

"It sounds like they have enough things to worry about," I countered. "If they have time and energy to come after me, then things aren't as dire as you say." I straightened. "I'm calling your bluff, Tyler. You can either help us, or you can fight us. Your call."

TRAINING

I watched Tyler from the window as he sat hunched over at the dock with his back to me. Looking out over the stillness of the lake betrayed the grief that ran rampant in this place. So much had been lost here. Tyler held some deep-seated grief that I couldn't even begin to understand.

Jules flitted around him like a firefly. With him going off-world, she'd reverted to her supernatural form. Now that he was back, mortality crept over her like a shadow. She'd lost her flower crown, so that was a start. But as she giggled behind her hand, I solidified my theory that her personality morphed to change the role she needed to play to ease her target's pain. Apparently Tyler needed a blonde dimwit who fawned over him.

Tyler ignored her and even from where I stood, I could sense his conflicted heart. He was doing his best and my heart panged for him, but it didn't matter, I had to stand my ground.

"You did the right thing," Will said, echoing my thoughts. I turned and curled into the warmth of his chest. His arms wrapped around me as if out of instinct. His throaty tone settled into my core and assured me that Tyler's suffering was necessary. "He'll just have to tell Odin I'm not going to help him," Will said. "I belong at your side, and you belong at mine."

My eyes stinging, I pulled away. "How can you say that?" I asked, my voice cracking with emotion. "After everything I've done to you, you should hate me."

He gave me a weary smile. "My mother is the one who got me into this world, remember? Not you. If anything, you're my guardian angel." His fingers trailed down my spine. "You have wings in there, somewhere. I've seen them."

I smirked. "Don't be ridiculous. I'm a Valkyrie, warrior bender of time and destructor of souls."

He swept me off my feet, his strength surprising me and I squeaked. He carried me away from the window—away from Tyler—and into my bedroom. My insides curled with anticipation. I'd held myself away from him for so long, but he was being stubborn. He wanted me to accept that we belonged together. What held me back was knowing there were memories that would eventually resurface. What if I remembered something terrible? What if I'd broken the first law of the Valkyrie not with Will... but with Tyler?

Will settled me onto the sheets and pulled away, his touch chaste but his eyes swarming with desire. "I'm not going to push you into anything you don't want to do," he assured me. He smirked. "Actually, I'm afraid of hurting you. This body is even a bit much for me to handle." He flexed and if he'd been a jock, I would have rolled my eyes. But he was Will and the muscles that rippled over him were made for a warrior—muscles that only a Valkyrie could handle.

My gaze fell over his majestic form. His strong arms, his Immortal leathers fitting to a defined ribcage, but then I noticed the glow at his fingers. It betrayed an ebbing light that was the spirit of his sword threatening to spring forth, and even now Will had trouble controlling it. He flinched away when he followed my gaze. "Sorry," he muttered. "I'm being stupid. I'm dangerous to you right now."

Tyler was right about one thing. Will was growing into his powers and without training, they could consume him.

Will sighed and retreated to the doorway, leaning on the wood and ignoring the scrawling smoke marks that drifted from his heat as he damaged the frame by just existing. "I'm going to go talk to him." The corner of his lips lifted in a smirk. "You know, Valiant-to-Valiant. Maybe I can see if there's some compromise we can come to."

My fingers curled into the softness of the sheets. I wanted to keep Will far away from Tyler, but I had to trust him. This was Will's life and I couldn't stand over him like the oppressive force my mother was to me. His gaze said that he needed to do this alone.

I found the strength to nod in agreement. "Fine, but if I wake up in the morning and find this house empty, I'll scour the universe to find you. Don't you let Tyler take you away. This is not your war to fight."

He laughed. "I promise I'm not going anywhere." He eased the door closed, leaving a crack as he peered through. "I'll see you in the morning."

I might trust Will, but if he thought I was going to allow him to talk to Tyler alone, he was insane.

I climbed through the window and eased around the corner of the house, peering until I spotted Will and Tyler sitting at the dock together as if they were just two dudes about to go fishing. It would have looked normal had they both not been glowing with Odin's unnatural power, their bodies garbed in golden leathers and swords steaming on the cracked wood, ready to be picked up at moment's notice.

I bit my lip as I strained against the glare to watch them. It seemed that Will had been holding his nature in. My chest stung as I realized that Will was having to control his new powers around me. With Tyler, he could just be himself—an Immortal that glowed with the power of the sun. He burned with such pure, unadulterated brilliance. If I didn't find a way to get him his mortality back, he'd be forced to learn to use the darkness like Tyler did to keep Odin's powers from consuming him. I knew that would break him. He could never embrace the same darkness that had turned his mother into the monster she'd become.

I had to get closer. Their voices drifted over the empty calm of the lake, but even my Valkyrie hearing couldn't pick up their words. My muscles tensed as I readied myself to hurry to the next tree, then I remembered Jules. Would she give me away if she spotted me?

After a quick scan, I couldn't find any hint of her. Perhaps Tyler had said something that finally got rid of her, at least for now. The trees creaked and wind curled through the pine needles just like any other night. Autumn had come and gone and now the evergreens towered in all their glory over the stark branches of trees that hibernated in winter. I was grateful for the pines that gave me enough cover to sneak through the brush and get just close enough to make out the words.

"Give me enough time to find out what my mother is up to," Will said. "If she's allied with Baldr, then that's just as much Odin's problem as anything else. You can help me do my training here and in the meantime, we can keep my mother from doing more harm. She might not have gotten to feed off of my sacrifice, but she took the Norn instead." His fingers twitched for the blade at his side. "I can't just leave her here. She's my responsibility now. I have to stop her from whatever plans she has in mind."

"I'll need proof," Tyler said, his words a growl. "And even if Odin concedes that you be trained here, that doesn't resolve Freya's demands. Aerie is her daughter. She wants her back."

"Then maybe she should have thought of that before she wiped her memories," Will countered. "And stop calling her Aerie. That's a girl that Freya destroyed. She's just Valerie now. She's just a teenage girl, no matter what she was before. She's in pain and she blames herself for everything. Freya needs to give her time to heal." Will gripped the sides of the dock and leaned as if restraining himself from grabbing his blade. "She needs to stay with me. You might be trying to protect her, but you're only making things worse."

My fingers ached as I clawed into the tree I was hiding

behind, leaning around it to catch every word until my neck complained from the angle it was twisted. A tap on my shoulder made me jump and I bit down on my tongue to keep myself from crying out and giving myself away.

Jules glowered at me and crossed her arms over her chest. "It's not polite to eavesdrop."

I grabbed my chest and sucked in gulps of air. "Jules, don't do that! You just about scared me to death." I narrowed my eyes. "And what are you doing here, anyway? Seems like I'm not the only one eavesdropping."

She waved away my accusation. "It doesn't matter. What matters is Tyler is suffering and he doesn't want my help." She sighed and the blooms that had opened around her neckline drooped. "Tyler has it in for you something fierce, I'm afraid. You're going to have to talk some sense into him. If you're not going to open your eyes and see how much he cares for you, then you need to set him loose. Stop stringing him on."

I balked. "String him on? What are you talking about?"

She rolled her eyes and twirled a vine around her finger. "Oh, come on. I saw how you were looking at him when he was telling you all about his heroic exploits. He's just a Valiant, you know. Negotiating with Freya and Odin are not tasks to be taken lightly. If I could see that there's something between you two, then Tyr saw it as well." She leaned in and hooked my blouse with a finger, pulling me in until I smelled the pungent jasmine of her warning. "As a Huldra, it's against my nature to want to cause someone pain, but the only way you're going to get Tyler mended is if you truly break him. Don't lead him on. Cut him free right now.

Take the next step with Will and show Tyr that there's no chance you two are ever getting back together."

Dizziness washed over me. When had Tyler and I ever *been* together?

A clash of metal on metal broke me free of Jules' trance. Twisting around the massive tree trunk, I clawed at the bark and spotted Tyler and Will face-to-face in battle. Their swords blurred and light flashed when their blades crashed onto one another. I screamed and launched myself out into the open. I had to stop this. What if Tyler killed Will? It would be all my fault.

Both Tyler and Will startled at my cry, blades poised above one another sending sparks flying over their faces. They parted and Will laughed. "Val, what're you doing here? I told you that Tyler and I were going to work it out."

Tyler rested his blade over his shoulder and glowered. "You wanted me to train him, right? That requires fighting, and lots of it. He needs to attune himself with his nature or he's going to burn up from the inside."

Embarrassed, I realized that I'd totally misread the situation and now I'd revealed that I'd been crouching in the woods listening in on a private conversation.

To my surprise, Jules appeared and beamed with an innocent smile. "It's my fault. I didn't trust you two and I got Valerie to come break you guys up. I've seen enough death in this forest and there's no way I'm going to let two Valiant kill each other."

Will relaxed at the excuse, but Tyler didn't seem to buy it. "Well, I'm just training him, so there's nothing to worry about." He tilted his head. "Are you guys going to let us get to business or are you going to make us sit out here all night?"

I threw up my hands. "Whatever, Tyler. Just make sure you don't hurt him or you're going to have to answer to me."

He grinned. "I'll be counting on that."

I was completely and utterly drained, both physically and mentally. Three days of non-stop training and Will still hadn't been able to best Tyler. Not that I expected a newly fledged Valiant to be able to defeat one of Odin's best, but it still made my stomach pitch every time Will came into the house soaked with sweat and fresh trails of golden blood streaking across his face and chest.

"You don't have to do this," I pressed him after yet another night of this nonsense. "This has to be Tyler messing with us. Beating you up can't be how you master your powers, much less how you learn to take on a mortal form so we can get you back to a real life."

Will grinned and wiped away droplets of sweat with the back of his hand. His hair clung to his forehead, but he laughed as if delighted with every moment of this torture. "I know you think it's crazy, but it's actually helping. I feel…" he searched for the word, "I hate to say it, but like I have a purpose."

I gripped his hands. "You mean getting ready to kill your mother? That's not your burden to bear."

His expression went somber and I sucked in a breath when his light dimmed, his features dwindling into a familiar visage of a mortal boy I'd given my heart to.

Will stared back at me, all trace of his Immortal life gone. Only the streaks of drying blood lined his face and chest to remind me that he had a different life now. "Like I said, Tyler is helping me. We won't have to stay here much longer."

I couldn't help it. Seeing him like that drew me in with an undeniable pull. My lips were on his and parting for him. At first he was stunned and his hands that had somehow found my hips squeezed, then he moved and deepened the kiss, bringing me in close as if he wanted to inhale me and fill his entire existence with me.

The door slammed open and I jumped away from Will, finding Tyler glowering from the doorway. He appraised me, then Will. "Good," he said at last. "You've finally gotten control over your mirage. I'll be able to move onto the next step of our plan."

I released the breath I'd been holding, but my chest felt tight. "What plan?" I asked, my voice wavering.

Tyler tried to pretend that he wasn't affected by what he'd just seen, but pain spiked behind the lights of his eyes. When guilt threatened to make me want to comfort him, I clung to what Jules had told me. I couldn't be selfish. This was what I needed to do in order to help him. If I let Tyler know that I still felt the connection between us, he'd never heal. He had to move on from me, just like Will did. I didn't dare think about what my life would be like without either of them, but it was the right thing to do. My love was forbidden, even if Tyler tried to tell me otherwise. I highly doubted that Freya had made an exception for any of her Valkyries, especially for me.

Tyler drew in a deep breath before speaking, as if he was struggling against drowning from the unseen sorrow in the air. "Will has informed me that his mother is Baldr's latest ally. I've already spoken to Odin and confirmed Will is more effective on Earth taking care of that new problem."

"And Freya?" I asked. "Does she still want me to come home?"

Tyler stiffened. "I'm not permitted to talk to her directly. Not after..." He shook his head as if clearing away a bad memory. "Odin talked with her about that. He agrees with me that you'll do more good here since this is a unique situation." He glanced at Will. "Will's progress is impressive. I don't think his training would be going as well as it has been if you went home. Even Freya has to realize it's because you're his anchor. If you leave, then Will is just going to regress. So, for the time being, Freya is permitting you to stay here, but that comes with a cost."

"What cost?" I asked, wary of any bargains he might have made on my behalf.

Tyler's light flared before he adopted his mortal form, dwindling into something so familiar that all my anger slipped right out of me. "When this is all over, I'm to dedicate my service to the Valkyries permanently," he said, his voice having lost the eerie Immortal hum. "Will can replace me. He has the strength and the darkness to handle higher doses of Odin's power."

My eyes went wide. Tyler was trying to pretend he was

doing us some sort of favor, but he'd neglected to acknowledge that this "bargain" meant I'd never see Will again... and Tyler would go right back to being my protector. Convenient—and a recipe for disaster. Didn't my mother understand I couldn't be around either of them? Maybe she thought that Tyler was the safer choice.

I didn't have a chance to complain. He jerked his chin towards the doorway. "Let's get going. Now that Will can appear human, we need to move." He turned and stomped towards the door, pausing to speak over his shoulder. "We go to New York. We have an ally there who will need protection when Leanne makes her move."

Tyler left, leaving me alone with Will and the tension that strapped around my chest like a straightjacket. As crazy as this was all getting, a room with padded walls was starting to sound appropriate.

"Who's Leanne?" I asked.

Will cleared his throat. "My mother."

NEW BEGINNINGS

*O*ut of all our Immortal powers, I imagined that it would take an army of Norn to stand in our way. However, of all things, money was actually an issue. We couldn't just super-speed our way up to New York and we didn't have the cash for gas. Our quest wasn't sanctioned by Freya—simply tolerated—so we were on our own. No using her forged books. No special lawyers or mysterious inheritances, much less rewritten memories. Getting a job was out of the question, so that left one sad option.

Selling the Porsche was bitter-sweet, kind of like saying goodbye but also like giving up the only piece I had of her.

"Sam would have wanted me to keep it," I protested as I handed Jules the keys. "And she wouldn't like that we're selling it to some random guy for much less than it's worth."

The stranger leaned against his current ride: an ancient looking thing with flames painted on the sides. I shuddered to think what he was going to do with a Porsche.

"No," Tyler said, his tone cold but his eyes as full of

feeling as they'd always been. "Sam would have wanted you to have enough money for Brooklyn pizza and some new clothes." He gave me a raised brow and appraised the ragged threads I'd been wearing and rewashing for the past few weeks. I didn't dare go back to the house to grab some things and I certainly didn't trust Jules to go through my stuff. It was all probably reclaimed by now anyway. "You'll want to make a good impression on your new ally."

I watched Jules totter away and make the trade. Bag of cash—probably drug money—in exchange for the last connection I had to Sam. She'd loved that car.

"Who's this ally?" Will asked as his arm slipped around my waist. The motion seemed natural, as if we fit together like a hand and a glove. He wasn't even aware of the shard of pain he stabbed into Tyler's heart every time he claimed me with his touch. I reacted to him out of instinct, sinking into the warmth of his chest, a secret, disloyal part of me wanting to pull away to spare Tyler the pain.

Tyler sniffed and tried to look indifferent. "You'll find out when we get there."

"Come on," Jules whined as she handed Tyler the keys to our new ride. "You're going to leave us hanging like that?" She plucked a twig from her hair. She'd struggled morph back into her mortal form and leaving her forest had made her go pale, but she wasn't about to let Tyler out of her sight. "I don't like surprises."

Tyler laughed and got into the driver's seat. He rammed the keys into the ignition and the car sputtered to life. "You're just going to have to deal. You're lucky I'm allowing you to come along, anyway."

She squeezed through the window and pinched his cheek. "It's almost as if you like me or something," she said, smiling. Then she got into the passenger seat and grinned like an idiot. An ember inside of me burned. How could she be so happy? Didn't she realize how hard this was for me?

Will squeezed my hand, because all of this was way harder than I could have imagined and if he could read my emotions as well as Tyler could read my mind, then he knew I wasn't handling this well. He waited patiently, knowing that I just needed a moment to absorb this epic shift in our lives.

The stranger who'd bought our car gave me a salute. "Have a nice trip," he said.

Our Porsche drove off with a stranger at the helm and I felt like a piece of myself went with it.

*

Sitting in the back of a car that smelled like cigarettes and beer wasn't my idea of a fun road trip. Will got me some cheese puffs, which my implanted memories said were delicious, and a soda to go with it. Crappy food for a crappy mood, he'd said. I wasn't one to argue and lamented my mixed feelings with powdered cheese and carbonated beverages.

A six hour drive didn't sound that long, but half-way in Jules started to sing. It was less a boppy-teen song that I expected from her and more eerie, queen of the wood, kind of music. When I fluttered my eyes closed and listened, I realized that she was leaving something behind too. By coming with us, she risked disconnecting with her forest. If she thought Tyler was really worth uprooting her life like that, literally, then maybe there was something to him that deserved a second-glance.

Will's fingers sought me out, squeezing the back of my neck in a slow massage. I'd been lulled into a trance with Jules' singing and hadn't even realized when I'd slumped into his arms.

"This ain't no love-boat," Tyler complained, glaring at us through the rearview mirror. "Do that on your own time."

Jules stopped her singing and laughed. "You certainly are the jealous type, aren't you?" She pursed her lips at him. "Were you jealous when you had to go off-world while they stayed here... *alone?* Oh, come on. You were a little bit, weren't you?"

Tyler growled and white-knuckled the wheel. "Of course not. I'm not jealous of anybody. I just don't want to do all the driving while Prince Charming back there gets the girl. I'm not that much of a pushover."

Will didn't respond, but his body went tense under my touch. I sighed and reclaimed my seat, wishing that this thing had a seatbelt. Just because I was a Valkyrie didn't mean I wanted to smash my head through the windshield when Tyler inevitably crashed paying more attention to me than to the road. "How much longer?" I asked. "This ally of yours better have good food. I'm starving." I was beginning to regret my road trip snack choices. Apparently powdered cheese melted on my tongue and gave me no sustenance whatsoever.

"We've got three more hours," Tyler said. "Just hold on. Once we're there, I know a place for dinner."

I'd expected fast food or something that we could grab on the go before we found a hotel, but I should've known better than to underestimate Tyler. Three long, silent hours later, he pulled our sputtering car up to a restaurant that looked more like a mansion. A gate separated the common-folk from the rest of the world.

"What kind of restaurant has a security gate?" I asked.

"One that caters to Immortals," Tyler said then drove up to the guard post.

"Friends of Dalia," Tyler said to a flat-faced dude in a suit who didn't seem very impressed with our ride. After an awkward moment of silence, Tyler sighed and splayed his palm, revealing a flash of a dark rune I'd never seen on him before. My memories fought to resurface to tell me what it meant. Only one word made it through the constriction of Grimhildr's programming. *Heimdall.*

"I see." The guard put away his notepad and pressed a button on the guardhouse panel. A gate lifted, allowing us entrance to the grounds. "Please accept our valet services at the front."

Tyler nodded and drove through.

We all fell into a hushed silence as we took in the stark contrast of the road basking in the dim light of dusk and streetlights to a white-washed building held up by columns intertwined with moss with spotlights of its own. Four blurry statues towered at the top, the night sky too clouded for me to make out the finer details. Only when the spotlights swept by could I see a familiar spear boasted by a woman dressed in battle leathers.

"Those are statues to pay homage to the gods," Tyler explained as he eased in behind a luxury car waiting for the valet. Our Porsche would have fit in much better than this piece of junk that was already winning open stares. "I'm guessing you only know about Odin and Freya, but there are four exiles in total that have been able to procreate."

"Wait a second," Will said as he leaned over the cracked leather seat. "You're telling me the way that an Immortal gets deity status is by having kids?"

Tyler chuckled. "Hey, it might be easy as a mortal, but once you ascend, you don't have the same plumbing anymore. Creating new Immortal life definitely qualifies for godship."

I peered up at the statues again as Tyler eased the car into drive and followed the line to the front of the restaurant. Odin sat atop his mighty steed, although he was missing the mechanical arm I remembered him having. I guessed that the Immortals thought it best to leave out that he was more machine than he was man.

The other two statues, though, I didn't recognize. One was a female with an antique telescope dangling from her hands. The last I tried to catch a glimpse of, but Tyler drove underneath the awning and put the car into park.

We were ushered out of our car and into the crowded restaurant before I had a chance to complain that I wanted to see the fourth statue. I bit my lip once we got inside. It likely would have made Tyler look ridiculous to introduce a Valkyrie who didn't even know who the gods were.

Low hanging chandeliers lit our path past secluded tables draped with velvet barriers. Immortals apparently liked to dine in peace, and while I could appreciate the concept, I found myself straining to peer through the shadows and catch a glimpse of what kind of Immortals gathered here. Were there more Valiant? Or was there some kind of truce here and I'd find a Norn or two? A shiver ran through me at that possibility. When we passed a table that hummed with feminine laughter, I couldn't help but think of Sam. Would I find Valkyries who remembered her?

"Here's your table," an usher told us and waved us up to the top level of steep stairs. At the end awaited an entire balcony that overlooked the restaurant which I hadn't realized was oriented in the same fashion as the glowing rune I'd seen on Tyler's palm.

"What are we doing here?" I snapped as everyone else took their seat.

Jules ignored me and folded a napkin in her lap. "Oh look!" she exclaimed. "They have maple appetizers." She grabbed one of the glazed balls and popped it into her mouth, her eyelids fluttering with bliss.

Tyler smirked as he held out a thick-walled glass. A waiter appeared out of thin air and filled it with golden, bubbling ale. I balked at the blatant display of Immortal powers, only to watch him vanish again, leaving only a flicker of shadows behind. Something about the magic made me shiver with dread.

"Figured they'd have maple treats. They saw you at the entrance," Tyler explained and tugged a flower that had bloomed in Jules' hair. "You do a poor job of hiding that you're a Huldra."

Will eyed his empty glass and held it up like Tyler had done. The waiter appeared again, filled the glass, and disappeared. Will barked a laugh. "Check that out!" he said, lifting his glass overflowing with froth. He took a swig and smiled at me, his lip rimmed with a foamy mustache. "I've only had beer once in my life," he said proudly, then his gaze went somber and he lowered his glass. "When my dad had let me take a sip of his." The moment passed and Will grinned again. "What do you Immortals say? Skol!"

Tyler barked a laugh. "Fitting in already." He lifted his glass. "Skol."

Everyone seemed to be having a good time, but underneath Tyler's swagger was a taut arrow ready to fly.

He caught my eye and gave the slightest nod of acknowledgment. *Good,* his eyes seemed to say, *there's still a Valkyrie in there somewhere.*

Food arrived and Will and Jules dove into their roasted duck and steamed veggies. I didn't touch my plate and stiffened as the mysterious waiter set a fluted glass of bubbling liquid by my plate. I almost spotted it too late. Inside the glass flashed a beacon with a yellow light. *Blink. Blink.*

I grabbed it and hurled the drink across the room. Jules shrieked in horror but Tyler watched me with an unwavering stare. When the glass hit the velvet curtain, the beacon turned red.

An explosion rocked the foundation of the balcony and flames burst to life, sending the curtains into a wall of inferno in a matter of seconds. Flames… I wanted to laugh. I was a Valkyrie and my homeworld was a pit of volcanic activity. My spear thrust into existence at my fingertips and flames burned at the edge of the blade. Wings itched at my back, but wouldn't come through. The hint of them drifted ash down the back of my shirt and I knew it would take a mental break to slam through Grimhildr's programming and regain all of who I was. For now, I faced new enemies that burst through the flames. Dark-pitted eyes glimmered like orbs of oil and fangs flashed, claws extended. A wave of fear churned in my stomach because even if I was a Valkyrie, I was still just a sixteen-year-old girl trying to stay alive.

Tyler shouted something at Will and then the two moved so fast their bodies blurred with lines of silver and gold. Armored leathers wrapped over muscle and gleaming swords appeared. Will followed suit behind Tyler, sword at the ready. Instead of fighting each other like they'd been doing for the past few days, they crashed into the creatures of shadow and slashed through dark blood and grime. Screeches filled the air and I studied the battle for my chance to strike. My heart pounded against my chest and everything seemed to blur together.

"Valerie!" Jules shouted as vines stretched through the cracks of the floorboards and wrapped around the nearest creatures' ankles, tipping them over as they roared with rage. As soon as she'd downed them her vines caught the embers and burned. Jules cried out in pain. "Val!" she called me again. "Help!"

I felt frozen to my spot. Instinct told me to move, but fear unlike any I'd ever felt wrapped around me with unseen shadows and squeezed.

I spotted an oily dagger going for Will's back and that was enough to unhinge me from my prison. Launching at the creature I screamed and drove my spear into his chest. Wide, shadowed eyes whispered with the last lick of life before disintegrating into ash.

Will whirled and stared at the blade that clattered to the floor. "Thanks," he whispered.

Tyler finished off the last of the creatures and reinforcements came just in the nick of time to be useless. "Nice try," Tyler said and twirled his blade through the air before it dissipated in a flash of brilliance. His Immortal body withered into his mortal one, leaving only my mortal friend with a handsome smile. "Tell Dalia we'll see her now."

I would have expected the place to be evacuated after a full-out attack like that, but the fire was put out by some ice-breathing creatures and the burned balcony sectioned off for repairs. The rest of the tables refilled with guests and mouth-watering smells overrode the smell of burnt wood within a matter of minutes.

"What was that?" I hissed as I followed Tyler into the restaurant's wine cellar.

"A test," he said and paused when our guide motioned for us to wait outside a door.

The guard growled at Tyler. "A test you nearly failed," he pointed out before glaring at me. "Some Valkyrie you bring us." His sharp features were distinctly human, but shadows glittered in the backs of his eyes, reminiscent of our attackers.

Before I could take offense, he slipped through the doorway. Literally—through it. I blinked as shadows whispered around the edges of the wood, protesting the traveler that had morphed its space.

"Do you recognize him?" Tyler asked. "His name's Shade. He won't remember you with your new body, but let's keep it that way. Don't tell him you're Aerie."

I made a face. "Only you call me Aerie."

Will wrapped an arm around my waist and gave me a peck on the cheek. "That's right. This is my girl, Val. Don't want any creepers getting ideas." He grinned, having pointedly been talking about Tyler.

Jules peeled off burnt layers of leaves and pines with an exasperated sigh. "Someone could have warned me that we were going to be attacked—by fire, no less. I'm too far from my forest. I can't just expend my energy like that."

Tyler surprised me by giving her shoulder a comforting squeeze. Light flared from his fingertips and the blooms along Jules' hair lifted. "My power stems from the sun," he explained at my perplexed face. "Sorry, Jules. I didn't mean for you to get hurt."

She giggled and blushed, swiftly changing from exasperation to giddy delight. She curled onto his arm and rested her head on his shoulder. "My hero in shining armor."

The door opened before I could gag. The black-eyed jock muscled us inside.

"Watch it," I complained when Shade shoved me low on my waist.

Will pushed him away, but I glared at him. I didn't need a guy to stand up for me.

Shade smirked at Will's protectiveness. "A Valkyrie with her very own Valiant pet. Cute, but cliché."

"Where's Dalia?" Tyler snapped. He crossed his arms. "I saw those shadows tracking us the moment we left the lake. She said that the magic protecting the outpost would hold, but she was wrong." His eyes narrowed with dangerous warning. "I have better things to worry about than dealing with a bunch of Skuld following me around."

Shade waved him away. "Come on. She's waiting for you. Don't get your leathers all in a bunch."

Tyler growled, but followed the black-haired man into a dimly lit room filled with telescopes and whirring gears. A woman, crouched over one of the devices, hummed as she twisted to get a better view. Her free hand scribbled something on a piece of paper. When she looked up, her pupils fluctuated as if adjusting to our proximity with the precision of a telescope. She smiled wide, revealing a set of golden teeth. "Tyr," she screeched and launched over her desk. Her arms wound around him as she gave him a big squeeze. She laughed and gripped him at arm's length, getting a good look at him. "It's been too long."

Tyler smiled and wriggled out of her grip. "Nice to see you too, Dalia."

I narrowed my eyes. Something about this woman told me to be careful. Her carefree demeanor was a mask, just as much as her golden teeth weren't real. Underneath there was something ancient and dangerous and her power hummed against my bones like a drill driving into my skull. I flinched when she set her gaze on me, her eyes wild and unique. Blue streaks spread out from her pin-pricked pupils and I had a feeling that she didn't miss much.

This wasn't just an Immortal. This was a goddess—Heimdall, the watchman of the Bifrost and capable of seeing all in her domain for a hundred concentric miles. Only thing was... I didn't remember Heimdall being a woman.

She offered me a hand and smiled. "Pleased to meet you, young Valkyrie. Tyr has told me much about you."

"Oh yeah?" I asked, infinitely glad that my voice held steady even as my heart thrummed against my chest like a frightened bird. "All good things, I hope."

She laughed. It was a hearty sound that could have put me at ease, if it hadn't been for the taut thread of danger underneath the surface that told me to be wary. "Mostly," she assured me, then she turned her attention to Will. "Ah, and our new Valiant. Handsome as they always are, of course." She grabbed Will before he had a chance to squirm away from the wet kiss she gave him on his cheek. "Welcome to the Bifrost." Her eyes glittered as we took in the magnitude of what that meant.

I turned and looked over my shoulder at the door. Shade opened it for me, revealing a hall that definitely wasn't the same as the restaurant we'd just been in.

This room wasn't part of the wine cellar. This was the Bifrost, the only entrance to Asgard and last line of defense against Baldr and his armies descending on Earth and destroying it from within.

"That woman is insane!" I shrieked.

Tyler rubbed his temples. Good, I hoped that he was getting a headache. I'd been berating him for the better part of an hour after Dalia had shown us to our rooms.

The Bifrost was under her control and could slip

through the various strongholds she'd established, which weren't just on Earth.

"She could have taken us anywhere!" I added. "Muspelheim, the Mojinir, even Asgard itself. And what then? We'd have been defenseless."

"Please," Tyler said. He beckoned to Jules. "Huldra, darling, could you do me a favor? Release some nightshade on this Valkyrie?"

Jules crossed her arms. "I'm none too pleased myself," she admitted. "Val has a point. We don't know anything about this Dalia. She might be your ally, but she's not ours."

Will hadn't said a word the entire time and gazed out the window as if he'd find what he was looking for on the dark streets below that glittered with raindrops and shadows.

This wasn't what I'd imagined New York to be like.

Of all places, the Bifrost had landed us in one of the most expensive hotels in the city. A massive wall kept out the worst of the blaring city lights. Gorgeous gardens sprinkled the grounds below. Jules spent her fair share of time at the window. At first I thought she was just admiring the view, but after she'd waved a few times I spotted other Huldra whispering through the leaves, laughing and dancing without a care in the world.

Easing up to Jules, I rubbed my arms and looked out the window with her. "Do you want to join them?" I asked.

She shrugged and glanced at Tyler who ignored us while he made himself a drink at the bar. "I do prefer my lake," she admitted. "It's quiet. Less... rambunctious." In spite of her dismissal, her gaze drifted back to the gardens and her eyes glittered with something I hadn't seen in her before. When she'd posed as Will's protective cousin, she'd been all business. But now she was wistful and full of hope… what did a Huldra dream about?

"Maybe when my work here is done, I'll visit the New York sprites." She gave me a sheepish smile. "Just for a little while, of course."

Will joined us at the window and pressed his nose to the glass. "I don't see them," he complained.

I laughed. "That's because you're not looking." Even though the Huldra were doing a poor job of blending in, they teased at the edges of the shadows, no doubt wanting to be seen. Yet, Will seemed to look past them, his gaze going somewhere I couldn't follow.

Will sighed and his breath fogged the glass. "My mother's out there, Val. I can sense her."

I found my fingers trailing over his arm, only to feel him shudder under my touch. "Can you describe it?"

His brows scrunched together, his face a dismantled reflection in the glass as he wiped away the streaks. "It was familiar," he admitted. "When those things… the Skuld, Tyler called them. When they attacked us, I felt the same thing." His chestnut eyes struggled to remain mortal as horror passed behind the crystal folds of his gaze where his Valiant side lived. "It's the same icy stillness I'd felt in my mother, as if she were an evil, dead thing that only knows how to suck in light and destroy it."

"Leanne is going to make her move," Tyler added, clinking glasses together as he mixed ice cubes, "but not yet." He popped open a can of soda and poured it into the glasses before slumping into the couch. He raised it and grinned. "Just soda," he promised, then knocked his head back and took a long gulp. He exhaled, satisfied. He dangled the glass and sloshed the ice with the bubbling liquid while he contemplated his thoughts. "We'll be ready for her when she strikes. We'll be safe here, for now."

Pinching my lips, I decided that I didn't like how Tyler was so cool with everything going on. It was almost like he… planned it.

Marching over to him, I snatched the drink out of his hand. "Hey!" he complained.

Frowning down at him, I glowered. "I think it's time you fess up. You've been working with Dalia all this time, haven't you?"

He shrugged. "Sort of, I guess. She might have helped me hide the lake house." When I gasped, he threw his hands up and added, "But it was my blood that powered the stealth spell, okay? She only helped me get it started."

I grabbed his wrist. "And this mark, then? Is that some cult symbol, or something? What kind of payment does an Immortal expect in return for that kind of magic?"

He twisted himself free and slumped into the leather cushions as if he were too exhausted to explain it all. "Come on, Aerie. You know it's worse than that." His gaze found mine and that familiar connection thrummed between us. For the first time in months, I felt the air shift around my skin as if time wanted to jerk to a halt. I hadn't tapped into my Frigg powers of bending time since I'd let myself get too close to Will. When I searched for the mortal that had stolen my heart, I found him completely enraptured with the mysteries outside our hotel room. He didn't seem the least bit interested in the argument Tyler and I were having, and neither was Jules. They made an appropriate pair, both looking for hope somewhere in the darkness.

Tyler's fingers grazed my arm and I jolted. "Hey," he said, his voice lowering. "The guy's been through a lot. His mother is a Norn-eating psychopath Hel-bent on sacrificing all of us. Give him some time."

I squeezed my stolen glass until my fingers went numb against the cold of the melting ice. Why *Tyler* was giving me boy advice, I wasn't sure, but he seemed genuine. I thrust the drink back into his face and he took it, setting it on the table. "I'm just tired of all of it, okay? My mother tries to control me. My father tries to use me. And everyone else? They just confuse me." I rolled small circles over my temples. "I need a break."

He patted the empty cushion at his side. "Then sit. Let's talk about it." He glanced at Will. "You don't mind, right buddy?"

Will grunted. "Huh? Oh, yeah. Sure." He glanced at me, guilt running frown-lines over his otherwise flawless face. "I could actually go for a walk, if that's okay, Val."

I swallowed and nodded mutely.

Will left, the door creaking behind him and Jules trotted gleefully behind him. "I'll join you!" she squealed.

Will's muffled voice complained, saying something about wanting to be alone, and I couldn't help but smirk when his hand appeared, holding the door open for her as he relented. He gave me a half-hearted smile and waved. "Be back in a bit," he said, then pointed at Tyler. "Don't do anything ungentlemanly-like, or I'll have to test my new sun-blade on your face."

Tyler gave him a salute. "Pretty sure she'll jab her flaming spear in my eye-socket first, so have fun."

Tension eased from Will's shoulders as he chuckled, waved again, then shut the door.

A lone with Tyler, I jumped up from the couch and promptly began pacing across expensive tile.

I decided that I didn't like this place. The low-hanging drapes and blood-colored walls reminded me of the rooms on the Einherjar. Freya was Odin's counterpart when it came to deities of war, but she'd also once been a goddess of love and beauty. That part of her shined through the different rooms of her ship. This place forced those memories to the surface and instilled in me a time where I'd been just one of Freya's daughters, happy and naive. Nighttime before bed consisted of a Roman-style steaming bath filled with rose petals and oils. My sisters would all bathe together and wash each other's hair. Their laughter still echoed pleasantly against my ears. It was the only time when my sisters took off their battle gear and gave their wounds a chance to heal in the rejuvenating waters our mother spoiled us with.

Tyler fanned himself with a throw pillow. "Of all the memories you choose to salvage from Grimhildr's programming..." He whistled. "What else you got in there?"

I glowered and slammed my thoughts closed. I pictured a door slamming in his face and Tyler flinched. I'd thought his skills a fluke, but now I knew that Tyler was getting inside my head. "Since when can you read my mind?"

Tyler shrugged as his cheeks went pink. "I've never been

good at it, especially with you. But you *are* more of an open book lately."

I slapped him on the shoulder. "Seriously, Tyler. Will can't read my mind. This doesn't sound like a Valiant skill." I chewed my lip. "I feel like I should know this about you already. Can't you just tell me what I haven't remembered yet?"

He sighed and shuffled to the window. Plucking a rose from the vase, he ran a finger over the thorns across the stem. "I'm not just a Valiant," he admitted and the hairs on the back of my neck stood on end. "I was actually an Immortal before I became one of Odin's soldiers."

"Dalia?" I asked.

Tyler nodded and turned the rose over, revealing one of the petals that had faded and withered. He plucked it free, but didn't let it fall. "My conversion was part of an alliance between Dalia and Odin. With the power I inherited from her, Odin would be able to hide his ship, and at times even Freya's planet."

"Inherited?" I asked. My eyes went wide. "... Are you related?" My gaze dropped to the unseen rune on his hand. "That symbol. It means you're Heimdall's heir... doesn't it?"

Tyler nodded and laughed when I swayed on my feet. He guided me to the sofa and sat me down. "Don't look so shocked. You're not the only one with a deity for a parent." He shrugged. "But you might be the only one with two." He sighed. "Odin and Freya have each other, even if they like to stay light-years apart. My mother, though, she only has her children. She's the weakest of the gods and it's my siblings and I who keep her safe."

"Siblings?" I asked, my voice turning into a squeak. "How many are there?"

He shrugged. "Who knows. I don't run into them often. The way we help her is by making alliances with other powerful Immortals. I'm lucky that Odin's work requires me on Earth so I can keep an eye on her." He frowned. "I can sense when someone wants her dead—which is more often than she likes to admit." He folded his fingers behind his head and leaned back. "Although, it's a strange position to be in now with Will's mother being our target." He eyed me. "Do you think he's okay with it?"

I didn't like talking about killing Tyler's mother. Hel, I didn't like talking about killing anyone. Some Valkyrie I was making...

Frustrated, I rolled off the couch and walked to the window, peering down to find Will wandering through the gardens. Jules bounced past him, running her fingers across the leaves as she danced and laughed. She might be having the time of her life, but a darkness clung to Will as if the Skuld had left a layer of their hatred on his skin.

"Those things," I asked Tyler, "the Skuld, you called them. What are they?"

"The Norns' pets," Tyler said. He joined me at the window, his gaze pensive on the pair below. "I'm sure Will can feel them better than you or I. His mother's the one that sent them, after all."

I shivered, not because that surprised me, but because a part of me already knew. "Was this why Freya assigned me to Will? He's a special case, isn't he?" Not that reaping a soul wasn't ever a special case...

Tyler nodded. "Now you're catching on." His gaze swept

over me and his fingers followed, trailing down the golden strands over my shoulder and over my back, stopping where my wings should have been. "Your mother didn't allow you to come back out of mercy. She sent you because she had no choice. You're the only one who can help Will stop his mother. Baldr is just gaining more allies and getting stronger. If he wins, then darkness reigns."

I should have pulled away. Letting Tyler touch me betrayed everything I felt for Will. Yet when I pictured the look on his face every time I rejected him, I couldn't move. The more my memories struggled to the surface, the more I realized that the bond Tyler and I shared ran deeper than I'd realized.

"So, why does my mother want me to come home now?" I asked, painfully aware that I was inches away from Tyler's body. Heat wafted off of him, hinting at the Immortal power that lingered under the sculpted, muscular lines.

"Because she's weak," Tyler whispered as he absently caressed my cheek. His forehead pressed against mine. "She's just as weak as I am. She wants to keep you all to herself and damn the consequences."

I swallowed the hard lump in my throat. Such raw admission made my knees wobble. "Is that why you've pushed me away?" My voice shook as I fought the urge to rise on my toes and brush my lips against his. "You said that I'm the only one that can help Will stop his mother. What happens once he does? Are you hoping he won't need me anymore?" I pushed my thoughts at him. *Are you hoping to have me all to yourself once he's gone?*

His breath puffed hot against my face. "Sweet Aerie. Your love is forbidden, be it to Will, or to me. Perhaps that's why I crave it so much." His lips hovered over mine and I held my breath. "When Will stops his mother, I hope he can stop me."

I closed my eyes, waiting with anticipation for Tyler to break all the rules he'd just laid out for me. His warmth vanished, replaced with licking shadows. When I opened my eyes again, Tyler was gone. I exhaled and my breath frosted the air.

NOT NOW, MOTHER

I didn't wait for Will to come back up, mostly because I couldn't face him with my cheeks red with guilt all over. Tyler and I hadn't done anything, but after he'd openly admitted his feelings for me, my heart roiled with my own conflicting emotions.

I settled into one of the rooms in the luxurious suite, opting for a smaller chamber with a single flatscreen and a whirlpool bath. The plush carpet thinned out to marble tile floors with a short wall surrounding the bath. Such an open layout would never have been possible with a roommate—at least, not with someone with an ounce of modesty. My heart pinched for Sam, remembering how she'd teased me about that. I closed the door and turned on the faucet.

Rummaging through the guest compartments revealed bath salts and soaps, which given how ripe I smelled opted for dumping the whole thing in. Soon the bath overflowed with bubbles that spilled onto the tiled floor. I marveled as the water gathered into the grooves and disappeared into camouflaged drains.

Shedding my clothes and slipping into the steaming waters, I sighed, glad to finally relax. Even if the knots in my muscles attempted to unwind, my mind was another story.

Tyler shouldn't have affected me like that... but he had.

How was it possible to have feelings for such two utterly different souls? I knew that I loved Will. We had a connection that sparked magic and tempted fate. Eventually, I'd grasp those lost memories I had of him and understand what it was that had brought us together. Yet, as I shuffled through the murky layers of Grimhildr's programming, what else might I find?

As my heart wandered, hoping to find a lifeline to grab onto, I closed my eyes and drifted into a state of relaxation as the steaming waters soothed muscles I hadn't even known were sore. I'd fought the Skuld and accessed my Valkyrie powers enough to call for my embers and my weapon. Using scalding powers that threatened to burn my mortal body to cinders always left me drained. Fatigue washed over me as I finally succumbed to the bath.

Just when I was starting to relax, a knock sounded against the walls I'd put around my thoughts ever since I'd learned that Tyler could invade them. I wasn't going to let him disrespect my privacy like that. Yet, I sensed it wasn't Tyler who'd given me a warning that I was about to be invaded.

Daughter...

Freya's voice crashed through my defenses. She could have destroyed me with a single thought, but I was far too precious to her. Her invasion came with her love for me that surprised me almost as much as her strength. She called for me again, this time her power singing through the burning metal of my locket as it radiated against my collarbone.

I clutched the necklace and scrunched my brows together at the twinges of pain as her voice vibrated through my body. "What do you want?" I asked through clenched teeth. "I'm trying to relax."

The air steamed as her connection to me strengthened and the flames of Muspelheim threatened to infiltrate the room. I growled and moved to get out of the bath, but slipped and caught myself on the edge. The bottom dropped out and the waters turned into a nightmarish vortex as I clung on for dear life. "Mother!" I shrieked.

We must talk...

An invisible force unlatched my fingers and I screamed as I slipped through to another world.

***

"I'm sorry," she began.

Freya didn't look sorry at all. She sat atop her throne, her spear at her side, and her chin upraised as if she had every right to pull me out of my one moment of relaxation. The air around her wavered, but it wasn't just the heat of Muspelheim that played with her hair. This wasn't really the volcanic world, and this wasn't really a place. I was inside her head.

"Let's just get this over with," I said and crossed my arms. I startled when wings brushed against my shoulders. I didn't turn to look at the fascinating appendages. This wasn't really my body. This was how my mother remembered me, garbed in battle leathers that followed the curves of my body. The flaps left my legs free to run and the leathers at my torso hugged the arches of my wings that extended from my spine. A tight headband hugged my temples and marked me as one of the Frigg, benders of time and beloved of Freya's daughters. My fingers twitched, remembering my spear, but this was how I looked before my time of trials and tribulation. I didn't have any weapons against my mother then. Just how she'd wanted it.

"You're reclaiming memories you're not supposed to have," she said as her gaze narrowed on me. "Why do you fight my attempts to save you from yourself? Don't you understand the danger?"

I wasn't sure if she was talking about Tyler or William—perhaps both. It didn't matter. I wasn't supposed to remember my feelings for either one of them. I wasn't supposed to *feel* at all... and neither was she.

Propping my hands on my hips, I decided to counter her question with one of my own. "If you want to help me *understand*, then why don't we start at the beginning? When did you first fall in love with my father?"

Her eyes widened. The red flames of Muspelheim licked behind her irises, her rage a mask for the compassion I knew she hid underneath. "I'm not the one who is suspect here." Her knuckles turned white as she clutched her spear, the symbol of her merciless power. "I am not the one who is endangering the entire universe based on selfish notions. I made a mistake by loving your father. It won't happen again. Odin and I are now powerful allies, but our relationship doesn't stem beyond that." She eased into the cold curves of her throne. "We wouldn't do anything to endanger you."

That statement opened my eyes to the truth Freya was trying to hide beneath her merciless demeanor. "You never stopped loving," I said, the words a bitter accusation on my tongue. "You're a hypocrite. You only transferred your love to me... and now you're smothering the instincts that you instilled in me."

She flinched at my words, but didn't retaliate like I expected. "Perhaps you're right," she said, her eyes glimmering with embers, "but it doesn't change the cost of our love. If you continue down this path, it will not end well."

The ground shook as if to emphasize the warning. The once pristine onyx walls cracked and heat broiled throughout the chamber. Shouts sounded from outside and metal clashed. I frowned at the breach of her thoughts as the realities of Muspelheim fed into my surroundings. "Tyler told me that Baldr found you."

Freya nodded. "We've always stayed a step ahead of him, or perhaps he didn't care to put in the resources to pin us down." Her shoulders rose as if every muscle in her tightened.

"What of father?" I persisted. "If he is such an ally, then why hasn't he come to you in your time of need?"

Freya's entire mood changed as if I'd said something ridiculous. She openly laughed and rose from her throne to glide down the steps and stand before me. "Your father knows that the small waves of Baldr's forces will only serve as target practice for your sisters." Her fingers drifted over my face. "Don't fret for me. We'll fight off the Skuld that Baldr sends to Muspelheim, but I fear it's only a distraction. Whatever he's up to seems to be focused on Earth."

I'd known that Baldr had been putting Muspelheim

under attack, but I didn't remember his forces being comprised of the Skuld.

Instead of asking about the darkness I was becoming intimately familiar with, I tensed, wondering how much Freya knew about Will's mother. That darkness in the lake was the same as the powers I'd used to conjure bodies... and it called to me to do so much more. Did she know that? Is that why she'd sent me to anchor Will, because I somehow knew how to fight it?

My lips parted to tell her, then my jaw clamped shut again when I glanced at the spear that gleamed with a humming power. This was the woman who'd taken my memories; everything that had made me who I was. Without them, I was left feeling confused, conflicted, and broken.

She appraised me as I fought my internal struggles. Her wings came into being, silencing my thoughts into a state of mute wonder. She didn't show them often. Great white arches without a single spot to mar their perfection fanned out behind her like a mirage. Most Valkyrie had black wings, and mine boasted freckles and flaws. Yet Freya was the best of us, our mother and the Immortal who would lead us through Ragnarök itself.

She flinched when the white feathers brushed my arms and I realized that she hadn't intended to summon them. "Oh, child, you still bring out a side of me that isn't supposed to exist anymore." She clung to the hilt of her spear as if it anchored her to the fiery rage of Muspelheim. "I've tried to mold you into what Valkyries are supposed to be, yet you all bear a mark that betrays my failure. Your hearts are in there, sprouting wings and telling me how you wish to be set free." She straightened and her wings flared with blue flames before turning to ash and trailing down the folds of her battle leathers. "We are Valkyries, warriors who keep the world a single blade apart from Ragnarök. Without us, without our sacrifice, the universe would fall into chaos." A click sounded as she pressed a button on her spear and the trembling walls around us turned into a glitter of stars. The universe unfolded before my eyes and my knees wobbled as she showed me world after world until we delved into the darkest pits of the cosmos. She pointed her spear to a seemingly insignificant void of black and it came to life, swirling with vibrant blues and reds. "The humans discovered the forces that only the Valkyries can control. Tears in time and space that come from another world, one unlike anything you could begin to imagine. It is full of color, wonder, and horror." She clicked another button, transforming the brilliant light-show to a swirling vortex of screams and pain. "The humans call it dark matter. They understand that an unseen force pushes the universe where it should collapse in on itself."

I waved my hand through the terrible display. "What is it?" I asked, my eyes wide with wonder.

"The echoes of the last Ragnarök trying to push this world apart. It wants to push and push until the universe itself tears open and allows a creature through that'll swallow the universe whole."

My mind spun trying to imagine a creature of that size. Feeling frantic, I clutched at the hard leathers that strapped over her wrist. "If humanity has already discovered it, then why don't you explain what it is? Maybe they could help."

She smiled, but it was a smile of a mother to her child

that had just asked for a star to be plucked out of the sky. "Humanity helps us in other ways."

I swallowed the hard lump in my throat. "Did you know Will's father was a scientist?" Perhaps he'd been too close to figuring out something Freya didn't want him to know.

"I know of all bright minds humanity has to offer. However it is the Norn who hold dominion over sacrifice, and to sacrifice knowledge is a great one indeed."

I frowned. "So you knew the Norn had targeted him, yet you did nothing."

She sighed and waved to the expanse of the cosmos that glittered like helpless sprinkles amidst the power of the echoes of Ragnarök. "This is what we are up against, my child. Sometimes we must endure hardships for the greater good."

My teeth ground together at her excuse for allowing Will's father to die. If he ever found out the truth, he'd never forgive me. To him, I'd always be just another Valkyrie who'd used humanity for their own agenda.

When I didn't respond, Freya pressed a sequence of buttons across the upper hilt of her spear. The movement made me flinch as if muscle memory had me trained to fear it. With a tap of her fingertips she could wipe out entire lives from existence, or she could bring forth the flames of Muspelheim and turn the cosmos into an inferno. When she held onto that spear, she held onto her excuse for justice and pitiless rage.

"Daughter," she said, her voice taut with emotion, "I brought you here because you're losing sight of the bigger picture. I sense your heart opening in ways that are dangerous for someone with your gifts." Her fingers brushed over the necklace. It hummed against her touch. "You have control over space and time itself. There is a reason I have made the first law of the Valkyrie. If you dare to love, if you dare to bring such weight into your heart as the crushing power of that emotion, you'll breach time and space itself."

I flinched under her warning. "I don't know what that means." I knew I sounded stubborn, but she couldn't just ask me to lock my heart into a box and hope it'd turn to stone.

She gave me a sympathetic smile. "It means you must trust me, Daughter. Promise me that you'll at least consider what I've shared with you."

I squeezed my eyes shut. She'd told me that my love could destroy the world and that terrified me to my bones. "I'll think about it," I said. Maybe Freya was just trying to control me… or maybe she was trying to save us all.

She tapped her spear against the floor and the echoes spanned out until my world was a roaring vortex sending me back home.

Be safe… my daughter.

A VALKYRIE'S LOVE

I jolted awake in a tub gone cold. Coughing and splashing, I crunched my toe against the porcelain edge and cursed as I stretched my neck back into a normal position. Rubbing the ache, I popped the drain and wobbled out of the bath before I wrapped myself in a fluffy towel. The whole ordeal had been a transfer of consciousness. I watched the waters swirl in the tub, reminding me of the ominous vortex that was out there in the cosmos right now, threatening to tear everything apart.

"Thanks, Mom," I mumbled under a hushed breath. "It's a wonder I didn't drown."

When no retort came from the empty bedroom, I sighed and shuffled to the long dresser and rummaged through the drawers. I found various sized clothes and pajamas ready for guests. Grabbing the fluffiest pink sleepwear I could find, my heart pinged knowing it was something Sam would've hated. Marshmallow pajamas, she would have called them.

After putting on the outfit that felt appropriately like a

cloud, I began brushing the knots out of my damp hair. A tap at the door sent me jolting out of my pensive thoughts.

"Come in," I said, expecting Jules. Without Sam, Jules was all I had when it came to girl-talk. Maybe she'd know how to unwind the truth from the lies Freya tried to force on me.

To my surprise, chestnut eyes peered around the doorway. "I just—oh…" Will paused when he saw my brush poised through damp hair. I blushed, sure that I looked ridiculous in my puffy pajamas, but his eyes didn't laugh. Instead his gaze went to the open folds of the loose buttons underneath my locket. "We can, uh," he rubbed the back of his reddening neck, "sorry. I meant to catch you before you got ready for bed. I guess I took too long."

When he moved to leave, I curled my fingers into the sheets. "Wait," I said. "You're already here. What's on your mind?"

He smiled and came inside, closing the door behind him. A fresh blush crept over my face. I hadn't intended to invite him in, but the connection between my mouth and the logical part of my brain didn't seem to be working.

His smile faded when he spotted the charred marks that streaked across the otherwise pristine porcelain tub. I hadn't even realized that my mother's visit had left its mark across my room like a scar.

Instead of joining me on the edge of the bed, Will sank down into the Victorian style sofa that sat adjacent to the dresser. "What happened?" he asked.

I mindlessly resumed brushing my hair, wincing when the prongs caught another tangle. The vortex that'd ripped my soul out of my body had done horrors to my hair. "Just my mother reminding me that my love is lethal," I said flatly.

His chestnut eyes found mine, as if daring me to deny my feelings for him. "Just because her love is lethal doesn't mean yours has to be too." He clenched a fist on his knee. "Her burdens are not yours."

I stared at him. It was as if he knew exactly the right things to say. My mother had just ripped me into another world to remind me how I'd inherited everything terrible that weighed on her shoulders. "It doesn't feel that way," I said, curling my legs under me. I couldn't suppress the shiver that ran up my spine. "What if she's right? Look what happened to Sam." My gaze found his. "Look what happened to you."

He blurred to my side, using supernatural speed that frightened me. He'd grown so much in the past couple of weeks, transitioning from a mortal boy that loved swim meets to one of Odin's Valiant. He wrapped his fingers through mine and rubbed my knuckles with his thumb. "What happened to me is not your fault. My curse began long before you were ever in the picture. And Sam?" His free hand grabbed my chin and forced me to look at him. Tears streamed down my cheeks and he wiped them away. "Sam made her choice. Her sacrifice was of her own doing. She wanted to give you something she'd never had herself: a chance to be happy."

We hadn't talked about Sam before. Just hearing her name spread fresh daggers through my heart. I'd been so busy blaming myself for her death that I hadn't stopped to consider that she'd made the conscious choice to attack

Will. Perhaps she'd just been trying to do the right thing, but whether she'd intended it or not, she'd saved my life.

When I searched Will's eyes that glittered with Immortal energy, I realized the other favor she'd done for me. If Will had killed me, he'd never have forgiven himself.

As if sensing my heart breaking, he leaned in and gave me a sweet kiss on the cheek. It felt so right, the way his lips formed to my curves. His touch wasn't like Tyler's. It didn't hold secrets underneath the surface or the sense of restraint that would tear anyone else apart. Will's love was open and honest. When he pulled away and he cupped my face, I saw a future in his eyes with so many possibilities. I didn't stop to wonder if it was my Frigg powers that searched his future, or my own imagination. I succumbed to the possibilities, either real or imaginary, and fitted myself to the curve of his neck.

I fell asleep in Will's arms, just like I'd done so many times before when he'd ascended as one of the Immortal. Our relationship had evolved into one of trust and security. A guilty part of me wanted to tell him about Tyler, but with everything going on, I knew Will was too fragile to handle the conflicting emotions of my heart. I couldn't even untangle them myself—just like the knots in my hair. When I woke up, I snagged my fingers through the strands and sighed. It was the perfect analogy for my life. No matter how much I tried, my problems tangled up into knots that were impossible to be undone.

I'd woken up a few times in the night, especially when

Will's warmth had disappeared when he'd retreated to his own room early in the morning. It would have been for the best that no one knew he'd spent the night with me—if Will had made any effort at stealth. The entire suite no doubt heard him stomping to his room. I'd rolled my eyes, knowing he was no fool. He wanted Tyler to know that we'd been together. Of course, Tyler would get the completely wrong impression.

After attempting to tame my unruly hair, I found an outfit suitable for a teenager. The tight fitting jeans and comfortable tee made me feel normal, at least on the surface. The girl looking back at me in the full-length mirror could have passed for happy—had it not been for the humming locket around my neck that betrayed a glimmer of Immortal power. I wrapped my fingers around its warmth, wondering why I couldn't bring myself to part from it. Just to run a test, I reached to the back of my neck to search for the clasp, but found that there wasn't one. If I wanted to take my necklace off, I'd have to break the chain. It was too small to loop over my head. When I gave the locket the lightest of tugs, fear coiled around my heart.

"Stop being ridiculous," I chided myself. It was just a necklace.

I had bigger things to worry about. Sounds came from outside my room and voices carried through the walls. When I ventured out and found the kitchen, I wasn't sure what I expected. Jules laughed, squeezing orange juice into glasses while Tyler cooked bacon and eggs. The delicious smells made my empty stomach twist. I hadn't had a proper meal in ages and Dalia's restaurant hadn't quite panned out for me.

I eased into a seat at the table and accepted a frothy glass of juice from Jules. My heart pinched, knowing that Sam would have loved this.

By the time Tyler pushed a plate under my nose and said I looked sickly so I had better eat something, Will wandered in and yawned. "Something smells delicious," he said and smiled. "Valiant powers include cooking? No one told me." He gave me a wink as he grabbed himself a plate.

Tyler rolled his eyes. "When you've been around humans as long as I have, you pick up a thing or two." He yanked the plate away and handed Will a spatula. "Here. You could use some practice."

I expected Will to take offense, but he flashed Tyler a handsome smile and walked over to the stove where a skillet of bubbling eggs waited. Tyler had apparently sabotaged the breakfast, putting the heat on high and soon the entire thing was burned. I guessed that he'd relied too much on his mother and Jules and now it was coming back to bite him.

"Guess your Valiant powers haven't kicked in," Tyler said with a smirk.

Will frowned and dumped the contents of the skillets onto his plate. "I burn it, I eat it," he said.

"You're such a martyr," Tyler complained and snatched away the plate, tossing the contents into the trash. "You can't take a joke, man."

Rolling my fingers around a warm cup of tea that Jules had given me, I zoned out, finding myself enjoying the banter between friends. I didn't know if Will and Tyler could be counted as friends, but as Tyler went on to explain the finer points of culinary arts and Will listened, I wondered if I wasn't in the picture, how close they might become.

Jules soon piped in, explaining that she felt nuts and berries were the best breakfast, but she wouldn't turn down hospitality and a crunchy piece of bacon.

It was only when Tyler started prodding about last night's events did I break out in a sweat. "So," he said, facing Will, "did you two learn anything out there?" He was talking about the gardens, but his eyes simmered with jealousy. He knew that Will had spent the night in my room.

Will bypassed the tension with a shrug. "Since Jules was with me, the Huldra seemed up to talking, but they were stressed. Kept going on about missing persons in Central Park and some kind of special, blue-colored tree sap every-where." He pointed a fork at Tyler. "You wouldn't happen to know anything about blue tree sap, would you?"

Tyler pushed his plate away, even though there were a couple of pieces of bacon left. He frowned, his appetite seemingly lost. "I only know of one kind of sap that the Huldra would care about. Yggdrasil's."

"What's that?" I asked. The term tickled something in the back of my mind. It was important... the world would stop turning without it kind of important.

He gave me a handsome smile that broke the tension of the room. "Yggdrasil's sap is what you and I are made of." He allowed the faintest light of his Immortal body to shine through. "Instead of flesh and blood, we're made up of the raw power of souls."

I narrowed my eyes at him. My biggest fear was that I didn't have a soul. "You're telling me that we're multiple souls put together?"

He tilted his head. "Sort of. It's complicated." I didn't know if he read my mind, or my horror painted across my face. "You're still you, Aerie. Nothing can change that."

Will cleared his throat. "But I killed Sam." Saying it aloud made him flinch, but he continued, "How could I kill an Immortal?"

"You didn't kill her," Tyler stated. "Not in the mortal sense of the word. When Sam took a Valiant's blade through the chest, she was sucked dry of Yggdrasil's sap. She's not dead—she's simply… less."

I shivered, but kept my eyes locked on Tyler. I didn't want to glance at Will and let him know that it still bothered me that he'd been the one to take Sam's life. No matter where she was or what she'd become, she was gone now in the sense of who she'd been. No matter what Tyler said, I knew the truth. She was dead and I'd never see her again.

Will leaned against the wall, seeming content not to share the table with us. I didn't like that he kept us at a distance, as if we were Immortals and he wasn't. When I met his chestnut eyes, it was as if last night hadn't happened at all. He broke my gaze and faced Tyler. "If the Yggdrasil sap is made up of souls, and people are going missing, then that means an Immortal is taking them." When Jules squeaked with protest, he added, "I don't believe it's one of the Huldra. They were too upset by it to be my first suspect."

"Do you think it's your mother?" Tyler asked as he crossed his arms.

Will nodded. "It lines up. If people have been going missing for the past couple of weeks, then that'd be around the time she ascended and allied with Baldr. She's up to something." His gaze darkened. "She's my mother. I need to stop her."

Unable to take it anymore, I got up from my chair and walked to him. I rested a hand on his muscled arm that tensed under my touch. "She's your responsibility just as much as my mother is mine," I reminded him. "Her burdens are not your own," I said, echoing his own advice.

Will frowned. "This isn't the same. Your mother's grievance is inaction, but mine—" He shot a pointed finger to the window. "She's out there taking people." He shuddered. "I can't even begin to imagine what she's doing to them."

With a sigh, I turned to Tyler. "What about Dalia? Will she help us?" New York was her territory and if what I remembered about Heimdall was true, she would have already seen who'd been taken and who'd done the taking.

Tyler shrugged. "Yeah, I suppose." He frowned. "She'll probably want something in return, though."

I nodded. I never expected to get anything for free. "We'll find out what she wants, and then we can either decide to accept her help or not."

Tyler rolled his shoulders back, as if preparing for a particularly difficult exercise. "You don't know my mother very well. We do this, we go to her, then she's got us by the balls either way."

I rolled my eyes. "Don't be such a jock." He'd spent way too much time at that high school.

After breakfast, we did the dishes and headed out as a group. Jules bounced ahead, trailing her fingers across the leaves. Her touch left a trail of glitter of green power across nature. Whispers echoed, the Huldra recognizing Jules as one of their own.

No one else seemed to notice, but underneath those indecipherable whispers echoed another voice, one that trembled with pain. I recognized it because it rang so familiar to my own feelings. I felt so locked up. No matter what I did, my memories were hidden from me. My true self was trapped in a place I couldn't reach.

Will walked at my side, comfortable with our proximity. A quick glance over my shoulder revealed Tyler, who promptly gave me a wink. I faced forward as a blush enflamed my face.

Both of them felt right. Tyler made life exciting. Will made life meaningful. I could see myself with either one of them, and that's what was so frustrating. If only I had access to my memories, I'd know what to do next. I made a fist, convinced that I'd been on the verge of figuring out these very emotions before Freya had made me start over with a clean slate. Perhaps she feared what would happen if a Valkyrie truly gave in to love... and maybe I should too.

"Absolutely not," Tyler bit off. "What kind of monster are you?" He gave her a low growl before continuing. "We're not just asking for help, you know. This shit is going down in *your* territory. If you don't stop this, then guess who benefits."

"Oh please," Dalia said. "Baldr doesn't scare me."

"No, Dalia. Nothing scares you." He growled again. "You see everything, yet you haven't even begun to see what I have."

Unfazed by her son's emotional response, Dalia twirled a miniature telescope across her fingers. She caught me watching and flashed a wide smile, her teeth startling me with their gaudy gold.

"That is the price, darling," she said, tilting her head to her son. She pointed the telescope at Jules. "The only reason I'm not able to protect all of those with Scandinavian ties is because I don't have enough Huldra to keep them safe." She sighed. "Central Park is the one beacon of life in this city filled with the color of nature." She tapped her telescope on the table. "And my only way to fuel the Bifrost."

My eyes went wide at that admission. I couldn't imagine the power it took to fuel the sole link to Asgard and the rest of the universe. "You killed those people?" I shrieked.

Dalia barked a laugh. "Sweetheart, no. I make deals. I observe. I trade." She tapped her telescope again. "I don't kill and neither do I approve the intruder who uses the kindred souls that are drawn into my domain. We can only feed off souls which have been attuned to us."

By now, Jules had nearly crawled into Tyler's lap like a frightened puppy. Keeping up the metaphor, she whimpered at the prospect of being one of Dalia's Huldra.

Tyler wrapped his arm protectively around Jules. The motion wasn't sensual, simply one of his nature as a member of the Valiant who was a part of the never-ending quest to protect the innocent. Tyler might not have been made a Valiant in the best of circumstances, but I knew deep down that it was a good fit for him. He protected things he believed to be wholesome and inherently "good." Jules was one of those things.

"Your price is too high," he said with finality as he gave Jules a comforting squeeze. "I will not play your games."

Dalia sighed, shrugging and twirling her chair back to her collection of telescopes. "A pity. Although, I can't say I'm surprised. We rarely come to a good bargain, you and I." She peered at him over her shoulder, her eyes smiling with pride. "You are my son, after all. You'll only take the best of deals."

"Were all your Huldra part of a deal?" I asked. There'd been so many Huldra in those woods.

She shrugged as she turned back to her work. "It's hard to say." She plucked out one of the broken telescopes from the pile. She tinkered with it until a lens popped free and she carefully held it up to the light. "Drat," she cursed. "Scratched." She tossed the damaged lens into a bin and it clattered with a collection of other discarded pieces.

"Why do you need more?" I pressed even though Tyler was shaking his head in warning. I glanced at Will, who nodded instead. As usual, Tyler and Will were on the opposite side of things. I chose to listen to my instincts. Dalia had information I needed.

Dalia hunched as she continued to tinker. I wondered if she wasn't going to respond until finally she popped out another lens, examined it, then tossed it. "You ask for my help in tracking down an imposter. The only way I can do that is with more Huldra, you see."

I tilted my head, getting a better view of the telescope she had in pieces on her desk. The minuscule parts glimmered under her lamp. "What do Huldra have to do with the culprit?"

She waved to the expanse of the room and her chair rotated with her movements. "This is the Bifrost. My forest is what feeds its power, and unfortunately, it's also what feeds Baldr." Her chair stopped so that she faced me, the full impact of her eerie gaze slamming into mine. "He's been taking his time leeching it from me, but now he's getting greedy. He wants to pluck off the Immortals one by one, fine by me." Her eyes glowed with internal power. It wasn't like Tyler's, a gold that burned with the sun. Heimdall's power glittered like the edges of the cosmos where time dropped off an invisible cliff and only a terrifying void remained. "The fact that he's trying to take the very power that fuels the Bifrost tells me he's coming after me, next. He wants me weak before he makes his strike."

Tyler peeled a whimpering Jules from his arm. "You have it all wrong."

Dalia broke the spell sparking between us, leaving me dizzy as she turned on her son with the full impact of her fury. She'd seemed composed, but the swirling heat in the room told me that Tyler had a way of getting under my skin. "Pray tell, *my son*, what I've misconstrued about this situation?"

He didn't flinch under a wave of power that would have made my knees buckle. "Just because you can see all in your domain doesn't mean you can understand it." He took a step towards her, showing he was either very brave, or very stupid. His short hair flew back against an invisible hot blast. "I've been among the other gods," he growled. "I know what they're like." He clenched his fingers into fists, as if enduring unpleasant memories. "They *all* think they're the strongest and everyone else is inconsequential. If you and those under your protection are being attacked, it's because they hold something of value, not because Baldr believes he can't defeat you without weakening you first." He braved another step and ran his fingers over Dalia's desk as he leaned. The wood creaked under his touch as if he held a weight that betrayed his own threatening tidal wave of power. "We're going out there. We're going to figure out who and what we're up against. You can help us, or you can stay out of our way. I don't give a damn."

I held my breath in the ensuing moment of tension that threatened to tear the room apart. Tyler broke it with a growl and took Jules by the hand. "Come on," he said. His gaze flashed to mine and my powers hummed on the edge of my senses. I suppressed them, in no way wanting to contribute my own power of time manipulation to a moment I didn't want lasting any longer than it already was.

Once again, the sting of rejection flashed like a supernova in his eyes and he left the room. An icy chill swept through my chest, reminding me that every time I hurt Tyler, I hurt myself.

Will ran his fingers through mine, a comforting warmth that tugged me out of a vortex of guilt that threatened to take me under. "You ready to go?" he asked, his eyes kind. He knew I didn't want to hurt Tyler, but as always, he was there for me.

I looked back to Dalia and she grinned at me, flashing her unnatural golden teeth that I suspected were quite real. "You go ahead," I said. "I have something I'd like to talk to Dalia about alone." When he gave me a raised brow, I squeezed his hand in return before pulling away. "I'll be fine. Just wait for me outside."

Seeming satisfied with that, he moved to leave, but paused at Dalia's desk long enough to give her a glare. It wasn't a threat, but a warning that said she'd better not do anything to me or she'd have to deal with him. He didn't care about his own life when it came to me—that much was already apparent by the fact that he was a Valiant and I was still alive when I'd been the one assigned to reap him. If he sensed what I had about Dalia, then he understood she liked to collect things. She wasn't going to collect me.

When Will left us alone and closed the door behind him, I turned to Dalia. She tilted her head to the side and swept an appraising look over my frame. "There's more to you than meets the eye," she said. Her eerie gaze transformed with bolts of blue as she used her powers to look deeper into my being until it felt like a thousand tiny electric bites fled across my skin. She laughed when I stiffened. "You don't trust me."

I propped my hands on my hips and hoped I looked brave even though I trembled under her scrutiny. I wasn't fooled by Dalia's appearance. She'd earned the title of 'god' by no small means. "You haven't given me a reason to trust you," I countered. "In my world, trust is earned."

She smiled, her teeth gleaming against the iridescence of her work lamps. "And in my world, alliances mean something." She glanced at my locket. "When you accepted my hospitality, you engaged an alliance between the house of Frigg and the house of Heimdall."

I groaned. I could kill Tyler. "It was just a night in a couple of beds you weren't using anyway," I complained. "If that's a problem, we'll go sleep on the street." We had plenty of money left over from selling Sam's car to find ourselves a place, but Dalia didn't have to know that. She might be all-seeing, but she wasn't all-knowing.

"No," she said. "You won't risk leaving my protection." Her eyes darkened. "I'm grievously familiar with the darkness that chases you."

I flinched under the haunting echo of her words. In such a small room, sound shouldn't travel the way Dalia's words did. "Is that how you know I'm a Frigg?"

She chuckled. "We have kindred gifts, little Valkyrie. I bend space, and therefore must bend time as well. The two are one and the same. Where my results are in teleportation of the Bifrost, yours seem to be the other end."

It should have unnerved me that Dalia could sense my latent powers, but she *was* an all-seeing Norse goddess and I was two-feet from her plethora of telescopes. "And what darkness do you speak of?" A shiver ran down my spine. I had a feeling she already knew what settled its icy claws in my chest every time I caused Tyler or Will pain. It had something to do with my powers over time and space, and the keeper of the Bifrost was one of the only people in the universe who'd be able to enlighten me.

"You'll find out soon enough," she assured me before shaking a broken telescope at me. "Now, we're allies until you break our truce with an act of violence." She grinned. "You're welcome to try, of course."

I sighed. Her relaxed posture didn't fool me. I knew that if I made a move to strike, she'd send me to the afterlife in two seconds flat—probably with a telescope shoved into my brain. "You already have an alliance with Odin," I countered. "You sold your own son to make that happen. If you're looking for an alliance with Freya, I'm afraid you're barking up the wrong Frigg. My mother and I don't exactly get along."

She laughed. "My son is even worse than you. It was his idea to become a Valiant so that he could impress some Valkyrie brat." She twirled a telescope across her fingers. "Not sure what happened to her. Lot of good it did him to give up his Immortal life for a creature that can't return his love." She sighed. "Hopeless boy. In any case, at least it wasn't for naught. He comes to visit his beloved mother now and again." Her eyes went soft as she looked at the door. "He's a good son, when he wants to be. I miss having him around."

By some miracle, I managed to keep my face expressionless. Had Tyler become a Valiant... for me? "I see." My words came out flat as I strangled my vocal cords by sheer will.

She wielded her telescope at me and narrowed her eyes. "Now, don't you go spreading rumor around to your Valkyrie friends that my boy is some sap. I'm telling you these things so that you know he's a good boy, but if I find out you been goin' out blabbing, you're going to find a pissed of Skuld in your closet the next time you go for a change." She grinned, the motion coming out menacing. "They like those puffy pajamas."

My lips twitched with repulsion. How much *did* she see? "Noted," I said, but I understood her protectiveness. She wasn't the only one who knew that Tyler was more than just his hard exterior. "Tyler has his secrets," I admitted. "I have no desire to share what little I know with any of my sisters." I straightened. "That's why I wanted to talk to you. I'm not looking to make alliances. I'm looking to break them."

She raised a perfectly smoothed brow. "Oh?"

While I imagined that Dalia didn't approve of Tyler being under Odin's power, it was nothing compared to how I felt about Will's predicament. I hadn't forgotten the fact that Tyler was here to bring Will back to Odin to begin his eternal servitude, the price for Immortality. I was just as trapped, constantly under my mother's determination to control me. It was time that I took a stand and took power over my own soul. "From what I remember of you," I said, shredding free a screaming memory from Grimhildr's programming, "you're a neutral party. I've fought the Skuld before and I remember you. All you did was watch us die." My sisters had fallen at my feet, their screams the last thing I heard before they turned to ash. It wasn't because Dalia was cruel, she simply did not fight in a war that wasn't hers in the first place. Now, though, that had changed. Baldr wasn't going to leave her be any longer. "You prefer the gods don't have alliances," I continued as I paced the small space in front of her desk. "You believe Immortals shouldn't govern themselves as monarchs with separate territories, but instead work together as a council of sovereigns."

Dalia leaned forward, her chair creaking on its wheels. "Go on," she said.

I ignored my locket that burned against my collarbone. Had it gotten hotter? "I want my memories back," I insisted. "If you tell me what you've seen in your forest, then it will help me stop this new threat that takes lives. You don't need another Huldra. You have me." Embers licked against my skin and I knew it wasn't my powers reacting to the threatening interest in Dalia's eyes. My mother's power knew my alliance went against everything she wanted for me. "Do you know how I can reclaim memories suppressed by Grimhildr's programming?"

Dalia hummed thoughtfully. "Yes, but you won't like it."

❧

*O*f course, the only way to reclaim my memories would be by using the most fundamental element in the universe: the sap of Yggdrasil. All souls coalesced in its power, eventually composing everything that cultivated Immortal technology. That realization made me sick to my stomach and was a segment of my Valkyrie training that Grimhildr freely gave.

The only way to get Yggdrasil sap was from the Einherjar... or a freshly sacrificed soul.

"That's unacceptable," I whispered, my voice having gone scratchy. I collapsed into the singular chair that sat across from Dalia's desk.

The shifting lights across Dalia's irises flashed. "I'll admit something to you, Valkyrie. The only thing I can't see is complete darkness. Baldr has discovered my weakness and now he exploits me with it. I asked for the Huldra because I knew it was a deal my son would never agree to. The truth is..." She hesitated as she sucked in a breath. "The truth," she tried again, her gaze fixated on a place beyond time and space that no mortal would ever see, "is that the darkness that chases you is what chases me, and it terrifies me."

I swallowed the hard lump in my throat. "So you can't help me?"

Her gaze cleared and her relaxed demeanor settled around her shoulders. She turned to her work again, seeming to find solace in her telescopes. "Perhaps. The Yggdrasil sap has many restorative properties. It could give you what you seek, and at the same time, rid me of a darkness that tromps in my woods unchecked." She shook her telescope at me. "If you see that sap just lying about, then using it is how you make sure those lives weren't lost in vain. Giving it purpose is how you stave off suffering and pain, for the sap of Yggdrasil will find itself roots, in one way or another."

I should have been afraid, but all I could think of was how the Yggdrasil sap could help me wrest my rightful memories from Grimhildr's oppression. I would know what I'd discovered before Freya had taken my memories. I could save myself from the downward spiral I found myself on with the foothold my memories could offer. "I'll do it," I said, straightening. "I'll find out who is killing people and I'll put a stop to it. Just tell me where to start."

Dalia's lips stretched into a grin, her golden teeth flashing before she jumped to her feet. I watched her, every muscle in my body taut with expectation. Heimdall was unpredictable and I knew better than to trust any deal we made.

She rummaged through a chest and tossed cracked and old telescopes onto the floor. "Ah." She pulled out a tiny, rusted tube with a foggy lens, then she tugged me to my feet before placing the cold metal in my hands. "There we are." She patted my hand. "Take a look. This is a special telescope I made when my boy went romping around looking for a Valkyrie's heart to break."

I gave her a raised brow. "Aren't telescopes for seeing things far away?"

Dalia rolled her eyes, the motion making her look mortal for a split second before the eerie effect of her irises made me want to look away. "I'm a goddess, remember? I don't make 'actual' telescopes. My creations see what isn't meant to be seen. Some search for violence. Others can spot love miles away." She tapped the metal in my hands, her fingernail pinging across the surface. "This one sees my worst fear."

I frowned, but curled my fingers around the device and

positioned it over my palm. Rusted splinters stabbed into my fingertips no matter how carefully I handled it, proving that Dalia had reservations when she'd crafted this particular telescope. If this device showed Dalia's worst fear, I had reservations of my own.

Curiosity winning over, I peered through the lens. At first, I didn't see anything other than a darker version of my skin. When I turned my hand over and looked at my palm, however, I gasped. An unmistakable blemish curled over the folds of my hand, settling into the crease directly beneath my thumb. It shifted like a shadow, but stayed in place even when I moved my hand to a different angle of Dalia's studio lights.

"What is that?" I asked, my face still pinned over the bronzed eyepiece.

"Suffering," she said simply. "Darkness thrives in pain. Her voice turned ominous and distant. When I pulled the scope away, I found Dalia's eyes unfocused and the blue spirals of her irises swirled like a violent storm. Mesmerized, I held my breath as she continued, and I realized she was speaking prophecy, looking through those folds of time and space that connected us. "An ancient god waits beyond, called by the one who will usher it into this world moved by the greatest force of all." Her eyes flinched to mine, an impossible power crushing into me and making me freeze. "Suffering that comes from love."

*D*alia's prophecy faded with the lights in her eyes and she slumped into her chair as if exhausted. "Sorry." Her voice dropped into a yawn. She lifted a hand to cover her mouth. "That happens sometimes when I'm around a Frigg."

I froze. She knew I was a Frigg. Did that mean she knew who I was?

"There's not many of you," Dalia continued, "but you're attracted to me like flies. Time benders can't get enough of the Bifrost." Relaxing, I moved to give her the scope back, but she waved me away. "Keep it as a token of our alliance." She glanced at the wall, her eyes swirling again with faint power and I knew she was looking through it at the sky. "Be sure to look at the heavens at night. Maybe you'll uncover more secrets that I've been too much of a coward to face myself." She gave me a golden grin. "Sorry, dear. I fear our time together passed more time than we realized."

With that sinking feeling, I left the Bifrost with Dalia's soft chuckles fading behind me. When the door swept closed at my back, a sudden thud hit my chest. I couldn't resist the urge to grab the knob and open it again.

My senses were right. The room had completely transformed. What had once been Dalia's workshop was now a small closet filled with wine bottles. I sighed and let the door swing shut again.

I don't know how long I stood there staring at the closed door that had once been the entrance to the Bifrost. I was glad that she was gone, but in a way, I felt trapped on the wrong side of the world. What good was I to anyone here, in my mortal body and with my weak heart?

As if in response to my doubt, Will's heat radiated behind me. I turned and looked up at him, unable to hide the guilt that streaked across my face. "Sorry," I managed to say. "How long was I gone?"

He crossed his arms and only the slight bulge of a vein at his forehead betrayed I'd concerned him. "A while." He glanced at the scope I still clutched in my hands. "Did she hurt you?"

I shook my head and my hair curled over my shoulders. I brushed it away. "No, I'm okay." I peered over his shoulder only to find an empty hallway. "Where's Tyler and Jules?"

He shrugged. "You were taking too long. Tyler didn't seem very concerned and Jules could only talk about food." He growled. "Might have told Tyler a thing or two of what I thought about his mother."

I bit my lip to keep a laugh from escaping. "Is that so?" I smiled, already finding myself relaxing in his presence. "I assume Jules got what she wanted if they're not here."

"Naturally," Will said, leaning against the wall. "Tyler took her to a local café. Apparently they have fresh fruit and berries fit for a Huldra. Unsurprising, seeing that Dalia has a hoard of them around here. Gotta keep the ones that take mortal bodies fed." Will shook his head. "You know, they'd make a cute pair if Tyler didn't have such an obvious thing for you."

I narrowed my eyes. Even though the jealousy in his tone annoyed me, I liked that he wasn't shy about showing his possessiveness over me. He didn't like it one bit that Tyler and I seemed to have a connection, and no matter how well I tried to hide it, Will knew me too well. "It's not —" I protested.

Will cut me off with a sharp wave of his hand. "It's not fair that he looks at you that way and you…" he trailed off before sighing. "I'm not blind, Val. I can see that he interests you and I know why that is."

My eyes went wide. "You do?" I wished that I did.

He nodded. "It's because we don't have our memories of each other. You and Tyler… I think you had something before I was in the picture. If there's an Immortal's worth of history there, then I doubt I can hold a candle to it." He flashed me a charming smile, defusing the tension that had locked against my chest. "Doesn't mean I'm not going to try." He winked and offered his arm. "Shall we get going?"

TYLER'S SECRET

After regrouping with Tyler and Jules, I sat through brunch, having lost my appetite. Jules gathered her assortment of nuts and berries into colorful arrangements before plucking one up and eating it thoughtfully.

"She likes to appreciate nature of all sorts," Tyler said as he leaned onto his elbow and watched Jules with an expression that mixed boredom with fascination.

"Not many Huldra where you come from?" Will asked before he took another bite of his sandwich.

I opted to sit next to Jules in the booth, only because Tyler was sitting across from her and I didn't want to give Will the wrong idea. However now seeing Will and Tyler scrunched together not trying to touch elbows made me regret that decision.

Tyler shrugged. "I didn't spend much time in New York, even though Dalia set up shop here in the early eighteen hundreds." He glanced at me before averting his gaze. "I joined Odin's service not long after that."

The blood drained from my face and I could feel Will's

eyes on me in accusation. Tyler and I had more history than I could even begin to imagine. I clenched my fists under the table.

"Not much nature in spaceships," I mused.

Tyler nodded as his lips slid into a smirk. "Not on the Mojinir, no."

When Will gave me an inquisitive look, I answered, "Odin's spaceship."

Tyler brightened. "How did you know that was Odin's spaceship?"

A blush crept over my face. Tyler thought it was because I'd reclaimed some of my memories of our time together. The truth was I'd already visited my father once on his ship. "Just a hunch," I said.

He sighed. "Right." As he stood, Jules gathered the remains of her lunch in her hand and pulled out a handkerchief. She smiled when I caught her eye. "It's for my sisters. They have to try this."

I wanted to say that I suspected the Huldra of New York were intimately familiar with nuts and berries, but decided to keep my mouth shut.

The sun smiled from overhead as we walked on busy streets towards Central Park. Everyone seemed to be in a hurry with a device plugged into their ears. No one paid even the slightest attention to us, a group of teenagers that would have been suspicious in any other venue. Will faintly glowed, his Valiant powers threatening to overtake him if I kept pushing his emotions. Tyler whispered with shadows and I knew it was an equal and opposite effect of whatever I was doing to them—and what they were doing to me.

Jules walked beside me while Tyler lagged behind,

watching our backs, and Will sped to the front, making me feel like a treasure trapped inside a phalanx.

"What were you talking to Dalia about?" Jules asked. She clutched her treasures to her chest as if she protected gold and silver rather than a couple of dried bits of fruit.

Will hadn't pressured me about my meeting with Dalia, but he knew that was because I didn't want to talk about it. Jules, on the other hand, blinked at me with the innocence of her question. When I didn't respond right away, I recognized a glimmer of fear.

I laughed and rested my hand on her arm. "It wasn't about you," I promised and she relaxed.

Once we reached the park, we all fell into silence, equally mesmerized by the people passing by. Children especially caught my interest as they laughed and clutched onto their mother's skirts. They weren't being raised to defend the universe or save the world. Their only job was to be happy.

Jules laughed as we passed a child that grinned up at us. "They're just darling, aren't they? The tiny humans."

It didn't surprise me that a Huldra loved children. I could see the kindred spirit of playfulness and mischief that came with youth. "Don't get many children in Mattsfield's forests?" I asked.

She nodded. "There are a couple of families that like to go camping in the summer, but it's rare I get to see such young ones." Her lips stretched into a smile. "I reveal myself to them, sometimes. The little ones find it fun." Her smile dimmed. "The adults just freak out."

My programmed memories hummed at that information. There were many fairytales about children being able to see things that adults couldn't. I imagined that there could be other Huldra out there like Jules who revealed themselves only to children because they knew they'd be accepted. The playful race thrived on emotions, especially joy and adventure.

Even Tyler didn't seem immune to the children's effect. We'd all stopped to watch children play ball for quite some time and the toy rolled to Tyler's feet. He picked it up and gently tossed it back to the youngest boy who came running. The boy laughed and thanked him before running off to join his friends, flashing Tyler a wide smile.

I wanted to enjoy the moment. Yet, now that I knew it was there, the icy stillness crept over my hand. The sensation was a constant reminder of what was coming for me. The scope Dalia had given me hung like a heavy weight in my jacket. I glanced up and peered through the filter of leaves at the puffy clouds that swept across the horizon. I hoped that when night came, I could see what else Dalia had been trying to warn me about.

Will brushed my arm and his touch sent a zing of assurance and warmth through my body. "What is it?" he asked. He followed my gaze. "Something I need to be worried about? I don't sense anything."

Just because Will was an Immortal now didn't mean he'd mastered his powers. I was glad that he could keep a mortal visage in front of the humans, even though a glimmer that streaked across his temple betrayed it cost him. I curled my fingers, resisting the urge to reach out and comfort him. He had every right to be worried about me. "Nothing's there," I lied. "I just don't like that there are children here. People are being taken. It's not safe."

Will threaded his fingers through mine and gave me a comforting squeeze. My touch cost him, sending another streak of light across his features. "Don't worry," he said, once again comforting me when he was the one about to break into a thousand pieces. "The attacks have only been attempted at night, according to Jules. The children will be sent to their beds long before any evil makes its way out into the open." He grinned. "Which means, while the sun is up, we can have some fun and look around. I've never been to Central Park."

We spent the better part of the day wandering and learning the park's turns and secrets. Countless vendors seemed to exist on every corner and Tyler looked about ready to smash every single one to pieces. "You know why they built the park, right?" Tyler asked no one in particular.

Jules hummed while she walked close to the leaves, seeming content to be so near nature. Will certainly wasn't going to engage in conversation with Tyler, so I decided to respond just to break the awkward silence. "No," I admitted. "Not even my programmed memories know that."

"That's because it's not important," Will offered.

Tyler dismissed Will with a wave of his hand. "It was because the Europeans thought Americans had dirty, pathetic cities." He waved his arms to the expanse of trees. "This was supposed to be America's proof that they could have a humane civilization, but they ruin it by making it a place of elites and trade. It should be about nature, plain and simple."

Jules interrupted her stroll to agree. "Without nature, humanity becomes dark."

I allowed Tyler and Jules to continue the conversation as

I came across a part of the park that was less than glamorous. We'd dodged the worst of the vendors, but now I sensed another sort of intrusion lingered on unseen corners. I spotted the glimmer of Huldra watching us as we moved through their woods. Slim, feminine bodies of spirits that hadn't experienced a dose of magic powerful enough to give them a mortal frame. Jules had experienced suffering, the one emotion that resulted in real, tangible power. If people were being taken, I wondered if the Huldra were tempted to use that pain for themselves.

Then I remembered, this was Dalia's territory. Even if the Huldra would stoop so low as to use the power of those who suffered here for their own gains, Dalia would know about it and I pitied any Huldra that dared to tick her off.

When evening fell, we found ourselves deeper into the lesser used areas of the park. I could see why no one wanted to come here. Trees twisted, looking pained. What had once been a fresh cement path was now a cracked and dusty spackle against dirt. I honed in on a splotch of deep rust that could have once been blood.

Even though I knew the sun was setting, it was darker here than it should have been. That's when I tasted the damp kiss of fog on my lips. I eased closer to Will and looked over my shoulder to find Tyler on full alert. Even Jules seemed to pay attention. Her shoulders curled as she shivered. Something bad had happened here.

"I don't like how this part of the park feels," Will said.

I pitched my voice low. "Can you sense it too?" My Valkyrie powers seemed sensitive to beings and acts of a magical nature. I wasn't sure what it was that I sensed, but if

Will could feel it too, it meant that this was magic that he'd felt before. "Do you think it's your mother?"

Will shook his head. "No. This feels different. My mother's power…" He tilted his head and the muscles at his jaw bulged. I knew he didn't like to think of what his mother was now, but he continued, "She feels like my mother… except wrong, twisted, and empty. This sensation, though… I don't know. It feels like something else. It's just… dark."

We had all worked under the assumption that it had been Will's mother who'd taken the helpless from Central Park. I thought back to what Dalia had told me.

I rummaged through my jacket and pulled out the scope. Tyler sucked in a breath. "Oh gods. Did you steal that? If my mother finds out—"

"Relax," I snapped before holding the eyepiece up to my face. "She gave it to me."

Tyler groaned. "That's even worse."

Ignoring him, I peered through the lens until my surroundings came into focus. I looked up through the filter of leaves, but there was still too much light to see past the obtrusion of clouds.

Shifting the scope down, I focused on the dense foliage of the park. The internal lens fluctuated, making me startle. I knew this thing didn't have batteries.

When my vision came into focus, I swallowed a scream.

Winding trails of glittering black slithered across our path like snakes. The tingling I'd felt at my ankles was tiny bites of a creature licking at the blue aura of our souls. My skin crawled.

The wisps of black choked the trees and forced them to

twist, bending them and squeezing strained cries from the branches that I'd missed before.

When I lowered the telescope, Will must have seen me blanch; He pried the device from my fingers and looked through it. He frowned. "I don't see anything," he complained.

"Let me try." Tyler snatched up the scope before Will had a chance to protest. He held it up to his eye and searched the woods, but mirrored Will's disappointment when he lowered it and glared at me. "Nothing, but, you're pale. Maybe only a Valkyrie can see it. Describe it."

The grim slate of his voice said he already had an idea what it was that only a Valkyrie could see.

The void. The shadow.

The echoes of Ragnarök.

*

Even though I hadn't been able to articulate what it was I'd seen, the unanimous decision to get back to the suite and mull things over sounded good to me. Only Jules didn't seem inclined to scale the steps to our suite. The moment we were inside the entry gates, she disappeared to deliver her treats to the Huldra who'd been too shy to reveal themselves during our visit to the park.

Once we were inside, I realized how exhausted I felt. I went to the living room and collapsed on the floor in front of an empty fireplace.

Will joined me and Tyler soon followed, both sitting on the floor on either side. I wanted to tell them that they weren't helping, but soon quiet conversation ensued that helped me take my mind off my feelings. Both Tyler and Will glowed as they talked, slowly shedding their mortal guises.

"I still think they're connected," Will insisted. He curled his arms over his knees and clasped his wrist. I kept my gaze on the shadows in the hearth that were an appropriate metaphor for the day's discoveries.

It wasn't cold enough for a fire, but I wanted one anyway to banish both the metaphor and the deep chill that crept into my chest and wouldn't let go.

Tyler drew his brows together. "I know your mother got herself into some dark magic, but what Aerie is describing is something else entirely." He tossed a toothpick into the fireplace. "The echoes of Ragnarök are scars on our world. They're everywhere, and they're actually a good thing." He glanced at me. "Without them, without the Valkyries who keep them in check, the entire universe would collapse in on itself."

I knew just as much as the humans what dark matter did for the universe. It kept it expanding. With an expanding universe, it would never die. But if that force was not there… it'd all go back to nothing and crush into an impossibly tiny, dense ball that had once been billions upon billions of galaxies.

"I never said it was an echo of Ragnarök," I protested as I crept closer to the fireplace. My fingers twitched, heat building in my center that wanted to light it.

Tyler shook his head, calling my bluff. "My mother gave you one of her telescopes. That's unheard of. She hoards those things like they're more important than her own children." He sighed. "It's part of her gift. She sees everything.

Her natural power is limited to a hundred miles of her domain, but she develops the telescopes to see more." His eyes dropped to the slight budge in my jacket where I kept the scope. I couldn't deny that I felt a bit of possessiveness for it as well, as if I'd inherited some great treasure that belonged to me and me alone. Perhaps some of Dalia's influence warped the object. I resisted the urge to tug it out and toss it across the room. I still needed it until I knew what this all meant.

"She wouldn't just lightly give it to you," Tyler continued. "I recognize that scope. That one shows her greatest fear."

I frowned. "Cheater." He didn't know I'd seen the echoes of Ragnarök because I'd been scared. He wasn't like Will. He couldn't read me that well. Instead he used his own knowledge against me.

He frowned. "It doesn't matter how I know what it is that you saw. The fact is, I know. Dalia is an Immortal that doesn't scare easily. There are only a few things in the known universe that get her on edge, and one of those are the echoes of Ragnarök." He leaned back against the edge of the couch.

I squirmed because I had a feeling I knew why they were called "echoes." It wasn't just because the dark whispers were remnants of the last Ragnarök, but because they were remnants of an echo that came from within the Valkyries. I felt it calling to me until my internal flames couldn't warm the cold core that settled into my chest. My Valkyrie spirit wasn't enough to keep it at bay, not if I let it keep spreading through me. The urge to set the room on fire just to feel warm again flashed through my mind, sending fresh terror once I pushed that terrible thought aside.

Even though I'd contained the stray compulsion, embers sparked at my fingertips and I shook them into the fireplace to keep the rug from lighting up. I'd hoped the flames would be small, but my power was more of a volatile nature. A flash exploded, sending heat billowing throughout the room and an instant fire roaring in the hearth.

Will shot to his feet as the flames reflected in his ethereal eyes, his mortal guise completely dropped. He looked at me and for the first time, I saw something other than concern there. I saw fear.

"I'm sorry," I whispered. I didn't want to frighten him. I wrapped my fingers around my elbows. I was so cold. My teeth chattered and I drew myself as close to the fireplace as I could without the flames catching my clothes.

"Let her be," Tyler said, not having moved from his reclined position against the sofa. He watched us through slitted eyes as if he were trying to fall asleep. "Don't be afraid of what you are, Aerie. You were born in the flames of Muspelheim and that power is all you have to fight against the threat of Ragnarök."

Will didn't seem convinced. "People don't just go around making ashes spontaneously combust." He kneeled so that we were eye-to-eye. "Are you okay? Did Dalia do something to you?"

"Oh please," Tyler said with a roll of his eyes. "Don't blame my mother." When Will glowered, Tyler snarled, his clothes morphing into battle leathers. He had such exquisite control over his gifts. It was easy to forget that Tyler was a powerful Valiant with centuries of experience.

"She didn't do anything," I said, forcing Tyler to lower his hackles. I reached into my jacket pocket and retrieved the scope. When I handed it to Tyler, he frowned. "Try again," I pressed. "This time, look at me." Maybe Tyler couldn't see the echoes of Ragnarök that infested a park, but if he had any connection to me whatsoever, he should be able to see the mark on my hand.

Will stayed silent as Tyler lifted the scope and took my offered palm. He turned it over as I splayed my fingers. He sucked in a breath and I knew that he'd spotted the mark. I bit my lower lip, but excited by the confirmation, and horrified about what the mark could mean. Was I really the harbinger of doom Freya was so afraid of?

He handed the scope to Will who took in a deep breath before taking a look for himself. The fact that he could see my mark didn't surprise me. My feelings for Will went both ways. "What is that?" he asked, although I had a feeling that he already knew.

"It's something that she's had for a long time," Tyler said. He made a fist and cursed. "Freya is an idiot. Suppressing your memories must have made it worse. It never was visible like that, not even with one of my mother's scopes."

I blinked at him as comprehension dawned. "You already knew?"

He nodded. "All Valiant know what Valkyrie truly are." He glared at Will. "Those who've gone through the training, anyway."

"And what are Valkyries?" Will asked, his voice holding a dangerous edge that Tyler had better be careful with his words.

Unfazed, Tyler explained. "Valkyries are born by the

suffering of men who die in battle and those who've already been sacrificed multiple times by the Norn. Because of that, they're innately in-tune with Ragnarök itself. Reincarnation is a paradox." He held up a fist in demonstration. "The gods as we know them don't create or destroy energy. They, too, must live within the bounds of physics. A soul is life, if one knows how to manipulate it. When a human is properly sacrificed..."

"The Einherjar," I murmured as a shiver ran up my spine. "I was supposed to take Will's soul to the Einherjar."

Will shook his head. "Don't look at me like that. You didn't take me anywhere."

The blood drained from my face. He meant to say, *I didn't dismantle his soul.*

I clutched at my elbows and trembled, then horror wound through me at the realization that I hadn't been born from the power of the Einherjar. I glanced at Tyler who seemed intent on watching me, his features unreadable. "You said that the gods can't create life, but Freya and Odin... they're my parents."

Tyler nodded. "And no one has known what to make of that. Maybe that's why Baldr is so terrified of them. Gods that can create life for real? That's a great power indeed."

I shook my head and closed my eyes, trying to focus on the emanating heat of the fireplace. Nothing could warm the stretching icy fingers that tried to dismantle everything that I was. Now that I knew what Tyler meant, I realized he was right. I clutched at the locket at my neck and wished that he was wrong. Most Valkyries would be burdened with suffering and pain, a darkness that called for Ragnarök. But me, I was born from the flesh of Freya and Odin, and if I had a mark of Ragnarök, it means that their suffering was worse than all the souls they'd ever reaped. "I don't know if I can do this," I said, my voice a shaking whisper.

Tyler growled with frustration as he got to his feet and began pacing. "This is our fault." His words were a sharp blade against my ears. I turned to look at him and found him shaking a fist at Will. "She's like a newborn without her memories. She doesn't know how to contain the pain inside of her and when we start tearing at her like a game of tug-of-war, it's just bringing all that out." When Will set his jaw in a hard line, Tyler straightened and turned to me. "Your mother chose to raise you on Muspelheim for a reason. All Valkyries need its flames to burn the cold pit inside of all of you." His eyes went wide. "Her daughters are the harbingers of Ragnarök and are a necessary force in the universe." He knelt and splayed his fingers over my arm. His touch felt scalding against my sweat-dampened skin. "You are the most vulnerable of all Valkyries. You are capable of true love. With love comes heartbreak. And with heartbreak, comes sadness that can eat you alive. When that happens, you will be tempted to accept the icy chill that exists in your kind." He curled his fingers away. "It's why a Valkyrie cannot love."

First Law of the Valkyrie... Don't Fall in Love.

My mouth went dry at the realization that those laws were in place for a reason.

A supernatural sheen broke out on Will's face and glittered like diamonds. He refused to look at me. "How do I know this is true?" His confusion turned to anger as he stood and faced Tyler. "You've been lying to us this whole time. Who's to say this isn't some elaborate scheme for you to get me away from her? To make me serve Odin to be miserable like you?"

When Tyler growled, Will shoved Dalia's scope at me. "Look at him," he insisted. "If anyone has darkness in their hearts, it's the spawn of Dalia."

Tyler's eyes went wide, and when he looked at me, I saw fear. His gaze dropped to the scope and I knew that Will had hit a nerve.

An icy chill swept through the room as I turned the scope over in my hands. That sensation meant Tyler's magic and his urge to disappear. Even though he shimmered, he stayed put and resignation fell over his features. He wanted to show me the truth.

I brought the scope to my face and sucked in a breath. Where I'd had a single black rune festering on my palm, Tyler was covered with them.

He closed his eyes and his jaw bulged before he turned and fled into a vortex of teleportation magic.

LOVE'S SACRIFICE

Tyler didn't return that night, leaving me confused and admittedly heartbroken. "Why would he hide that from us?" I asked, and my thoughts echoed, *from me?*

Jules still hadn't returned, leaving only Will and me to ponder what this all meant. Will paced an endless circle at my back while I huddled as close to the fireplace as I dared. The flames had died down, but not much.

Tyler's revelation only seemed to make the cold grip on my chest worse, supporting what he'd said that my connection to Ragnarök was tied to my emotions, particularly those of a romantic nature. I'd never realized how much I'd cared for Tyler until he'd looked at me like he'd lost me forever. Now that I knew he bore the mark of Ragnarök, there was no way we could be together. If I truly let myself love him and something happened, it could be a tipping point that would bring about the end of the world. Yet, the thought of abandoning him to his suffering clawed at me until it left physical pain and my mouth parted in a silent cry. I couldn't deny my feelings for him anymore. I wouldn't.

As if he sensed the shift in the room, Will's footsteps stilled behind me and his warm hand rested on my shoulder. Where Tyler caused me anguish just thinking about him, Will was a constant that would never falter. I turned and crushed myself into his embrace. "I'm sorry," I muttered as my fingers curled into the vibrant glow of his Valiant leathers. He was far too worked up to keep a handle on his human mirage and I didn't blame him.

"For what?" he asked, his fingers automatically threading gentle strokes through my hair.

"This isn't fair to you," I said. If I was going to admit my feelings for Tyler to myself, then I had to admit another truth I couldn't deny: my heart belonged to Will.

His hands went low on my waist as he pulled me hard against him. The motion was of a possessive nature and he knew what I meant. "I'm not angry with you," he said and raised a hand to continue his gentling strokes. "I'm not blind. Tyler is an Immortal and so are you. Before I was in the picture, you two must have had something." He forced me to pull away and to look him in his eyes. Rainbow lights glittered in the back of freshly Immortal irises. "I think this was exactly how it went down in my last life. This is why Freya wiped your memories. You loved both of us and it was tearing you apart."

To hear it aloud made my heart thunder in my ears. It was true. I was falling for them both… and perhaps that's because it had already happened before.

He cupped my face. "That kind of pain left unchecked… it would be enough to usher in Ragnarök, wouldn't it?"

I swallowed hard, because I knew he was right. Guilt seemed to be my worst trigger against the icy claw in my chest and the final straw that made me want to lower my defenses and let it consume me until I couldn't feel anything anymore.

I forced myself to look up into his eyes that glittered with hope. Even now, knowing what he knew, he wanted to love me. I found my fingers gliding over his as I leaned into his touch. "Even without my memories, my heart remembers," I admitted. "You're right. I care for both of you." I shivered because I was being so selfish. It wasn't fair for me to feel for Tyler what I felt for him. Pain and guilt ripped through me and I winced, pulling away and pressing my hand against my chest where an icy dagger threatened to pierce through. "Will, I'm so sorry. What should I do? It's not right for me to put you through this."

Unfazed by the threatening shadows that licked at my fingertips, he pulled me close to him again, allowing his warmth to banish the cold that wanted to devour me. "I would say choose me, but I know it's not that simple." He lifted my chin and gave me a tender kiss without any warning, making my toes curl as the breath of the sun of his magic spread across my face. The icy pain retreated, replaced with the unadulterated thrill that he gave me. I knew that it would be a short lived elation and would come crashing down with guilt the moment I saw Tyler again.

"Then what?" I asked, breathless.

He sighed. "You're going to have to do it again."

I blinked at him with incomprehension. "Do what again?"

He ran his fingers through my hair, bringing me in for

another tender kiss before pulling away. "You're going to have to let us both go, before you fall too hard." When I made a sound of protest, he raised a hand. "If you make a clean break now, you can survive this pain." His hand fell as he chewed his lip before asking his question. "You haven't slept with him yet, right?"

I squeaked. "What? No. Of course not."

His shoulders relaxed. "Good."

An awkward silence swooped in to mix with the tension that grew between us. We'd never crossed that line, and from my perspective it'd been because Will had already been going through too much. Back at the cottage, I'd been more concerned about helping him adjust to his new Immortal life while I beat myself up for being the cause of him losing his mortal one. Yet, now, I saw that Will had held himself back because he'd seen the hesitation in my eyes. I couldn't make that step with either of them. Even without my memories, I knew if I did, I'd form a bond so deep that breaking it would destroy me.

"It's settled, then," Will said, raising his chin in defiance. "Once I take care of my mother, I'll go with Tyr to the Mojinir." He'd called Tyler by his Immortal name, making me frown. "You," he said, landing a heavy hand on my shoulder, "will go back to Freya. You have a mother who loves you. You must hold onto her for the strength you need." His hand fell to his side as resignation settled around him like a shadow.

Anger made my heart thunder in my ears. "You're going to give up, just like that?" I grabbed his arm, but it felt like a rock under my touch. He was unearthly and unmovable when he wanted to be. I'd wanted him to be able to adjust to his new Immortal body, but not like this. "Did you think about why my mother would send me to reap you, knowing everything that happened between us?" I snapped.

His features hardened. "Because she wanted to break you. If you reaped me, then your capability of love would have died with me."

That thought hadn't occurred to me and his words came at me like a slap across the face. "No," I stammered. "I refuse to believe that." I curled my fingers into fists. "If that's what she really did, then damn her. I'll prove her wrong to doubt me."

Will's gaze finally broke from mine, shifting to the window as silver moonlight broke through the tension of the room. His voice turned low and ominous as he quoted the second law of the Valkyrie. "Don't question the gods."

I gave him a humorless laugh. "Or what? She'll fail me again?" I shook my head and embers flew from the tips of my hair. I hadn't realized that my Valkyrie powers had started to seep through, although I wasn't sure if it was to suppress the shadow budding in my chest, or to fuel the flames of my anger. "No, Will. I'm going to question them." I began counting on my fingers. "Freya. Odin. Dalia. They've only managed to make things worse." Invisible wings sent a warm draft across my shoulder blades as my rage built into an inferno in my chest, driving away the icy chill of Ragnarök. "They've only ever kept Ragnarök on the edges of the universe, keeping it at arm's length and just hoping it'll stay there." I straightened. "Perhaps it's time to face our fears." A cloud blocked out the moon, leaving only the flicker of flames from the hearth that had roared to life. I growled with determination. "It's time to fight."

Fighting something that could swallow entire worlds seemed an impossible concept, but I was determined to try. The alternative was unacceptable. I couldn't just ask Freya to wipe my memories again and I couldn't fall into the trap of believing that I could trust her. She didn't have my interests at heart, even if she was only trying to protect me. Taking away my capability of love would destroy me all the same.

I could never give up on love.

Even though my heart tugged me in two different directions, I had to give myself time to sort out my feelings. As much pain as it caused me to consider losing either Tyler or Will, it would hurt so much worse to lose them both.

Having been unable to steer me away from my dangerous course, Will left me alone with my thoughts. "Going to bed," he'd said, clearly annoyed with me, then disappeared into the dark hall.

Clutching my fingers into fists, I stormed outside. I wasn't sure if I was looking for Jules or Tyler, but decided that perhaps it was best if I were alone for a little while. I moved deeper into the foliage and wandered, hoping my chest would unclench, but it only seemed to get worse.

I hadn't realized what had drawn me out at first, but now I sensed it. There was a wrongness in this forest that resonated with the darkness clinging to my soul.

Approaching a tree, I pressed my fingers to the peeling bark. I'd expected the graze of rough nature. Instead, an unexpected icy jolt of power made my jaw clamp shut as electricity slammed through me.

There was so much pain here. I stifled a cry as my heart remembered things my brain couldn't Grimhildr's programming bucked under the jolt of power, but held onto my memories in its vice grip.

I wanted to know what had caused so much pain in this forest. I couldn't imagine this kind of suffering could build up from the instances of kidnappings, even if they'd been taken right here under my fingertips and dragged away into the darkness. This was something deeper... more ancient and terrifying that suggested centuries of pain. When I focused on the sensation that wafted through the woods, I found that I'd been following its trail through the forest. If I kept going, I might find its source.

Swallowing the hard lump in my throat, I followed it. A few ragged steps into the journey, the hairs on the back of my neck stood on end. I wasn't alone.

I trailed back as much as I could, realizing that the source I sought could very well be a person. I sensed another presence whispering amongst the leaves. Footsteps sounded, too light and swift to be a human's.

Squinting into the darkness, embers burned in the backs

of my eyes and offered me a better view through the darkness. A female silhouette walked through the trees, the
branches parting as she went. Her fingers grazed the edges,
helping to push the brush aside as if she were swimming
through the suffering to get to the other side.

I'd never been good at stealth, but I tugged at any
suppressed training I might have had to keep my footsteps
light. The further we delved into the woods, the more dead
and crunched leaves threatened to give me away. I opted for
the softer soil, hoping to keep my presence hidden. I
stepped on a twig, the sound reverberating to my sensitive
senses and I froze. The silhouette kept moving, oblivious to
my error.

A few moments in I realized why I hadn't been spotted.
We'd almost reached the source.

A blue glow emanated at the end of the long trail. I drew
in a long breath and forced myself to appraise my
surroundings. When I'd come with Will and Tyler to investigate Central Park, we'd made sure to go through every
trail. We'd been sure to check every corner and bush. I
would have remembered this path, but I was certain that I
hadn't been this way before. The twisted trees bent and
intertwined into an arch, making me shiver when I stepped
under it as if I'd trespassed into new territory. I kept my
eyes on the blue glow that illuminated the waxy branches
that were so dense, I couldn't even see the stars.

Blood thundered in my ears when the silhouette paused,
as if considering she might have been followed, then
continued on. I gripped my locket for confidence before
following her into the blue glow.

I was glad I'd turned my eyes to my feet to look for

leaves or twigs that might give me away. I stifled a gasp at the specks of glass that littered the dark path. When I picked one up, carefully turning it over to inspect it with my molten gaze, I realized it wasn't glass at all. The fine veins showed that this had once been something alive.

I'd never seen the sap of Yggdrasil, but I had no doubt that this was what it was… at least, what was left of it. Life should have emanated from the translucent husk that stole the heat from my fingertips, but it'd been licked clean.

The silhouette halted and I jumped behind a tree before she turned around. I went still when I finally made out her features. This girl who looked so frightened had a single line of determination running across her jaw was none other than my friend, Jules.

I refused to believe that Jules could possibly be involved in whatever I'd uncovered. I'd trusted her with so much. That kind of betrayal could tip me over the edge.

A part of me wanted to jump out and confront her right away. Surely she had some sort of explanation, but I knew better. I recognized that look on her face because it echoed the same pain that weighed heavy in my heart every day.

Guilt.

The emotion tainted her and permeated the air, helping me to dispel what I had once believed to be innocent. I shouldn't have underestimated a Huldra.

Jules seemed satisfied and turned back to the wall of thorns, sending them unfurling with a wave of her hand. The limbs glowed green with the power of nature and life. It was such a stark contrast to the suffering and death that surrounded us like a fog.

When the thorns parted, it revealed the sickly treasure

trapped inside. A body twisted and bloody twitched with the thorn's movement and my stomach dropped. Disbelief rooted me to the spot. There was no way this could be real. Jules wasn't a killer.

A groan escaped the victim… still alive.

I couldn't deny what was right in front of me. Huldra reacted to the suffering that permeated the air with its heavy stink and whispered through the trees like a mirage. Their fingers were the thorns and they dug into their victim. He cried out, the sound pathetic and weak as if he'd been screaming for hours.

I had to act. I had to do something to save this poor soul from the Huldra… from Jules.

I burst from my hiding spot and embers came to life at my fingertips without a second thought. When someone's life was on the line, I embraced my Valkyrie. This time, I could be what my mother wanted me to be. I could dole out justice where it was deserved.

My spear sprang to life in my grip. My final transformation whispered a shadow of wings at my back. The flash of them must have alerted Jules; she whirled and went pale at the sight of me.

What I saw in her eyes wasn't madness or guilt, but desperation and fear. What could have been wings immediately sent ash crumbling down my back. It could have been the mercy still inside of me that prevented the full shedding of my mortal form, or it could be that without my memories, I was more mortal than I was a Valkyrie warrior. I growled, because I still had my flames, I still had my spirit, and I still had my fight for justice. I ran at Jules with all my strength. "Release him immediately!"

Speechless, her jaw slacked in awe of me and her hands came up in surrender.

The other Huldra abandoned her as quickly as they'd arrived. They were nothing but parasites come to feast on their victim. A blue glow left the man with them and the human's body slumped into the hardened thorns that drooped with him. Blood trailed down his broken body and he looked at me with a glimmer of hope in his broken eyes before he closed them forever and took his last, strained breath.

I knew that I'd seen death before. As a Valkyrie, I'd watched William over his multiple lifetimes before I'd come to claim him for the Einherjar. Even though I'd seen his death, I couldn't remember it. To my mortal brain, this was the first time I'd seen such finality and loss. This man would never live again. Whoever he was, he surely had loved ones who would be crushed by his absence. He wasn't like Will. Reincarnation was the curse of the Norn and I didn't smell the shadowed stink of dark magic on him... just pain and suffering that dissipated into the air along with his soul.

Jules fell to her knees and tears welled in her eyes. I hadn't realized that I'd poised my spear at her face, my knees bent in a trained fighting stance. I might not have all of my memories, but my Valkyries instincts were still there.

"Please don't kill me," she begged.

Jules trembled as frail blooms continually budded in her hair, only to wither and fall to the ground at my feet. I found my spear lowering. This was all wrong.

"Tell me what's going on," I demanded. Heat swirled at my ankles and I knew that my power was threatening to take over. There was an ancient mercilessness inside of me that demanded justice. I couldn't deny the suffering before me. Stilling my hand against delivering justice sent crushing pain through my temples. "I'm going to need an explanation," I warned as I grit my teeth together.

"All the Huldra's lives are in danger," Jules squeaked. "If they don't find enough sacrifices, then Baldr is going to take twice of what he's asked for. Two Huldra for every human they've failed to find for him." Tears fell freely down her round cheeks. "I came here to offer myself, but I was too late."

Self-sacrifice was the pinnacle of honorable acts and was enough validation for me to dismantle the power of my spear. Heat flashed and ash trickled across my fingertips. "Baldr is here?" I asked, my voice pitched low as I quenched the flames within me.

She shook her head. "They said he doesn't come in person anymore." She glanced at the thorns behind her and winced at the carnage. "He's sending someone in three days to collect the tribute." Her gaze turned to me, full of pleading and desperate worry as lines marred her face. "They need one more human to fulfill the quota. What're we going to do?" She shook her head and tears flung from her cheeks. "Huldra are a kind and gentle race. Suffering gives us purpose because we *must* fix it... it's in our most basic instincts. We believe in life and beauty." She dug her fingernails into the dark soil that glittered with spent souls. "This is destroying the Huldra here. They'll lose their minds."

From the twisted whispers that echoed through these woods, I imagined that they already had.

"Show me this tribute," I demanded. The blue light was

gone, which meant that the Huldra had drained this soul dry. That kind of power solidified into crystals and would have to be stored someplace safe.

At first Jules hesitated, then she gave me a shaky nod. She glanced at the ash still trickling from my fingers. I didn't like that she was helping me just because she was afraid of what I might do. "Hey," I said and knelt to lower myself to eye-level. "I'm not going to let anything bad happen to the Huldra, okay? I'm going to help. You should have come to me first."

Her shoulders relaxed and she gave me a weak smile. "I know, but these are my sisters. They're not your problem."

I reached out to her to offer a comforting squeeze. She flinched and her reaction felt like a slap, but then she took my hand. Where I was flame and chaos, she was softness and nature. "I forget you're not like your sisters," she explained.

Those words stung, even though I knew that Jules meant it as a compliment. Any of my sisters would have slaughtered her on the spot. Justice demands death for death. I'd stilled my anger and rage, giving her a chance to explain herself. Those weren't Valkyrie instincts... but something that came from within my flawed heart. It turned out those instincts were right. Something far worse was going on here than met the eye.

The forest shifted and Jules allowed me through the brush, giving me one last glance of the victim before the branches curled over his body in a possessive embrace. I knew that nothing would be wasted. His body would feed nature, springing forth new life. But the death and suffering

I'd seen had not been peaceful. "Do you know who he was?" I asked, my voice shaking now that my Valkyrie justice and strength trickled away with the ash trailing across my skin.

"I didn't know who he was, but I knew what he was like," Jules said. "My sisters have some sanity left. They've only been taking the worst of the worst… rapists, muggers, even murderers." She looked back the way we'd come. "Didn't you sense the injustice in him?"

I widened my eyes. I'd indeed sensed a great injustice, but I'd thought that the act of his sacrifice. Now that I stopped and considered the full situation, it was entirely possible that the injustice I felt had been his crimes. All the more reason that a Valkyrie should weigh all possibilities in a situation. "I guess I did."

I followed Jules as she walked and motioned me to follow. Magic swept over us as we trailed down the path and passed through an invisible veil. It was not unlike the magic that had hidden Tyler's home. I didn't know what I expected in the center of the Huldra community, but the grandeur that revealed itself was beyond any imagining.

It wasn't quite a city, but rather an intertwining of tree limbs and gleaming branches that glowed with power. Two types of magic thrummed a new heartbeat in this place… emerald green for the nature that lived here… and a deep, vibrant blue that betrayed the souls that lingered here until Baldr would come to claim his tribute.

Huldra didn't have mortal bodies, not unless they needed to venture out into the human world under a moment of greatest need. They traveled through the trees, their effigies watching every step I took.

We ventured deeper into what I could only call a nest and Jules held tight to my fingers. Suffering and sickness lingered on the edges of the path, revealing that the Huldra were slowly losing themselves to their cruel acts of violence. Cracked leaves broke free of fractured limbs and dusted the forest floor. Healthy parts of the forest worked with emerald light, attempting rejuvenation. I followed the stems of power until we turned a corner and I sucked in a breath. I'd never seen Yggdrasil before, but I imagined if the Tree of Life had a heart, it would look something like the center of the New York Huldra nest. What had once been shards of glass swirled in a ball of light kept in place by hovering tree limbs. Glowing veins shot out and hummed with life across the center of power... the power that had been built of souls.

This kind of magic could be used for countless things. I knew what my mother would use it for. My memories tugged at me and escaped Grimhildr's programming, allowing me a glimpse at the center of the Einherjar where my sisters were born, their souls woven and their flesh knit together. Human spirits were Immortal on their own and that power could be transformed. Energy was neither created nor destroyed. A goddess like Freya knew how to give it life again, but the truth was, she was only molding what was already there.

It was so beautiful that for a moment, I was mesmerized and watched the streaking blue lights dance with the Huldra whispering through the trees. Then I remembered why this was here and clenched my fists. Baldr had made this happen and he was going to come to claim his prize.

If my mother would make new Valkyries with this kind of power, I shuddered to think of what Baldr might do with it. He was no god. He didn't know how to mold this power into new life. If he couldn't create… then there was only one other option; he would destroy.

Now that we closed in on the gathering of Yggdrasil sap that swirled with blue mesmerizing power, I noticed specks of dark holes. Huldra continued to reach in and settled their harvested power in the voids, and I realized that the ball was held together like a giant honeycomb. There were still a few voids left and they needed one more sacrifice to complete the orb.

"You said that Baldr was coming in three days?" I asked.

Her fingers squeezed around mine and this time I couldn't mistake the burst of power that traveled up my spine. Jules wasn't holding my hand because she was sentimental. I was in Huldra territory. Their whispers and curiosity swirled around us with warning. It was Jules who kept me bound here and fought off the waves of compulsion that I would be tossed out like an unwelcome guest. The Huldra's voices grew louder, but I couldn't understand them. It wasn't just Old Norse, but a dialect that only Huldra could understand. "Yes," Jules said, "Baldr will be sending someone." She looked at me, her eyes full of pleading. "You can't let my sisters sacrifice another. They're holding on by a thread. I'm afraid another sacrifice will make it impossible for them to come back from this."

By the sensation of cold bites on the back of my neck, I knew that some Huldra had already crossed a line into madness, but I couldn't let Jules know. It was hope that kept her in one piece and I wasn't going to be the one to break her.

The maddened Huldra tested me and filled my mind with words that spoke with impulse. They pushed me to let go of Jules. I could slip away with them deeper into their nest and be free of worry and fear. I could become one with nature and I'd never experience death again, for a forest lived its own version of eternal life.

I shivered and shrugged the compulsion off. "I'm afraid they're already too far gone," I told her and squeezed her hand a little bit tighter. There was no way I was going to let go.

There was also no way in Hel I was going to allow the Huldra to fill those empty honeycomb slots with another suffering life.

In fact, I knew what I had to do. I had to take my share of the power of Yggdrasil for myself. Guilt filled me at the prospect, but the sacrifices were already done. This power was here, and somebody was going to take it. That somebody might as well be me.

I tugged Jules towards the light. "You're going to have to make sure they don't attack us."

"Why?" Jules squeaked as she stumbled after me. "What're you going to do?" Her voice shook, because there was only one reason I'd be walking closer to the glowing orb.

I didn't answer her. I wasn't going to allow Baldr to gain strength and threaten this world, the place where Will was supposed to grow up, find a family, find happiness.

The idea of him finding a family without me made my heart pinch, but I knew that's what could make him happy.

A future was the one thing I couldn't give him and I wanted that for him more than anything. But first, I had to get him his mortal body back and eliminate any threat to his world. I wasn't too naive to realize that I was the largest threat of all, but I couldn't just stand by and do nothing. The second Will was safe, I'd do what I had to.

I paused when we were within arm's reach of the Yggdrasil orb. Its power thrummed with life in my ears and reminded me of memories of the Einherjar. My mother had taken me there on occasion. Her main throne room was on Muspelheim, but she also had chambers on the Einherjar where she welcomed her newest daughters. I liked to spend time there and I often was allowed to play with the other children. When I'd come of age, she'd separated me from the others, keeping me closer to her side when my empathy began to show my true, unnatural nature.

Grimhildr's programming overcame the thrum of magic around me and kicked in, preventing me from remembering anything after that. I wasn't sure how old I was when I'd met Tyler. The strongest layer of Grimhildr's programming prevented me from remembering both Tyler and Will with a wall so thick I couldn't even begin to contemplate how to break through to the other side. Freya had blocked those memories for a reason. If breaking the first law of the Valkyrie had been a mistake, then was I right in breaking the second one?

Second law of the Valkyrie... Don't question the gods.

I had to believe in myself. Questioning my mother meant shaking off the chains she forced on me. She didn't know what I was feeling. She didn't know what it was like to be separated from a core part of myself. If I listened to her, my worst fears could be realized, and the guilt would eat me alive that I'd done nothing to stop Baldr from unleashing death and destruction onto those I loved.

Raw determination spurred me to reach out to the swirling ball of power. Branches barred my way and embers sprinkled from my fingers, burning them until a high pitched screech sounded through the woods and the branches retracted.

I pushed through to touch the smooth surface and scaling heat grazed my fingertips, threatening to burn away my mortal flesh. I did something I hadn't thought possible in my current state; I transformed my arm from the elbow down to my true Valkyrie form. Perfect marble skin layered over with an impenetrable shield. I didn't need armor to protect me. A Valkyrie was a weapon of war and the embodiment of grace and merciless power.

"You can't do that!" Jules screeched, her voice turning frantic.

Angry whispers echoed through the leaves, approaching us like a tidal wave that would come crashing down right on top of us.

Jules searched the leaves, her eyes wide with fear. "They don't understand," she said, interpreting the mangled Old Norse for me. I didn't need her translation. Snarls and flashes of teeth amidst the leaves told me what the Huldra thought of my blasphemy.

"Just keep them away long enough," I demanded, then closed my eyes to focus on the raw life that spilled into me. I dug my fingers into the molten layer of blue and realized why it held such a vibrant color. Where I was the red burning flames of Muspelheim, the sap of Yggdrasil was the core of that flame, a burning heat so hot that it was blue, the base of any flame and the source of its power.

My Valkyrie skin layered over with blisters at the heat that rivaled my own, but I set my jaw and kept my free hand latched onto Jules as the ground shook in warning.

The forest exploded with enraged cries and snapping of ancient oaks. I thought that the Huldra didn't have a physical form outside of special circumstances, but I'd been wrong. They could take a physical form any time they wanted and creatures of nightmares burst from the woods. Living embodiments of leaves and twigs bundled together to make horrifying beings that clawed their way towards me.

"I can't!" Jules protested and yanked on my arm. "Don't do this! They'll kill us both!"

Jules' fear confirmed that the Huldra were too far gone to be saved. To kill me was one thing. I was a Valkyrie and an intruder. But to take Jules down with me crossed a line. She was their innocent sister who'd only tried to help them. It set my rage into overdrive.

"No," I growled and my voice grated with fiery power. "We're not going to help Baldr gain a foothold. I don't care if your sisters are too insane to see that I'm trying to help. I'm going to take this power and we're going to use it against him."

Jules didn't seem entirely convinced, and I had to admit it was rightfully so. While I claimed I was taking this power to save the world, I had a selfish agenda to restore my memories. I argued with myself because how could I fight an enemy I couldn't remember? I needed to overcome Grimhildr's programming at all costs.

The first Huldra slammed into us and my knees buckled at the impact. With one hand still plunged into the super-natural honeycomb like a kid stuck in a cookie jar, I took the brunt of the blow with my shoulder. A flash of spark splintered against bone and made my teeth rattle. I'd enforced my body with my Valkyrie power, but I couldn't fully transform. Not until I had enough memories and all my years of controlled training came back to me.

The Huldra that had attacked wrapped thorned fingers around mine and tried to pry me away from Jules. The way she carelessly tore at my skin, making us both cry in pain, told me that this wasn't about helping her sister. Jules was the only force anchoring me to the Huldra's nest and the creature that speared sharp points into my skin knew it.

I needed more time to absorb Yggdrasil's sap, but I wasn't going to get it. Two more Huldra twisted to life in the shadows and staggered towards us, gaining momentum as their legs hardened with power drawn up from the soil.

Cursing, I yanked my hand free of the honeycomb and used it to block a serrated arm that would have taken off my head with a crude blow. I flashed with rage and my own spear materialized. I lashed out, but I couldn't fight trees with a spear. Every branch I chopped off regrew another.

I needed flames.

"Close your eyes!" I commanded, and to my relief, Jules obeyed. Her free hand shot up and guarded her face just as I unleashed the eternal embers inside of me with a scream.

Memories flooded back as I touched that blue-hot flame within me. Each one seared my mind like a blade. I'd only known loneliness and frustration all my life—until I'd met Tyler. I was over a hundred years old, but the memories that slammed into me felt as if they came from someone else. Someone sad, pathetic, and weak.

I could have fought Freya, but I'd accepted my punishment with the selfish desire to see Will again, and the stubborn vigilance that I could regain my memories on my own. What a fool I'd been. I'd almost taken Will's life because I didn't know who I was. I should have fought back and claimed my right as an Immortal with my own rules and my own mind.

Screw the last of the Valkyrie. They didn't apply to me.

Something snapped in me at that fierce realization. I'd claimed to stand against Freya, but I'd never meant it with the ferocity that I held now.

A deep roar sounded from my throat, but it wasn't from me. The beast to which I was connected echoed through time and space to announce its presence. I allowed it its moment of triumph. It sensed my rebellion to the gods and to anything or anyone who would stand in my way, but it believed that was its opportunity to use me. I would let it think me weak and malleable. I would use this power for myself and free the bonds that suppressed my sisters. No longer would Immortals like Odin push poor souls like Will into service, forcing them to fight for their very lives or else be used as a power source to create the Valkyries. This wasn't the way things were meant to be. This was an injustice that needed to be righted. Valkyries were made for that purpose, but the deep irony that they were borne out of such injustice made a humorless chuckle rumble in my throat.

The Huldra stilled at the sound, recognizing me as a greater threat than I'd been a moment before. I was glad they couldn't see I was close to losing consciousness. Black dots sprinkled over my vision as memories continued to pummel into me as if I'd open the gates to my mind and I was drowning under the ocean of my past.

The otherworldly beast sent tingles up and down my arms, wanting to control me like a puppet while I was distracted. I allowed its efforts to keep me upright. My necklace burned with warning, a scalding ember barely able to keep the shadow away. I shamelessly used my mother's power to keep a monster from controlling my body and mind.

I should have been terrified, but an immovable confidence wound through me that said my mind would stay my own, just as it always had through everything I'd been through. I had too much love there for a shadow to understand. It couldn't touch those parts of my mind which were the same parts my mother feared. She shouldn't be afraid of the power of love. It's what kept me safe in the face of the destruction of the universe… in the face of Ragnarök.

Even though embers burned my heart, my fingers frosted over with ice and Jules finally found the strength to detach herself from me. She was my only foothold in the Huldra's nest. An invisible force knocked the wind out of my chest and the trees blurred as I catapulted backwards. I soon lost sight of Jules and the watching Huldra that glowed with an array of green. The blue light followed me out.

The glow, I realized, emanated from my chest and was a reminder of the power I held within myself now. I hadn't taken everything, but I'd taken enough from the collection of Yggdrasil sap to unlock my memories.

I let darkness close around me as I was tossed out onto

the street. When I fluttered my eyes closed, a touch grazed my shoulder. I didn't have to look up to know that both Tyler and Will were here for me. They'd sensed my break.

One of them picked me up, and I didn't care who it was.

I knew I was safe.

RAGNARÖK'S TOUCH

When I woke up in my own bed, a headache thundered through my skull with such ferocity that I squeezed my eyes shut again. I gripped fingers through my hair and found the strength to squint one eye open, only to find Will curled up in a chair. I knew that someone would have watched over me during the night, but a part of me hoped I would awake to Tyler. He'd been with me for a hundred years and perhaps knew what to make of the mess I'd found myself in. Now that the intoxicating power had eroded into reality, I knew I'd made a mistake.

Asleep, Will was unable to maintain his mortal form. Soft ivory leather covered his body and for the first time, I noticed the silver roots that swept across his neck in the most vibrant tattoo I'd ever seen. That certainly hadn't been there before. It reminded me of the branches of the World Tree from a memory so deeply rooted in my mind, I wasn't sure if I could retrieve it even having broken Grimhildr's bonds.

I wanted to reach out and touch his skin, but when I lifted my fingers, I drew in a deep breath. The black rune was visible now, a stark contrast to Will's icon of life and purity. My mark was of Ragnarök itself.

I lowered my fingers to the bed and pulled aside the sheets. I was still in my clothes from last night, the guys probably too prude to change them for me. I laughed, both at their chivalry and in relief that my mark hadn't spread to the rest of my body. My body was still my own… for now.

Unsure of what to do, I watched Will for a while. The slow rise and fall of his chest mesmerized me and I wondered how he could sleep so peacefully knowing that the threat of Ragnarök was just inches away. If I reached out, I could brush away the silver strands that fell over his eyes. Maybe he would wake up, but I was scared of how he was going to look at me. I wanted to peer into his innocent chestnut eyes, but he was losing that part of himself. In this form, I'd be met with the star-struck rainbow irises filled with crystal and Immortal power. I could almost imagine how he would look at me while intoxicated with his new life. William the mortal might view me as a victim or someone deserving of being saved. But William the Valiant? I only imagined disgust, fear… rejection.

The door creaked open, ending my debate to wake him, and his eyes flew open at the sound. He didn't fulfill my fears. He didn't even look at me. His gaze flew past me and zeroed in on the sound, every muscle in his body suddenly tense as veins stood out along his arms.

Tyler stepped inside, looking as if he hadn't slept all night. His hair spiked on the ends and he gave Will a raised brow. "Calm down, lover boy. I sensed she was awake." He glanced at me, his face completely unreadable as usual. For once, I was glad of it. If he hated what I was becoming, I didn't have to see the judgment in his eyes. I kept my gaze on him, using him as a shield against the inevitable heartbreak I'd see in Will.

"And where have you been?" Will asked, his voice surprising me with its sharp anger.

Tyler narrowed his eyes. "Scouring the area for enemies." He pointed at my hand. "The Mark of Ragnarök doesn't show itself to the naked eye unless she was under dire threat. I don't know what or who attacked her, but I intend to find out." He frowned. "Not to mention, Jules is missing." The full force of his gaze fell on me. "Now that you're awake, perhaps you could tell us what happened?"

My fingers trembled and I clutched onto the sheets. Unexpected tears welled up in my eyes and I felt so pathetic. I'd been so strong the day before, but now that I was facing my protectors, they looked at me as if I were a victim. How could I tell them that I'd brought all of this on myself?

It was Will's touch that brought me down from my rising panic. "Shh," he said and his thumb stroked over my knuckles.

I finally found the courage to look at him. My chest tightened as I prepared myself for the brunt blow of his rejection. Instead, I found the ferocity of his protectiveness as his touch ran up my arm and squeezed. "Who did this to you?" he asked, his words encouraging.

I bit my lip, because I knew when he learned the truth, he wouldn't want to protect me anymore. Yet, hiding in lies wasn't the answer to this. "I found out who was taking the victims," I said, my voice hoarse and scratchy from sleep.

"Dalia's Huldra have been under siege by Baldr's forces. He's been making them sacrifice humans and gather their souls to create Yggdrasil sap." I shivered. "All of it was in one place like a giant honeycomb. I…" my words halted and I forced myself to finish telling him the truth, "I pulled some of it into myself. I needed to become stronger. I…" My voice broke, because Will's face had already begun to change. Horror streaked across his Immortal eyes.

"You… fed on souls?" His voice lowered with a dangerous edge as he pulled away, leaving me feeling alone and cold.

Tyler growled. "I can't believe the Huldra are the culprits. That doesn't make any sense."

"*That's* what you're focusing on?" Will asked incredulously. "Did you not hear what she just said?" He glanced at me as he leaned back. "That's… how my mother became…"

My heart twisted at Will's judgment. I wanted to say I was nothing like his mother, but Tyler defended me before I could. "I heard her just fine. You're overreacting."

Will scoffed and shot to his feet. He pointed at my hand in accusation. "So you're not concerned at all about *that?* It didn't materialize because she was in danger. It's there to warn us that she's about to fall off the edge. You're really going to tell me you're not worried?"

Tyler crossed his arms. "Nope."

Will shook his head with disbelief. "I need some air," he snapped, refusing to look at me as he slammed into Tyler's shoulder on his way out.

Tyler righted himself as the door closed behind Will. He seemed unimpressed by Will's freakout.

I'd fully expected Will's reaction and my heart burned at

his rejection, but Tyler's calm demeanor completely baffled me. "Why aren't you upset?" I asked. My voice was scratchy from sleep, but my throat tightened further with tears that threatened to overflow onto my cheeks. I'd been seduced by the power in the Huldra's nest and now that I was free of it, I felt like I'd made the wrong choice.

Tyler released a long breath and settled onto the edge of the bed. He glanced at my hand. The black rune stretched across my knuckles and before I could hide it under the sheets, he reached out and laced his fingers with mine. "Because I've waited for this day for a long time," he admitted.

My eyes went wide. Memories churned of what Tyler had been like from the beginning. The only reason he'd been on Muspelheim was to keep me from being seduced by the echoes of Ragnarök. It was his light that could keep the shadows at bay. He was a Valiant, and one of the most ancient and powerful of Odin's forces. Having been a member of the House of Heimdall before his conversion, he knew the darkness better than anyone. Heimdall had gained her gifts from peering into secrets that weren't meant to be uncovered. Her Sight was a gift of Ragnarök itself.

His eyes glittered as he recognized the way I looked at him—like someone who truly knew him. "You're getting your memories back," he observed. When I gave him a slight nod of confirmation, he retreated his touch, leaving me alone with the hunger that clawed inside of me.

Now I understood why Freya had tolerated any feelings I might have harbored for Tyler.

He was the only one who could save me from myself.

yler and I talked for the better part of an hour as he helped me to pluck new memories free from Grimhildr's fragmented programming. My mind couldn't handle regaining all my memories at once, so it compartmentalized them like a sea of locked boxes. Each one that I opened dosed me with a part of myself I'd lost.

Today, I opened boxes about Tyler, how he'd helped me, and how we'd become close over the years.

Valkyries aged much slower than humans. Our minds and bodies prepared ourselves for an Immortal life with the graceful aging Freya instilled into us. I'd feared what it would be like to regain a hundred years as a Valkyrie, if it would change me, but in so many ways I felt exactly the same… just more… complete.

As a hundred-year-old Valkyrie, my mental state wasn't that far off from a sixteen-year-old human girl. I was still finding myself and learning what I wanted in life. That decision weighed heavy during the long years as an Immortal. Without the looming promise of death, it felt like anything I chose would be painfully permanent.

After Tyler had fallen into silence, my brain buzzing with the boxes I'd already opened, I wanted to focus on the present. The past hummed at me and I wasn't sure I was ready to process all of it yet.

"Why hasn't Will come back yet?" I glanced at the door. After learning what kind of connection Tyler and I had, I longed to know what it was that drew me to Will.

He shrugged. "According to you, Will's always been a hothead."

I blinked at him. "I talked to you about him?" I asked. "I mean… before?"

He nodded. "I was there when you went through your training and when you decided to reap Will."

My spine went taut as I straightened. "You mean, when Freya decided?"

"No," he said, the single word making my blood run cold. "That was your decision. You wanted to prove your mother wrong. You thought you were capable of becoming a true Valkyrie."

I was never more glad to be wrong.

"Will cares about you more than he'll admit," Tyler continued. "He doesn't want to see you falling for the same dark magic that took his mother." His gaze fell to the mark on my hand. "It's powerful. I can understand why some would want to use it."

There were some boxes in my mind that lingered with the icy shadows of the House of Heimdall. Tyler wasn't afraid of me because he knew that power for himself. Even if I couldn't see it, the same mark that was on my hand wound over his entire body, only kept in check by his power as a Valiant. I wanted to ask how he'd gotten them… but didn't dare risk unlocking those memories.

"When I was in the Huldra's nest," I said, my memories going back to the night before, "I felt like I knew everything." Tyler leaned back as he listened to me. I felt like I could unleash any truth on him and it would still be okay. "I felt like I knew exactly what to do and that everyone else had been wrong." I reached out to Tyler just as I had for so many years. He'd been a source of strength when the darkness had taken me and it was his light and understanding that had called me back. "We have to tell Dalia what's going on," I said. Her name was the only word that made him stiffen. "She needs to know that she's breeding trouble by collecting Huldra," I pressed. "It's not protecting her territory at all. She's inadvertently helping Baldr get stronger."

I pulled at him, but he didn't budge. "I know," he said flatly.

I stared at him. "What do you mean... *you know?*"

He swallowed. "Why do you think I brought you here?"

A chill ran down my spine as I put it all together. "You wanted me to regain my memories," I said, biting the words off with accusation. I wanted to be truthful with Tyler, but he'd been lying to me this whole time. I yanked away and he flinched. "Even though you knew I'd fall deeper into the echoes of Ragnarök, you brought me here anyway." Anger stirred in my chest where hopelessness and fear had once been. A part of me felt better at having someone to blame, even if it was Tyler. "How selfish can you be? You'd risk Ragnarök just so I'd remember you?"

Pain cracked across his face with jagged lines and he reined in his emotions as fast as they'd appeared. "It's no less selfish than what you did."

I didn't have to ask what he meant. The only reason I was here instead of being with him on Muspelheim was because I'd fallen in love with Will and abandoned Tyler and my Immortal life. I'd known that it would bring me closer to unleashing Ragnarök by pursuing a human... but I hadn't cared.

I snarled. "Ever heard the phrase 'Two wrongs don't make a right?'"

Tyler glowered and then stood. "Do what you want," he

said, his words turning cold. He might as well have been a wall of steel for all the compassion he showed. "Now that you know who you are, you can't keep running away from me. I'll be here when it all goes to shit and it'll be me who puts you back together again, just like I always do."

He left me alone and I wanted to scream. I yanked off the sheets and crawled out of bed. Heat burned my tongue and I knew there was only one way I was going to quench this rage.

I marched straight for Dalia's restaurant and didn't care that I left gleaming embers in my wake.

DON'T TRUST A HEIMDALL

One look at me and the restaurant's security crossed their arms like immovable sentinels that guarded the front doors of Dalia's fancy-schmancy restaurant. When I lifted my hand and showed my rune, one guard pressed a device on his ear and muttered something in Old Norse. I waited for the marbled response.

"She says to go through the back route," he replied, shrugging when I glared at him. "We can't let the guests see you like this. Bad for business."

I had blood and dirt caked all over me. It wasn't like I had time to stop for a shower when the end of the world was on the line.

Growling, I brushed past him and rounded the building, finding a blotchy red door on the other side.

I tested the knob and found the door unlocked. I jerked it up and yelped when I found Dalia staring right back at me, which was a startling image indeed with her golden grin and eerie blue-streaked irises. Now that I knew what the color blue meant... I was afraid of where she'd gotten her power.

"What a nice surprise," Dalia said and ushered me inside. "Please, come in."

Holding my chest, I stepped inside and the door closed behind me with a thud that reverberated through my body. I glanced at it, not wishing to test it to see if the dusty back of a restaurant was still what I'd find on the other side. Magic hummed, telling me that Dalia had already moved us to someplace new.

"What brings you here?" she asked as she settled behind her desk and picked up the new scope she'd been working on. Brass melted under her fingers and smoothed over the rim, molding into place and Dalia examined her work, then glanced at my haggard appearance. "Hope my son didn't do that."

I cleared my throat. "No, it wasn't Tyler."

She rolled her eyes. "I do hate his human name. Tyler. It sounds so forced. Tyr just rolls off the tongue."

I made a fist. My memories told me that Dalia liked to go off topic, not because she was stupid, but because her inner mind was seeing everything in her domain right now, every second of every day. She was as close to mad as an Immortal could get. It was her innate fear of the darkness that chased her that kept her in control. Ironically, it was the mark on my hand that made her respect me.

"What if I told you it was your Huldra that did this to me?" I asked.

Dalia put down her scope. "What? My Huldra wouldn't attack you. Not unless you went into their nest." My lips flattened into a thin line and Dalia's eyes widened. She shot to her feet and the blue streaks of her irises went wild. "What were you doing?"

I slammed my hand onto the desk and she stared at the black mark that wound over my knuckles. "Did you know that they were working for Baldr? They're the ones who've been kidnapping humans and sacrificing them, sucking them dry like some kind of damn parasites."

She leaned back in her chair, not looking as upset as I expected, but she certainly was surprised. She steepled her fingers as she slowly rocked back and forth. "I should have known that Baldr would get to them. The poor dears."

I growled and dug my nails into the wood, sending embers flying as my rage got the better of me. "You need to get them under control. Baldr's sending someone in two days and they're going to expect a full orb of Yggdrasil." I leaned and the wood protested under my weight, sending a crack through the frame. I knew I was unleashing the stolen power that wound inside of me, but I didn't care, not now when Dalia was looking at me like she had nothing to do with any of this. "Don't you even care?"

She stood and faced me, not a single line of fear in her face. "I've gathered the Huldra for years to protect these woods. What kind of humans have they been taking, hmm?"

I balked. Jules had told me that the Huldra had only taken criminals, but... "It doesn't matter," I shot back. "They're going mad. If you let them kill even one more person, deservedly or not, you're going to break them."

Dalia shook her head. "I knew what I was doing when I cultivated the strongest Huldra for my territory. They're easily manipulated, but they will not stray from their core values. Even now, when Baldr tries to get them to work against me, they only take scum off the streets. No harm, no foul."

"And the magic they're giving to Baldr?" I shot back. "What about that? You don't care that he's getting stronger?"

She laughed. "It doesn't matter how strong Baldr gets. He's already won. I'm just trying to make sure that I survive whatever games he's playing."

I gaped at her. "What? This doesn't sound like the Heimdall I remember." The House of Heimdall was known for its infinite power and recklessness. No one messed with Dalia or her people. No one.

She grinned and a pink tongue flashed behind her teeth. "Oh, have we met before? I'm not the only one keeping secrets around here, are we?"

I growled. Tyler had warned me not to let Dalia know who I was, and now I knew why. He'd become a Valiant because that had been the only way to save me. It took Odin's light to calm the shadows that threatened to eat me alive. My mother's flames weren't enough to subdue it and I hadn't been raised with my father. It took a Valiant who understood what I faced to bring me back from the edge. I swallowed, because if Dalia knew that I had been the one to take her son from her, she'd have my head.

"Just the stories I remember." I motioned to her array of scopes and weapons. "From what I heard, you never gave up like that."

Her shoulders relaxed, seeming satisfied with my explanation. "Well, after I faced the darkness, I lost my son, and this small reprieve where he's returned to me hasn't been the reunion I'd hoped for." She let out a long sigh and rounded the desk. "No, child, I'm not giving up. I just know when I'm beat." She grinned again. "I'm old and tired. I'm certainly not the Heimdall you 'remember.'"

I frowned and looked at the array of trinkets again. She holed herself up here like it was some kind of prison. "Why don't you shut down the Bifrost?" I asked. "If it didn't exist, then Baldr would be trapped in Asgard and you wouldn't have to worry about him anymore."

Her eyes went wide with warning. "One does not just 'shut down' the Bifrost, child. The only time I will ever leave my sacred duty is when Ragnarök threatens at our door. Even then, it will try to rip the Bifrost open." She straightened. "I've prepared centuries for that day. It will try to break me, but I'll be ready."

While I appreciated her resolve to fight against the end of the world, it didn't change the fact that Baldr was coming after the Huldra and there was still plenty of Yggdrasil sap left over. "We can't let Baldr get his hands on any more power," I insisted. "If you shut down the Bifrost now, then your sacred duty will have already been completed, yes?"

She shook her head. "No, the Bifrost can never be closed, not permanently. Even if I drain it of power, its connection between all points of space and time can never be undone. It is a fundamental link that cannot be broken, only utilized."

I tilted my head. It sounded like how Immortals made new life. They didn't create new souls, but remeshed what was already there. The Bifrost was a link that already existed, but Dalia had figured out how to make it a doorway and keep its control for herself. If what she was saying was true, then without a guardian, a force as powerful as Ragnarök would use it in horrifying ways.

"Okay," I sighed. "Fine. You don't close the Bifrost. What

then? We just let Baldr get away with this? We let your Huldra claim another life and lose what's left of their sanity?"

She bit her lip, then waved her hand. The walls shook and a faint, golden light streamed in through the creases in the walls I hadn't even known were there.

My eyes went wide and I whirled on the door. The ground shook and light spilled around its perimeter. "What'd you do?" I shouted over the growing hum of power. "Where'd you take us?"

"I'm sorry," Dalia said, her words a whisper that I almost missed in the roar of noise. She curled her fingers into a fist and power swept through the room, sending the door crashing open.

A city of gold streamed its brilliance into the room and Dalia pushed me out. My knees slammed to marbled streets and I cried, turning with Valkyrie speed only to find the door closed.

When I turned back to face a crowded audience of over-dressed Immortals, I knew where Dalia had sent me and my blood drained from my face as a cold chill settled into my stomach.

Asgard.

The crowd parted and a man towered over me. The way the people shrank from him wasn't out of fear, but respect. He offered me a hand and his face lit with a charming smile. Across his knuckles scrawled the same black mark that afflicted me.

I swallowed the lump in my throat and took his hand. He pulled me to my feet and I tried not to look as petrified as I felt.

This was Baldr.

He wasn't what I expected. Everything in my memories told me that name held with it horror and merciless rage. Yet, the man at my side who waved the crowds away with a smile didn't look frightening at all. In fact, he was quite beautiful. He took my hand with such familiarity that I found myself rummaging through those boxes in my brain, searching for any memory that I could possibly have of him. Surely we'd met before.

"So, you finally took a mortal form," Baldr observed with

an approving nod. "It's a good choice, if I have to say so myself, Sister."

... Sister?

I barely had a chance to digest that as a city of golden spires and brilliant lights glittered around us. Baldr took me across a glass path that spiraled with rainbow lights. It led straight to the largest set of spires that collected together to form what could only be called a castle. I staggered when the ground beneath us molded and moved, bringing us closer to the entrance with increasing speed.

He laughed as I bent my knees in a battle stance. "Mother warned me you wouldn't be yourself. It's all right. It's just a moving highway."

I looked over the edge of the "highway" and found a cascade of waterfalls and sea creatures with glimmering horns cresting the surface. My stomach pitched and I scrambled back, finding myself in his arms. "I don't understand," I blurted. None of this made any sense.

He shushed me. "Don't worry. I know it's overwhelming, but I'll explain everything."

Once past a line of fierce warriors that reflected the city's grace in their impenetrable armor, I felt crushed by the unnatural silence of the castle. There was no carpet to absorb the sounds and I realized why it all felt so eerie. No foliage or plant in the place. Just metal and gold and light.

Our footsteps echoed as Baldr handed me off to a girl with fire in her eyes and a brilliant red cape that hid the supernatural appendages at her back.

A Valkyrie.

He walked ahead of us and waved his hands, sending the

walls morphing and revealing a room that hadn't been there a moment before.

I clutched at the Valkyrie that guided me. "What's he done to you?" I hissed. "Are you his prisoner?"

The Valkyrie gave me an obnoxious laugh that echoed through the new chamber. "What? No. I've served your brother for years." She pulled me onto a puffy cushion that sat at the edge of a table filled with delicacies fit for a Roman feast.

Baldr sat across from me and plucked a grape from the closest platter, grinning at me before popping it into his mouth. "You look hungry. Why don't you eat?"

My gaze swept over the collection and my stomach growled. There was no sense in fighting my enemy on an empty stomach. I took one of the finger sandwiches and placed it on my tongue. I tried not to show my enjoyment as the delight nearly melted.

"She thinks I'm your prisoner," the Valkyrie said, leaning over the table as if it were all some big joke. "Isn't that adorable?"

Baldr smiled, the motion making him unabashedly attractive. "My sister has always been known for her antics." He winked at me. "Why don't you tell me what you did to piss off Dalia enough for her to send you here, without your memories, no less." He tilted his head and grinned. "I hope it didn't have anything to do with me."

I swallowed the stolen morsel and knew as the cold chill ran up my spine that Baldr was every bit the horror I knew him to be. This was what he was good at. He knew how to appear to be charming and alluring, but in his heart, he was as dark as they come.

I leaned onto the table, ignoring the fact that my legs had gone numb. "Dalia's been working for you all this time."

He threw his head back and laughed. The Valkyrie at my side glittered with her clear adoration of him, but I didn't miss the streaks of shadow that ran like sickened veins across her neck. The glimpse disappeared as if I'd imagined it, replaced with the marble skin of an Immortal, but I knew what I'd seen. This Valkyrie was certainly Baldr's prisoner, both in body and in mind.

"Dalia's a smart girl. She knew what you were going to try and do." He took another grape and examined it. "So after you'd activated your rune, she sent you to me, just like we agreed."

Fury wound through me. I'd been set up twice now. It seemed like everyone had an agenda to get me on the knife's edge that risked Ragnarök. Tyler wanted me to regain my memories so that we could rekindle some estranged love story. Baldr... I wasn't sure what he wanted from me, but it wasn't anything good. The only person who was innocent in all of this was Will and I regretted disappointing him. If I made it out of this... When I made it out of this, I would tell him he was right all along. I'd messed up, big time.

I shot to my feet, sending the low table rattling. "You're going to send me back," I demanded. "I'm not like your Valkyrie pet. You can't control me."

The woman at his side gasped in horror, but Baldr seemed amused. "You're right," he said, righting a plate that had overturned. "I can't control you. Do you know why that is?"

I narrowed my eyes. "Because I know who you really are?" My memories hadn't kicked in, but a deep knowing filled every fibre of my body. Baldr was my brother... but he wasn't Odin's son. There wasn't any light in him at all to fight Ragnarök's power. He accepted it willingly. Behind the confidence and handsome poise hinted a deep-seated madness that consumed him from the inside.

Baldr waved me away like an unruly child. "Perhaps you know who I am, for we are siblings, after all, memories or no." He leaned one elbow on the table and entertained an expression that was supposed to look sincere, but came off horribly sarcastic. "No, sweet sister, the reason I cannot control you is because you already have a master." He reached across the table with such lightning speed that I didn't see him coming. He held my hand up and pressed a light kiss to the mark that stretched shadows across my skin. "And now that you've accepted him, there's only one step left to trigger Ragnarök."

My skin crawled. His words felt like an omen. I'd already broken the first two laws of the Valkyrie. There was only one more and I couldn't believe that I'd ever entertained it.

Third Law of the Valkyrie... Don't Trigger Ragnarök.

Baldr dismissed his Valkyrie pet and took me into a room filled with glowing panels. On Earth, it would have looked like a futuristic 360-theatre. Here, it was Baldr's personal spy chamber.

He showed me the Huldra's nest with the Yggdrasil orb being drained by a shifting shadow. Broken bodies littered around her that had once been Huldra. She'd taken her fair share of lives to account for the missing slots in the honeycomb. Each sliver of blue liquid glass that seeped into the creature layered over flesh and bone until I recognized Will's mother.

"Leanne," I breathed and looked up at Baldr as my eyes widened. "You've been the one behind everything."

He tilted his head to the side. "I suppose so." He glanced at me, a smirk tugging at his lips. "But you chose the boy, dear sister. You wound the magic that sent his mother mad with hunger for eternal life, so much so that she was willing to sacrifice her son over and over again." He crossed his arms and whistled. "I have to admit, even I'm not so cruel. And then you dared to play with your toy. Such audacity even I must admire."

Ash ran down the back of my shirt as wings threatened to burst through. "Don't feed me lies," I warned. "I'll go all Valkyrie on your ass and I won't be sorry."

He laughed, which only served to stoke the flames in my chest. "I would never dare lie to you." He waved his hand and the screen flashed, revealing two Valiant warriors crouching in the brush.

Will and Tyler.

"You better not—" I began, rounding on Baldr with my fists.

"Shh," he said. "Just watch. You'll enjoy this."

I held my breath as they crept up on Leanne. This was the only moment they'd have a chance against her while she was distracted with draining the Huldra's bounty.

There were two things working against the two men who held my heart. This was Will's mother and every second that passed she regained more of her mortal appearance. Would Will truly be able to strike her down when she had her human face?

Then there was Tyler... I would have thought him Will's saving grace, if it hadn't been the look of raw pain that streaked across his features. The screen turned and zoomed in on what had grabbed his attention and a cry escaped my throat. Jules' body, broken and bleeding, lay still on the forest floor.

"This is highly entertaining," Baldr whispered behind his hand as if we could be heard. "I put my money on the Norn. What do you think?"

Rage blasted through me with such raw strength that something deeper than shadows and flame touched my soul. I'd felt it once before when I'd been willing to give up everything that I was.

Eternal love that could consume me with undying flames.

I screamed and reached through the screen, sending blue fire across time and space to ignite the brush at Leanne's feet.

She stopped feeding on Yggdrasil's sap and screeched as her raw, pink flesh melted under the heat of my rage.

Will whirled and faced me as his chestnut eyes cleared with realization. Although I knew he couldn't see me, he looked straight at me. "Val?" he cried. "Are you all right? Val? If you can hear me, I'm coming for you, okay? Don't give in to the shadow!"

"Stop yelling, you fool!" Tyler shouted and drew his sword. He approached the screeching Norn that was already melting back into a shadow. She retaliated with wisps that lashed out and left scars across the ground. Tyler dodged and growled. "We have a Norn to kill!"

I watched in horror as Will let go of the mortal part of himself and his eyes glazed over with duty. Sunlight streamed through the broken forest as he drew his sword and called on Odin's power. Thunder cracked in the distance as they unceremoniously sliced at the creature. She fought back, whips streaking harsh lines across Will's flawless armor.

I wanted to tell Will he didn't have to do this, that it would crush him if he killed his own mother, but that thing wasn't his mother anymore. Baldr said that I'd been the one to make her this way. Guilt rooted me to the spot as I watched the two Valiant warriors work to dispatch the Norn, for that's all she was now. She spat and growled at them, what was left of her face flashing with rage.

"You're my son!" she yelled and clawed out at him. "You *will* obey me!"

Her voice shook Will's hold on Immortality and red blood streaked across his chest at her blow. He staggered and I waited for Tyler to swoop in with the killing strike, but he sheathed his sword and took a step back. "This is your battle," he said.

Will drew in a deep breath and nodded before his armor gleamed again. "My mother died with me," he said, holding his sword high and a metallic hum sang through the broken woods. "You have stolen her face, and you will pay for that crime."

Leanne screamed as Will's sword mercilessly sliced into her chest, splitting her ribcage open. She didn't have blood anymore, but a thick, black liquid oozed out of her and steamed onto the ground.

Will turned the blade, dismantling the creature further. "With this kill, I become a member of Odin's army. I have banished the darkness and embraced the light."

Leanne withered and melted until nothing was left at all. Will's sword hung limply from his hand. I wished that he would cry or tremble, but he simply stared at the empty place where she'd been.

Tyler rested a hand on his shoulder. "Well done, Brother. It's time we go home."

Will broke his gaze from the kill and stared at Tyler. An array of emotions passed over his face.

I turned to Baldr as the scene continued to unfold. "Can they see us?"

He smiled. "No, Sister." His smile turned to a frown. "Although, with the way you were able to cause flames, I'd say your Frigg powers of bending space and time are coming back to you." He pointed. "They're leaving. Watch this."

I didn't like the giddy tone of his voice. Tyler and Will followed the path that would lead them out of the woods, but I recognized that shimmer that threatened at their feet.

The Bifrost.

"No!" I screamed and reached for them, but it was too late. Will and Tyler disappeared through the veil and by the look on Baldr's face, I wasn't going to like where he'd taken them.

"Where are they?" I demanded.

Baldr laughed and whirled, pointing at the screen behind us. "Look. They'll come out on the other side."

With my breath caught in my throat, I watched as the screen came to life with flames and screams. A battle raged and I immediately recognized the scene.

Muspelheim.

Without my help, Freya had failed to keep the volcanic planet out of Baldr's grasp. An army of shadows descended on my people. Valkyries fell by the hundreds and blood soaked the ground. They were unable to fight against a creature they couldn't see. These weren't regular Skuld. Somehow, they were stronger and dark fingers stretched the blazing sky.

Memories burst out of boxes in my brain and I winced as I gripped onto my head. This was one of the last prophecies of how the world ended.

Tyler and Will appeared in a blast of ice and shadows. I knew now why Baldr had wanted such a bounty of Yggdrasil's sap. This was all about getting to me. He needed enough power to transport two Valiant warriors across time and space with the link offered by the Bifrost. They'd never go willingly, not when they found out I was missing. This was how Baldr was going to get to me... and it was working.

Rage tinted my vision red. They were Valiant, but they were no match for the army that crashed onto the molten sands. Tyler's black runes became visible as he delved into powers he shouldn't have. Screeching shadows dove down from the skies and slammed into the pair. Tyler blocked the onslaught with a shield of black ice.

"Oh," Baldr mused, "looks as though Tyr has a few tricks up his sleeve. Kept a grip on his Heimdall Curse, I see."

I growled and wrapped my fingers around Baldr's throat, hating how he smiled at me as if he'd already won. "Why are you doing this?" I demanded. "Did I do something to you? I don't even remember meeting you."

He wrapped his fingers around my wrist and squeezed. I'd underestimated his strength and cried out at the power of his grip as he pulled me away. "No, Sister. It's what you haven't done for me that makes me enjoy the look on your face." For a brief moment, the sickening glee disappeared, replaced with anguish. "You're not the only one who's loved. You took her from me, and now you're going to get her back." He twirled me and held my hands behind my back, forcing me to watch Tyler and Will fight for their lives. "Or you're going to watch them die."

I didn't know what Baldr wanted or how I was supposed to help him get it, but in that moment all I knew was that Tyler and Will were about to die if I didn't do something. Tyler was a Valiant and using the shadow that lived inside of him brought him closer to a void he could never return from. I knew it, because it lived inside of me. Ice spread out on his feet, a near-impossible act on the volcanic planet and I rushed to the screen. I took a few short breaths before digging my fingers into it.

Like Dalia had melted her brass, time and space molded around my hands and an invisible force threatened to pull me through. I had to control where I wanted to go and right now, that was home.

Muspelheim was a place I'd spent the majority of my life. I'd found love and loss there, grown to learn who I was and what I was willing to sacrifice for what I believed in. Right now, there were two men who had my heart and I believed in them. I believed in the love that threatened to change me forever. I let it engulf me and the blissful agony of it strapped around my core, molding me from the inside.

My flesh threatened to melt away at the raw, frigid power that wrapped over my form.

"Don't let it devour you," Baldr instructed. "Let it in, but hold onto the ember that is your heart. The fires in your soul aren't the merciless flames of Muspelheim. It's the love our mother fears that drives you. Use it." Whatever he wanted, I needed to be alive for it, so I heeded his advice.

I latched onto the fierce love I held for both Tyler and Will. They had both suffered because of me and I wasn't going to let it end like this. I wasn't going to fail them so utterly and completely.

A scream erupted from my throat, my own voice mixed with the call of Ragnarök, a creature that devoured worlds. No matter its reputation, I wasn't going to let it devour me.

Time and space wrapped over me like a cocoon and my lungs constricted, unable to breathe. I focused on the core of my heat even as a blackness deeper than any cold I'd ever experienced threatened to freeze me solid.

Wings sprouted from my back and my skin glazed over with my Valkyrie form. I still couldn't shed my mortal skin, but that's because I knew if I did, I'd never get to see Will again. I had to do this without giving up that crucial part of me I'd discovered. Mortality was where I'd found my love for Will and the drive to defy the gods. I couldn't let it burn away and drift its ash through the cosmos.

Flames ignited and I tumbled out onto the molten planet of Muspelheim. Spear in one hand and the other steadying me against the ground, I sucked in a deep breath. A battle raged around me and ash stung my nose. The air wavered with heat and movement, and even though I should have been terrified, a smile erupted across my face.

I'd done it.

⚊

"Val!" Will cried, his words garbled from the icy layer that Tyler held around them like a shield.

Tyler's eyes went wide, snapping onto me with disbelief swarming over his face. "Aerie?"

I wanted to cry with relief. They were alive. I wasn't too late.

The creatures they fought off were coming back for another blow and they screeched battle cries through the roiling red clouds.

There was only one way to fight these things. My sisters had already fled, ran back to the Einherjar for a desperate escape. Fools. I couldn't believe they'd abandon their world.

The dead littered the ground and the dying made it seem like the cracked layers of soil moved. I crouched low, my stomach dropping when I realized that the ground actually was moving. It trembled as if the very core of the planet growled with rage.

I didn't have time to consider what that meant. A wave of black blotted out the brilliant red hues of Muspelheim's clouds and I tossed my spear into the sky, filling it with all my guilt and betrayal.

Freya had set me on this course. She'd had a son and never even told me. It felt like entire worlds revolved around me and now they were all about to be destroyed. Before the guilt crushed me, I sent the icy emotion into the sky and watched it crack open space and time, sucking in the threat of screeching creatures until only an unnatural silence remained.

The sky sucked in all light as if I'd opened a vortex. Panic rose in me. The crack I'd created was powered by all of my suffering and guilt. What if that was an endless source of power? What if my guilt had no end?

I rushed to Tyler and Will, Tyler dropping to his knees as the ice finally melted. "No, Aerie," he breathed, his eyelids fluttering before they closed and he collapsed.

I fell to the ground and coddled his head into my lap. "Tyler?" I cried.

Will gripped my arm. "He's just passed out," he assured me, then looked up at the vortex that seemed to grow, taking in it all sound and light. "What is that?"

I wanted to answer him, but I felt like I was being watched. I surveyed the grounds littered with broken bodies, only to sense Baldr's laugh echoing somewhere in the distance. I frowned when the vortex sucked it up.

The ground shook again, and this time I clutched onto Tyler to keep him off the scalding soil. He was so cold to my touch. I didn't know if he could take the flames of Muspelheim.

Will's face gleamed with Immortality and sweat. "Look," he whispered and nodded at a mountain in the distance that spewed with lava.

Forms moved at its base, staggering towards us until I could make out the army of Valkyries that had risen from the ashes.

I froze when I recognized the one who led them.

"...Sam?"

BOOK 3: VALKYRIE UPRISING

Ragnarök

Embers floated across a barren landscape and even though I had power over time and space, that moment stilled on its own. The heat wavered dusty air and my gaze settled onto a staggering Valkyrie with withered wings. She limped and growled, half her flesh replaced with the glittering scourge of Ragnarök's dark power. She drew it in with great, gulping breaths as she continued to stumble across ash and lingering flames. Sam's glassy eyes reflected my horrified face as she came close enough that the putrid stench of decay and ash tinged my nose. She bared her teeth and growled.

This wasn't Sam. She'd lost all the snark and grace I loved about her. This was a shell of what was left. Darkness filtered through her skin and seeped from her eyes, leaking across her defined cheekbones like a war tattoo. I reached out to touch her, but stopped short when the icy chill of Ragnarök's harsh kiss grazed my mortal fingertips like razor blades.

It was Will who finally brought me back. His fingers dug

into my shoulder and forced me to fall back against his hard chest. My gaze lingered on my lost sister and I scrunched my eyebrows at the soft yearning that wrapped around my soul.

Ragnarök wanted to draw me in with the rest of my sisters it had already claimed. In an instant, I knew what it wanted and a deep, primal part of me yearned for it to succeed. In order for there to be life, there must be death. Like my sisters, new life could rise from the ashes. Worlds would be reborn and given a fresh slate. Ragnarök had achieved that thrice before, the lore retold through generations by the Valkyries who had survived the end of the world. Freya was one of the only ones and she'd tell me those nightmarish bedtime stories as a warning. Even if Ragnarök ended our world, the suffering wouldn't dissipate. And so it devoured the darkness until it had become a sentient being. It stared back at me through my fallen sister's eyes and for a brief moment, its heart touched mine.

Then Will whispered my name and pulled me back from the brink. "Val," he said, his voice a pin drop in the silent room of my heart.

I turned away from the draw of glittering darkness. This was my reality. Tyler half-dead at my feet. William's eyes alight with panic. And darkness seeping up from the grainy sands of Muspelheim that were about to take us under.

I closed my eyes and concentrated. I was a Frigg and a daughter of two gods. I knew the extent of my powers now and the source of my strength.

Love.

It's what my mother had feared. It's what had given

Ragnarök a window to enter into our world, and it's what would save Tyler and Will so that we could fight it together.

*W*hen I opened my eyes again, I blinked as a cool blast of recycled air swept my hair over my shoulders. A ship's ancient groans sounded along the abused hull. I scented the rot of Ragnarök in the air. I'd slipped through time and space, bringing Tyler and Will with me to the Einherjar.

I knelt and swept my hands over their mouths to make sure they were still breathing. They didn't move, but soft puffs against my fingertips told me that they'd survived. Will glowed with the protective hue of Odin's power, while Tyler glimmered with dark runes visible to the naked eye, betraying his Heimdall connection to the mysterious matter that made up of turmoil and darkness, I scented the rot of Ragnarök's power.

Pain and suffering was the weight that drove Ragnarök. It's what gave Tyler his strength, and even though I had the same gifts, I was a Frigg. Love was my strength. Time and space warped when I commanded it to, but to bring others with me broke more than just the laws of physics. There were the three laws of the Valkyrie… and then there were the unspoken rules of the universe.

I shivered and stood as I hugged myself. Who cares what new law I'd broken? I should be used to it by now.

My memories were on my side for once, letting me know that this ship lazily orbited Muspelheim and kept its eternal watch over my Immortal sisters. I'd landed on the viewing deck where'd I'd spent hours just staring at Muspelheim before I was old enough to live there.

I turned to find a broad wall of glass separating me from the void of space. A horizon view showed me the Einherjar reluctantly drifting away from my home. I could see why. Glittering black jaws closed in around the ruby world and threatened to swallow it whole.

"No," I whispered as tears sprang to my eyes. Muspelheim thrummed with its heat and red gleam like a beacon in the universe. I couldn't imagine it being snuffed out, along with all the Valkyries who lived there and trained for the final battle. Most of my life, I'd just wanted to be a part of them and make them proud. Now, that final battle was here, and they hadn't been ready... because of me.

"You shouldn't be here," a warning voice said from the end of the room.

I whirled and tears flung from my face. "Mother?" I asked.

She seemed smaller in person as if the trials of the end of the world had diminished her greatness, but she straightened and kept a tight grip on her spear. Ash drifted down her dress, betraying that she'd recently summoned her wings. She loved her daughters, even if she wouldn't admit it. I couldn't imagine what this was doing to her and I wanted to run and hug her and tell her that it'd all somehow be all right. Love was what gave her the purest white wings I'd ever seen and I wanted to have that part of her back. Yet, it was the look on her face that rooted me where I stood.

"You're beyond redemption," she snarled and her eyes flashed with a ruby gleam, burying any hope that I'd reclaimed the goddess of love I knew her to be. Freya stood before me now, the scorned goddess of war. She stabbed the butt of her spear to the ground and the sharp echo against the ship's hull made me wince. "You've broken all three laws of the Valkyrie. Was that not enough? Now you shred through time and space, bringing your toys with you?" Her gaze fell to the two Valiant warriors at my feet.

A flash of gold brilliance came to life at her side and made her startle. The motion put me on edge and all the hairs along my arms stood on end. The goddess of war was not easily frightened.

The father of the Valiant appeared as a hologram, magic mixed with technology, and glimmered with eerie translucence as he took in the scene. His mechanical left arm whirred as he clenched a fist. "Why are two of my soldiers asleep on your deck?" he growled.

I realized that he'd addressed Freya and not me. "Father?" I asked, wishing I could wipe out the pathetic waver of my voice. If he was going to yell at anyone, it should be me. Freya had an entire planet to worry about.

He continued to ignore me and turned the full wrath of his gaze on Freya. "How could you have allowed this to happen? I thought you said that you had things under control?"

Freya's lower lip trembled and she clamped down on it hard before lashing out her reply. "She's just as much your daughter as mine. Perhaps that's why she's so attached to those fools she's brought with her." Embers streaked through her immortal body, evidence of the power of flame that coursed through her veins. Sweat broke out on my forehead and I wiped it away. I'd almost forgotten that I still had my mortal body.

As if sensing my distress, Freya turned to me. "Why did you bring them?" Her words cut off short as if my answer terrified her.

I swallowed. "Because… I love them."

Both Odin and Freya, deities of war and wrath, stared at me as if I'd just broken their hearts.

TYLER'S SECRETS

Freya left me alone with the two sleeping Valiant and a view of the destruction my love had wrought. I sat cross-legged as I watched the glittering grains of Ragnarök seep through a rip in space and time, its fingers slowly wrapping around the ruby planet like a snake constricting its prey.

I don't know how long I sat there, but it was long enough for Freya's embers to have retreated and the mournful darkness to wrap the chamber in a cold chill. I didn't notice that I shivered until Will wrapped an arm around me from behind and hugged me to his chest. I leaned into him and didn't try to stop the fresh tears that bubbled up. I'd thought that I was all cried out, but he seemed to awaken something in me that was buried so deep, it broke through fresh love and pain.

Tyler had awakened as well, but he didn't complain at the protective hold Will had on me. He straddled me with his legs and pulled me to him and hugged me tight. His cheek pressed against mine and he just held me, and I knew he'd be there for me as long as I needed.

Tyler sat across from me and took my hand in his. I couldn't believe that he'd be so kind to me when Will was right here, but his features didn't hold any jealousy or anger. His crystal eyes went soft as he stroked his thumb over my knuckles. "I'm sorry," he said, his voice a low, husky whisper.

Will hugged me tighter. His breath puffed on my neck as he spoke. "Val?"

I shifted and snuggled into the crook of his arm, keeping Tyler's hand in mine. "Yes?"

He glanced at Tyler, as if for the first time acknowledging his rival was there. Yet, he didn't look annoyed or angry. Instead, a whisper of a smile tugged at his lips. "I'm glad you saved us."

Tyler shook his head. "It's not worth the price." He glanced at the span of destruction through the viewing shield. "Ragnarök has staked its claim and nothing can stop it now."

I didn't want to face that horrible truth. This couldn't be the end of the universe.

I chose to study the harsh, beautiful lines of Tyler's face. The attack on Muspelheim had torn at his armor, leaving it to stick itself back together as if an invisible seamstress worked her needles before my eyes. The gashes left open revealed hard abs and the bulge of his bicep tearing through the fabric. His skin still boasted the dark runes, but they flickered against the golden sheen of power that draped over him like a soft aura. I looked down to my own stretched mark that had hardened on my hand. "Is this why you became a Valiant?" I asked. I hesitated, then ran my fingers over the gold film that drifted over his skin. "Odin keeps it at bay, doesn't he?"

He stared at me for a moment, then nodded. "I'm a Heimdall. I think you know what that means now."

I didn't know what it meant, not entirely. All I knew was that his mother was the caretaker of the Bifrost. That was the only place where time and space didn't have rules.

Will stroked my arms as if trying to banish the chill that refused to leave my bones. "The echoes of Ragnarök," Will said. His words came out distant as if he were piecing a puzzle together. "What if that darkness settled into souls?"

Tyler stiffened. "Yes," he said. "You're getting warmer, lover boy."

A new kind of chill ran down my spine. I covered the black rune on my hand, wishing I could banish it from my body. "Ragnarök is here because of us."

Tyler nodded. "Right again."

I thought that I'd been the harbinger of Ragnarök, but it wasn't just me. It was those I loved, and my love was drawn to others like me.

I turned to Will and frowned. While he didn't have dark runes, he'd only recently become Immortal. He had experienced more darkness than I cared to admit, a byproduct of his time trapped under the Norn's curse.

Tyler stood and offered his hand. "Can I show you something?"

When I glanced at Will, he smiled his encouragement. Somehow, the two had formed a bond and were on the same side. I guess they had a point. With the universe about to end, there wasn't much purpose in fighting over a girl.

I took Tyler's hand and he led me down the hall. Will remained behind. He clasped his hands behind his back and gazed out of the viewing shield, surveying the damage that we'd done. As Tyler eased me around the corner, I thought I caught a wisp of shadow licking at Will's fingertips.

I sensed Freya and Odin, but I had no doubt they were off arguing whose fault it was that I'd triggered Ragnarök. Leaving me with Will and Tyler meant they knew I was in good hands. Even though my parents had forbidden me to love, it gave me a small comfort that they trusted those I'd given my heart.

As Tyler guided me down the halls, I realized that we'd been holding hands this whole time. It felt so much easier to love now that the threat of Ragnarök had already come to fruition. Even though the end of the world should have terrified me—and it did—I indulged the forbidden pleasure to allow myself to do something I'd never done before. I was allowed to *feel.*

Tyler smirked at me. "You're staring."

A blush heated my cheeks. "I know." I squeezed his hand and he stopped. I didn't care if he knew how I felt now that I'd already broken all of the rules.

"What about Will?" he asked, his mischievous tone turning serious. "He loves you. It'd take a blind man not to see that."

I nodded. "And I think I love him too."

Tyler winced at that admission. "Okay, then, why are you looking at me like I'm your knight in shining armor?"

I swallowed hard before pulling him closer. My fingers ran up the strength of his arms and flattened against his chest. His heart thundered under my fingertips. "Is it possible that I could love you both?"

He blinked, his crystal eyes flitting between the magics of Odin and Heimdall, resulting in a rainbow of gold and black. The effect mesmerized me. "I think you know how I feel about you, Aerie." As if against his will, he curled me closer and his fingers ran through my hair. He had no reason to fight his feelings anymore, but something sent his jaw flexing before he spoke again. "The difference between us is I know why you might love me, and it's not because of who I am." In spite of the sting of his rejection, his lips came closer, the prickle of ice and magic sprinkling over my entire body as his desire filtered through. "You love *what* I am."

"What if you're wrong?" I asked. I drifted closer to him, closing the minuscule distance between us. I hesitated when his breath caressed my face, but he didn't pull away. I gave in to the need to taste him until our lips met.

His entire body went stiff, then he curled into the kiss as his tongue grazed against mine, suddenly passionate as if I'd managed to flip a switch off his resistance to me. His presence engulfed me, hot and hungry. He gave me that brief moment to know him and the passion he was capable of before the magic between us shut off with a snap. He pushed me away as darkness clouded over his eyes until only a terrifying void remained. I couldn't see the crystal or the spark of his beauty. There was only a glassy black that came from within his soul and glazed over the love he held for me. "Ragnarök isn't the worst that could happen," he warned.

I swallowed hard. I'd always known that Tyler had a secret. "What could possibly be worse than Ragnarök?" I didn't want to be afraid of him. There was a kindred connection between me and the darkness that brought his runes to life across his skin. His armor threatened to disintegrate as it became translucent, giving me a blush-worthy view of his perfect body.

"This is a darkness that threatens to consume me. I've survived it, but at a cost. I would not have you pay that cost."

I ran my fingers across his cheek. No matter what he was, he was beautiful to me. "Does it hurt?" I knew he wouldn't tell me what it cost him to keep the madness that overtook the Norn out of his eyes, but I could sense the deep weight of suffering in him.

He leaned into my touch and closed his eyes. "You're drawn to me because my bloodline is a direct lineage of the power that fuels Ragnarök." His eyes flashed open, somehow a deeper shade of black than they'd been before. "To love me is to reject peace. So many would die if you and I..." His words drifted off.

I forced myself to let my hand fall. "If I chose you," I finished for him. There was a reason I found my heart belonging to both Will and Tyler. They represented two distinct futures and I had yet to make my choice.

Tyler emanated darkness and chaos, a boon of the Heimdall line. He was the true descendant of the power that kept souls permanently bound to this world. Darkness, suffering, and pain were what prevented a soul from returning to Yggdrasil. That power shone through him and sang each trait with glaring realization. I found its significance when I looked into his eyes. Without it, there would be no life at all. There would be nothing to ground new souls to this plane and life would never have started in the first place. I drifted closer as I admired him.

Immortality. Strength. Beauty. *Terror.*

"You cannot choose me," he growled. He grabbed my hand and tugged me along with him. "Perhaps if you see it, you'll come to your senses." He glowered at me over his shoulder. "I cannot fight what I feel for you if you are not fighting it too."

Panic surged in me as Tyler all but sprouted wings and flew down the constricting halls of the Einherjar. We took twisted turns, going through airlock walls that flew open at our passing and sent fresh blasts of cold air over my face.

When we reached a chamber with winding pipes and a low melody that I recognized from a distant memory, I forced Tyler to stop. "I know that song."

Tyler released me and I wandered closer to a door that vaulted all the way to a two-story ceiling. This was the center of the Einherjar and I'd only been here once before. I couldn't remember what was on the other side of this door, but it both enthralled and terrified me.

"You should," Tyler said. "It's the song of Yggdrasil."

Heartbreak was the only description for the way this song made me feel. "Why is it so sad?" I asked as I ran my fingers over the crystals embedded into the door. Pipes surrounded the frame as they twisted over one another and delved into the floor. Mechanical groans and hissing sounded when I stepped on the thin panels that separated the ship from the contents of the chamber beyond.

"It's a lamentation," he explained and pressed on the crystals. Unlike me, they came to life under his touch. The walls rumbled, and then the door began a slow ascent.

I fumbled with my tattered clothes as I waited. "Does Freya know we're here?" I asked. This was her ship, and if my memory was right, this was the Einherjar's core. We were definitely not allowed to be here.

Tyler shrugged. "I'm shielding us. If she's monitoring us, then she thinks we're still on the viewing deck with Will."

I blinked at him. "Really?" My gaze swept over him again, taking in the sizzle of magic that hummed under the golden sheen of Odin's light. He was working the dark magic of Heimdall, and that both enthralled and terrified me. "Is that safe?"

He glanced at me. "No, but you must see this, and Freya wouldn't allow it."

The door fully raised, then he stepped inside. I drew in a deep breath and followed.

EINHERJAR'S CORE

nlike the honeycomb of tattered souls I'd found in the Huldra's nest, Einherjar's core was full of life and wonder. Orbs swirled around twining roots of a giant tree that spanned up into an impossibly long core that speared through the center of the Einherjar.

"This must go through the entire ship," I said, my neck arched back as I stared upward in awe. I'd always imagined the core of the Einherjar to be like any other spaceship which was a singular ball of light and plasma. The Mojinir and the other smaller ships that ferried the Valkyrie to the various outlier planets had such cores. But this? I ran my fingers through the fine mist of the air that tingled with life and mystery. I'd never felt anything like it.

Tyler frowned and reached out to grab my fingers and lowered my hand to my side. "Don't be deceived. These souls suffer. They'll never move on to the real Yggdrasil."

I blinked at him. He still watched me with that eerie black gaze. I didn't like it when the darkness overcame him.

It felt like he was cut off from me. "These are the souls that my sisters have reaped."

Tyler nodded and took my hand, guiding me down the silver path to the center of the tree. Great, winding roots walled in around us and pierced the metallic hull. That's what the pipes were for. The roots spanned the entirety of the ship.

Tyler tugged me close as souls whispered by us. Slight stings radiated across my arm where the faint blue power ran over us. Tyler shrouded me with his darkness and soothed the faint hurt. "Souls trapped by the Norn's curse can't make their way back to Yggdrasil," he said, keeping his voice low. "I can't approve what the Norn do to them. Eventually souls are destroyed under the weight of their dark magic. But Freya's version of the afterlife for such lost souls isn't much better." He forced my hand onto the rough bark of the tree's lower trunk. I flinched as raw power tingled through my mortal skin and grazed the Valkyrie embers in my soul… as well as my own darkness.

I closed my eyes as the voices filtered in. Young men through the ages who'd suffered under the hands of the Norn, and now were trapped in this place until they too would be torn apart, not to feed the Norn's lust for eternal life, but to feed Freya's need for vengeance against them and her desire to create her daughters. My sisters, I realized as a chill swept through me, were recycled bits of these souls and sorrows.

My eyes flung open and Tyler released me. I couldn't look at him. Instead, I gazed up at the span of streaking light that glimmered through the tree. My mother used these souls, and no matter her reasoning, the end did not justify the means. "What can I do to fix this?"

Will's booming voice was my answer through the forbidden chamber. "You break me free of Odin's bond so that I can tear this abomination down myself."

I whirled to find Will marching towards us. Shadows whispered at his fingertips and left a trail of smoke along his footsteps. Tyler was not the only one who boasted dark magic. Will had suffered under the Norn and survived. Perhaps all Valiant had the darkness at their core. It's why Odin's power of light was so useful to them.

Will growled as an invisible wall hit him and he crashed to his knees. Sweat broke out on his brow and a snap sounded through the air. Tyler cursed, and I knew that his shield over us had banished with Will's attempt to intrude on the sacred chamber.

"Fools!" Freya's voice boomed and Valkyries appeared at her side. They filtered into the mist and souls screeched their rage at the winged abominations that had destroyed kindred souls. The blue lights dove and left searing scars along my sister's faces. They growled and swatted at them as if they were but a nuisance.

"I'm the one who brought her here," Tyler said, his voice carrying the expanse between us and my mother.

Her eyes blazed with the fires of Muspelheim. "I know, and you will pay for this. The young Valkyries are forbidden to come here."

To my surprise, Tyler smirked. "Of course. You want to make sure they're nice and brainwashed before they see what we really are."

Freya bared her teeth and pressed a sequence of buttons on her spear.

The air hummed, and then everything went black.

GROUNDED

When I awoke, it was to Freya stroking hair from my face. I sat straight up in the plush bed that threatened to engulf me with its silken sheets and goose feather stuffing. I searched the room, my memories telling me that this was my chamber on the Einherjar. My favorite obsidian statues gleamed on a shelf. Each one was a different depiction of the birds Tyler had told me about on earth. I'd been so fascinated with other creatures that had wings. It forced a smile to light my face. At the time, I'd treasured his gifts, but now I could appreciate them for what they were. Obsidian was not easily carved.

"Daughter," Freya said. The word came out smooth and apologetic.

I faced her and drew in a breath at her beauty. I couldn't remember the last time I'd been this up close to the goddess of love, for that's what she was in this moment. All the fiery rage had left her eyes, leaving them an emerald sheen that glimmered with adoration. White wings brushed at her back and her touch lingered along my arm.

Then I remembered what Tyler had shown me and I closed my heart to her. I saw her for what she really was and I leaned away.

She frowned. "Tyler should not have shown you that place."

I stiffened. Tyler hadn't placed all the blame of the horror I'd learned at Freya's feet. He'd said "we."

"Did you force Tyler to help you recruit those souls?" I don't know why he'd included himself in the admission. A Valiant couldn't recruit souls, could they?

She tried to stroke my face, but I flinched away. "He's a Heimdall. He cannot survive without feeding the darkness that torments his bloodline." She sighed. "His mother used to have an alliance with us, but it seems Baldr has offered her a better deal. I can only hope her son will not betray us as well."

My fingers dug into the sheets. "What are you talking about? What do you mean 'feeding' the darkness?"

She tilted her head and gave me a sympathetic smile as if I were so sweet and naive. "He must periodically feed on the souls we have reaped. Did he not tell you?"

The blood drained from my face. That's why Tyler had brought me there. He was going to show me why he hated himself... why I could never embrace the darkness he'd been forced to endure.

"Lies." I snapped and flung the sheets off my body. I growled to see I'd been changed into Valkyrie leathers in my sleep. They fit too snugly against my mortal curves. "Never lie to me."

She shook her head and stretched for me again, but I leaned out of her reach. "Daughter. The Norn are the villains here, not me. I only make use of their carnage for good. I take death and give it life again. Tyler has been useful to us. He's helped you manage the darkness that plagues you."

I marched to the full-length mirror and took in my appearance. Scraggly hair. A sprinkle of freckles across my face. Embers sparked at my fingertips, the Valkyrie side of me wanting to summon my spear. I indulged my rage and let the weapon come and I enjoyed the sound of surprise from Freya as she stood and fanned her wings.

"Daughter, why are you so angry?"

I didn't have time for this. Ragnarök was destroying our world and my mother was wasting time trying to justify an unpardonable sin. Perhaps Tyler had no choice, but she certainly did. I gripped my spear before turning and pointing it at her. "Where are Tyler and Will? I need to talk to them."

Her wings folded in at her back as if I'd deflated her with that statement. "You love them," she acknowledged. "I can see that. But there is a reason it is the first law among us, my daughter. Love opens up emotions that are dangerous to our kind. Love is blind. With love comes light, and with light, there is always darkness."

I frowned, but didn't lower my spear. "Ragnarök is the result of that darkness." I tilted my head. "But you already knew that."

She stared at her hands. "Yes."

"How many times have you seen Ragnarök destroy the universe?" I asked. It seemed like a ridiculous question, but instinct made me speak it aloud.

Her gaze snapped up to mine and a whisper of embers

glowed in the backs of her eyes. "You are asking the wrong question."

I shook my head. "No, I think it's the right question."

The tips of her wings disintegrated, the primaries wilting and drifting ash to the floor. "You should ask me how many times I have prevented this world from being destroyed by Ragnarök." Only the goddess of war knew Ragnarök's weakness. Even speaking of it threatened to dissolve the visage of peace that stood before me now.

There was only one way that my mother knew how to stop a force as powerful as Ragnarök. "It's your fault that it exists at all," I accused. My voice shook and tears sprang to my eyes.

Her gaze darkened and the rest of her beautiful plumage turned to ash.

I didn't want to be right. Unfortunately… I was.

Freya refused to speak to me after I'd figured out the truth. Ragnarök was the culmination of darkness drifting in the universe until it had become an angry, sentient being.

I had to know more about it. When Mama says no, try Dad.

Freya had programmed my room to stay locked, but it didn't prevent my summons of the god of war.

He appeared when I called him as a burst of golden light that sent shadows scurrying from the walls.

His rainbow eyes glittered as he appraised me. "It seems you've angered your mother," he said. His gaze went the spear that hung loosely in my grip. "Luckily yours doesn't have buttons."

I frowned. Freya tormented me with her ancient software that could do anything to a mind. She could wipe my memories, make me see things that weren't there, or just knock me out. No telling what she was doing to Will and Tyler right now.

"I need your help," I said. It was a statement, not a request, and my father straightened.

"What kind of help?"

There were a lot of things that my father could do for me, even as his apparition, but primarily what I needed now were answers.

I rested my spear against the wall and pulled up a chair. "You never did tell me bedtime stories," I jested with a smile.

He raised a brow. A long scar streaked through it as if he'd taken a blow to the head. I remembered that my father liked his scars. It gave him character—his words, not mine.

"What kind of stories would you like to hear?" he asked.

"Ragnarök," I said immediately. "Tell me why my mother created it, and why she doesn't have the power to stop it."

He frowned, but didn't chide me for accusing my mother of such a heinous act. To my surprise, he answered me. "Your mother isn't the only one guilty of contributing to Ragnarök's current state. It is the culmination of all darkness in this universe and all the worlds that came before this one."

I bit my lip. "So you've survived Ragnarök before?"

He nodded and rubbed his mechanical arm. "Not without a price."

"Can I survive it?" I asked. I hated how hopeful I sounded. If I could survive, then maybe others could too.

Odin's gaze went distant and lines marred his face as he grimaced. "Daughter. I cannot give you hope when there is none to be had. Once Ragnarök is triggered, it will devour until it has destroyed the last of this world. Your mother and I, as well as a handful of gods, take shelter in the end days in a seed of Yggdrasil. From there, we bring forth new life. Your mother has a great burden to create life from darkness, but that was a choice we all had to make. The first time Ragnarök came for us, it was too late. When we found out its cycle, we prepared as best we could for when it would come, and put rules in place to stem off its return as long as we could."

I ran my hands over my thighs. Already my skin tingled from fighting against my Valkyrie form that threatened to break through. I couldn't lose this body. I couldn't lose hope that there could still be a chance to put things back the way they were supposed to be. "So what is Ragnarök, exactly?"

Odin's gaze remained fixated on a spot on the wall and I realized he was likely watching the glittering black fingers continue to wrap around Muspelheim. "It's the negative experiences souls have endured. Its weight cannot leave this plane. When souls leave this world behind, they shed darkness like a second skin and return to Yggdrasil. When your mother and I figured that out, we learned how to use that darkness to make ourselves Immortal. By giving the darkness form, we gave it new life."

My eyes widened. "So the two of you created Ragnarök?"

He nodded. "That's why it is our duty to keep it sated

with fresh sacrifices. The Norn are a necessary evil in this world we've incidentally created. Reaped souls are valuable. They fuel our ships, create our sons and daughters, and keep Ragnarök itself at bay." His mechanical hand fisted. "We've imprisoned Ragnarök in another realm. It takes the power of the Frigg and the Bifrost working in tandem to pull the creature outside of its realm. When you opened yourself up to love, you created a fissure in the space-time web, and allowed it back in."

I snatched my spear and pointed it at him. "Don't you dare try to blame me for the destruction of the universe." That was a bit much for a father to put on his daughter's shoulders.

Odin stared down at me over the bridge of his crooked nose. "I don't," he assured me. "You weren't supposed to exist at all."

I glared at him. "You're not making me feel any better."

He continued as if I hadn't said anything. "Freya and I were not supposed to love one another. When she became pregnant, we knew we'd pay the ultimate price for our violation." He closed his eyes. "The last time we had a child, we were thrown out of Asgard. Freya thought you could be different, but we should have known better. Where Baldr was all of our hate, you are all of our love and it crushes you with the pain that comes with that burden. Now, I fear, Ragnarök will be too strong, and the Bifrost is out of our reach while Baldr puts us on the defensive. For once, the darkness might just win."

The blood drained from my face. I knew that Baldr was my brother, but it hadn't occurred to me that my parents viewed him as their punishment. Freya had tried to suppress my tendency for love, but she'd failed. If I was all their love… then what was Baldr?

"Maybe if you'd shown my brother and me more love instead of the boundary of laws and rules, things wouldn't be like they are now."

Odin's eyes glittered with raw power. "Freya and I are the result of Immortals who've lived without boundaries. That's how Ragnarök was born in the first place." His gaze darkened. "You are our weakness. We loved you and allowed you to test those boundaries. Now the universe will pay for our failure."

I wasn't going to let Odin frighten me. "Stop being so pathetic," I snapped, and he blinked at me in surprise. "I wanted answers, and now you gave them to me. Now tell me where Will and Tyler are being held and help me bust them out. If I'm the one who set Ragnarök free, then I'm the one that's going to shove it back in its prison."

Odin faded, and I could have roared with rage as he left me alone. I stood there in silence as I wondered if my father had just abandoned me.

Then the door clicked.

LIGHT AND DARK

A faint golden trail hovered in the air and wound down Einherjar's hallways. I followed it, hoping that my father would lead me to Will and Tyler and not into one of Freya's traps. She'd shoved me in my room like a disobedient child. Even if she didn't expect me to break free, I made sure to cover myself in a sheen of darkness like I'd felt Tyler do. Ragnarök was the result of suffering and pain, something that was the flip side of the coin of love. I had plenty of that burning in my heart. Guilt. Betrayal. Need. It all gave me a dark strength that fueled my control over the space-time web, and gave me enough strength to create a ripple around me that hovered just above my skin.

Whispers accompanied the dark magic, but I ignored them now that I knew what they were. My suffering wasn't alone. I attracted the unseen bits of broken souls that filtered through the cosmos. And on a place like the Einherjar, there were a lot of lost souls hidden in the walls. The tree in the center of its core spanned the entire ship and trapped those souls here until Freya was ready to use them.

My list of things to burn was growing larger, and this ship was certainly one of them.

The golden trail stopped at a locked door, and then another click sounded as I approached. The heavy vault lifted and revealed Will and Tyler bound in iron chains and shoved against the wall. Burn streaks spattered across the metal, telling me that Will and Tyler had not gone down without a fight.

Tyler snapped his head up at my entrance and his lips lifted in a mischievous grin. The dark void of his eyes still remained and the black runes glimmered underneath his torn leathers. "About time," he said.

Will rattled his chains. "I'm so glad you're here," he said, his words on the exhale of pure relief. "I can't take another second with this asshole. He's a hundred times worse with the creepy runes making him nuts."

Tyler glowered and his skin flashed with a dark glimmer that reminded me of the stretching fingers devouring Muspelheim. "Your girlfriend brings out the worst in me. What can I say?"

Will growled. I summoned my spear and stabbed it against the ground. "Enough!"

Both guys looked at me, their enraged expressions becoming sheepish. "Sorry," they said in unison.

My lips twitched, wanting to smile at how cute they could be. I kept my composure, trying to keep my upper hand of authority in this situation—which was pretty easy to do when I wasn't the one in chains.

I walked to Will first and he offered his wrists. "Don't move," I commanded and lashed down with my spear. Sparks flew as the chains broke under the power of my magic. Will raised a brow at me. I was getting stronger and I wasn't the only one who'd noticed.

Ignoring him, I walked over to Tyler and dismantled his chains as well. He shook them off as they withered into a pile of ash at our feet. "Impressive," he remarked and his grin widened.

I resisted the urge to take a step back when his canines extended into sharp points. "That's new," I said.

He reached up to graze his tooth and winced when he pricked the sharp point. "Well, that certainly isn't good."

Will took my arm and pulled me away from Tyler. "I don't know what's going on with him, but I'd keep my distance if I were you." He leaned in closer to my ear and lowered his voice. "Did Freya do something to him?"

I shook my head. "This is my fault. I—" I couldn't say the rest out loud. What I wanted to say sounded too much like my father's lament—and would only hurt Will.

My love did this.

I couldn't think about what damage my love could do. I'd gotten so much stronger since I'd learned how to love. Slipping between the folds of space and time, as well as bringing Will and Tyler with me, showed how far I'd come with the power all attained through love. Perhaps the world wasn't doomed. Perhaps I could even learn how to stop Ragnarök.

The first step was to escape this ship. My skin crackled with dark magic that kept me hidden, but its weight was already making my eyelids droop. I couldn't keep this up forever, and I certainly couldn't step through the space-time web again... not without a little boost of magic. "Tyler," I said in my most commanding voice, "you need to get us back to that tree."

*W*ill voiced all his concerns with my plan—and loudly.

"Enough," I hissed. "I'm cloaking us, but Freya isn't deaf. You keep that racket up and she's going to hear us, then it's back in chains."

"Yeah," Tyler added. He gave me a wink. "Only one girl is allowed to tie me up."

Will scoffed and wedged himself securely between Tyler and me. "You're disgusting when you've gone all dark side."

Tyler's magic whispered over him in a wave and he grinned as if he was doing it on purpose. Was it actually getting stronger?

I glared at him. "If you're going to indulge him, then why don't you cloak us? I'm getting tired." I only had the one rune along my knuckles, but it was growing larger. It stretched long fingers up to my elbow and wasn't showing any signs of stopping.

He glanced at it and winced. "Aerie, that thing is reacting to me. Being around me is only making it worse."

I took Will's hand. He raised an eyebrow, but I had a theory. "I'm going to ask you a weird question. You need to answer, and honestly."

Tyler moved as if to fall back and leave Will and I alone, but I shook my head.

"You can ask me anything," Will said. The honesty in his

voice bit like a viper. I didn't want to hurt him, but I needed him to remember what we had together.

I kept a tight grip on Will's hand. "Do you remember the first time we met?"

"Which time?" he asked. Now that he was a Valiant, he would remember his past lives.

I bit my lip. "The best one."

His eyelids fluttered closed and his fingers clenched around mine. "It was on a beach."

I knew that beach. Both pain and pleasure filled me through the memories bound between us. It's where we'd fallen in love in another life… and where we'd been ripped apart in the most horrible of ways.

As if I'd turned off a switch, the darkness writhing over me solidified into tiny bits of ash and drifted grains over my skin. The space-time web fluctuated, sending the walls around me bowing. Normally I would have triggered a time freeze—but now I knew what I was doing.

Instead of letting myself be dragged in by the immense weight in the space-time net fueled by my shock and sorrow, I commanded it. I reeled it in and secured it into the center of my chest where I'd always thought my flame as a Valkyrie resided. The heat wasn't because I was a Valkyrie. It was my capacity for love.

Tyler stretched out and sent a wave of darkness over us, effectively shrouding us before the ships scanners could detect our presence. "That was foolish," he remarked, but he tilted his head, looking both pensive and intrigued.

I straightened. "It was necessary." I needed Tyler to see that I was capable of controlling my darkness. With Will to bring me back and remind me about the mortal part of myself, I could undo even the weighty power of Ragnarök. There was *hope.*

"Now come on," I insisted and tugged Will with me.

He stumbled, still stunned at what had happened. "Where are we going?" he asked.

"We're going to free some souls."

<hr>

I should have known it'd been too easy to free Will and Tyler. The moment we stepped around the bend and arrived at the glittering doors that separated us from the Einherjar's core, two scowling gods stood in our way.

I kept my grip on Will's hand. He was my anchor to the rage that bubbled up inside of me. If Odin had betrayed me just to see what I'd do, then he knew where my alliances were now.

"I expected you to choose one," Odin mused.

Freya's spear glowed with embers and the edge of its blade licked with tiny flames. It only did that when she was very angry. "I expected her to reap them both after what they made her do." She lifted her lip in a snarl. "It's because of them that you triggered Ragnarök. Why would you bring them here? Why would you defy me?" She growled and streaks of red ran down her arms and spidered out at her feet. "You break the laws of the Valkyrie over and over again as if you've learned nothing at all. I've been too easy on you."

It was the glimmer of tears in her eyes that betrayed the source of her anger.

She was afraid. Afraid of losing me—or having to put me down.

"I am not Baldr," I said through clenched teeth. "I didn't want to trigger Ragnarök."

I'd never seen Odin summon his weapon, but a great axe appeared and flattened against Freya's stomach to prevent her from lunging at me. "Calm yourself," he commanded.

Apparently, my brother's name was a trigger-word.

Freya seethed, and in that moment she was not my mother. She was the goddess of war who'd been challenged. In war, challenges needed to be removed.

Will released my hand and took a brave step, putting himself between two gods and their target. "Odin," he said. My father raised his chin and acknowledged the latest addition to his army. Will splayed out his fingers and the golden magic of his Immortality danced over his skin. "I didn't ask for this gift, but you gave it to me." His fingers clenched. "If the power of suffering souls is what keeps the Einherjar running, if the power of a soul is what will give your wife what she needs to save Muspelheim and her daughters trapped down there, then I give my own freely."

I clenched onto Will's wrist. "What're you doing?" I hissed.

Will glanced at me and gave a slight nod as if to say *Trust me.*

Freya seemed to be jolted out of her rage by the offer. The blaze of red in her eyes calmed to sizzling embers. "I lost a daughter," she said, almost numbly. "There is nothing that can be done to save her—not even your sacrifice."

I stiffened, wondering if she'd seen what was left of Sam and the undead Valkyries still trapped on Muspelheim.

"You're right," Will said. "But you have daughters down there still alive. And the souls trapped in the Einherjar's core have suffered long enough. You torment them and drain them dry." He pointed at the wall that glittered with crystal and took another step. "You don't need the souls that couldn't survive their Valkyries. You need someone who did." He opened his arms again and leaned his head back, exposing his neck. "Take what you need, and in exchange, you will set them free."

Will was right. All of those broken souls were useless trinkets compared to the burning blaze of his soul. The Valkyries had never reaped an Immortal's soul—not that I was aware of. Whereas a mortal's soul had limits... a soul like Will's had none.

Freya clenched her spear until her knuckles went white. I had a feeling that it was a motion made to restrain herself from pressing a deadly sequence of buttons. "Ragnarök is already upon us. You dare to offer me a deal?" She snarled and her eyes burned until I couldn't even recognize her anymore. "I will never give up the power that is rightfully mine. Your soul was supposed to have been ours, but you fell into Odin's service by my daughter's sacrifice. Perhaps I should just take you for punishment of what you've done."

"Mother!" I snapped and shoved Will aside. A wave of heat exploded at my shoulder blades and my wings threatened to burst through delicate mortal skin. I couldn't allow myself to lose my human form. If I embraced all the rage and fire that came with being a Valkyrie, I'd turn into the very thing I was growing to despise. "As your daughter, I am begging you to give me this chance to fix the damage I've caused." I lowered my voice. "I'm asking you to trust me."

My mother's fingers twitched and I didn't hesitate. I summoned my spear and tossed it. My aim had always been good, but landing the blow so that I broke her death-grip on her weapon without hurting her took skill—and a bit of luck.

The weapon clattered to the floor and every Immortal just stood there, stunned.

I moved fast before they could recover from their shock. I embraced the deeper part of me that fueled my Immortality and my connection to Ragnarök. Time and space warped, sending me catapulting towards the spear lying on the ground. I snatched it up and pointed it at my mother. "Stand aside."

"Daughter. You don't know how to use my weapon," Freya said. As strong as her words sounded, her voice strained until taut.

I hovered my finger over one of the buttons. I didn't know how to use it. I could just smash away at it and I had no doubt terrible things would happen. "Just get out of my way and you can have it back."

She didn't move, but her eyes glowed with embers as she watched me. "I have survived Ragnarök before only because I'd prepared for the day when it would return. Those souls are how we survive, Daughter. You cannot have them."

I growled. She wasn't looking at the bigger picture. "For once in your life, will you listen to me? After everything I've been through, I learned what it meant to deal with the darkness inside of me. I've overcome Ragnarök every single day I've been alive."

Freya flinched. "I tried to protect you from it." Her gaze

fell on Tyler. "That's why I allowed the Heimdall anywhere near you."

My eyes narrowed. "Do you even understand why he stabilized me?"

She raised an eyebrow. "He holds the same darkness of Ragnarök inside of him." She glanced at Odin and gave him a slight nod of appreciation. "It is my husband who knows how to filter out the shadows."

Odin agreed with a stomp of his foot. "I discovered the power of sunlight early in my years of Immortality. It subdues Ragnarök and any echoes it might leave behind."

"No," I said, the word a final thud against my ears. Both my parents straightened at the challenge. "You've only learned how to suppress it. I have learned how to *fight* it." Tyler had helped me because he awakened friendship and hope in me. When I'd come of age and was threatened to be dragged under by the ugliness of reaping souls, it was Will's love that grounded me.

Ragnarök only knew loss. It sank into the weight of space and time created by humanity's suffering and pain. Love gone wrong could easily make that pain a hundredfold deeper… but it was also love that gave hope. There was another side to Ragnarök. I saw it every time I looked into the eyes of someone who loved me. I saw it in Will. I saw it in Tyler. I even saw its glimmer in the backs of my mother's eyes as she watched me with her breath caught in her throat. The universe was too balanced for there to only be doom and gloom.

There was love. There was Yggdrasil.

I was going to get there. If heartbreak was how I fell,

then love was how I soared. Love was how I'd get to Yggdrasil and end Ragnarök's course of destruction.

"We do this my way," I said and lifted my chin. I brandished the spear at my mother. "You've run from Ragnarök for too long. It's time that the cycle is ended."

Freya hesitated, then looked to Odin for guidance.

My father lowered his weapon and frowned. "We've tried it our way," he said after a long moment of silence. "Perhaps we should humble ourselves and give our child a chance to do what we never could."

Freya's brows drew together as if she were pained by his response. "But what if she fails?" Her voice broke on the last word. A Valkyrie's failure against Ragnarök meant the end of the universe itself. "There will be nothing left."

Odin shook his head and his weapon vanished in a flash of light. He took Freya's chin in a gentle pinch as he leaned in. "You know that's not true. We've watched Ragnarök destroy the universe over and over again. We hide like cowards until it has devoured every last atom. We rebuild what's left and start anew." For the first time, the glimmer of sunlight in his eyes dimmed. "I'm tired of starting over."

Freya didn't look convinced, but she allowed him to pull her out of the way so that the crystal door to the Einherjar's core was free. I edged around them and pressed against its sharp edges, but it wouldn't open for me. I looked at Tyler and he understood my unspoken need. He rested a hand against the wall, and I paid attention to what he didn't this time. He drew on the suffering of darkness inside himself, and that's what the Einherjar reacted to.

My stomach churned and nausea threatened to overcome me. This was how I knew that the Einherjar had perverted the basis of Yggdrasil. A true resting place for souls wouldn't be capable of recognizing suffering, but the core rumbled at the hint of it as shadows spiraled around Tyler's fingers. Suffering was all it ever knew.

The door hissed open and I followed Tyler inside with new resolve.

I was going to do exactly what Ragnarök did every time it demolished the universe, except this time, I wouldn't leave only suffering behind. I'd take it all away until only raw, innocent humanity was left.

TRUST

*O*nce inside Einherjar's core, souls whipped in panic at the sight of Freya's spear still in my grip. I leaned it against the wall, trusting that my mother wouldn't come rushing in after it. I suspected that if she really hadn't wanted me to enter Einherjar's core, she would have stopped me—spear or not.

Will followed us inside and the door hissed closed, leaving me with a sense of entrapment. The power and suffering in this place weighed the space-time web harsher than anything I'd ever felt. Now that I knew what to look for, I sensed the mass that could call Ragnarök through worlds. It was no wonder Muspelheim had been its first target. The Einherjar held all the souls that Valkyries had reaped... but it was Muspelheim that held the grave of a thousand dead Valkyries that had devoured those very souls at their birth and lived with the guilt and suffering of their duty every day.

I shifted closer to the winding roots that formed the base of the long tree that soared through the center of the ship.

Blue spirits glittered around it and sang their low lament, settling down now that I'd released my weapon.

Will's fingers wound around mine as Tyler pressed a hand against one of the roots that arched high above his head. He scratched at the bark, revealing oily grime that flaked away to reveal the wires buried underneath. The ship itself fed off of these souls and I shivered.

"Shine bright," I said through the pain that clenched around my chest.

Will blinked at me. "What?"

I held his grip tighter. "Burn hot with the power of Odin. Take away their pain."

I'd seen Tyler do it over and over again. He seared away the darkness with the power of sunlight. It wasn't love, but it burned hot like love and kept the icy chill at bay. I could do that for these souls... and maybe it'd be enough to set them free.

Tyler came to my side in an instant, his eyes the crystal worry of one of the Valiant who only wanted to protect. "Are you sure?"

I nodded and stiffened my lower lip to prevent the tears that threatened to spill over my cheeks. "I need to do this. Don't worry. I will survive."

Tyler offered his hand. "You'd better."

With my left grip on Will, I gave my free hand to Tyler and drew him to my side.

I'd never felt more loved and protected than I did right then with both Valiant warriors opening their hearts and their love to me. They were two halves of my heart and I was just a husk without them.

I closed my eyes and nodded. "I'm ready."

They hesitated, but then the heat came. It grew in low, rolling waves like thunder of a storm. Then it seared against me, running up my fingertips to my elbows until the fiery fingers threatened to disintegrate me from the inside.

I opened my heart to the pain and the souls gave a high-pitched trill in recognition as they penetrated my chest and curled up in the open space of my soul where the echoes of Ragnarök lived.

I was the conduit. I was the weight in the space-time web that would draw them in…

and it was my Valiant who would set them free.

The scent of sunlight and embers embraced me… and then I died.

YGGDRASIL

*D*eath. But only a temporary death. This was the glimpse of Yggdrasil I needed to capture a weapon against Ragnarök and its never-ending hunger.

I opened my eyes, but regretted it the moment I did. The impact of purity and love soared into the heavens in the form of a great, golden tree that exuded not sunlight, but pure and unadulterated love and joy. It gleamed with radiance and souls free of suffering and pain danced through its leaves, sharing all they'd learned in their journey to earth.

Crystal blooms budded under its leaves, reminding me of Odin's gifts. He'd harnessed sunlight, but that crystal is what I saw in a Valiant's eyes. Perhaps my mother wasn't the only Immortal who hid behind her title of god of war. There was a heart in there somewhere, even if it was one encased by steel.

A yearning lifted my spirit up, threatening to tear me from my body so that I could join the souls dancing through Yggdrasil's branches. How I wanted to. This felt like home. This was a place where I'd never know pain.

Two strong hands held mine on the mortal plane where space and time threaded together in an overlapping tapestry.

Will.

Tyler.

I couldn't leave them to Ragnarök and the jaws of its dark fate.

I forced my eyes to roam lower among the branches that glittered with blooms until I got to the low-hanging fruit of souls full of the golden weight of Yggdrasil's sap. A minuscule breeze sang through the limbs, sending the crystal leaves clinking against one another in a beautiful symphony.

The largest of the golden fruits broke free... and dropped.

I dove for it. If that fruit made it into the space-time web, it would become a soul with a mind and a life and a conscience. It'd have a purpose... but I had greater plans in mind.

I snatched the fruit up and the tree groaned as if it'd just noticed the disturbance. The low mist at the base covered the thin layer of soil that separated this realm from that of my own.

"I'm sorry," I whispered and my voice disappeared into the weightlessness of an afterlife I'd never get to see again.

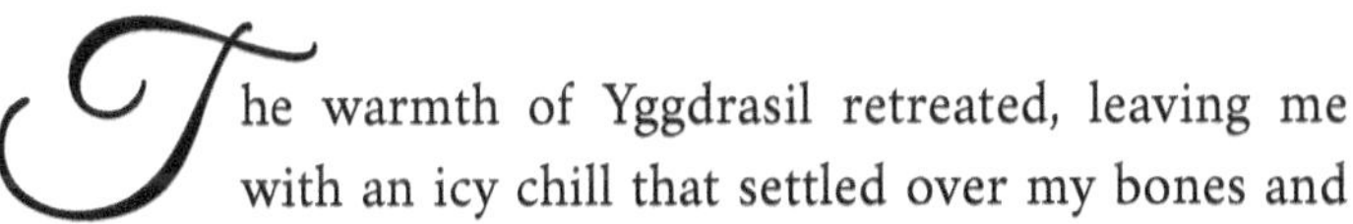

The warmth of Yggdrasil retreated, leaving me with an icy chill that settled over my bones and made my teeth chatter so hard I was sure I was going to dislocate my jaw.

"Tyler," I cried, the name coming to me unbidden as familiar pain wrapped spiked claws around my body. This is what it felt like when I was ripped from the promise of love and hope, only to find myself immersed in darkness.

Time and space vibrated around me like a weeping thing trapped in sobs. Needles pricked against my skin as my limbs fell asleep against the cold that struggled to reach inside until it grazed my soul. My stomach dropped and my hands shot out looking for something to grab onto as the sensation of falling made me panic.

Tyler's strong arms wrapped around me and I curled into his chest and his warmth, the helpless sensation immediately easing under the undeniable promise of his strength. I pressed my entire body as close to his as I could as I greedily drew in his heat. Memories unlocked with a soft *snap* as another box opened, filling me with all the times Tyler had done this for me before. He stroked my hair and shushed me as he pulled the darkness out of me... and into himself.

I cringed when I realized this was why my mother had allowed him anywhere near me. Something had to give when I tampered with space and time. I'd learned the price of opening my heart to it and attracting the weight of sorrow that existed in the echoes of Ragnarök. That price was Tyler's suffering, as well as my own.

Torment clawed at me and I found the strength to try and pull away, but Tyler's arms were solid iron and wrapped around me like prison bars. "You're not going anywhere," he chided in a hushed whisper. "You pushed yourself too far."

I knew he was right. The other times I'd used my gifts to this extent had been accidental—but my trip to Yggdrasil was beyond anything I'd ever attempted before.

That's when I remembered the hum of heat I still clutched in my hands at my chest.

I wriggled in Tyler's grasp and looked down as I forced my frozen fingers to open.

A golden fruit with the purest light of life emanating from its core gleamed back at me.

"What is that?" Will breathed.

I'd almost forgotten that Will was still with us, and that we were in Einherjar's core with a tumult of souls still whipping around us... but there was less of them. I craned my neck up to peer at the small gathering of blue dots that twinkled like stars. I hadn't managed to save all of the souls, but at least I'd helped some of them escape this place.

When I looked back at Tyler... he would not meet my gaze.

DEGRADATION

Freya wouldn't face us for the rest of the evening. Even though there was no sun to guide our days, and only a perpetual darkness that clouded my homeworld of Muspelheim, the ship continued its cycle of natural lights that lined the walls. It dimmed into the soft hue of evening and my stomach growled for dinner.

Even though my body was starving after expending so much energy, nausea prevented me from even the contemplation of eating food.

I'd settled for a warm bowl of soup which a Valkyrie had placed in front of me. We'd come to the mess hall which was small in comparison to a ship of this size. A handful of tables boasted the few Valkyries who still had their mortal form, having returned from reaping their souls. Their skin was pale and their lustrous hair turned scraggly as it hung about their chest in clumps.

"What's wrong with them?" Will asked.

Tyler had gone with Odin and Freya to "discuss matters," whatever that meant. I'd refused to part with my magical fruit and it rested on the inside of my jacket, out of sight, but it continued to hum its otherworldly song against the wall of my chest. The other Valkyries seemed to sense its healing power and glanced at me, nervously looking away when I caught their gaze.

"They're shedding their mortal bodies." I swirled my spoon in the contents of my soup that'd long gone cold.

A Valkyrie assigned with making sure I finished at least a few bites by Freya herself walked to us and frowned. Her wings draped over her shoulders in slow, drifting waves. "You're not eating," she observed.

I glowered at her. My stomach couldn't possibly process food. "It's cold," I complained.

Her shoulders relaxed. "Oh, is that all?" She reached over Will as if she'd forgotten he was there and he leaned to keep from getting an elbow in his face. Embers fluttered to life at her fingertips and then a flame appeared. She gripped the bowl, sending the contents frothing with heat before she released it. "There," she said, satisfied with her handiwork. "Now make sure you eat up. Freya is not in a good mood."

"When is she ever?" I growled.

The Valkyrie smirked. "Hang in there, Val. We're all just trying to get through this one step at a time." She bowed, then her wings fluttered before she left.

"What was that about?" Will asked as he leaned closer. "Do you know her?"

I tried to watch the Valkyrie as she sauntered away, her gait majestic and graceful as was native to the race... except when it came to me. Her wings, black as midnight, shimmered and looked beautiful even against the ship's harsh lights. "No," I finally admitted. My memories of the

Einherjar were fragmented at best. I'd been trying so hard to reclaim my life on Earth that I'd let so many things about my Immortal life slip away. She was just one of many Valkyries to me now. Their perfection and poise blended together until they were nothing but a pristine race that represented my torment and my imprisonment to an old way of life.

Then my gaze went back to the Valkyries still struggling to eat. The one who'd helped me found a few more with cold soup and set their bowls warming with her touch. They smiled their thanks, but their eyes were tired and their shoulders hunched as if already feeling the weight of their wings.

"You said they're shedding their mortal bodies," Will said, lowering his voice so that only I could hear him. He eyed my bowl of soup, seeming to concentrate on it far harder than he needed to. "Does that mean you're going to lose your body too?"

I startled and dropped my spoon. It clattered to the table and Will picked it up, wiping it off with my napkin before offering it back to me. I stared at the twisted metal that reflected my human face. Every Valkyrie was linked to her soul, and when Will died, the deterioration should have begun. I'd been clinging to my mortal body with such ferocity that I'd almost forgotten I wasn't supposed to have it at all.

He lowered the spoon back to the table and wrapped his fingers around mine. I hadn't realized that I'd started shaking. I met his gaze, suddenly feeling frantic as fear gripped my heart. I couldn't save the world, I couldn't save him, and what if I couldn't even save myself?

"Val," he whispered, bringing me back to the present just as he always did, "you're doing it again."

"What?" I asked and my voice shook.

He grinned and his thumb stroked over my knuckles. "You're spiraling and trying to hold the universe on your shoulders. You're really good at that."

He drew me in and I allowed myself to curl into the curve of his chest where I fit perfectly. He stroked my hair and we watched the other Valkyries go about the mess hall until the lights eventually dimmed and we were the only ones left.

"Do you think it's because of the rune on your hand?" he asked.

I hadn't realized that he'd been stroking the black mark that continued to grow. I knew what it was now. It was the same darkness that ran in the Heimdall line and the same power that had made my parents Immortal—and spawned Ragnarök. "Is it a bad thing to hold onto my mortality?" I asked. Even though I felt my mortality acutely in this body—the hunger, the fatigue—I didn't want to let it go. Resting against Will's chest reminded me why I'd fallen in love with him. It was this very moment. Sitting together, *being* together, even when the world around us was falling apart and death loomed around the corner. This was part of what it meant to be mortal and it made the moment even more precious. I peered up at Will, unable to resist the urge to run a finger across the perfect arch of his cheek. "Is it wrong to hope you can get yours back?"

He winced as if I'd stung him and I pulled away, realizing that I'd summoned an ember and burned him. "I'm sorry," I murmured. Even though I was still a Valkyrie, he was a Valiant. I shouldn't have the ability to burn him.

The warmth radiating across my chest wasn't just my feelings for him. It was the power of the stolen fruit I'd taken from Yggdrasil. I pulled it out and its golden glow cascaded across the table as if its light was a tangible substance set free into the world. It drifted and rolled until it reached the floor, then finally dissipated in a fog of glitter.

"What do you plan on doing with that?" he asked. He ran his fingers around mine, but didn't venture near the fruit's flesh.

"I believe there are two possibilities this fruit can offer." I turned it in my hand and marveled at the golden glitter. "I could stop Ragnarök…"

Will leaned his cheek against my head. "Or?"

I folded the fruit into my jacket, dousing us in the gentle darkness of the sleepy mess hall.

"Or, I could save you."

ill tried to assure me that there was nothing to save him *from*, but I'd seen the glimmer of hope in his eyes. He didn't want this life as an Immortal. He wanted to go back home and live a life he'd been denied multiple times over.

I wanted that for Will. I wanted him to live a full life and then return to Yggdrasil with all the wondrous things he'd experienced. With the power of the stolen fruit, perhaps that vision was within my reach… if only Ragnarök wasn't devouring the universe.

No matter how I looked at it, Ragnarök had to be stopped first, and I certainly wasn't strong enough to stop it on my own.

Somehow I'd fallen asleep after Will had guided me back to my room. I barely remembered him laying me down on the plush bed. Blankets stuffed with Valkyrie feathers coddled me in comforting warmth until sleep overwhelmed me. I dreamed of Yggdrasil and the souls that slipped freely through her leaves. It could have been the best dream I'd ever had in my life—except for the fact that Ragnarök itself woke me up.

A crash buckled the ship, sending it pitching and toppling me off the bed. The gravity wells lurched trying to compensate and slammed me back the other way.

Bruises blossomed across my arms as I blocked a wave of crumpled furniture tumbling right onto my head.

Will's voice shouted, muffled by the chaos that surrounded us, but I couldn't even release a scream. I put all my energy into grating my bones against the heavy iron that threatened to flatten me into the ship's hull.

Yggdrasil's promising warmth radiated against my chest, tempting me to use the power to save myself. I ground my teeth against the fleeting thought. Even if something happened to me, the fruit could still be used to stop Ragnarök. I couldn't be so selfish to save myself, only to doom the universe to certain death.

The next thought that slipped into my mind was of the swollen darkness that festered in my soul. If I wouldn't use the light... perhaps I should use the dark.

My bones crunched as I failed to hold up against the weight of the bedroom furniture bearing down on me. Of course Freya had to garnish the room with weighted weapon cases, likely filled to the brim. Devices meant to protect us were about to crush the life out of me.

Another rumble shook the ship and the sound of metal on metal rang against my ears. Will slashed away at the bulky object and continued to shout, but he wasn't going to get to me in time.

I closed my eyes and took a deep breath as I tried to escape the deep ache that ran through my arms. Slicing pain jabbed as the weight crushed me just a little bit more and my mortal body strained to hold up against a losing battle.

The darkness offered reprieve against the pain. I also knew that accepting the darkness was a step towards Tyler, towards Ragnarök and a future that couldn't possibly have a good ending. But dying right now would mean Ragnarök won all the same. I felt its icy claws wrapping around Muspelheim and reaching for the ship. Its disturbance against space and time rattled the ship's sensors and threatened to pull us under an invisible well from which there was no return.

A sound escaped me, and I realized it was a cry of frustration. I was so tired of losing. I was sick of Ragnarök and the constant threat looming over my head.

I was sick of love tearing me apart.

A rip sounded across my back as my Valkyrie wings burst through and I groaned against the wave of pain. There was a reason Valkyries shed their mortal bodies slowly in the form of a slow degradation until the flesh peeled away like old skin. The transition from mortality and a biological form designed for a beginning and an end couldn't be something less than subtle. To adopt something so foreign as Immortality and the fiery, Immortal body that came with it meant shredding yourself apart from the inside out. The pain could be enough to make someone go mad.

I'd shed my Immortal skin before on my trip from Muspelheim, and while that'd been rough, it was nothing like this. I embraced the powers inside of me, the Immortality, the flames, and most of all, the darkness that fueled my deepest skills over space and time. It should have been a gradual reacceptance of the things I'd forgotten, but my Immortality came crashing into me with the force of a thousand blades and a burn so raw, it was as if I'd been set aflame.

My wings stretched and flames engulfed my back, sending my beloved jacket disintegrating into ash that tricked down my arms. I caught Yggdrasil's fruit before it fell and wasn't surprised my flames couldn't even mar its glory.

My transformation didn't slow even with the power of Yggdrasil in my grasp. My shadows swirled and writhed across my arms and bound my wrists like chains. The once heavy furniture toppled to the side as I shrugged it away, only to reveal a shocked Valiant staring me down with a blade dulled against the onslaught he'd given my bedroom.

The ship continued to pitch, but my legs moved with it and my wings fanned out to give me balance. My world tinted in red as the flames of Muspelheim awakened in my heart. The pain ebbed and delight rushed in to take its place. How could I have fought this? Why would I have denied myself my true form? Power surged down my arms and my world lit up with a thousand lights as I drew on my external senses that caught the ebb and flow of the stars, of space and of time.

"Once again, you show me I'm not worthy." Will dropped to one knee and bowed his head. "You truly are a goddess."

If I hadn't quite literally been on fire, I would have felt the blush that crept over my face. Here I was, completely topless, being called a goddess. "Don't be so dramatic," I muttered as I rummaged through the remains of the room. One closet built into the wall held a small bounty of Valkyrie vests and I wrapped one around, tucking it tightly against my protesting wings until they squeezed through.

I turned to find Will watching me. His gaze averted. "Sorry. It's just, you're…"

I rolled my eyes. "Yes, a Valkyrie." I gripped his arm and yanked him to his feet. "There's no time for that," I assured him, even though my voice came out musical and strange to my ears. I rushed to the window and searched the darkness for any sign of our attackers. "Do you see them?"

He shook his head. "Nothing."

Flames lit the backs of my eyes and seared my irises, warping my senses until I spotted the heat signatures… or lack thereof.

A cold, terrifying void wrapped around the volcanic planet. The Einherjar could have been raining flames down onto it, but that wouldn't have done much good. This wasn't an enemy we could fight with weapons… but the onslaught that disrupted our gravity wells didn't have such strength.

A sprinkle of ships descended on us and disappeared beneath my window, going under and around the ship. Tiny arms extended and gripped against the hull. Lights flashed, followed by zaps as the enemy worked to drill its way in. Air hissed and alarms blared. They'd breached the hull all over the ship.

Tucking Yggdrasil's fruit into a secure pouch at my hip, I grabbed Will by the arm. "Come on. We're going to the bridge."

If I'd still been human, there was no way we could have gotten to the bridge. Freya and Odin effortlessly bypassed the light-speed airlocks, going to and from secure areas as they pleased. As a Valkyrie, it was tough, but I could do it. I pinned my wings close to my back and concentrated on the blips of space-time before each door before ripping it open and dragging Will through with me.

By the time we got to the open room that glittered with crystals and hologram stars, two gods glowered down at me, followed by Tyler who was decked out with what I could only describe as a crystal suit.

"What on Earth are you wearing?" I asked and curled my lip. Rainbow was so not his color.

He gave me a raised brow. "I could ask you the same." Even though his mood was somber, I sensed the excitement in his tone. I'd embraced my Valkyrie... I'd embraced the darkness that brought me one step closer to him.

"This is no Earth," Freya snapped. She pointed the spear

at me, but her fingers stayed clear of its buttons. "Tyler has agreed to take care of our Skuld problem." She rested the butt of her spear on the ground. "Why didn't you tell me you wanted to shed your mortal form? I could have eased your transition."

Will growled and stepped in front of me. "She nearly died. She was forced to transform. This ship of yours is a deathtrap."

To anyone else, Freya would have seemed unmoved by the statement. Her finger on her spear twitched, a sure sign that she was reigning in emotion she wasn't supposed to be feeling. "My daughters can take care of themselves, most of all Valerie."

I wasn't interested in a debate of my capability, or everyone's thoughts that I'd sprouted wings and flames mixed with shadow at my feet. I was supposed to be a creature of fire, but I was something else, too. My parents had rejected the darkness until it created Ragnarök. I wouldn't make that same mistake. I'd deal with my pain instead of trying to bury it in another dimension.

"How is Tyler going to help you?" I asked.

Tyler proceeded to ignore me as he climbed into a glass tube.

I'd seen other supernatural creatures use it before—or rather, be used by it. A space-time actuator compressed and expanded the power placed within it, and when it hummed to life, I knew I wasn't going to like whatever Tyler had planned. By the look of approval on Freya and Odin's faces, it wasn't anything good.

Odin stopped me when I moved to unlatch the actuator.

"He's already begun. You are Yggdrasil's chosen and Tyler is doing this so that you may have a chance."

I frowned, but my hand absently moved to my pouch where I'd secured Yggdrasil's fruit. Freya's ember eyes followed my movements and she frowned. "Don't think I don't know what you've taken from Yggdrasil. Don't bring out that blasphemy here."

I balked at her. My mother, of all creatures, couldn't lecture me on morality. "I won't," I snapped. "I'm saving this for Ragnarök to clean up *your* mess."

She opened her mouth to retort, her knuckles white as she gripped her spear, but Tyler slammed his fists against the crystal barrier of his cage. "Enough," he snapped. His armor cracked all over and a piercing hum made me grip my ears. Light billowed from him, bled over his eyes, and Tyler embraced the one thing he hated the most: the suppression of Odin's gift to his Valiant. Only Will was strong enough not to flinch away when the Einherjar drew on Tyler's offering.

Space and time buckled around us like a web. The drilling and groans of the ship ceased against the invasion of the Skuld trying to get inside. It wasn't because Tyler had done anything to protect the ship... he'd stopped time.

As a Frigg, I could walk through manufactured bubbles of space-time. Tyler's light continued to engulf the room, and for the first time, he was able to join me in the stolen moment.

"Take Will to Muspelheim," he ordered. "My mother has betrayed us. If you can reach the Bifrost, you can stop Baldr and you can reach Ragnarök's core."

I strained to look at him through the filter of my fingers.

My wings wafted behind me and my Immortal form did little to protect me from the power of Tyler's onslaught as he expanded the breach in space-time to engulf the entirety of the ship and out into space. I watched as the rainbow hue, like the edge of an Earthly soap bubble, swept through the void and wrapped around Muspelheim itself, stopping Ragnarök in its tracks. The power to hold this shouldn't have been possible. What strength was Tyler drawing from?

"What'll happen to you?" I asked, shouting over the frozen hum. Sound shouldn't have been able to travel, but this wasn't a frozen pocket of time. This was a new layer in the universe that Tyler had dragged us to, one where we moved freely and the space in our immediate vicinity reacted, but out in the distance the world had stopped spinning and the universe had been put on pause.

"I'll hold this as long as I need to," he said as he pressed his fists against the barrier. His armor gleamed and shadows licked through the cracks of his armor. "You're our only hope, Aerie. Do what must be done."

I bit my lip and wanted to tell him that this wasn't right. Whatever he was doing required nothing short of sacrifice... multiple sacrifices. Those souls I'd seen vanish from the Einherjar's core... I'd thought that they'd found peace in Yggdrasil.

I was wrong.

I looked past my bias and my love to see Tyler for what he really was. He glowed with the tell-tale sign of souls, the sickly gold that dripped from his fingers and bled through his eyes.

He was a devourer of souls.

Pain mixed with grief and incomprehension. How could Tyler be even worse than my mother? She'd used souls to create her daughters and as much as I hated her for that, her actions came out of a desperate need. Ragnarök always came back. Without her daughters, without her army, it would wipe through the universe in a split second. It'd been attracted to Muspelheim and it'd stayed long enough for us to plan a course of action.

I ripped open space and time and grabbed Will's hand. Tyler gave me a final nod before I stepped through and dragged my Valiant soul with me.

Perhaps he had no choice either. He was a Heimdall, part of a line consumed by the weight of pain and suffering. If he didn't feed on souls, what would happen to him?

There were so many questions that needed answers. Answers that I couldn't hear from Tyler right now. That left only one other person… Dalia, the goddess of the Bifrost.

Stepping through a void, my stomach dropped and disorientation nearly overwhelmed me, but I kept a tight hold on Will as I concentrated on holding the portal open. The Einherjar couldn't move, not while under Tyler's spacial distortion control. When I looked back and moved my freckled feathers out of the way, I saw his light gleaming like a beacon at the end of the tunnel. I whispered prayers that he'd be okay.

The lurching portal ended and I stepped onto the hot, ashy ground of Muspelheim. This time I'd brought us to the outskirts of the city. Golden spires broke the sky and distant volcanoes made the perfect backdrop to what had once been my home.

Will stepped out behind me, his body blurring as time and space fought the foreign entity. A flash brought my attention to the sky and then a sonic boom swept the clouds sprawling until I could see the glimmering blip that was the Einherjar. A thousand glittering black dots closed in around it and my heart thudded against my chest. He'd helped me break free of the Skuld and their hold on the ship, but now I had to hope that the Valkyries and my mother, as well as my father, could keep him safe.

"He can take care of himself." Will squeezed my hand that was still holding onto his like my life depended on it. "Tyler is the strongest person I know, aside from you, of course," Will said, surprising me with his honesty.

"Yeah," I said. "It'll take more than a couple of Skuld and the echoes of Ragnarök to slow him down."

Will's eyes roamed my body, clearly getting distracted. "You're beautiful."

I rolled my eyes. "Glad to know that becoming Immortal didn't dampen your teenage hormones." I tugged him to the outskirts of the city. We called it the Jewel, the one place on

Muspelheim where we could find luxury and comfort. It was a jewel indeed, a glimmering indulgence surrounding by the claws of reality that held the stone in place. Towards the outskirts resided the barracks that blended with the red hue of the landscape... and then there were the natives.

Tyler had told me to find Mr. Jefferson. I'd nearly forgotten the Jotun and collective of natives that were a natural part of the volcanic world. Like the Huldra communed with the forest, the Jotun communed with flame.

My wings twitched as we walked and I stretched them, allowing myself to adjust to their slight weight and how they changed my balance. I finally released Will's hand to give myself some space. He matched my pace as we kicked up dust and marched to the caves where I'd find the Surtr, the fire-born race of the Jotun.

"You seem content to have your Valkyrie form back," Will observed.

I curled my fingers into my palms and instinctively squeezed my wings to my shoulders. There was magic in this form and it wasn't entirely biological. The appendages would have been massively heavy if a human had somehow found a way to sprout wings. An invisible force brushed through my feathers and lit up my nerve endings with the power of the Valkyrie. I frowned, because I knew where that power came from now. How many souls had been destroyed to give me this body? "Just because I like it doesn't mean I have a right to it."

Will fell into pensive silence as we continued to walk. Then he looked up and surveyed the lazy dunes. "Why is it so quiet?"

I didn't turn back to look at the scar across the sky. "Baldr has sent his forces against the Einherjar. He believes he's already claimed Muspelheim." I shuddered when I thought of the undead Valkyrie that still roamed this planet. I had no desire to come across Sam again and the empty shell she'd become. "I don't know where the risen Valkyries will be. We should keep our eyes open."

He nodded and light flickered at his fingertips. If any trouble came our way, his sword would be ready to take care of the problem. "So where are we going?" He glanced over his shoulder. "I saw a city that way."

"Some of my sisters might still be there hiding out and waiting for Freya's orders." We'd been given countless training sessions on what to do if Muspelheim was ever under attack. The city had a maze of underground tunnels and they all led to our allies who had their own residence a few miles out. "If they're smart, they'll follow protocol."

We continued the long trek. I couldn't have directed the way out loud, but my muscle memory kicked in and knew exactly where to go. Freya had dropped us all over the planet and told us to find the caves. It sometimes took weeks, but as an Immortal I didn't need food. Rest and nourishment were only luxuries.

Luckily this trek wasn't a long one. After two hours, and two stops to hide from drifting black clouds that repre-sented the patrolling Skuld still left on the planet, I spotted the divots in the red clay and ash that meant doorways to the caves.

I flared my wings and vaulted to one, looking back at Will when he made a sound of surprise. He laughed. "Sorry.

I just forget that those wings aren't just for show. You really know how to use them."

I tucked them to my back again, wishing it wasn't so easy to slip back into my natural form. I recognized the way Will looked at me. It was the same way I'd viewed him when he'd changed from his human form to the perfect hard edges of one of the Valiant. He'd seemed too perfect, something I couldn't touch and kept lifted on a pedestal. "Once this is all over, I'm going to figure out how to get my mortal body back. You don't have to look at me like I'm something majestic."

He swept fingers over my feathers, the caress making me tremble. The nerve endings along the supernatural appendages were incredibly sensitive, designed to help me sense shifts in the air. "But you are majestic," he insisted. "Why would you want to be human again?"

I frowned and pulled away. "The same reason you want to be human again, I imagine."

Guilt swept over his features, his brows drawing together and his fingers folding into fists. "That's different. I see how you look at me like I'm something to be pitied. This body only makes you think of Tyler and he does such a better job at being an Immortal than I do."

I hadn't even thought that Will might compare himself to Tyler in that way. I knelt and swept away the ash, revealing a hatch with rusted hinges. I lifted, and what would have been impossibly heavy for me in my human form was a featherlight motion for a Valkyrie. There was some benefit to losing my mortal body, at least.

A draft of cool air burst through the tunnel and swept my hair from my face. I fluttered my eyes closed at the refreshing breeze. Cleaner drones filtered the air and fluttered through the darkness like fireflies. Keeping my wings close to my back, I slipped inside.

Will dropped down beside me, then looked up at the square hole we'd come through. "How are we going to close the hatch?"

Waving him away, I found a panel and popped it open. Grateful for my memories finally returning, I plugged in the code to electronically close the hatch. A fan sounded as it worked to reorient the ash over the hatch and keep it hidden from view.

Will nodded, his eyes a dim glow as his Valiant form fought against the darkness. "Impressive."

I allowed my vision to adjust to the long hall that led through the maze of caves. Once inside, the network could be a trap if one didn't know where to go. The Surtr were adept at mimicking the way volcanoes worked, sprouting roots as the lava fought to escape its chamber. Except this time I didn't want to escape; I wanted to find the molten core.

Will took a few steps and paused at the first intersection. Both tunnels looked exactly the same. Lights flickered as the cleaner drones continued their business of purifying the air, gathering near the hatch to expel the contaminants we'd brought inside. A few flickered around my wings and I vibrated my feathers, flinging them off.

Will turned and gave me a raised brow. "You got us this far. Do you remember the way?"

I searched through the array of boxes in my mind, both open and closed, and ground my teeth together. Unfortunately, none of this was ringing a bell.

While straightening and trying to look confident, I picked a tunnel at random. "This way."

※

After about an hour Will started to ask questions. "Are you sure we're going the right way."

I fluttered my wings, noting the shift in air currents that could have been a sign of an open cavern that would take us to the Surtr city, or it could have just been a swarm of cleaner drones doubling back and picking off the lasting particles of the outside world from our path.

I took another turn, following the hint, then jerked to a halt when I spotted one of the Surtr traps. If I hadn't been looking for it, I would have walked right across the spot across the floor that lit up against my thermal senses. Paper-thin tiles would give way to a vault of lava burning from underneath. A Valkyrie perhaps could survive the heat, but I wasn't going to test that theory.

When Will sighed in frustration and moved to step around me, I grabbed him by the arm just in time. His feet grazed the trap and molten heat swept up and engulfed the room. I flared my wings as much as the constricting tunnel would allow and vaulted us out of harm's way.

When he gave me an incredulous look, I released him and sighed. "Okay, fine. I have no idea where we are."

Instead of yelling at me, he smirked. "I figured as much in the first five minutes when you took us in a complete circle."

I bit my lip. I'd hoped that he hadn't noticed that. "Right." Dropping to the ground, my wings brushed around my shoulders like a cloak and I put my head between my knees. "Everyone thinks I'm some kind of champion. The fate of the universe resting in my hands is kind of a stress trigger."

He laughed and unfolded my fingers, stroking across my palms with his thumbs. The skin glittered against his touch, my Immortal form hardened and metallic, but against his Valiant marble, we made a good pair. "You're not responsible for any of this," he said.

I gazed into his eyes and saw what I always did, my reflection that countered his statement. I could have saved him had I been stronger, wiser, more capable. Instead he was trapped just as much as I was. "Do you believe in fate?"

He cocked his head. "That we're all destined for a purpose?"

I nodded. "My mother wasn't supposed to have me, but she did. Then she wasn't supposed to love me, but she did." I stroked his face. "Then I found you, and I wasn't supposed to love you, but I did. What if my fate is just an echo of my mother's failures?" She'd created Ragnarök and doomed the universe to the cycle of life and death. I didn't want to speak aloud that I felt like it was my fate to undo her mistakes. That was far too much pressure, but it was starting to weigh on me until I thought I might be crushed by the responsibility.

He smiled, encouraging and calm as always. "There's this memory I have of us together. You were always so worried about what was expected of you and the future." He swept a strand of hair behind my ear. "Even as a powerful Frigg, you can't control the future, and trying to will only eat you up from the inside."

My heart swelled at the drifting memories. My gaze

went distant as I remembered how his touch on my face felt just like it did right now. Reassuring and solid. "You told me I should live in the present." My gaze went back to his and I tried to look past the rainbow glitter of his Immortal irises. Beneath the magic was a boy with chestnut eyes with a gaze that could hold me captive and quite literally stop time. I huffed a laugh when I realized the irony. "Did I ever tell you that when I was human and I'd forgotten our history, you triggered my Frigg powers? I would stop time when you looked at me like you are now."

He leaned closer. "Even if I couldn't remember, something in me remembered you." His lips brushed mine and warmth in me stirred. "You've always been my light against the darkness."

My heart broke to hear the adoration in his voice. The raw honesty told me everything I needed to know about my relationship with Will. An unexplainable force drew us together. There wasn't anything forbidden or dangerous about it, no matter what kind of rules my mother had put in place for the Valkyries. Without him, I was lost in darkness. With him, he reminded me why life was worth living, not to focus on timelines I couldn't control. As a Frigg, I focused far too much on the timeline. I searched and prodded space and time in my desperate attempt to make the world a better place. I kissed him again, taking his advice and living in the here and now. No matter what the next five seconds, five minutes, or even five years brought me, it couldn't take this away.

A flicker of light caught our attention and we broke from the kiss that made me feel whole again. I turned to find a Surtr glowering down at us. The lengthy creature was what some might call a Minotaur, complete with bullhorns and red skin. But this Surtr wasn't going to chase us through the tunnels and eat us for dinner. I broke out into a smile and jumped into his arms. "Billy!"

Billy was around my age—a little over a hundred, and had been one of the first Surtr I'd ever met. He hugged me in return. "Our little Aerie returns to us."

He grinned, giving me a full view of serrated lines of teeth layered like a shark's. Will gripped my arm and protectively pulled me away.

I laughed. "It's fine. Billy, this is Will."

Billy eyed the human turned Valiant and sniffed. I never knew what the Surtr smelled us for, but he only seemed to tense after getting a good whiff. "Reeks of guilt."

I rolled my eyes. "He does not." I smiled and went to nudge Will, but his features had darkened.

"It's nice to meet you too," Will said, not sounding the least bit amused. He extended a hand and cleared his throat. "If you're a friend of Val's, then you're a friend of mine."

Billy gave him a slow nod of appreciation. "Come. You two have triggered enough of our traps."

Will gave me a raised brow. "What else did we trigger besides the lava pit of doom?"

I grimaced. There'd been a few spring-loaded walls that could have been triggered had I not spotted the stains on the ground. Muspelheim was under constant attack by Baldr's forces, and even though it'd never been anything strong enough to unseat my sisters from the city itself, we'd always had to deal with the Skuld and those they possessed. I shivered.

Billy narrowed his eyes. "Enough to alert us that we were either in trouble, or there was a hapless Valkyrie wandering around with half her memories on freeze." He motioned for us to follow. "Looks like it was both. C'mon."

Will stuck close to my side as we trailed behind the Surtr who clomped his way through the halls. He seamlessly chose corridors and hit invisible buttons as we made our way through the maze. Tunnels shifted behind us, ensuring that even if we were being followed, a pursuer would have a heck of a time keeping up. They'd have to stay right on our heels.

"How do you know this creature?" Will growled.

He didn't trust the Surtr, and I didn't blame him. The race did kind of look like something out of nightmares in their natural form, but I'd grown up with them. Those parts of my memories were fluttering to life, making me dizzy as boxes unlatched in my mind and filled me with a life before

Earth, before Will and before my duties as a Valkyrie had taken away an otherwise pleasant childhood. Where my sisters had been kept at a distance, it was Billy who'd been a companion. I hadn't been around him as much as Tyler, but Billy was the one who'd taught me the tunnels and the way of flame. It was a near cult-like fascination the Surtr had with Muspelheim's core.

My nose crinkled at the tinge of burning cinders as we reached the epicenter of the tunnels, and the home to the Surtr. We rounded the last tunnel and the walls opened up to the expanse of the underground city that teemed with life. Lava drifted in lazy pools around the perimeter, dipping back into the rock and leaving the life-giving energy of its heat to spin the massive turn wheels that powered the way of Surtr life.

"Wow," Will breathed as he stepped out on the long ledge that built a single bridge that was used to enter and leave the city.

Instinctually, I spread my wings, wanting to ride the massive updrafts of heat as I'd done as a child.

Billy straightened and grinned, showing his serrated row of teeth again and beaming with the pride of his people. The Surtr were one of the Jotun and could adapt to any element. I'd never truly understood what that meant until I'd learned that Muspelheim hadn't always been a volcanic planet. What would have melted the flesh from my mortal bones was now a life-giving resource to the adaptive nature of the natives.

Billy spread his arms. "Welcome to Jotunheim."

"Great," Will murmured as we navigated the terrifying walkway that led to the core of the city, "more Norse nonsense for me to remember. Surtr: Minotaurs with shark teeth, check. Muspelheim, planet that doesn't know when to stop producing lava, check. Jotunheim: a mysterious city inside said planet with even more lava."

I snorted and covered my mouth with my hand. It seemed that even though I didn't have my mortal body anymore, I still had some embarrassing traits. Will smirked at me and I nudged him to keep walking. "I'm glad you're keeping track because there's going to be a quiz later."

Billy peered at us from over his shoulder. His spine made him hunch, his body built for long leaps across lava pools. "What's a quiz?"

I gasped. "Oh, a terrifying earth atrocity. They come when you least expect them and leave you rattled for days."

Will nodded, an expression of complete seriousness making his jaw rigid. "Absolutely. You don't want to come across a quiz."

Billy's eyes went wide. "Wow. Good thing I don't have to go to Earth. Life there sounds tough."

We giggled behind our hands while Billy led us into the heart of the city. A part of me was grateful to have my natural form so that I could walk beside Will and make progress towards ending Baldr's hold on my homeworld. As much as I wanted to pretend my brother wasn't my problem, Ragnarök had other plans. I frowned when I noticed the specks of glittering black running through the layers of

Jotunheim like gems. "How much longer do we have until we have to evacuate?"

Billy followed my gaze and sighed. "Ragnarök burrows deep and Baldr's forces keep coming. They drill through the caves and try to bypass our traps. Something has their attention and the majority have left, but I have no doubt they'll be back."

My stomach dropped, remembering Tyler and that flash of light in the sky. Will's hand slipped into mine and squeezed.

We continued to wind through the city, the Surtr natives only dropping us curious glances before going about their business. The Surtr were the ones who built Valkyrie spears and armor. Where they were talented at weaponry, they were even more skilled at software. We entered into a room alive with lights and buttons that lined the walls. One Surtr strapped into a revolving chair spun around the room, pressing sequences all at once as if he were Freya smashing buttons until something happened. I didn't realize it was a female until she lifted her goggles and her gleaming ruby eyes caught mine. "Ah, Valerie Frigg. Billy informed us you were wandering the tunnels." She glanced at Will. "And who is this handsome Valiant?"

Will straightened. "Just someone who wants to stop Ragnarök as much as you do."

The female nodded. "Indeed. I'll take all the help we can get." She continued her work and spun through the room, making me dodge out of the way when she rounded towards a panel next to my head.

Billy pulled a lever and made the chair stop. "Now that Val is here, don't you think we should show her?"

The female frowned. "Oh, right. Yes. I suppose." She unbuckled herself and dropped to the ground, her hooves clomping hard against the stone. "This way."

As she pressed another sequence of buttons and a door opened on the other end of the chamber, she gave me a smile. "I see that you don't remember me, child. That's all right. I heard about your run-in with Grimhildr."

I swallowed hard. The sassy Surtr did seem to ring a bell, but my memories refused to surface. Just like when I'd met Will, I simply had gut feelings to base my decisions off of. The feelings swarming in my chest told me I could trust her. "Sorry," I murmured.

She waved my apology away. "Don't be. My name's Ymir. Your mother and I don't always see eye-to-eye on things, but we both love this planet. We loved it enough to keep the most important thing in the universe safe, should it ever fall into the wrong hands."

That made me raise a brow and I glanced at Will. He shrugged. "What could be more important than the Einherjar? Or the Valkyries?"

Ymir grinned. "How about the key to the Bifrost?"

***

*Y*mir took us through, yet again, more tunnels. My wings twitched as the sensation of being closed in by rock and stone started to get to me. "Here we are," Ymir said as she stopped at a panel and plugged in a code so fast that I couldn't have even hoped to remember it. She glanced at me and grinned. "Just because I have hooves you think my fingers aren't nimble?"

I fumbled at the constricting wall of my leathers that hugged my ribcage. I missed my old jeans and T-shirts. "You're having way too much fun poking fun at the Valkyrie with amnesia."

Will crossed his arms. "What's behind door number one?"

Ymir pressed the final button and two doors pressed together hissed as they unlatched. When they slowly drifted apart, I drew in a gasp.

A thick glass wall separated us from raw, molten lava. Heat should have been billowing into the room and cooking us alive, but I realized the encasement wasn't glass at all. I walked up to it and ran my fingers over the pristine material.

"Fascinating, isn't it?" Ymir remarked, clearly proud as she straightened. She pressed a hand to the wall and closed her eyes. "I can almost feel the power it took to build this. Such a massive undertaking."

"What's it made of?" Will asked, sounding curious in spite of himself.

"It's a form of diamond, carbon compressed until it's so tightly bound that even heat can't penetrate it." She shrugged. "Perhaps there's a bit of Yggdrasil sap in it as well. A little magic goes a long way."

I pulled my hand away. "Great. So this is a giant grave." I knew what it took to draw Yggdrasil's sap from a soul. The Huldra's honeycomb form had taken merciless sacrifice one after another to build enough power to fuel the Bifrost. The Surtr likely worked in the same fashion, being just another race of the collective Jotun.

"Don't get your feathers all in a bunch," Ymir said and

clacked her hoof against the stone. "Valkyries return to this planet after their death, remember? That's plenty of sap for us to work with. Your mother had no use for it, since she can only work with mortal souls, and she wants the Bifrost just as badly as we do."

I raised an eyebrow. "You're telling me that you can get the Bifrost under our control?" That'd be a game changer. Even Ragnarök didn't have control over time and space to that degree. And once Ragnarök was taken care of, perhaps even Asgard could be reclaimed.

I shook my head, finding myself going down the path of a Valkyrie who served Freya. It wasn't my responsibility to take control back from my brother. I was going to do what needed to be done to give Will the life he deserved, then I was done.

Ymir waved her hand and the wall emanated with a soft blue light, sending the lava parting to reveal the golden hull of a ship. "We have the Gulltop."

A memory triggered at that name. "It's what fuels the Bifrost." Or, at least, it's what used to power it before Dalia used whatever souls she could find. Realization swept through me. The Heimdall line, that was why they controlled the Bifrost. Only they had enough darkness and the capability to devour souls and fuel something as powerful as the Bifrost without the help of the Gulltop.

Will paced in front of the massive wall. "How do we get to it?" The lava swarmed around the Gulltop, revealing hints of tunnels that acted as release valves for the pressure, keeping the flow of lava constant.

Ymir laughed. "You can't drain this chamber, not without blasting through the vent chambers and being disintegrated by the lava that would be released. This is lava from the heart of Muspelheim. Not even a Surtr or a Valkyrie could survive it. The Bifrost is a terrifying force and the Heimdall who controls it can only do small jumps. She can't send entire armies between worlds. If she had the Gulltop, she could do just that."

I frowned. "What if *we* had the Bifrost?" The original Bifrost worked not only in space, but in time as well. I could take Will back to before any of this happened. Perhaps I could even prevent his mother from selling his soul to the Norn.

That would mean that I'd never have met Will in the first place and dread sank to my bones, but I knew if I ever did get control of the Bifrost, that's exactly what I'd have to do. Ragnarök would never have been triggered, Will would get his human life he deserved… but what would happen to me?

Ymir frowned at me as I struggled to keep my face under control. I wasn't very good at hiding my emotions. I cleared my throat and pushed hair that escaped the tight band of my headdress aside. The armor seemed to summon itself the longer I was in my Valkyrie form. I looked down, seeing leathery boots wrapped over my thighs. My spear hinted its presence with a flurry of embers at my fingertips.

"What did you have in mind?" Ymir asked, still watching me with that scrutinizing gaze that I had a feeling didn't miss a thing. "There's a reason we encased the Gulltop behind impenetrable diamond and surrounded it with molten lava."

I bit my lip and looked to Will for strength. He was the one soul who was innocent in all of this. He didn't deserve to be here with stress and fear glimmering in the rainbow sheen of his armor that crusted over his body. I wasn't the only one on edge. "Where is the Bifrost now?" I asked instead.

Ymir pulled a device from her tool belt that was about the only garment on her Surtr body. The rest of her was covered in a light sheen of fur that kept her otherwise decent to my human-accustomed eyes. Her brows furrowed as she watched the screen. "It's still over the city, but its cold signature is growing. It's trying to jump something." Her ruby gaze met mine. "Something big."

mir took us to the mortal transitional quarters, a place similar to the rooms on the Einherjar designed for Immortals shedding their Immortal skin. I brightened when I spotted Mr. Jefferson.

My history teacher couldn't have looked more at home in the small nursery where children Surtr and human alike played together. He laughed when they collectively grabbed his book and tried to rip it from his hands.

"Another story, Jeff-Jeff!" said a small boy with two little horns that curled over his forehead.

A human girl tugged on one of the horns and got him to release the prize. "No! He said he was going to show me how to dance!"

Mr. Jefferson still had his human form, and I wondered if he'd ever let it go. He seemed content in his skin, even if the tell-tale sign of fire streaked through his veins. He didn't try to hide it here, and the Surtr children with human faces did the same. The fire-blood of Muspelheim transformed them and molded them, making them the only creatures I knew who could hold a fire in themselves better than a Valkyrie.

Mr. Jefferson's smile grew when he spotted us. "Ah! Val, and Will? What a surprise."

Will blinked, and I realized that he didn't know Mr. Jefferson had been an Immortal. I laughed and prodded him in the ribs. "C'mon, don't look so surprised."

Will shook his head. "Is everyone I know inhuman?"

Mr. Jefferson stood and shook off the children that clung to his legs. He coaxed them with promises of more stories if they would be good and go with Ymir to complete the rest of their daily lessons.

I expected the clinically scientific Surtr to be offended by the children, but Ymir drew the girl up onto her hip and laughed when the child tugged on her more impressive horns. "Come, children. Let's leave Jeff-Jeff to talk with our guests."

"Will you do the melting trick again?" a boy asked hopefully as he trotted at her heels.

She smiled and a wicked gleam glimmered in her eye. "Only if you behave. Now come along."

I watched in fascination as the children swarmed around her, screeching with delight when she ran a finger along the wall and left a molten streak in her wake. So that was the melting trick.

"She does like to show off," Mr. Jefferson said with a touch of fondness to his voice. He situated himself at a short table designed for much smaller Surtr and folded his hands. "Now, what brings you two here? Was it just Ragnarök?" His gaze fell to my pouch. "Or did you have something about Yggdrasil to share?"

I slipped into one of the chairs that was barely knee-high. My wings draped over the back and grazed the floor. Instinct born of the endless chiding from my mentors had taught me to pick the appendages back up, but I couldn't even lift a finger right now. I was so tired and weighed down by secrets. I didn't want to hide them from Mr. Jefferson.

"I went to Yggdrasil," I said, my voice low with the admission. "I'm a Frigg and I have the same powers as a Heimdall." Something deep within me told me that I'd taken my one and only shot at setting foot on Yggdrasil's soil. After my thievery, I was not welcome back there again.

I glanced at Will, guilt returning with the knowledge that if I failed, he'd never get to find peace there. Even if I was doomed to wander the world for eternity, he wasn't born into this fate. He'd been betrayed by the one supposed to care for him the most.

Will joined us at the round table littered with rocks that I now realized glowed red. The table itself was a shade of limestone, strong enough not to be blistered by the fiery toys. I picked one up, indulging in the surge of blistering heat that ran up my arm. As a Valkyrie, I communed with fire. It's why the Surtr and the Valkyrie were a good match.

"Do you believe Ragnarök can be stopped?" Will asked.

Mr. Jefferson stroked his chin, managing to look like an ordinary teacher as if we were sitting in his classroom at Mattsfield High. That life seemed so far away and so long ago. "No. I don't." When our faces fell, he lifted a pointed finger. "However, I do believe it can be buried. The universe is a large place and there are pockets deep enough for even a mass of that size to be put to rest."

I continued to turn the ember over in my fingers, keeping myself busy so I didn't go for the more precious treasure in my pouch. The fruit of Yggdrasil lingered a soft melody that drifted in the background of my senses, and I knew the longer I kept it in this world, the more it would wish to return home. "Isn't that precisely what Freya and Odin have done during past cycles?"

Mr. Jefferson stiffened. "That's what I suspected. They don't admit to past cycles. Until now, that had been my theory."

I bit my lip. I hadn't intended to spill any of my mother's secrets, but I let the guilt wash away. Leaving the rest of the universe in the dark and trying to manage Ragnarök all on her own was precisely why she'd failed. I wasn't going to make the same mistake. "She told me that Ragnarök is the culmination of suffering and darkness that gave Immortals life in the first place." I left out the part where she and Odin were actually its initial creators, having been the birth of Immortality in the first place. I would leave Mr. Jefferson to figure out that one on his own. "After it was done devouring the world, she trapped it in a pocket of space and time."

Mr. Jefferson nodded gravely. "That would line up with my theory. The power of a Frigg and a goddess like Freya would be enough to trap the beast in such a prison."

I leaned over the table and my wings draped over my shoulders. "Do you think we could replicate it before it devours the world?"

Mr. Jefferson hummed. "It has already begun its feed on

Muspelheim and it'll stay here until it's drained the life-force of fallen Valkyries."

My stomach lurched. "What'll happen to them?"

He shrugged. "It seems Baldr made use of them as foot soldiers, but now that the majority of Freya's forces have fled, I suspect he's begun Ragnarök's feed."

Will scratched his nails against the table and growled his frustration. "What does this Baldr have to do with Ragnarök? I swear, this bastard plagues me in every area of my life. First he twists my mother with promises of Immortality until she becomes a monster. Now he wants to play god of Ragnarök? What does he gain by destroying the world?"

Mr. Jefferson's eyes gleamed with the power of his race. I wasn't fooled by his collected demeanor. Ragnarök had shaken his race to the core. "Let me ask you a question, Will. When you look at Valerie, what do you see?"

Will leaned back and glanced at me. "What do you mean?"

"Just tell me how she makes you feel. Then try to tell me why she makes you feel that way."

Will shifted uncomfortably, and even through the gold hue of his Valiant magic, I could have sworn I saw his cheeks tint red in a blush. "Valerie is the only light in my life. She's been there for me when no one else was. When I feel hopeless or like everything around me is about to collapse, I can just look into her eyes and live in the present. It's what's kept me sane."

Rocked by how much I meant to him, I wanted to tell him he was wrong. I wasn't the light in his life. I was the darkness that had blotted it out.

"And why do you think that is?" Mr. Jefferson asked thoughtfully. "What is it about her?"

Will looked into my eyes and smiled. "It's the love we share. Even through death, it's kept our bond strong. Even through the loss of memory and the loss of our bodies, my love for her will never fail."

I swallowed hard. "Will."

He took my hand. "There's nothing wrong with me loving you," he insisted. "If it's about Tyler, it's fine. I was childish to be jealous over it. He's been there for you a hell of a lot longer than I ever have been. How could he not fall in love with you?"

Tears sizzled in my eyes and I was grateful I didn't have to wipe them away. A Valkyrie never cried, for tears never survived the heat of our nature. "But you deserve so much better," I insisted. "It's my fault you're a Valiant. I failed you. You should hate me."

"What?" He slipped off his chair and knelt at my side. "Why do you insist to place this burden on yourself?"

"She's right," Mr. Jefferson said, the validation making my teeth grind together. I wasn't sure if I was ready for this, but I couldn't fight Ragnarök if Will followed me blindly into the fire. I needed him to let me go for the next step of my plan to work. "Freya and the Norn have a deal. The Norn entice humans with Immortality and the Valkyrie reap the souls. Of course there were disagreements over how many souls the Valkyrie would get until it turned into an all-out war. Baldr now leads the Norn and Freya fights for every soul she can get." His ruby gaze landed on me, burning with merciless fury. "Ragnarök was due to come, be it from Valerie's love or some other event. Fate cannot be avoided. Freya knew that when the echoes of Ragnarök began to spread across the universe."

Will shook his head. "So what does that have to do with me? Why does this put any blame onto Val?"

Mr. Jefferson turned his gaze to Will. "Don't you see? Valerie is a Frigg. She could have reaped your soul and prevented Ragnarök's return. She's strong enough to imprison it, but she let you go. She allowed you to kill her sister and become a Valiant." He sneered. "Now you're useless and just as damned as the rest of us."

Ymir appeared from the doorway, as if summoned by Mr. Jefferson's rudeness, and startled me by slapping him on the back of the head. "Jeffra!" she sniped, using his native name. "What's the matter with you? I thought you were supposed to be good with children."

The fire left his gaze and he rolled his shoulders back. "My apologies. I simply was taken off guard by learning a dark truth I'd always suspected about Freya." He gave Ymir a raised brow. "Did you abandon the children just to come and berate me?"

She glowered. "They're with Billy. He's just as good a mentor as you or I."

That surprised me. I'd always viewed Billy as a comrade, but it seems after a hundred years, he'd grown into a position of respect and leadership, guiding young Surtr just as he'd done for me.

Satisfied, Mr. Jefferson nodded. "Very well. I shall retire to my quarters, if you'll excuse me."

We watched him leave and Ymir gave us an apologetic smile. "I don't know what's gotten into him." She sighed, then gave us a wistful smile. "I'll show you two to your rooms."

We followed Ymir down the corridors and I'd stopped trying to keep track of where we were. If Ragnarök chased me right now, it would win, because there was no way I could find my way out again.

"Why do you think Mr. Jefferson asked me to clarify why I loved you?"

I shrugged and made an effort to keep my wings from trailing the ground behind me. "Perhaps he was pointing out that you're in love with your own death."

He shook his head. "No. There's more to it than that." Will took my hand as we walked. I liked being close to him, but right now I just wanted to pull away. Even after everything we'd learned, he still hadn't come to the conclusion that I was toxic to him.

"You're light. You're warmth. He was trying to show me that you're everything good." He gave me a raised brow. "Perhaps you're everything Freya was supposed to be."

"Yeah, so?" Freya had told me that I was all her love, which meant I was the culmination of her failure and weakness.

"Then what does that make Baldr?"

I stopped in my tracks. Ymir and Will paused and stared at me. "If I'm light, then Baldr is dark." I met Will's gaze. "But I'm darkness too, Will. The only difference between my brother and I is that I'm trying to stop Ragnarök."

Will grinned. "Maybe not. Maybe you're just going about it differently."

Ymir piped up. "Are you telling me that Baldr thinks he's

trying to save the universe?" She buckled over and laughed. "That's a good one."

I chewed on my lip before making a decision. "I think Will's right." When Ymir stared at me like I was nuts, I flared my wings, hoping it gave me a sense of authority. "Do you have any hologram screens I can use?"

It felt very twenty-first century to call up my brother, but that's exactly what I'd decided to do. If I'd gotten him wrong all this time and his goals were the same as mine, at least on the larger spectrum, perhaps there was some reasoning with him.

Standing in the hologram room with a three-sixty wall that wrapped around me, I glanced at Will through the translucent screen. He nodded, offering me encouragement and strength, but staying off the platform so Baldr couldn't see him. No matter my hopes, Baldr would only use him against me again.

The extravagant dining hall appeared when Baldr picked up the call. I swallowed, recognizing the luxurious low drapes and unending platter of delicacies. An Immortal didn't need to eat, and the display of fresh fruit and wine only boasted Baldr's stature. Asgard was alive and well and as of yet, untouched by Ragnarök.

"Sister," he said, his voice already grating on my last nerve. "How unexpected. Have you called to plea for surrender?"

I glowered and flared my wings, which only served to make him laugh. Before he could comment on my Immortal form, I summoned my spear in a burst of flame. My powers came to me so much easier with my feet on Muspelheim soil. Lava and the magic that burned through my veins roared to life and whispered the desire to burn. Flame always changed anything it touched down to the very molecular level. If I found myself face-to-face with Baldr again, I'd show him exactly what kind of power I had for those who crossed me. "You attack our mother, you attack me, but you yourself remain lazing about on Asgard. Why is that?"

He examined his nails. "Oh, I don't know. Perhaps I'm bored with the thought of such an easy victory." He lowered his hand and grinned. "Of course, it's exactly what I expected. I'm good at understanding my opponent's weakness."

I gripped my spear, resisting the urge to form a portal and jump right through the screen and impale his face. "You wanted me here for this, why?"

He laughed. "Ah, yes. That was a fun trick. Your love is your weakness, dear sister." His laughter faded. "As it is mine."

That got my attention. "You're capable of love?"

He clutched at his chest. "Oh, how you wound me." He waved over someone who was off the screen. The same graceful Valkyrie I'd seen before that seemed to like to fawn all over him now draped herself over his chest. "What is it, Baldr?" Her voice came through the speakers just as musical and pure as the rare selection of Valkyries who inherited our mother's grace and beauty at its finest.

He ran a finger across her neck before gripping it and putting her in a chokehold. "Would you care to show my sister what happens to those I love?"

Her eyes went wide, but she didn't struggle. She gurgled something, but Baldr didn't let go. Then her eyes flared with flame, a warning sign that a Valkyrie was about to draw on the strength of the powers of Muspelheim that ran through her blood. For the same reason we didn't need food or water, we didn't even need to breathe if we accepted the raw magic that gave us our bodies.

Baldr growled. "I gave you an order."

"Stop this!" I shrieked. I didn't even know if it was possible for a Valkyrie to deny herself the life-giving force that came naturally to us from birth. "What point are you trying to prove?"

He responded by wrapping his other hand around the Valkyrie's throat. She twisted at an odd angle until he squeezed hard enough for her neck to snap. The light immediately died in her eyes, fading as fast as the light of her body.

I watched in horror as Baldr drew shadows from her flesh. He inhaled what was left of her soul that should have returned to the pits of Muspelheim.

I rocked back on my heels. Baldr had just shown me what we were capable of. We were Freya's children, but we also belonged to Odin. That made us gods of another kind. Instead of giving life... we could take it for ourselves.

Images of Tyler flashed, those tell-tale shadows creeping across his skin. Each black rune that marred his perfect body was a soul he'd devoured.

I stared down at the rune that stretched an ugly scar across my hand and realization swept through me.

"Yes. You get it now." Baldr dropped the Valkyrie's body

to the ground and it fell with a soft *thud*. "You understand what we are."

Baldr didn't care if Ragnarök devoured the world… because those with this ugly power would be all that remained once it was done.

⌇

My mouth went dry and I licked my lips. "What are we?" I asked, my voice raw.

"Our parents have staved off Ragnarök so many times that they finally started to become like it. They've been devouring souls longer than we've even been alive. It makes sense that we'd inherit their darkest secret and turn it against them."

I didn't want to listen to Baldr's logic. "So you *want* Ragnarök to destroy the universe? Are you insane?"

He shook his head. "You think so small, my sister. We let Ragnarök do its work, but we won't let it finish." He twirled the wisp of shadow around his finger, commanding it to dance for him across his knuckles. "Haven't you tried feeding from Ragnarök itself?"

My eyes went wide. "Feeding?"

He laughed. "I know you've fed before. I see the rune."

He hid my hand behind me. There had to be some mistake. "I haven't fed on anyone."

He gave me a raised brow. "No? Not even that human you supposedly loved so much? Where is he now? Have you asked him if he feels like something is missing?"

I glanced at Will and he was shaking his head. I knew

what he was thinking. *Don't let him tell you this is your fault. I'm fine. I'm here.*

But Will wasn't fine. He wasn't all here. Every time I looked at him, I saw how fractured he was. I'd thought what was missing was his mortality. I'd been wrong. It was a piece of his soul.

I licked my lips again, desperately wishing I had something to drink. That's when I ran my fingers across the hidden fruit still in my pouch and hope blossomed in my chest. Whatever I'd taken from Will, this could give it back to him.

"Sister. You are indeed hopeless. It was probably an accident. That's why he's still alive. You could have taken everything, but you only took what you needed."

What I needed. The truth in that statement shook me to the core. Ever since Will's death I'd begun to regain my memories. I'd found the strength to overcome Grimhildr's programming and I'd even been able to step through space and time with ease. Such a leap in ability wasn't because of some inherent strength. I'd fed on Will's soul.

I squeezed my eyes shut. "I called you because I wanted to work together. I want to stop Ragnarök and find a truce." I opened my eyes and met his. The man who looked back at me was wild and uncontrollable. He stood tall and proud, pensively watching me as if he were Odin himself, but I sensed the frustration and pent-up aggression in the lines of his jaw. "What is it that you really want, Baldr?"

"I told you before," he chided. "I want Sam."

I shook my head. "And you know that she's gone."

He huffed a laugh. "Haven't you been paying attention?" He turned to the body that had already started to harden.

He swept his fingers over it, releasing the shadows that he'd drawn in.

My entire body went still as I watched. The glittering black was reminiscent of Ragnarök as it twisted and moved like tiny claws as it gripped the Valkyrie and lifted her up. It burrowed into her and made her convulse.

Then her eyes opened.

At first her irises were the purest of black, and then the shadows faded, leaving the ember purity of a Valkyrie renewed. "Baldr," she breathed, her face softening into relief. "You brought me back."

I balked. Once again I searched for Will through the screen, but he was gone. My blood ran cold. Was he afraid of me now? I couldn't deny that I was exactly like my brother. The only difference was that one of us had embraced what we were.

Gods.

WILL'S CHOICE

"**Y**ou know how to reach me when you're ready to accept our fate."

Baldr's last words still shook me to the core. I'd been staring at the blank hologram screen for what seemed like an eternity before Ymir gently took my hand. "Aerie?"

Calling me by Tyler's nickname for me jolted me back into awareness. He was still up in the Einherjar fighting for me while I was supposed to be figuring this all out. The truth, however, wasn't so easy to unravel. According to Baldr, stopping Ragnarök was a simple matter of accepting what I was. If I fed on it, if I drew its darkness into myself, I could save everyone... but I feared what would happen to me.

"I can't do it," I whispered.

My hands shook and Ymir drew me off the platform. "No one is asking you to."

"What's going on here?" Mr. Jefferson snapped. His veins

illuminated in the dim light with harsh ruby tones. "Will told me to tell Valerie not to feed on Ragnarök. Did I hear him right?"

I blinked at him. "Where's Will?"

Mr. Jefferson frowned. "How should I know? He rushed past me and shouted orders at me as if I hadn't been his teacher for the past two years. No respect these days."

I looked to Ymir whose features had gone unreadable. Even if I had no memories of her, that seemed suspicious. Ymir was the kind of Surtr who always had an opinion and always knew what was going on. "What aren't you saying? Where's Will gone?"

She released me. "I suspect he's gone to the Gulltop."

"What?" I asked. "Why?"

She released a long breath. "If he thinks the Bifrost will save you from having to sacrifice yourself to save the rest of us, then he's going to break the seal on the Gulltop for you to do just that."

❧

I ran as fast as I could, but I didn't get very far. I cursed when I reached the first split in the tunnels. "Which way?" I demanded.

I'd dragged Ymir with me. Even though she protested, I wasn't going to let her go. "I can't tell you that," she bit out.

I gripped her wrist until her bones grated together. She winced, but clacked her hoof. "Yes you can," I insisted. "Will is hanging on by a thread. If I'm going to restore his mortality, then I need him alive. There's no telling what breaking the Gulltop seal will do to what's left of his soul."

She ground her teeth but didn't seem inclined to budge. "He loves you. Allow him to protect you the only way he knows how."

The tunnels shook and a male cry echoed through the corridors. I released Ymir as desperation made black stars sprinkle across my vision. "What was that?"

The lights wavered, turning red, then blue and going into a low hum as energy swept through Jotunheim.

I was too late.

Will was dead.

I was already in my Valkyrie form. I'd lost my mortal flesh. I'd lost Sam.

Now I'd lost Will.

I let go of the last hold I'd kept on my Immortality. Fire unlocked in my soul and ignited, releasing my internal rage and darkness I'd kept at bay for so long.

Tyler wasn't here to save me this time. He understood my darkness better than anyone, and now I knew why. The dark scar running along my arm blistered and solidified, becoming a permanent scar as the remnants of Will's soul found me and absorbed into my body. Feeling the surge of power that gave me only enraged me more. I was Will's death and no matter how much everyone tried to tell me none of this was my fault... I was the one to blame.

Tears sizzled into steam in my eyes and my wings caught fire. Ymir screamed in the distance, but I couldn't decipher her words. Even a Surtr couldn't withstand the full force of my rage and grief. I was the child of two gods, and not everything that was good about them. I was the birth of their secrets and their sin. I was an abomination.

I should have joined Ragnarök in that moment and merged with its glittering black fingers that devoured this world, but one small piece of sanity found its way into my mind.

Why did Will just sacrifice himself?

I ran through the corridors and followed the scent of his sacrifice, coming upon the chamber to the Gulltop completely emptied. There was nothing left of him, but the evidence of what he'd done was in the massive split in the wall that diverted the lava through the venting corridors that were intended to reroute the lava, but he'd opened them all. He'd gone inside those tunnels and put a crack in each one, being devoured by flame to release the final seal on the Gulltop.

My fingernails bit into my palms and every muscle in me shook with the wrecking grief that he'd do this to me. He couldn't be reborn, not if I had devoured his soul. I was his curse, and now he was a part of me. That wasn't enough.

But the Gulltop, it rested on the bottom of the chamber lopsided with a single panel glowing with warning. I approached it and stared at the buttons.

Ymir drifted behind me, followed by Billy and Mr. Jefferson, as well as a small herd of Surtr I didn't recognize. Some of them had weapons, and I didn't underestimate the primal spears they pointed my way. This race was the one that had fashioned Freya's spear and given the weapon such powerful cruelty. I had no doubt their own weapons had a few secrets in their software.

"Help me open it," I growled. My voice grated through my throat with the pain I couldn't express. Shadows licked over the flames sprouting across my arms. My Valkyrie armor was having a hard time holding up against the onslaught and hardened into black leathers.

Ymir stepped forward. "The Gulltop was caged for good reason," she insisted. "One wrong move and you could change everything."

My vision flared as flames licked in the backs of my eyes. "That's precisely what I want to do." When she gave me a blank stare, I motioned to the cracked and burned surroundings. "Is this the timeline you want? Ragnarök on our doorstep, Freya and Odin trapped on the Einherjar with the Valkyries who have survived? Your people hiding in caves awaiting Ragnarök and the Skuld to finally find you?"

Her lower lip began to tremble. "No, of course not, but—"

"Then open this door," I snapped.

She glanced over her shoulder at Mr. Jefferson who hesitated, then gave her a slow deliberate nod. Billy motioned to protest, but Mr. Jefferson lowered his hand. "She's right." His words were so low that they were barely audible. "This is not the timeline we should be living." His eyes met mine, matching my rage with their fiery red. "Daughter of Freya, daughter of Odin, you inherit the Gulltop, the Bifrost, even Asgard with every right. Baldr is not our ruler." He knelt to one knee. "You are our Queen and I recognize you with the authority of all the Surtr have to offer."

Ymir stiffened, but finally relented and knelt as well. The

rest of the Surtr followed suit, dropping to a knee one-by-one.

My wings flared. "Thank you," I said, then pressed my hand against the blazing metal of the Gulltop. "Now help me fix this."

THE GULLTOP

$\mathcal{I}$ didn't think about the consequences of going back in time. If I stopped to consider what I was doing, I wouldn't have the strength.

I climbed into the confined space of the Gulltop alone. Buttons glowed to life and there was just enough space for one more person.

I gave Ymir a hard glare through the hatch. "You're coming with me."

She went pale, but climbed in.

Only a Surtr would know how to operate this thing. Like most of the technology that dictated the Immortal world, I suspected it was Ymir who had built it.

Confirming my suspicions, she plucked away at the buttons and the hatch closed in behind us. "When I made the Bifrost, I thought that I was helping our race. Traveling through the universe and colonizing other planets was our dream."

I listened patiently. This was the kind of information I

needed in order to save the world. "The Bifrost was a prototype?"

She nodded. "It's still my best work yet. Only one device can link into the slipstream of space and time." She patted the hull of the Gulltop fondly. "But this device can enforce it, grows upon it and manipulates it. Instead of just transporting the individuals in the room through space, the Gulltop opens time as well."

I nodded. "I know exactly where... when, I want to go."

Ymir gave me a mournful look. Her hand rested on mine, her red-hot claws feeling cold against the raw heat that burned inside of me. "I warn you, time cannot often be changed. And when it can, the consequences aren't typically what you'd expect." She placed my hand on a sequence of buttons. "But you and I are not the same. Perhaps you will succeed where I failed."

I wondered what attempts Ymir had made that had resulted in the permanent seal of the Gulltop behind deadly lava. "What makes you say you failed?"

She gave me a weak smile. "The Jotun are the result of my experiments. Instead of Terraforming planets to suit our needs, I experimented on freshly Immortal bodies, mine included. We were supposed to adapt to any planet we called home. Instead, we became enslaved to it and changed on a fundamental level that we cannot survive without it." Her gaze went distant as she ran her fingers over the length of her horns. "The Surtr didn't always look like this. We were once beautiful, but when I bound myself and my clan to Muspelheim, I learned that we could never leave." Her eyes glimmered. "Until Freya came into the picture, that is. She gave us Yggdrasil's sap and Muspelheim itself fueled

Jotunheim with new power. Some of us are able to resume our more natural human forms. Without Freya, though, we all would have been trapped here forever, doomed to Muspelheim's fate." She drew out a vial of glittering gold liquid and popped it open. She downed it in two seconds flat and her form twisted and shimmered. Her horns retreated into her head and her skin lost its metallic, red hue. When she fully transformed into a beautiful woman, I openly stared. She laughed. "Oh, right." She popped open the hatch at the floor which revealed an assortment of packages. She opened one and shimmied into the tight suit. She offered me a bag. "Helps with the distortions. Think of it as anti-g-force. Acceleration is always a component of time, and when you're going in reverse, it has a Hel of a punch."

I grimaced at it, then flexed my wings. They couldn't extend all the way before hitting sensitive machinery. "I'll pass."

She shrugged and returned the bag to the hatch before flipping the lid closed. "Suit yourself."

She cracked her knuckles, then started dancing her fingers across the glowing lights. All she was missing was her revolving chair.

I watched, mesmerized, and then a hologram screen popped in front of our faces, revealing the watchful Surtr standing outside the hull.

She cleared her throat, then hit an orange button. "Our Queen would like to say something before we embark." When I widened my eyes at her, she motioned for me to speak.

I sighed. I hated speeches. "I'm sorry for everything that's happened. My mother is supposed to protect this planet and its people. You are our allies, and you don't deserve for Ragnarök to be breathing down your necks. I'm going back to the beginning when this all started and make sure the timeline is corrected. Wish me luck."

A cheer sounded before the screen blipped off. "Well done." She gave me a wink. "You'll make a fine Queen." She pointed at scroll knob with eight runes glimmering beside it. I recognize the Norse style merged with the modern date system. "Plug in when you want to go. Just remember, once you successfully change the timeline, it'll take the space-time net a period to adjust. You won't be able to use it again —not in this lifetime, anyway."

So, no pressure then. Great.

❧

I'd been watching Will ever since he'd been assigned to me. His first life was his dedication to the Norn and the first moment he'd appeared on our scanners. I'd been so young then that I hadn't understood what it meant to be dedicated to the Norn, but I knew the date by heart. Those Norse runes were etched into my memory as the day I'd gone from being a child to becoming a fledgling Valkyrie.

I dialed in the date: February 4th, 1955.

The Gulltop hummed to life, singing that familiar high-pitched scream that was all too familiar. When the Einherjar had sent me to Earth and fitted me with a human body, the same invading sensations rattled my bones, but this wasn't just travel through space. My Frigg powers reacted as the Gulltop drew its strength from me. The

Bifrost was powered by the souls trapped on Asgard, but the Gulltop had no such resource. It was now powered through me.

I sensed Dalia when the Gulltop made its connection to the sister ship. Her shouts rang in the background of my senses, warning Baldr that the Bifrost was being manipulated. I grinned, because there was nothing that he could do about this. He wasn't a Frigg and he had spurned the Surtr, the one race that could have helped him gain control over time itself.

I was glad the Surtr were on my side. I wanted to tell Ymir as much, how much I appreciated her help, but the Gulltop's screech ended and my vision went black as pain streaked through my body.

Another scream sounded, and this time I realized it was my own. Every atom in my body protested the reverse movement through time as the Gulltop gained momentum, ripping into me and pulling out the dark powers of my Frigg nature to unseat us from the present.

How ironic, I thought, that this was how I would save Will. He'd always loved the present.

❦

Scandinavia, 1920

The hilltop where Will had been dedicated as a child was just as I remembered it, but my memories were from a grainy hologram screen that had spied on the aftermath of the contract Leanne had made with the Norn. The darkness that had cemented the bond had distorted the image, leaving me wondering what Will had looked like as a child in this life. I'd been submerged in my training at that time, Tyler close on my heels trying to make sure I learned how to defend myself against the power of the Norn. He had firsthand experience with them and it was his fear of them that had driven me. I'd been so focused on protecting myself and learning the skills I would need that I hadn't even paid attention to Will during his first, short life.

Now, though, I marveled at the serene calm of the wavy hills topped with bright grass that made it look more like a velvet carpet than something born of nature. The sky glowed with a healthy blue and puffy clouds lazily danced across the horizon.

I'd arrived during the cheery part of the day. Wildlife bounced through crags and a chill wind tangled invisible fingers through my hair.

Then a twig crunched behind me and I whirled to find Ymir grinning. Panic filled me as I searched for the Gulltop. Where was it?

"Relax," she said. "This is how it works."

"How do we get back to our time?" I asked as dizziness swept over me. My feathers brushed my shoulders and I startled, nearly forgetting that even though I was surrounded by Earth's air and soil-scent, I was still a creature of Muspelheim.

"The Gulltop hasn't moved, it's still in the heart of Jotunheim. It's transported our bodies through time and space and we'll be yanked back like a rubber band when you call for it."

"And how do I call for it?" I asked.

She paled. "You mean you don't know? It's the same way that you got us here."

I grimaced. "You put far too much faith in me, Ymir."

She sighed and stepped through the grass, but then she stopped and curled her toes. "This feels amazing." When I glowered at her, she laughed. "Don't worry. I'm sure you'll figure it out." She pointed at an assortment of vertical stones atop the highest hill. Tufts of moss and grass stuck out of its sides. "I assume that's where we're going? I sense something familiar there."

I sensed it too. The pull of a portal drew me to the place that housed the weight of suffering and pain—an Immortal's cocktail for power.

"Come. Let's check it out before Leanne arrives." I marched up the hill and Ymir followed me.

She was a scientist, which meant that her calculating eyes were documenting every step of this journey. She should have been terrified, even just a little bit, but everything seemed to fascinate her. I remembered the first time I'd come to earth, how the abundance of nature and life mesmerized me. Even without my memories, and the addition of a few new ones thanks to Grimhildr, I recognized how special this place was. Humans had no idea how good they had it.

A path of cobblestones and footprints led me to the top of the hill which was more of a rundown temple to the Norse gods. Fresh offerings of mint and flowers settled on the offering stone and I stared at it. Leanne came here often.

Ymir bent and examined the offering. "Do the Norn eat this?"

I laughed. "No. I suspect that humans have their own idea of what the Norn want." The Vikings were the closest to true followers of the Norn. Sacrifice and constant bloodshed were what had given them a place in history, and what had kept Immortals like the Norn going strong for centuries.

"Leanne is going to dedicate Will. I need to stop her." I sat on the stones and stared at the sky. It would only be a few more hours before she'd make her way up the cobbled path. I flexed my wings. There was one thing about being in my native form. She would listen to what I had to say.

❦

*Y*mir hid in the bushes by the time Leanne arrived. I'd planned out exactly what I was going to say. The crazy woman I remembered didn't care a speck for Will or his future. She was coming here to kill her son, and I was going to do what Grimhildr should have done. Wipe her mind, make her a vegetable, and then I'd make sure Will would find a new home that cared what happened to him.

The shy, wide-eyed woman who crested the hill wasn't how I'd imagined the terrifying creature that would be willing to give her son as sacrifice to the Norn. She stared at me as the blood drained from her face and she clutched a baby to her chest.

"Leanne," I said, hoping to win her over by showing that I knew her name.

She looked more like a frightened rabbit ready to bolt. She froze and her mouth bobbed open and closed, but no words came out.

I shrank my wings to my back as far as I could and crouched as I offered a hand. "It's all right. You don't have to be afraid." I tried to remind myself that this woman was evil beyond evil, but she looked so terrified. I managed a smile.

Shaking, she unlocked from her frozen stance and tugged an amulet from underneath her blouse. *"Ofre."* Sacrifice.

My mind worked to translate her tongue, instantly replacing the Danish with English that I was more accustomed to.

I didn't know if I was capable of speaking her language, but I tried anyway.

I cleared my throat and then flinched when a soft hum swept through my body. I glanced back at the brush where Ymir was hiding, only seeing two eyes peeking at me over the foliage. She held up a device that blinked.

I turned back to the woman whose gaze hadn't left my wings. She was still as white as a sheet. "Leanne," I tried again, this time my lips wrapping around an unfamiliar accent as her language and muscle training of how to form her words downloaded into my brain, "I know why you're here."

She startled. "You speak my language?"

I relaxed, glad that Ymir was able to pull through for me. Trying to talk to Leanne without speaking the same language would have proved difficult. "That's not the question you should be asking."

Her gaze went to my wings again. "You've come for my son's sacrifice?" She pulled the child away from her bosom and offered the boy. I melted when I saw Will's face. Little eyes opened, revealing chestnut irises that had always held me captive.

"No," I snapped, and she clutched the baby back to her

chest. I forced my anger to simmer in the low heat of my core that begged to be set free. This woman didn't deserve explanations. Here she was freely offering her child to me. "I've come to ask you not to sacrifice your son."

Her eyes brimmed with tears. "But, he is sickly." She took a brave step forward and I knew it cost her. Her knees wobbled, but she stood her ground. "You're a Valkyrie, yes? Does Freya not demand my son's life, just as she's taken my daughter's?"

My wings flared of their own accord, the feathers scraping against stone and sweeping away the small offerings on the pedestal. Leanne shrank into herself in fear. "A daughter?"

She nodded vigorously. "I would not expect such a warrior as yourself to know of it. Freya does not honor those who die from sickly illness and succumb to weakness." She squeezed her eyes shut as if trying to block out the memories. "I vowed, should I ever have a child again, I would make sure they lived forever and earned a place in Valhalla." She clutched at me with her free hand. "Please. Do not let this child be lost too. He has the same illness."

That's when I sensed the darkness in the child that had been masked by my own rage. I wrapped my fingers around the bundle and Leanne released him.

Holding the baby who cried against my overwhelming warmth, my heart crushed under the inevitability I hadn't expected.

It was just as Leanne had said. I sensed a biological flaw in this child, one that could not be undone. I could knit flesh anew, build new bodies for Immortal souls to inhabit, but I could not mend that which was broken. Tears sizzled in my eyes as I returned the child.

There was something to be said about humans who died of illness. Such suffering weighed down a soul so that even they could not return to Yggdrasil.

If I prevented Leanne from bonding Will's soul to the Norn, he would die in a few short years anyway, denied Yggdrasil and the life I wanted for him.

No matter what I did, I couldn't save him.

*P*inned with indecision, Leanne asked me over and over again what she must do. If she could not bind her son to the Norn, how else could she save him?

I had no answer for her. I also couldn't explain that she would turn into a twisted creature unrecognizable from the kind, fretful woman I saw before me now. She was a victim in all of this just as much as the rest of us, just as much as the innocent child in her arms.

Eventually I gave in to the hum of grief in my soul, inwardly activating my connection to the Gulltop and hoping I hadn't done anything to change this timeline. I needed another shot to get this right.

Ymir and I vanished from Scandinavia, from 1955, and returned to the heat of Muspelheim.

*I*f I couldn't save Will by undoing the Norn's curse before it even began, I had to think deeper.

"What if I stop Will from unlocking the seal to the Gulltop in the first place?" I asked Ymir as we huddled in the cramped confines of the time-traveling ship.

She shrugged. "You could try that, but the moment you did the timeline would be rerouted and we would be stuck in a timeline where the Gulltop is still inaccessible."

I growled. "Why did you seal it away in the first place? We need it to stop Baldr, especially if he tries anything." Having time travel on our side gave us a distinct advantage I wasn't ready to give up. It wouldn't matter if I saved Will, only to lose him again to Baldr's insane plan to release Ragnarök on the universe. The bastard actually thought that he could control it.

Ymir bit her lip. "I told you, I've failed my people before. The last god to steal the Gulltop from me kicked the gods out of Asgard."

My eyes went wide. "Baldr had control over the Gulltop? How did you get it back from him?"

Her gaze darkened. "With enough sacrifice, anything is possible."

Now I understood the weight of guilt Ymir carried around with her. It wasn't just the creation of the Jotun that rested on her shoulders, but the reason the Surtr were nearly an extinct race. Their cavernous city of Jotunheim held only a mere few hundred Surtr. Jotun like the Huldra numbered in the thousands.

"I see," I said. "So, if we're to keep control of the Gulltop, we need someone to manually release the lava." Why did it have to be Will. I would have offered myself, but if anything happened to me, there'd be no one to stop Ragnarök or my insane brother. Ymir couldn't do it. I needed her to run the Gulltop. I certainly couldn't ask any of the other Surtr to give their lives so that Will might live.

There was one last weapon in my arsenal. The Yggdrasil fruit still in my pouch.

The concentration of raw life lived underneath its soft flesh. Perhaps if I got him to take a bite before he sacrificed himself… I could still save him.

I glanced at Ymir. "I have an idea, but you're not going to like it."

We dialed in the time stamp to just a few moments after I began my call with Baldr. Traveling through time with the Gulltop wasn't any easier the second round and my screams echoed through time and space as we ripped through the natural world and followed the threads to where I needed to go.

My feet met the smooth, warm stone of Jotunheim and Ymir joined me at the tunnel's entrance to the hologram room. We'd stop Will before he ran out.

"Are you sure about this?" Ymir asked.

I'd explained my plan to her in its entirety, but I couldn't be sure if it would work. Yggdrasil's fruit traveled with me and I wouldn't be able to restore it after its use.

I nodded and spread my feet. "I'm sure."

Baldr's mocking voice echoed through the corridor and

I scraped my fingernails against my palm. Will came barreling into us a moment later, nearly plowing us over on his way to the Gulltop.

He balked at me. "Val?" He looked back at the room, the dark silhouette behind the screen being my past self, then he looked back at me. "What is going on?"

I held both hands. "There isn't much time to explain, but you're on your way to unlock the Gulltop. It worked."

His shoulders relaxed. "Good." Then his jaw flexed. "If you've come to try and stop me, you're wasting your time. This is the only way you can fight Ragnarök and you know it."

I nodded. "I'm not trying to stop you. I think you're brave, stupid, and heroic, and you're right." I pulled the golden fruit from my pouch and offered it to him. "But you don't have to die."

He stared at it. "You need that."

I shook my head. "No. This is why I took it in the first place. It was all to save you."

He flinched, but reached out and ran his fingers over mine as he took the fruit. He didn't let go of me. The rainbow specks glimmered, hope flickering in the backs of eyes that should have been chestnut brown and warm. "I'm not worthy of all that you do for me."

I pushed the fruit at him. "Just take it. We don't have much time."

I slipped my fingers away from his and he lifted the fruit to his mouth. The golden skin glowed against his lips… then he took a bite.

Light exploded and Ymir dashed behind me to avoid the worst of the blow. I flared my wings to protect her. I didn't know what the fruit of Yggdrasil would do. All I knew was that it was power and raw life. It would give Will a chance against the lava that would come bearing down on him when he went to free the Gulltop.

He handed the fruit back to me with a small piece missing. He'd barely taken a bite and tiny teeth marks glowed around the wounded fruit. I lifted it again, about to tell him that he should eat the whole thing, but he dashed around me, faster than he should have been.

Gold blurred through the corridors, and then Will was gone.

Time distorted and pain snapped through my spine.

"You did it," Ymir breathed. "You changed the timeline."

I clenched my fists against the fresh waves of pain as I struggled to stay in one piece. It felt as if tiny claws raked against the inside of my ribcage, threatening to tear me apart. "What'll happen to us?" I was the product of my timeline. Would I simply cease to exist?

I looked too Ymir, but she blurred. My vision distorted as dizziness swept over me, and then my body began to disintegrate. Bits of ash ran down my fingers and burning agony swept through me.

I'd been through this before. This was how I'd felt when the Einherjar sent me to earth. When I'd shed my Immortal skin in favor of a mortal one. Except, this time I wasn't getting a human body. I was merging with my Immortal self in this new present.

I blinked a few times, readjusting as I found myself on the platform with the screen around me gone black. Baldr had just informed me that I was a god in my own right, capable of commanding Ragnarök and feeding off of its power. I could give life where I'd taken it, the trait of any god. Life was like any other energy in the universe. It could never be destroyed... only transformed.

When Wills screams rocked my body and the caverns trembled, I ran after him just like I had before. When I slammed into Mr. Jefferson, he tried to tell me about Will, but I didn't need to hear it this time. I knew exactly where to go.

I sped down the halls and found the chamber with lava freshly drained and the Gulltop lopsided, ready for me once again.

But this time Will had survived the onslaught. His blackened body trembled on the edge of one of the massive drains. I ran through the broken diamond wall and to his side. Had I saved him, only to watch him suffer?

He lifted a hand and tried to speak. No words came out.

"Will?" I asked, my voice breaking.

His hand fell to the black rune across my knuckles, and then I knew what I had to do.

I absorbed the remains of Will's soul, but I didn't draw him into myself like I had before. This time I held him in one piece and carried him as carefully as a breakable porcelain statue in the heart of my mind.

I opened a portal through space and time, using the lasting power of Will's sacrifice to fuel the trick. I only needed a small jump. I didn't need the Bifrost to step between the folds of space, not when I had the fuel.

I only used a sliver for the small step to the surface of

Muspelheim. I walked out into the center of the great city of Valkyries. Golden spires towered all around me and a shocked group of traitors stared back at me.

Skuld… and my undead sisters.

They came at me in a wave of snarls and teeth. That's exactly what I wanted. Now that I knew what I was capable of, I had no qualms about feeding on the tattered remains of their souls.

I drew in the darkness and the first wave fell around me in a pile of ash. The rest of the army stopped in their tracks, halting at the dusty circle.

I ignored them while they cursed and snarled. They were all made of grief and torment and they had no concept of right or wrong. A moment ago, I was their enemy, but now that I'd decimated their comrades, I was something to be feared.

The sacrifice of shadow swirled in the air and I did something I'd only done once before. I opened up to it. Without even knowing what I was doing, I'd created bodies before. At the time, they'd remained empty shells, decoys to throw at the bottom of the lake and get the humans off our trail.

This time I recreated Will's flesh down to the finest detail. I imagined how he was before all of this. He was a swimmer, lean and strong, but with the growing form of a human that would eventually age and die. I hated the thought of Will dying, but that was the cycle of life and how it was meant to be. He would live a full life, and then he would be free to return to Yggdrasil.

I settled a forcefield around us to keep out the worst of the radiation and heat while I did my work. I wasn't going to give him the curse of a Valiant's form. He'd never wanted Immortality. Will's flesh formed from the ash, swirling and writhing until it formed an arm, then a leg, then the slow embodiment that was the mortal shell to his soul.

His spirit rested inside my mind and carefully I pulled it out and pushed it into the new body I'd formed. It wasn't that I'd created life, but I felt a sense of accomplishment and awe when he drew in a deep breath, the first in his new body.

He stood, and I'd expected him to be shaky as a newborn. Instead his thighs flexed and his muscular arms wrapped around me, embracing me as he drew in another breath.

His low voice sounded like music against my ears. "Val. I'm alive."

FULL CIRCLE

$\mathcal{I}$ was so amazingly happy in that moment that I nearly forgot there was an army of Skuld and undead Valkyries flanking us. Finally, one arrived that wasn't afraid of me.

Sam snarled and marched up to us. She glowed with the fires of Muspelheim, but she wasn't like I remembered her. She jerked in ungraceful movements as if her muscles were too stiff and flesh rotted off her bones, only for the wound to burn with cinders and knit back together. I realized that it was the power of Ragnarök that kept her alive.

"Sam?" I asked, wondering if I could reason with her.

She growled a low, guttural sound that wasn't even close to a word.

"I don't think that's Sam anymore," Will whispered as he covered himself, realizing that he was naked. "Good thing, or she'd be making fun of me right now. Naked in the middle of a Valkyrie city surrounded by ghosts. Talk about nightmares."

I waved him into silence. "Just be grateful you're alive."

Sam stalked us in a slow circle, looking as if she were debating the best way to hack into my skull and eat my brains.

I didn't have time for this. I'd saved Will, but now I needed to save Tyler, the Einherjar, and everyone inside of it. I glanced up at the haze of red clouds that blotted out the sky. The Einherjar was up there, somewhere, and I could only hope that Tyler had been able to hold on. If he'd fallen, I wasn't sure if even the Gulltop could save him while he'd been in the middle of distorting the space-time web in order for me to get to Muspelheim.

"Get out of my way," I barked, not caring anymore if this thing that impersonated Sam could understand me. I summoned my spear in a flash of heat and pointed it at her. She snarled at it. "I'm like Baldr. If you serve him because he can control Ragnarök, then you should serve me."

To my surprise, Sam grinned as if I'd said something hilarious. The edge of her lip lifted, revealing teeth and bone.

That's when I felt it. A heartbeat thrummed through my body and nausea made me buckle over.

"You're not ready," Sam whispered, the words barely audible through the garble of her broken vocal cords.

Will steadied me, but hissed as the raw heat of my flesh left his skin blistered. "What's she talking about? Val? What's wrong?"

It felt like I'd eaten something bad, then multiplied that feeling by a thousand. Baldr had opened my eyes that I could feed on the darkness... but then I realized, wasn't that exactly what the Norn did?

Shadows sprouted across my arms like weeds bursting

through my flesh and I cried out. I gathered a fistful of the sprouts and ripped them from my body. There was no way I was going to get this far and turn into a Norn!

"Not ready," Sam hissed again. She cocked her head to the side as if listening, then nodded. "He sends you home."

I didn't have time to ask who "he" was. The glittering black fingers of Ragnarök that lingered on the horizon zeroed in on the city and dove down straight for us.

I held my forcefield tight. I wasn't going to let it be broken and the inhospitable atmosphere rip Will up from the inside. I'd worked so hard to get him back into a mortal body. I wasn't going to let anything take that away, not even Ragnarök.

But the fingers weren't trying to destroy us. Darkness enveloped the sphere I held around us until only my internal flame illuminated our surroundings. I knelt and held onto Will. Nausea and pain continued to streak through me, but Ragnarök's presence was... actually soothing.

I felt the slip of time and space underneath us shift, then we were falling, and even though I should have been terrified, I held onto Will's hand, and he held onto mine. No matter what happened, we were together.

***

Ragnarök spit us out onto a dusty trail in the middle of a forest that looked suspiciously reminiscent of Central Park.

When the darkness retreated, leaving us only with silver

moonlight filtering through the trees, I heard laughter in the distance.

Human laughter.

Still holding onto Will, I slowly stood. My wings flared out of instinct to keep me balanced.

I couldn't believe it. We were back on Earth.

Will released a long breath. "Well, that was unexpected."

I released him as I took a few steps and then paused. "Yeah." I tilted my head and listened, but there was no sound of Baldr's laughter or any sign that this was a trick. "Why would he send us back to earth? He totally had us." And whatever he'd done, he'd soothed the nausea winding in my stomach that would have turned me into a Norn.

"Who?" Will asked.

I turned and almost laughed. He was still naked. I blushed and looked away. "Uh, Will."

He looked down. "Oh, crap." He covered himself. "Well aren't we the pair. A naked dude with a Valkyrie. We're not going to stand out at all."

Leaves rustled and glittered, and then I heard another kind of laugh. The tinkering joy of a Huldra. I ignored the fluttering of my heart hoping that it would be Jules. The unwanted image of her lifeless on the ground shoved itself to the front of my mind.

Brushing aside the painful memories, I followed the trail of glitter and motioned for Will to follow. One of Dalia's Huldra, whether they could be trusted or not, was a better guide than hoping I could find my way out on my own. To my relief, the flutter of the leaves led us straight to the luxury condo we'd stayed in what seemed like a lifetime ago.

The door buzzed at my touch, opening and allowing us in.

"What do you think?" I asked when we entered into the familiar room. The fireplace was just as I remembered it, surrounded by a jumble of pillows enticing for a group to just sit and talk. My heart yearned for those days when it'd been all of us. Tyler, Will, and Jules. I hadn't appreciated having them all together, but now I missed it.

Will closed the door behind us. "I think Dalia realizes she chose the wrong side."

I hummed thoughtfully and flexed my wings, grateful to finally be able to properly stretch them. I wouldn't be able to go for a leisure flight around here, not without activating Thor as it wiped thousands of human minds after being spotted. Even if my mother wasn't around to enforce it, the A.I. program would still keep tabs, especially during Ragnarök. The last thing my mother needed was for one of her worlds to go on full-out panic during the end of the world. That would only feed Ragnarök more and make it more difficult to imprison.

"If Dalia has really switched sides, then I want to talk to her," I said.

I turned when there was no response, finding Will had already disappeared down the hall. All I saw was the flash of a handsome male buttocks before he disappeared into a room. I grinned, shamelessly filing that memory away for when I was feeling down.

Will returned shortly in customary jeans and a loose fitting Tee. He smiled his warm, sensual smile. "Why're you looking at me like that?"

Happiness bubbled out of me like a fountain and I had to

keep my emotions in, lest they seep out as flame and singe the carpet. After everything we'd been through, Will was right here in front of me, mortal, and free of the Norn's curse.

It wasn't over, not by a long-shot. Ragnarök was still out there and once it was done with Muspelheim, I knew Baldr would have no qualms about letting it destroy this world. I didn't want to turn into a Norn myself, and until I figured out how to feed on darkness without that happening, Baldr and Ragnarök were still my greatest threat.

"I'm just glad you are finally human again," I said. Effortlessly I moved to squeeze his arm, but he flinched the instant I grazed his skin. "Oh, sorry."

His mood turned sour. "When I imagined getting my human body back, I didn't expect you to be in your Valkyrie form. I can't even touch you." He ghosted his fingers over my arm, then made a fist. "Do you think you can do for yourself what you did for me?"

I slowly shook my head. "Not any time soon. You saw what happened. When I fed on darkness, I almost became…" My words drifted. I couldn't say it out loud.

He grimaced and slumped into the sofa across from the fireplace. "You would become like my mother."

I curled up on the floor and hugged a pillow to my chest, releasing it when it began to smolder. With a sigh, I released the heat that wanted to get out and directed it to the fireplace. Long dead logs engulfed in a flame that burst to life.

I'd never imagined my future with Will to be anything permanent. But now that I was here, living this new present with him, I wasn't sure what was going to happen next.

COMING OUT OF THE CLOSET

I insisted that Will go to bed, but he refused to leave me alone. I wasn't going to leave the fireplace. My emotions were a wreck and the metal grate full of flame was the only safe spot I could release the embers dying to get out of me. I wasn't on Muspelheim anymore and I had so much pent-up energy inside of me. I thought of Elena and Michael. She'd lost her wings, but not the flame that lived in her heart. She'd become something closer to human than I certainly was. I recalled her sitting on the couch sipping tea.

I glanced through the room, sweeping my gaze over a sleeping Will on the couch. Even if he'd refused to leave me, he still had slipped into unconsciousness. Coming back from the dead must have been tiring.

I wandered through the condo and looked for a phone, then laughed. Elena was probably halfway across the world right now. I didn't even know her number.

A low hum brought me out of my thoughts and I frowned. Tilting my head, I heard it again, a buzz that didn't sound mechanical. I followed it into one of the bedrooms. It was coming from the closet.

I was glad the knobs were metal. They wouldn't disintegrate under my touch. I grabbed it and yanked it open, not sure what I was going to find inside.

Instead of a walk-in closet filled with clothes, a familiar room appeared, one with telescopes and a particular immortal with a golden grill for a smile.

"Well, hello dear. Aren't you a sight for sore eyes?"

***

T'd wanted to speak to Dalia, but this was not how I'd imagined it. "Did you seriously just use the Bifrost to teleport to my bedroom?"

Dalia held up a finger. "Actually, it's my bedroom. You're only borrowing it."

Glowering, I stepped inside. Time and space slipped over me like a blanket as I entered the pocket realm of the Bifrost.

"What do you want?" I snapped.

She grinned. "I want what I've always wanted. I'm a simple creature."

She motioned for me to sit across from her desk and I glowered before yanking the seat out and sitting on it. I allowed the heat of Muspelheim to billow from my body, but the chair stood up under the onslaught. I draped my wings over the back and a shower of embers flew across the ground. It didn't surprise me that the Bifrost was Valkyrie-proof. "And what is it that you want?" I asked. "Power?"

She laughed. "Hardly, dear." She leaned onto her elbows

and sighed. "I just want a place my children can be free. Is that too much to ask?"

I narrowed my eyes. The Bifrost shook, sending the telescopes clinking against one another. "What's that all about?" I asked.

She leaned back in her chair and propped her boots up on the desk. "Just Baldr getting a little fussy that I'm talking to you. He thought he was so clever sending you to earth." She winked. "He doesn't want you dead, or turned into a Norn. He wants you to join him."

I crossed my arms. "Well that's not going to happen."

"And I tried to tell him that," she said with a nod. "But you know how he is. He thinks everyone will bow down and worship at his feet." She rolled her eyes. "I'm quite grateful he's no longer at the top of the food chain. Even if he had agreed to spare the Heimdall line, it almost would have been worth extinction to slap him across the face."

A smirk came to my lips and I tried to douse the amusement Dalia always managed to awaken in me. She was likable, but she was dangerous. I wouldn't forget who I was dealing with. "You know, I remember outside your restaurant there were statues of the gods. My memory isn't so good. Who was the fourth one? Was it Baldr?" Technically, after I'd seen what he could do, he was a god by definition. Converting energy and bringing life into being was the only requirement. Dalia, Odin, and Freya had their own strengths that accomplished that task, but Baldr and I, we were wrong. He didn't deserve a statue.

She smiled. "You think I'd have a statue of that creep?" She slammed her hand on the desk and bellowed a laugh. "Hilarious!"

I frowned. "Then who is it?"

Her mood turned somber. "You really don't remember, do you?"

Now I was starting to get impatient. Another boom rocked the Bifrost, but I ignored it. Let Baldr have his little tantrum. "No, I don't."

Her smile mixed with her usual sarcasm and a hint of mournful sadness. "The fourth god is an ideal, a leader among us who doesn't exist yet." She pulled out her phone and shoved it across the desk. "Here. Take a look."

I leaned over and peered at the image that displayed her restaurant. It was an ad online depicting "food to die for," which was a horrible pun. But then I spotted the row of statues and frowned. The last one was a man covered in runes. Hair swept back and even through the stone gaze, I could sense the mischief behind it. "That's Tyler," I said. "You think your son is a god?"

She laughed. "You know, I had that statue built before he was even born." She took the phone back and smiled at the image. "Perhaps one of my visions saw him and was hopeful." A click sounded as she locked the phone's screen and returned the device back to her pocket. "Or perhaps, Tyler will be the one to save us all."

❧

The idea of Tyler coming to my rescue wasn't so far-fetched. He'd done exactly that for me a thousand times. Every rune he bore on his body was a scar of sin he took so that I didn't have to. "So how does he do it?" I asked, half-fascinated and half-mortified. "How does he feed on a soul without turning into something like a Norn?"

I'd only known Valkyries to be able to manipulate the energy of souls, but the Heimdall line was a unique case. They acted as servants to the gods and each had their own skills. I'd met a few of Tyler's brothers on occasion. Now that my memories were returning, I recalled they didn't appreciate one of their own playing bodyguard to a Valkyrie that only put him further at risk. If he gave in to the darkness because of me, he'd turn into something worse than a Norn.

"Tyler is strong," Dalia said, pride dripping from her voice as she swayed her chair back. "As are all of my sons. We're a form of the Jotun, but when I discovered how to manipulate energy and create life, that's when I became a god and the Heimdall became a new race. The Bifrost was given to me by Ymir herself to safeguard. That was back when she trusted me, of course."

I nodded. "Right." Now that I thought about it, Tyler had gone out of his way to make sure I hadn't seen that fourth statue. I frowned. "What does Tyler think of this?"

Her golden teeth flashed as she laughed. She twirled one of her telescopes across her fingers. "He's always been arrogant, but the idea of being a god appalls him. He'd rather 'eat embers,' as he says."

A smile twitched at my mouth at Tyler's phrase. He loved to tell mouthy Valkyries to eat their own embers.

Warmth radiated down my spine as I thought about the Einherjar. "So the alliance with Freya, that was to feed Tyler the souls he needs as one of the Heimdall."

Dalia's smile faded. "He told you?"

I shrugged. "He tried to, but I figured it out. Are all the Heimdall soul-sucking monsters?"

The room darkened and another boom shook the Bifrost, but I had a feeling it wasn't Baldr this time. "My son is no monster."

"No," I agreed. "He was just unfortunate enough to inherit the family trait."

Dalia all but launched at me across the desk. She grabbed a telescope and chucked it at my face. I dodged just in time to catch another in my wing. "You will speak of my son with respect!"

I held up my hands in surrender. The Bifrost was a small enough room as it was without an enraged mother throwing telescopes at me. I rubbed my wing. "Fine, all right." I shook the appendage and worked out the bruise. "Tyler is trapped on the Einherjar, did you know that? Baldr is attacking him and everyone on board." I knew why Baldr didn't want the Einherjar to survive. It was the one force in the universe that held the power—and the people— capable of stopping him. With the strengths of all the gods combined, there was a chance to do the impossible and stop Ragnarök itself. No Ragnarök, no darkness, and no Baldr.

"Why do you think I'm helping you?" she snapped and slammed another telescope on the desk instead of throwing it at me. The lens shattered and glass fell across the desk. "I'm the caretaker of the Bifrost and I can see everything that transpires within a hundred miles of my vicinity. I saw the Skuld and the Valkyrie head straight for him and that human of yours." Her lower lip quivered before she sank her teeth into it. "Do you know how helpless it feels to have the power of space and time at your grasp, but to be unable to help your own son when darkness befalls him?"

I shrank my wings to my back. I knew exactly what it felt like to be unable to help those you loved. "Darkness haunts me," I admitted. "I want this all to end."

She straightened. "Darkness doesn't have to haunt you, my dear. As a Heimdall, I for one know how to turn it into a strength."

KINDRED SOULS

Lessons from Dalia, the goddess of the Bifrost, and a gangster who ruled New York, as well as few select planetary provinces—from her own testimony—led me to believe that we had a fighting chance against Baldr. There was one last thing I needed to stop him, and that was to get Tyler to admit he was a god.

He was going to love that.

I found Will sitting on the edge of the couch when I arrived. He stared into the dying flames and looked pensive with his hands folded as he rested his elbows on his knees. When my wings sent the fire flaring back to life, he finally glanced at me.

"You were gone," he said, his voice raw from either sleep or emotion, I couldn't tell.

I bit my lip. "Yeah, sorry. Dalia paid me a visit."

He frowned. "You should have called for me. We're supposed to be in this together."

I swept past him, careful not to brush my feathers

against his skin, and pulled the drapes aside. I frowned when the fabric blackened under my touch.

Outside, the morning sun cast cheery rays onto an emerald forest that spanned out in a long line between the metallic spires of civilization. Modern sky rises looked almost out of place next to the trees and greenery. "I meant to tell you that I met your mother in Scandinavia."

Will shot to his feet. "What?"

I leaned so close to the glass that the heat of my breath fogged it. "I tried to stop her from dedicating you to the gods."

He came to my side and moved as if to touch me, then curled his fingers away. "When you used the Gulltop, you gave me the Yggdrasil fruit. I wondered what could have happened that you'd allow me to go through with sacrificing myself, even if you knew you could bring me back. But to go back to my first life..." I saw the pain in his eyes. He considered it a betrayal to even think about altering the timeline so that we would have never met.

"She was different, back then. You were sick, and you had a sister who had died before you." The truth spilled out of me like a wave and tears sizzled in my eyes. "I couldn't stop her from dedicating you. I thought that if I did, none of this would happen, and you could have lived a normal human life like you were supposed to." I sniffled and looked at the length of him. He was perfect, just the way he was, but I could sense the darkness running through his veins. I'd caused him so much suffering. Even now, wisps of torment glittered across his skin. "Why are you in so much pain?"

He cornered me against the wall and slammed his fist against it. "Because, Val, I can't touch you. I can't make you stop grieving this life that you wanted for me. I can't do anything."

Helpless. I understood what Dalia meant now, how it felt to see everything that you wanted to fix and being powerless to do anything about it. I matched Will's gaze, relaxing under the familiar chestnut calm of his mortality. "You know," he continued, "when I first realized how I felt about you, it wasn't because I felt a surge of passion or a wave of joy. It was the thought of being without you wrecking my insides until I felt sick. Being apart from you torments me, but I ignore it. I do what I think is right."

He spread his fingers out against the wall and leaned as close as he could. The heat sizzled off my skin and turned his skin pink. His lips hovered over mine and I knew he wanted to crush into me, speak to me with his body when words wouldn't work anymore. But I was a Valkyrie, and he was human. We could never be together and make it work.

His mouth parted, his words crushing me instead. "That's not love, Val. That's duty."

With the sting of his rejection hanging in the air, he shoved off the wall and stormed out of the room. The door closed behind him. He didn't slam it. He simply closed it, and I'd never felt anything so final in all my life.

I expected Will to come home at least by nightfall. I rummaged through the refrigerator and found it stocked with sodas. In the freezer were plenty of dinners to tide a single human over as long as we needed. Until I figured out how to rescue Tyler, I had no plans on resuming my mortal form, as much as I missed frozen spaghetti.

A part of me never wanted to feel what it was to be human again. It was better this way. If Will could touch me, then I'd forget everything we'd just said to each other. I didn't want to forget.

Even though I'd poured myself a carbonated drink and watched the ice swim around in the glass, I didn't sip. The moment I touched it the ice would melt and the soda would turn into a bubbling frothy mess. I knew that Elena had somehow managed to control her heat, but she'd spent lifetimes on earth acclimating to this world. I didn't have that kind of time.

When Will finally returned, I snapped my head up and blinked at the doorway. He wasn't alone.

I'd just been thinking of the powerful Valkyrie with torn wings, and there she was, smiling at me until I almost didn't recognize her. I'd never seen Elena smile like that, like she was truly happy.

Then I saw why. Behind her stepped out a man and he slipped an arm around her waist before giving her a kiss on the cheek. "Well would you look at that. This guy wasn't nuts after all."

I nearly swallowed my tongue. "...Michael?"

🦇

*A*pparently our little venture through time and space had a little consequence of twenty years passing us by. Ragnarök had such weight and mass, we'd slowed down while the rest of the world had kept spinning.

It boggled my mind that even without the Gulltop, I still had to worry about slipping through time.

Michael hadn't stopped grinning. Even though he wore a different body, I'd recognize that soul anywhere. He'd once been a vegetable and a mind trapped in a loop of permanent nightmare... but something had changed.

That's when I had enough sense to check my leathers. "Where's the fruit of Yggdrasil?" I snapped.

Will plucked it from his jacket and handed it back to me. "About burned off my hand trying to get that."

Rage turned my vision red and Elena stepped between me and Will. "Calm down, sweetie. Will just did a good thing."

I allowed her to drag me away to the kitchen. It seemed to be where humans liked to talk and Elena had been around them long enough to adopt their quirks. Two male voices hummed in the background.

"He stole it," I complained as I sat onto a chair. It creaked with warning under me, but I didn't care if it burned to pieces. "He let me think he wanted to kiss me, and then he just stole it."

Elena smirked, which didn't help my mood. "Sweetie, that boy wants to kiss you more than anyone I've seen. I'm sure he can multitask."

I narrowed my eyes, but the heat drained from me, leaving a low warmth in my chest. "So, how did he find you?" I shifted uncomfortably in my chair. "Don't get me wrong. I'm happy for you. You finally have Michael back."

She beamed. "It's just, it's incredible. I never imagined I'd get to talk to him and he'd know who I was." She reached out and took my hand. I flinched, but then relaxed when I realized she couldn't get burned. She was just as much a Valkyrie as I was. "Will went to Dalia's restaurant and asked for her help to find us. Dalia keeps tabs on all Immortals, especially those like myself."

I raised an eyebrow. "So, there are more out there like Michael?" Perhaps it wasn't so uncommon to break the first law of the Valkyrie.

She nodded. "Yes, and with your help, we can find them and help them like Will helped Michael. It's incredible."

I untangled my fingers from hers and pulled the fruit from my pouch. A slice was missing now, the wound next to the teeth-mark where Will had taken his bite. "Do you know what this is?" I asked.

She folded her hands. "I believe I do. What I don't know is how you got your hands on it."

I tucked it back into my pouch. "I'm a Frigg, remember?"

Her eyes went wide. "You must be a powerful one if you can travel all the way to Yggdrasil and make it back alive."

I told her the whole story, not leaving out the bit that I didn't think I could ever travel to Yggdrasil again. I got the one shot—and we had the one piece of fruit. I couldn't just go squandering it on lost souls, as much as I wanted to.

Elena opened her mouth to protest, but then the table's centerpiece, a vase with a wilted rose, lifted on its own and floated in midair. I stared at it. "Are you doing that?"

She shook her head slowly from side-to-side.

The vase crashed to the table, breaking into splintered pieces and tossing the contents to the ground. I jumped when Michael cleared his throat.

Will grinned. "Turns out Michael has a little secret."

Elena shot to her feet. "You have telekinesis?"

Michael blew her a kiss and she flinched, her hand flinging up to her face. By the look of shock, I suspected he'd just made sure she'd felt that. "You bet I do, and we're going to kick some serious Norn butt. It's about time the tables have turned."

ichael's powers were only the start of the weirdness. What worried me the most was that Will hadn't seemed surprised by Michael's inhuman ability.

When I tried to talk to him about it, he told me that he had to find the others. When I asked him what he meant, he sputtered and said Dalia had told him—but had she?

I paid the Heimdall a visit myself, which revealed that there were three other cases of Valkyries who were exiled and still watched over their charges. Will ventured out, determined to find each one.

Still looking like a freak who'd just walked out of a comic convention, I couldn't leave the condo. I'd never felt so confined in all my life, not even when I'd spent five years training in the caverns of Jotunheim.

Each time Will returned, Yggdrasil's fruit had a little bit less power, and our household grew until everywhere I turned was a friendly face.

The other Valkyries looked similar to Elena. Freya had ripped off their wings and banished them to earth. I would have expected them to hold some sort of resentment against me. I still had my wings even though I'd broken the first law of the Valkyrie, but they weren't like my sisters. They were loving and kind and quick to embrace me as one of their own. That just made everything worse.

The new couples were so amazingly happy to finally be together that their bliss gave no room for sorrow. They'd experienced the horror of Elena and Michael's same situation for lifetimes.

Iris and Paul. They'd been the closest and easiest to find. Dalia had taken Will off to Windsor, one of the provinces of Canada to pick them up. Iris mesmerized me with the way her eyes changed. One green and one a ruby red. Even though she was ancient, she had the body of a fit, but mature thirty-year-old and she claimed she was becoming more human every day. She wanted to age, and I wondered if she was starting to succeed. Most Valkyries looked to be around sixteen to twenty. Her goal had always been to embrace mortality so that one day, she could find a way to free Paul from his torment and join him in the bliss of Yggdrasil. It was a novel concept, but I didn't have the heart to tell her that even if she found a way to become truly mortal, her soul would always belong to Muspelheim.

Nina and Henry. They took Dalia a few tries to locate, as they were buried in the deep lush of the Amazon. Nina prowled like a wild animal, playfully snapping at anyone who dared venture too close to Henry. He encouraged the primal behavior, petting her as if she were a cat. What made her stand out the most was that her eyes weren't red at all, but an aquamarine blue that matched her exotic appearance.

Helena and Daniel. Now they were an even odder pair. Helena sat straight with her hands folded over her knee as she sat across from Daniel. They both reeked of sophistication and wealth. As seemed customary, they challenged each other with a game of poker that no one else was allowed to play. Helena took an elegant finger and slid a chip across the table. Straight out of Vegas, she'd made sure that Daniel had every luxury. What had started as a dancer gig where even a Valkyrie might fit in had turned into a long-term game where she played backdoor poker games and lost just enough hands not to get thrown out of the house.

They were the latest addition to our growing cluster of weirdos, and now that it was all said and done, only a single sliver of Yggdrasil's fruit remained.

Will had taken me aside to return it to me. We'd hardly spoken these last few days while he'd been out on his "field trips."

He held out what was left of the precious fruit. Having saved the final soul on Dalia's list, I suppose he thought he had no use for it anymore. He grimaced, having the nerve to look apologetic that perhaps he'd squeezed all the use out of it.

I snatched the core back from him. I couldn't hold it in anymore. The words spilled out of me on their own as rage glimmered in the backs of my eyes, tingeing my vision red. "I know I'm supposed to understand, or whatever, but I went all the way to Yggdrasil to get this fruit for *you*, not anybody else. I'm not some kind of charity. And not to sound selfish about it, but we still have Ragnarök to worry about." I hadn't told him, but I'd felt its icy fingers growing ever closer to this world. Once it drained Muspelheim dry, there'd be nothing to hold it back. Not even Baldr—no matter how pompous and arrogant he thought he was—could stop a force like that from devouring entire worlds. "None of this matters if we all die."

Will crossed his arms and leaned against the wall. Normally he would have immediately sniped back at me, but he was exhausted, even if he wouldn't admit it. Dark circles under his eyes betrayed how little he'd slept while he'd been off playing hero. Being human again took its toll and as much as he pretended he could keep up, he couldn't fool me.

"Just look at them, Val," he said, his voice gravely, but stern.

I followed his gaze through the thin glass that separated us from the rest of the living room where the odd matchup of Valkyrie and human pairs seemed to all get along. The Valkyries took turns lighting the wood while Nina doused the flames with water, just to see if they could still burn it. The contents of the fireplace sizzled with protest and Nina squealed with delight when she managed to snuff it out. Even though smoke billowed into the room, Henry smiled at her as if she were the most adorable thing in the world.

My new housemates had been cooped up in this condo nearly as long as I had been, but they didn't seem to mind. Even if the other Valkyries had learned how to contain the majority of the supernatural heat in their bodies, they certainly couldn't pass for human. Metallic skin and gorgeous glowing eyes made them stand out, as well as their supernatural grace and beauty that came with being one of Freya's daughters.

"Yes, they seem happy," I admitted, although the edge of my voice made it clear that was irrelevant to this conversation.

Will narrowed his eyes. "Isn't that enough? If you've learned anything from me, it's that I believe in the power of the present."

He was starting to get on my nerves, and he knew it. "News flash," I snapped, "I'm a Frigg. I live in the constant flow of time and space. There is more to the universe than the present. Without the future, you have nothing, and I intend to make sure there's a future for all of us if I can help it."

Will frowned. "I know you're angry."

I tossed the fruit to the ground. It didn't bounce like I'd expect fruit to do. Instead it ricocheted and sent a crack through the tiles. I glanced at the Valkyries and their men and found them watching us now. "I'm not angry. I'm pissed."

Will knelt and picked up the core. His fingers turned pink at its raw heat before he wrapped it in a towel. "I'm sorry I used so much of it. It's just, when I heard there were others like me—"

"It's not about the fruit," I snapped, then lowered my voice, hoping the others couldn't hear me. "I just." I looked down at my hands. The perfectly smooth skin glimmered as embers blazed through my veins. "I don't get why things are like this between us now." I met his gaze, hating how pathetic I sounded. "Is it because you can't touch me?"

He sighed. "I know it's hard. We both misinterpreted what we are to one another."

"*Misinterpreted?*" I squeaked.

"Just hear me out, Val. We thought we were soulmates, that we completed each other just because it hurt so much to be apart, but ever since I took a bite of that fruit…"

My eyes widened. "You lost your feelings for me."

He wouldn't meet my gaze. "I don't think it's that I lost something." His eyes shot up and those chestnut irises met mine, full of hope and longing, but this time he wasn't longing for me. "Our attraction to one other, it's there, I won't deny that." He moved so that he backed me against the glass. My feathers crunched against my back, but I didn't complain as he pressed a hand and leaned so that our breaths mingled. "You're my Valkyrie. I'm your soul. That's our bond to one another, and when you gave me what the Norn took away, you gave me back my freedom."

Pain made my vision blur. I couldn't listen to Will talk this way as if a bite from some fruit could destroy his feelings for me. "Then what about them?" I asked, not caring anymore how my voice grated with the thousand tiny daggers that plunged through my bruised heart.

He watched them and a low murmur of voices resumed as they pretended not to be dying to know what we were talking about. Daniel cheered, having won his latest hand against his mate. "Their bonds are too strong. Those humans have been reborn so many times with nothing but their Valkyrie to guide them that they don't know any other way of life. I won't deny it's something akin to love." He turned to me and stroked away my hair, his skin just far enough away from mine so as not to get burned. "The difference is, Val, your heart doesn't belong to me. It never did."

My stomach twisted and I clutched at it. I wanted to tell him that he was wrong, that I didn't love Tyler, but for some reason my voice wouldn't dare utter those words aloud. "I don't get it," I whispered. "They don't burn anyone who tries to touch them." I met his gaze. "Yet you and I, we burn each other until one of us turns to ash."

He huffed a laugh and I hated how sexy it was. "After a few centuries, I'm sure even a Valkyrie can learn to contain her passion, hide who she is and pretend." He dared to press a kiss against my hair, pulling away with a hiss. "But not you, Val. Never forget who you are."

ALLIES

*D*alia surprised all of us by showing up at our doorstep with a bedazzled telescope in one hand and a giant bottle of wine in the other. She gave me a golden smile as I stood there like an idiot. "Do you always answer the door looking like that?" she asked, her grin only growing wider.

I flared my wings, reluctant to admit perhaps it was pretty stupid to be answering the door, but with so much going on, I forgot that I wasn't human. "That's what Grimhildr is for," I muttered and moved aside so that she could enter. "What brings you here, on foot no less? My closet not good enough for you anymore?"

She laughed. "Ah, don't sound so sour, dear. It's not often that I leave the comfort of the Bifrost. Take honor where honor is due."

"Dali!" Nina screeched and ran on all fours before sweeping the small woman up in her arms.

"You two… know each other?" I asked as I shut the door, more than a little bewildered. "What's an outcast and a

Heimdall got in common?" I grinned, because that sounded like the start to a terrible joke.

Henry followed his mate and laughed. "Well I'll be damned, it's the goddess herself."

Dalia gave him a fond smile, shoving the bottle of wine into my chest before giving his cheek a pinch. "It's a down-right miracle. I can't believe it." She waved in welcome as the rest of the couples entered the room. "Iris and Paul," she said, marveling. "Helena and Daniel." She swept across the room and gave each of them a kiss.

Will stood in the doorway and smirked. "You should just tell her, Dalia, before Val turns this place into an inferno."

I realized that the wine I was holding was starting to boil. Dalia frowned. "Well that's unfortunate, dear. I do prefer my wine chilled."

"Would you care to tell me how you all know each other?"

Dalia smiled. "You know, the way your mother treated her daughters who broke one of her precious laws that she herself couldn't even uphold always baffled me. I took it upon myself to care for them and help them find their mates during the recycle process."

Paul, Henry, and Daniel collectively shivered at the term. Paul gripped his mate's arm. "Tell her not to call it that. She makes it sound less horrendous than it was."

Daniel straightened his bowtie, and it was the only sign that he'd been fazed. "Agreed. You shall never use that term in our presence again."

Dalia rolled her eyes and shoved her way past them. "Fine. But enough chit-chat. I've come here on important business."

Curious, we followed her to the living room. The hearth with flames that never died—not with four Valkyries in the room—illuminated the jeweled telescope that Dalia placed on the floor, the ruby flames sending lights scattering across the polished stones. "I've been saving this one for quite a while. Ever since I started picking up echoes of Ragnarök entering the atmosphere, I knew it was a matter of time before Baldr brought the fight to us."

My wings flared at that. "Ragnarök and Baldr are here?" I wasn't ready to face them. All I had was a lot of anger and a chewed up pit of Yggdrasil's fruit in my pouch.

Dalia nodded and motioned to the telescope. "You're a Frigg. I built this especially for you."

I looked to Will for reassurance. He knelt and gave me an encouraging smile. "What damage can a little telescope do?"

Narrowing my gaze, I glowered. "When it comes to Norse deities, I wouldn't put anything past her."

Dalia might claim to be on our side, but she'd betrayed me before. If Baldr was coming here, I knew I wouldn't put my bets on the Valkyrie who hadn't even washed her hair in three weeks because the water would just evaporate before it got anywhere near her scalp. Not that I needed to bathe… but being on earth without being able to do earthly things just made me feel even more out of place.

Before I had a chance to stop her, Nina crawled over to us and plucked up the telescope. She frowned and turned it over before looking through the eyepiece. "I don't see anything," she complained before tossing it back down onto the carpet. "Must be broken."

Helena waved her away. "That's because you're a Gina,

not a Frigg. The only thing you're good at is making it rain." Nina growled and Helena sighed. "And biting people."

Appeased, Nina smiled. Now that I was getting to know her better, she looked the least like a Valkyrie out of the group. She boasted pointed teeth and her nails were unusually long. I'd just chalked it up to her primal nature, but now that I thought about it, perhaps the reason her nature was primal was because she was a division of Valkyrie I didn't often come across. The Gina weren't permitted to live on Muspelheim. They were the only lineage who revolted against our fiery nature and embraced the opposing element. My mother had once talked about them, looking both fond and melancholy about her distant daughters. "The universe cannot be all fire and heat. There must be balance, and that is why the Valkyrie have the Gina to douse the destruction of our flames when we forget not everything deserves to be burned."

My mother's words made me soften towards Nina. She'd been an outcast long before she'd met her human.

Helena, poised as ever, elegantly extended her arm and offered me the telescope. "Why don't you tell us what you see? I will vouch for Dalia, if that helps to change your mind."

Relenting, I accepted it. "Fine."

Dalia watched me with the intent of a predator as I lifted the eyepiece to my face. Blocking out the watching eyes as best I could, I focused on the end of the scope… and into the swirling black void that ended with the flashing maw of Ragnarök itself.

I saw Baldr, handsome as ever, stepping out onto a platform as he greeted an enormous crowd. I frowned, because as the vision came into focus, I realized that he wasn't on Asgard. The glowing lights and lazy waterfall were part of a sky rise resort just a few blocks down from Dalia's condo. I'd seen it on the television being advertised as the "party to be." I'd just flipped the channel every time, uninterested in a social event with a bunch of humans who'd freak out the moment they saw me.

But in this vision, the humans all wore elegant wings and painted themselves with glittering, metallic layers until the more graceful among them might pass as a Valkyrie if I didn't look too close.

What was Baldr up to?

A single dark spot in the vision caught my attention and I focused on it. My magic worked with the telescope to bring the point at the far end of the venue closer. I drew in a shocked gasp when the darkness cleared, revealing Tyler chained to the platform. He strained against the cuffed restraints, jerking when a flash of glittering black swept through his body like lightning. He cried out as the darkness pierced through his skin, ripping off one of the runes he wore on his flesh.

The crowd was oblivious of him, the air alight with the power akin to Grimhildr's soft reprogramming. There wasn't anyone suffering on the platform. There wasn't a dark form ripping Tyler to shreds before their very eyes. There was only fun and dancing and drinks.

I lowered the telescope and a wave of dizziness swept over me. The hairs on my arms stood on end as my powers as a Frigg hummed. I hadn't even realized I'd been using them. "There's going to be a party."

Iris leaned forward, mesmerizing with her mismatching green and red eye. "The one that's been playing on TV?"

Nina bounced up and down. "Does saving the world include going to a party? Because I'm in."

Helena frowned at Nina. "You really are a Gina, completely hopeless and incapable of taking anything seriously. You don't even know what this means, do you?"

I blinked at her. "Are any of us supposed to know what this means?"

Helena rolled her eyes and waved over her mate.

Daniel seemed to calm her and had she still had wings, they would have settled against the agitation that lifted from her face when he was around. He wrapped an arm around her shoulders, seeming to know the calming effect he had on her. "I think what Helena is trying to say is that Baldr's going to try and set a trap." He gave me a wink. "He didn't count on you having allies."

IT'S JUST A NECKLACE

J'd been both jealous and suspicious of my new roommates ever since Will had started bringing them in. They all seemed so happy and content, whereas I just felt left out and confused.

The guys, especially, were growing into themselves after lifetimes of living a terrible curse. Where Michael had telekinesis, the others began to display signs of supernatural gifts as well. I wasn't sure if it was because they'd tasted Yggdrasil's fruit, or because they'd been freed from a centuries-long curse. Whenever I approached Will about it, he managed to change the subject.

Paul opened up first. I liked him and how easy he was He was older than the rest of the group, seeming to have been an oddity with the Norn's curse. He'd met Iris in his late thirties, which also would explain why she looked a bit older to me. Perhaps she was so closely bonded to her mate, she's matched the age of when he was supposed to die.

It still baffled me that all of these men would have died, over and over again, if it hadn't been for Will. As Paul gave me a friendly smile, guilt wafted over me, because I would have given them all up if it'd meant Will would have been safe.

"You've been quite distant," he remarked. We reclined on chairs that looked over the city, resting on a long balcony with the soft breeze slipping through my hair. It was refreshing to be outside. The iron chair beneath me managed my heat and I tried to concentrate on the wind, allowing it to sweep away the worst of my embers. "I just recently lost my mortal body," I said.

He nodded knowingly. "My memories started to return after Will fed me the fruit." He twisted, revealing a long scar along his neck that I hadn't noticed before. "This was given to me when Iris lost her body." He covered it up again with the long layered sweaters he seemed to prefer. Now I knew why. "I've kept it as a birthmark through every life since. It was a burn from one of her feathers when Freya cut off her wings."

I grimaced. "You were there for that?"

He laced his fingers and the only evidence that recalling these memories bothered him was the twitch at his jaw. "Iris should have reaped me during that life, but she didn't. She spared me, and then she broke the Norn's curse." He waved away the memories as if they were a stench that lingered in the air. "Anyway, you can guess the rest. Iris was banished from her homeworld and doomed to watch me turn into a vegetable over and over again. All the while trying to live on a planet incompatible with her nature."

I frowned. Even though this planet didn't have molten lava spewing all over the place—for the most part—I wouldn't call it incompatible. "I find it quite nice, actually."

He gave me a weak grin. "I didn't mean the atmosphere. I meant the people. If Iris ever slipped up, Thor would show up and wipe everyone's memories. Even people she'd turned into friends. When I would turn forty years old, that's when I was slated to die or turn into a vegetable. Sometimes I'd take my own life because I knew it was coming. I didn't have the memories, but my heart knew. Other times I'd let the end come, and then she'd have to suffer until I died of old age." He ground his teeth before continuing. "She's had to endure so much worse suffering than I ever did. If she wanted any sort of friendships to get through those rough times, she had to hide who she was, on top of everything else."

I pressed my lips together. "How?"

Taking that as his cue, he struggled to his feet, and I realized his birthmarks weren't just for show, but lasting deformities that caused him pain. "I usually hide it better than this. I must be tired." He gave me a wink. "I'll send Iris in. She'll be glad to teach you, just as she's taught me."

He opened the glass door and called for his mate. She came to him in a flutter of smiles and soft kisses. "Paul. I hope you've been kind to Valerie."

He smiled and cupped her face, giving her a kiss. "Of course." He slipped inside and ushered her out onto the balcony. "Now you two have your girl talk." He jabbed a thumb over his shoulder. "I'm going to play a game with Daniel and wipe that smug smile off his face. He thinks he's some poker god. It's time that someone give him a dose of humility."

I thought Paul was joking around, until I spotted the

wicked grin on his face. He had a trick up his sleeve he wasn't telling us about.

"Oh dear," Iris said as she rested her elbows on the rail. "He's going to get us in trouble, isn't he?"

I couldn't help but be put at ease. Iris, with her joyful smile—as if she'd gained the whole world overnight—which, now that I thought about it, is basically what had happened. She'd been living a nightmare for gods knew how long.

Her smile dimmed and she looked back out over the city. "So, this party. What do you think of it?"

I got up and joined her as we leaned along the rail. My wings swayed behind me. My feathers grazed her shoulder, then I jerked it back with a grimace. "Oh, sorry, are you okay?"

She laughed and brushed away the ash, revealing flawless skin. "A little touch of home isn't going to hurt me."

I stared at her shoulder where I'd burned off the edge of her blouse. "I feel like a walking inferno. I'm not used to everything around me being so... delicate."

She gave my arm a squeeze and I relaxed. I'd nearly forgotten how much I'd missed touch, just a quick embrace or something as simple as a comforting gesture. "Are you committed to walking into Baldr's trap? Because that's exactly what this party is."

Images of Tyler being drained of his life up on a platform for everyone to see made my stomach churn. "I can't just leave Tyler defenseless." I hadn't told anyone about what I'd seen, but there was something about Iris' softness and friendly bi-colored gaze that made me want to open up to her.

"Tyler," she repeated the name and her brows furrowed. "Why does that name sound so familiar?"

I couldn't remember Iris, but Tyler was a lot older than me. There was no telling what kind of trouble he'd gotten into before he'd become a Valiant. "He was my guardian for a long time. He went by the name 'Tyr.' Before that, he was working under Dalia as a Heimdall."

Her eyes went wide, giving me a glimpse of the silver ring that surrounded her irises. I laughed, because now I understood where she got her name. "I remember now. I met him once when Dalia first found me." Her gaze unfocused as she dug up the ancient memories. "He went by Tyr back then, too. He was the first to help me understand the darkness that powers my sisters. It helped me understand that my suffering could ease Paul's pain. I'm grateful to him."

I raised an eyebrow. "What is it that he showed you?"

She propped her hands on her hips. "He showed me a nifty trick that you're going to need to learn, because if you're really going to this party, we can't have you walking around a crowded venue in your true Valkyrie form."

I frowned. "But it's an angel costume party. The telescope showed me that. I thought the whole point of Baldr's trap was so that I wandered around a crowded venue in my Valkyrie form where he can easily spot me."

Iris shook her head. "We can't do much about your wings and beauty, but that's not what I'm talking about."

Before I could correct her that she was far more beautiful than I could ever be, she tore up a napkin and sprinkled it over my arm. It immediately caught fire and the remaining ash drifted to the ground.

"Oh." She had a point. The moment I bumped up against someone, I'd give them third-degree burns, and any chance of saving Tyler would go up in flames, along with anyone who ventured too close to me.

"As you've seen, we outcasts have learned how to suppress our natural form."

As Iris continued on with the technicalities of how to suppress Muspelheim's raw heat that ran in my blood, I couldn't help but think of what Will had said. I shouldn't deny who and what I was, but if it meant saving Tyler, wasn't it worth it?

"Is it reversible?" I asked. If I did this, I wanted to be able to return to Muspelheim. I didn't belong on earth anymore. Will and I were over, that much was apparent. If I managed to save the universe from the clutches of Ragnarök, I wanted to return to my old life—with some improvements, of course. I hadn't thought too much beyond saving the universe, but as a Frigg, the future was always on my mind. I could teach my sisters how to use their powers without reaping souls. Perhaps I could even find a way to reroute suffering that already existed in the universe and help Freya continue to grow her army while being able to finally put an end to the Norn. I knew the necessity of military might, so I would not deny my mother her daughters. Even if I managed to defeat Ragnarök, Baldr was going to be a permanent, Immortal thorn in my side. I never wanted to be unprepared for him again.

Iris bit her lip before replying to my earlier question. "I'm afraid it's a permanent alteration. This isn't a mortal skin you can just shed. This is your true self that you must change on a fundamental level."

"I know why you did it," I said, my voice lowering. I glanced through the doors and spotted Paul at the table with Daniel. I sensed something supernatural humming through the air and Paul grinned before turning over his cards. Daniel's face flushed red. He opened his mouth to speak, but the glass used in Dalia's condos was akin to one of Ymir's inventions and I couldn't hear a thing. Paul threw his head back with a laugh.

Iris sighed as she watched her mate thoroughly enjoy himself. "He's my everything. When I met him, I just couldn't imagine going back to Muspelheim. I couldn't pretend that reaping a soul was a necessary evil. I'd done it for a long time, but when I met Paul, I just couldn't go through with it."

"Was it love?" I found myself asking. I desperately needed to know if what Will and I had shared was just my imagination, or if he was pushing me away.

She squeezed my arm again. "You know, at first I think it was just our bond, the one that forms between a Valkyrie and her soul. But over time... love grew to replace what we'd both lost." Her gaze flicked to Will who sat at the fireplace with Henry and Michael. Michael used his powers to hover one of the burning logs while Nina clapped her hands. Henry ruffled her hair and even if he hadn't shown signs of his powers yet, he seemed quite content. "You and Will have something, but I think he knows how you feel about Tyler. He's not the kind of guy to stand in the way of what you two had before he was in the picture."

I startled and pulled away from her. "What do you mean? Tyler and I—"

She laughed, the sound musical and gentle on the cool

breeze. "I didn't know who your heart belonged to, but it was obvious you've been pining away for some boy out there." She grinned. "Don't worry, sweetheart. We're going to get Tyler back." She offered her hand. "You just have to be willing to have a little faith."

❧

The process to douse the sharp edge of being a Valkyrie wasn't as hard as I'd imagined. All I had to do was rip off my necklace.

I gripped the locket. I'd hardly given it a single thought except for when my mother had used it to remind me I was still under her scrutiny. It burned under my touch, the core of my heat resting inside it.

I'd never questioned that it didn't have a clasp, or that I never took it off. I'd slipped it under any blouse I wore as a mortal, and it had its own space underneath my battle leathers when I was in my Valkyrie form. As a human, it'd kept me grounded, kept all of my Valkyrie's heat strapped safe inside it for when I would shed my mortal skin.

But now... now I gripped it as if I held on for dear life. "I don't know if I can do it," I whispered.

All of the Valkyries had come out onto the balcony when they'd notice embers erupt across my wings. The guys stayed inside and made themselves busy, pretending not to notice that I'd gone into full crises mode.

"You just gotta yank it," Nina said helpfully, jumping up and down with excitement.

Helena glowered at her. "Don't rush her. She has to make

the same decision we all did. Even you had a necklace once, even if you didn't live on Muspelheim."

Nina rolled her eyes. "I ripped that thing off so fast. Being a Gina sucked. It's all 'be one with water and fire' my friends," she said, wiggling her fingers. "I got out of there and headed straight for the closest forest. It was a bit of a jog... but can't say I regretted it." She grinned. "Henry was a missionary, you know that? He thought I was some savage that needed his lectures." She winked. "He's lucky he's cute."

As much as I wanted to hear more about Nina's history, Elena gripped my hands. My locket burned underneath my fingertips.

I gazed up into her ruby-rimmed irises. "I'm afraid I'll lose everything," I admitted in a low whisper. If I gave up the deepest part of me just for a chance to save Tyler, what if I was wrong? What if I lost any power to save him just like Baldr wanted, and then Ragnarök devoured the world, all because I acted rashly?

"You're overthinking it," Elena said. "No one is going to make you do anything you don't want to do, and if you ask it of us, we'll go after Baldr ourselves. You don't have to do a thing."

Immediately I shook my head. I couldn't send them off to face Baldr alone. He was a Frigg... just like me. I was the only one who could face him and make it out alive.

"No. This is something I have to do." I closed my eyes and tightened my grip around my necklace. Elena pulled away, but then her hand rested on my arm. Another touch grazed my skin, until all the Valkyries gave me their support with their touch on my blazing skin.

I drew in a deep breath, and then I tore the necklace off my body.

*T*he cascade of unbelievable cold that flooded in to replace the gaping wound in my soul made me gasp.

My sisters gave a collective shudder, but didn't yank away as if they'd known this part was coming.

"Fight through it," Elena offered.

"We're here for you," Iris added.

I opened my eyes and my breath frosted the air and my teeth chattered. I'd never been so cold in all my life. "W-when does t-this pass?" I asked, my jaw nearly clacking off my face as I tried to speak.

They held on tight, offering me what meager warmth they had to give. "Just a few seconds," Nina said through gritted teeth, and at first I thought she was trying to comfort me, but when she dug her nails into my skin I realized she was talking to herself.

When the sensation of icy daggers passed, leaving me dizzy, the Valkyries helped me inside.

"Make a spot on the sofa," Helena said, barking orders and making sure that the guys adjusted the pillows to perfectly hug my body as they set me down.

Darkness faded in and out of my vision as my consciousness threatened to collapse, then one more familiar touch caressed my cheek.

I fluttered my eyes open to find Will smiling down at me. "Rest, Val. We'll be right here when you wake up."

THE UNKNOWN

For the first time in… ever, I slept in a dreamless sleep. As a Valkyrie, we slept just like mortals did, but as a Frigg I dreamed of different layers in time. A reoccurring dream trapped me in the pits of Muspelheim with gushing lava spewing into a giant cavern, likely a place I'd found myself in when I'd gotten lost playing with Billy in Jotunheim.

Tonight I didn't have my necklace to feed me the constant fuel of my race, and I realized that the fires of Muspelheim didn't come naturally to the Valkyrie. We were Freya's weapons, forged with the hottest of flames.

Without her oppressive guidance, I was left with what I was on my own, which was a ball of determination and emotion, and the Immortal drive of a Frigg scorned.

I awoke to the scent of coffee and waffles. A human breakfast if I'd ever smelled one, but my stomach surprised me with a gurgle of protest that I wasn't jumping off the couch and devouring everything there was to eat right now.

Groaning, I sat up and clutched at my head. In spite of

Will's promise, exactly no one was waiting for me when I woke up. Well, Nina was curled in a ball in front of the fireplace, but by the slow rise and fall of her chest, and her slack-jawed posture assured me that nothing short of an explosion was going to move her from that spot.

Feeling sore and stiff, I wobbled to the kitchen and leaned against the doorframe. Everyone had crammed inside, crowding around the bar to find a task to prepare the feast.

Iris spotted me first, her bi-colored gaze flashing with excitement. "She's awake!"

I groaned when they shouted. "Not so loud," I complained. "It feels like I got hit with a boulder."

I flinched away when Will came to my side and moved to take my arm. My feathers brushed against his face and for a moment I watched him, horrified, just waiting for his beautiful features to scab over with blisters, but nothing happened. Instead he swatted away my feathers with a laugh. "Don't be skittish. You're safe now."

Feeling sheepish, I took his offered hand and let him guide me to the closest stool. Daniel shoved a plate full of delicious food in front of my face. "The girls say you become a little bit mortal when you take off the necklace. That means you need to eat."

Without even asking, I grabbed a fork and shoved half a waffle into my mouth. I groaned. It was so unbelievably delicious.

He slid a bottle of maple syrup. "It's even better with this."

Murmuring my thanks around a mouthful of food, I popped off the cap and doused my waffles with the goop my memories said would be quite sweet and indeed scrumptious. Another mouthful fulfilled that promise and my toes curled.

"How are you feeling?" Will asked.

I tore my gaze away from my food and realized that the entire room had been watching me gorge myself. I swallowed my final mouthful and dabbed away the crumbs with a napkin. It was nice to be able to use napkins again. "Other than starving and willing to eat my own arm, pretty good." Guilt washed over me. Here I was, indulging, meanwhile Tyler was out there somewhere as Baldr's prisoner. Was he making him suffer even now, or would he save that for the party?

"What day is it?" I asked, suddenly worried I might have slept through the whole thing.

"Relax," Elena said, pushing a glass of orange juice at me. "Gather your strength. The party's tonight."

Another waffle fell onto my plate and I looked up to see Michael grinning at me.

"Do you think she'll be ready?" Helena asked, always practical, as she gave Elena a raised brow. "She slept two days while she was undergoing the change."

"I'm fine," I growled before stabbing my waffle with my fork. Less talking. More food.

Nina joined me with her own plate as she happily ate with her hands. She opted for a plate full of oranges. "I just love fruit," she commented as she split a peel and the scent hit me right in the gut, making me think of Sam.

I continued to eat, but slower this time. Will gave me a pensive look, but I ignored him. I'd already been through so much, and now I could never go back to Muspelheim.

For the first time in my life, I didn't know what the future might hold.

*M*ichael had turned on the television and flipped through the channels, only to find all of them talking about Baldr's party.

"You sure he doesn't have a hacked version of Grimhildr?" Helena asked to no one in particular. She sat cross-legged on the couch and frowned at the screen that glowed over the mantle.

Nina, seeming to have formed a bond with Helena, swatted at her ankle—at least as much as Henry would allow. Her mate wrapped his arms around her until she squealed and finally relented, falling into him with a contented growl.

"Why don't you tell us?" Daniel asked Paul with a scowl. "You're the one who can read minds."

Paul grabbed his chest in mock-surprise. "Whatever do you mean?"

Daniel crossed his arms and joined his equally serious mate on the couch. "No one beats me at poker. That's the only way you could have possibly won."

"Shh," I hissed and grabbed the remote from Henry as I turned the volume up.

Abnormal weather reports black-out all over the skies as a strange phenomenon means stargazers will need to take a night off.

The serious reports turned to encouragement that said

stargazers should attend Baldr's party. I scoffed and turned off the TV.

"Hey," Michael complained and the remote flung out of my grip of its own accord. He caught it in midair and grinned. "I wasn't finished watching."

"No, Val's right," Will said, standing and offering me his hand. "It's time to make our game plan."

We tallied up our strengths. Paul could read minds and tell us who was working for Baldr and who wasn't. Michael could follow me and react the fastest, taking any weapons out of enemy hands with a mere thought. The other Valkyries would attend, garbed with their own faux-wings Dalia had so kindly contributed. We didn't tell her that Tyler was the star of the show, or else she might have insisted on coming herself—and ruining any efforts at subtlety.

"I appreciate the help," I began, making my third attempt to go it alone. "You don't need to help me, none of you do." I stood at the door with Dalia's outfit for me, something closer to my Valkyrie leathers that hugged me. The gold trim around the waistband was soft against my fingertips and the flowing folds of the dress hugged my thighs all the way down to my heeled boots. Not the best wear for fighting, but it helped me fit in at a human party.

Nina propped her hands on her hips and smiled, although it was more of a show of pointed teeth. "You gave me Henry back. If you think I'm letting you walk into that place alone, you're a neon frog."

When I gave Henry a raised brow, he waved me away. "Don't ask. She liked to pounce on the poisonous frogs back home and 'test her mettle.'" He scooped her up in his arms and gave her a squeeze. "Regardless, Nina has a point. You gave us our lives back, but we know it's not over yet. That black-out the humans are talking about is Ragnarök, isn't it?"

I hesitated, but all eyes were on me. I nodded.

Helena adjusted one of her fake wings, fussing with Daniel to stop touching it. "Then let's get going." She brushed away invisible dust and then gave me a smile. "Where I come from, fashionably late isn't a thing. You're just late."

Filtering out the door and getting hit by New York's chill air reminded me that I wasn't a daughter of Muspelheim anymore. I shivered and wrapped my feathers around myself. When I noticed Will shivering too, I opened one wing and drew him into the cocoon of warmth.

We bypassed the limo that Dalia had waiting for us. I preferred walking, and I wasn't interested in facing the end of one of her telescopes. If she wanted to spy on us, she'd have to do it from a safe distance. Just the fact that we hadn't heard from her cemented my theory that Dalia couldn't see past Ragnarök's shadows. Tyler was unreachable, even to a goddess and that should have scared me, but I felt like I finally had my head on straight. No matter what happened, I was doing the right thing.

Will's shivers eased as we walked together. He matched my stride and my wing brushed up against his back. The nerves were sensitive, and I wouldn't allow myself to get this close to just anyone, but Will wasn't just anyone. No matter our falling out, I cared deeper about him than I'd ever thought possible.

"What do you think Baldr will try to do, once you're inside, I mean?" he asked.

I didn't know if he was just trying to make conversation or if he was concerned, but there was no sense in lying to him. "He's going to try and bait me with Tyler."

His eyes widened and if it hadn't been from the encouraging shove of my wing, he would have stopped in his tracks. "He's got Tyler?"

I nodded. "He must have breached the Einherjar." I didn't know what that meant for my parents, but if the ancient Norse gods hadn't been able to stop Baldr from coming to earth, then I didn't want to think of what might have happened to them.

There'd been an entire army of Skuld bearing down on the Einherjar when I'd gone to Muspelheim. I shouldn't have abandoned Tyler there to fend for himself, but he'd ordered me to go. There hadn't been any time and Ragnarök was still my greatest threat—at least, I'd thought it was. Now I was beginning to question that. If Ragnarök could be controlled, then it mattered more who was at the helm.

The ground beneath my feet seemed to jump to a low bass that rumbled the streets the closer we ventured to the venue; an old building with a crowd and velvet rope blocking off the entrance. I paused to take in the sheer number of people that spilled out into Central Park. "Wow," I breathed.

Nina jumped up and down, nearly skipping down the street as people started to filter past us. At first I panicked, wondering if Thor would crash down onto us in retaliation of breaching mortals witnessing a Valkyrie in the flesh, but they hooted their marvel at my "costume" and grabbed the edges of wings attached to their back, spreading them and pretending to flap away.

"How are we supposed to get in?" Iris asked, her brow knitting with concern. "There're so many people. The main event can't hold so many."

Will seemed unconcerned. "Baldr wouldn't have gone through all this trouble to lure Val out if he wasn't going to let her inside." He turned to me and leaned in, lowering his voice. "This is where you're on your own, Val, but you have to find a way to get us all inside. Baldr won't expect you to be coming with friends."

I pinched my lips together and nodded, withdrawing my wings to allow Will to back away.

I matched each gaze in return, marveling how I'd made such close friends in such a short time. Paul smiled. "You can say it out loud, Val. The others would like to hear it."

Iris punched him in the ribs in punishment for reading my mind and he doubled-over, but I was already smiling.

"Paul's right," I said. "I've grown to care about all of you, and you care about me, even though I don't think I deserve it." I straightened and a breeze kicked away my metallic locks. I drew in a deep breath of New York's crisp night air. Something else was on the breeze. The tangy blood-sweet scent of Ragnarök drew close. "Even as a Frigg, I can't tell you the outcome of tonight. All I can say is that I know Baldr intends to use Tyler, and if he succeeds, Ragnarök will be unstoppable."

I glanced at Will, hoping to sense if there was any spike

of bitterness or jealousy, but I only sensed his calm resolve to help me in any way he knew how.

We marched on, myself in the lead and the array of my allies trailing behind me. When I reached the bouncer, I did a double take.

Shade, one of Dalia's men and a friend of Tyler. He gave me a grim-faced greeting. "Thought you might be here. Dalia sent me to make sure you gained entry." He unlocked the velvet rope and glanced over my shoulder. "Brought your friends, too?"

Tyler had warned me never to tell Shade who I was, but it sounded like word had somehow gotten out. I was the reason that Tyler had become a Valiant in the first place. He'd fought his Heimdall heritage any way he'd known how, and that included selling his soul to Odin, my father, for a chance to quell the misery of his curse. Each soul Freya fed him added another scar to his collection, and another promise that he would take the darkness in my stead.

I sensed the darkness now, its pull stronger without the purging fires of Muspelheim to keep it at bay. It called to me, whispered for me to reunite with Tyler and accept Ragnarök's cold embrace.

I shook my head and faced Shade. "Yes, we are all looking to get inside." I bit my lip before adding, "Tyler's in there. Whatever Baldr has told you, he plans on killing him and taking this whole planet down next."

Shade's face paled. He reminded me of Tyler in the way his midnight hair fell into his eyes and he had that kind of murderous look that was sexy all at the same time. He leaned in close. "I know. Baldr thinks he paid me off with a couple of vials of Yggdrasil sap." He shoved a vial into my hand. "Take it, and get rid of that bastard."

I closed my fingers around the prize and grimly nodded.

Flaring my wings, which awarded oohs and aahs from the crowd thinking I boasted some mechanical garb, I stepped into the darkness and prepared myself for the one thing I'd never faced before... the unknown.

*D*arkness swarmed inside the venue so thick that I couldn't even make out the crowd farther than a few feet in front of my face. Music thrummed and made the people sway as if it locked them into a trance. Wings moved, making me feel like I was in some kind of nightmare with the undead Valkyries of Muspelheim. My breath caught, expecting for Sam to launch out at me at any second and thrust accusations of my failure in my face.

A gentle touch at my arm brought me back to awareness. Will, flanked by our new allies, moved through the shadows. "You can do this," he whispered, then blended in with the crowd.

I hated how quickly I lost them and my fingers clutched at the empty space at my nape. I wilted. My necklace was gone and for the first time, I was going to have to do this on my own.

Then I heard a cry, the same one from my nightmarish vision that had brought me here. The shadows flashed as they surged with new power, and I spotted Tyler for just a split second before the platform went dark.

His gaze had met mine, and in that split second I knew what he was telling me to do.

Aerie... get out of here.

I wasn't going to listen to him and I clenched my fists as raw determination swept through me. I marched straight towards the platform. Pain ricocheted across my face when I slammed into an invisible wall and a chuckle sounded on the speakers.

"Well, sister, so glad you've decided to join us. I was just thinking your boyfriend was a poor excuse for a snack. Ragnarök would truly become unstoppable if I fed it a Frigg."

I slammed my fist against the invisible wall, awarding myself only strange looks from surrounding patrons who danced in a daze. When they refused to move, I shoved them out of the way with my wings.

Baldr appeared on the edge of the platform and grinned, looking manic and wild with his hair sticking out at all angles. Apparently using hair gel was his idea of a fashion statement. "I'm so disappointed that you haven't decided to join me. It's unfortunate, but I can rebuild this world with or without you." His grin widened. "Unfortunately, I'll have to destroy it before there's something worthy to rebuild. That's where your boyfriend comes in handy." Another male scream overrode the music and I beat against the wall as rage took over. Even without Muspelheim's link, my vision tinged with red. "Let him go and perhaps I won't kill you," I snapped.

He buckled over and held his stomach as he laughed.

"You really are my sister. Arrogant and oblivious to the very end."

Before I could retort, someone bumped into me from behind. I blinked at Paul.

He pretended to be drunk and laughed, tangling with my wings as we both tumbled to the ground. "He's terrified," he said, just loud enough that the music drowned out his words from anyone else who might be listening. "He's fed Ragnarök too much, and now it's out of control. Tyler is the only thing keeping it in check, but when it's done feeding on him, it's going to come after the next most powerful object."

I swallowed hard. Baldr had managed to unlatch Ragnarök from Muspelheim, meaning it'd already devoured what was left of the undead Valkyrie and the power offered by the planet's core. I could only hope that the Surtr still huddled in the protection of Jotunheim and I hadn't been too late. But now Ragnarök was here, and if Tyler was the only thing distracting it, the next most powerful object in Ragnarök's vicinity would either be Baldr... or me.

"And how many souls have you fed on?" I asked, shooting to my feet. "If I'm so oblivious, then why can I see you shaking?"

His spine shot rigid at my taunt, rage tinting his expression with a mixture of surprise. That's exactly the kind of reaction I'd been going for.

I used his hesitation to slam into the invisible wall again, because I knew it was some magic of his own creation. It hummed and dipped with the wrongness that reeked of his power. All I needed to do was break his concentration long enough to get through the barrier.

I didn't have to know that Michael was behind me. His mental shove sent me reeling into the wall hard enough for my head to spin… and to form a hairline crack.

Baldr snarled with primal rage and snapped his fingers, enacting the first round of his attack.

Half the crowd shifted before my very eyes. Flesh melted away, revealing the horror of the Skuld and their white bones shining through shadow. The other enemy was one I hadn't encountered before. Ice creatures with faces frosting over with splintered eyes screeched and the high-pitched cry made me buckle to my knees. Then I recalled the race of Jotun that had betrayed the gods long ago. The Skaoi, ice elementals that had settled in the folds of Neptune and likewise inhospitable planets frozen to the core—just like their hearts.

The crowd exploded and my Valkyrie allies launched into action, forming a barricade around me as I worked on the barrier.

A flash, another cry, and Tyler yanking at his chains. I had to hurry. This was the part of my vision that, if it came to fruition, meant Ragnarök would get exactly what it needed to become unstoppable.

"You are only making this worse!" I shouted. Rage tinted my vision red and I found the strength to summon my spear. I was so grateful that the weapon wasn't attached to the necklace I'd detached from my body and my soul. I wasn't a daughter of fire anymore, but I was still a Valkyrie; I was still a weapon that would seek justice.

I pierced the crack in the barrier with my blade and steadied my foot on the wall as I levered it back and forth. I thrust my wings to give me balance as I worked.

"You know nothing of Ragnarök!" Baldr bellowed, but I recognized the tinge of panic in his voice. "I've studied it all my life. What have you done? Played footsie with a Valiant and a human. You're pathetic."

I slammed the spear into the crack again and the barrier finally fell. I glanced over my shoulder once to check on my friends. They were holding off the attack, but just barely. Nina clawed at the face of one of the Skaoi, sending ice splintering everywhere. Red tinged the floor, betraying that not all humans had survived the onslaught. Michael levitated one of the Skuld in the air, containing the wisps of violent darkness before flinging it at another. Its neighbor invaded one of the humans, sending the man roaring towards Will. Will punched the man in the face and it went down, sending the Skuld unravelling with him. He glanced at me over his shoulder and gave me a nod.

I had to let them fight, and while they did their job, I had to do mine. I spread my wings and I did what a Valkyrie does best.

I launched, spear in hand, straight towards my enemy.

✴

Baldr grinned, and I knew at the last moment that I'd made a mistake.

He vanished, leaving me to fly face-first into yet another barrier. This time it snapped around me with finality and I found myself embraced by a familiar glittering darkness.

A male groan drew my attention and I crawled across broken glass until my fingers met chains.

I dismissed my spear in a puff of flame and ran my touch over the iron until I found ice-cold skin.

"Tyler?" I whispered, the word a desperate plea.

His hand gripped me with unexpected strength. "Aerie," he responded and the shadows cleared just enough for me to see his bloodied and bruised face. "You shouldn't have come here. It's a—"

I waved him away. "Yeah, yeah. It's a trap. I got that."

He smirked and my toes curled. Even now, with chaos rampaging all around us and certain doom hanging above our heads, he could make my breath catch with one of his wry grins. Then his gaze fell to my collarbone and his eyes went wide. "You don't have your necklace." His eyes shot back up. "You gave that up… for me?"

I swallowed hard. Of course I had. The only hesitation had been if it would be enough to save him, and now I wasn't so sure. Yet, as I wrapped my fingers around his and felt my heart slide into place alongside his, I knew that choosing Tyler would never be the wrong choice. "I couldn't just let you suffer."

He drew me in close and buried his face in my neck. He inhaled as if I was air itself and he'd drown without me. "Aerie. You're a beautiful fool."

Ice spread around my knees and a piercing cold made my legs go numb. "What is that?" I asked as a vibrant hum sounded all around us.

He held me tighter. "You don't have your mother to protect you anymore. Ragnarök can feed on you now."

Just before the glittering black descended on us, I drew out the vial that Shade had given me. I popped off the cork and downed it in one shot.

Heat blasted through me and my wings flared out with renewed embers. My eyes went wide, because this wasn't just some harvested sap from a Huldra honeycomb nest. This was the same stuff that had made up unadulterated Yggdrasil fruit.

I didn't question where Baldr had gotten his hands on such a rare and precious commodity—then again, he was a Frigg as well. It shouldn't have surprised me that he'd made his single trip to Yggdrasil and grabbed a fruit or two. He'd even found a way to harvest it into vials, enough to bribe Immortal bouncers to make sure the right people got into his "end of the world party."

Ragnarök wailed with such agony as it slammed into me, then bounced right back off. It wasn't just the power of Yggdrasil that gave me the strength to withstand its blow, but my acceptance of Tyler's hand in mine. His dark runes stood out stark against the pale marble skin of his body. Corded muscles boasted the scars and they slid over his knuckles and onto me. He'd taken on the shadows of the world for far too long. It was time that I accepted what I was. It was time that I accepted the dark connection that Tyler and I shared.

I stood, hand-in-hand with Tyler, as my skin glowed to life. The flames of Muspelheim renewed in me three-fold and shadows scurried away from my feet. Ice melted and the air steamed as I blazed. "I am your commander!" I bellowed up at the writhing void.

The glitter inside of Ragnarök's dark mass twinkled like a thousand stars, and now I knew what they were. Each diamond speck was a lost soul, a piece of a heart torn asunder and bound with so much suffering that it would never find peace. Ragnarök was a poor, pitiful creature that only knew how to devour, to destroy, all in an attempt to rid itself of its sorrow.

"Freya has trapped you for millennia and made your suffering grow," I said, my voice lowering.

The mass crooned and bellowed, snaps of black ice whipping around my face. It wasn't going to try to feed on me again, now while I glowed with the strength of a hundred suns. It lowered as if trying to get a better look at me and I stared, face-to-face, looking into the eyes of the underworld.

A thousand voices permeated my mind as Ragnarök tried to talk to me. In there somewhere was Sam, my lost sisters, even Will's mother. They all just wanted the suffering to end and my wings flared with embers at the distaste their rot left in my mouth.

There was only one way to save them. Only one way I'd been trained to deal with lost causes and enemies.

I summoned my spear and I slashed.

Ragnarök split in two and the wound I'd left behind glowed with a bright scar of purification and light. The blackness cracked all around, sending streaks of lightning followed by ear-breaking thunder to crash through the building. The upper floor peeled away in the crash of a tornado that hadn't quite touched down, leaving me an open view of the star-speckled sky.

Across Central Park humans cried out and the skies churned in response to their suffering. I swept out a hand, my powers as a Frigg humming to life as I slowed time for them.

The world kept spinning. Ragnarök continued to fall apart, but at least those impacted by the rampaging screams of chaos wouldn't have to endure it for much longer. I protected each one in a bubble of their own present moment, a gift that Will had taught me.

I banished what was left of Ragnarök to the low weight of the space-time net. With Yggdrasil's power running through my veins, I connected with the universe on a level I'd never experienced before. I knew its layers and its secrets and where Ragnarök could find its own present in time, away from suffering, away from worlds it only knew how to destroy.

When it was gone, I released my time stop on the humans. Distant groans sounded, followed by the low hum of Grimhildr kicking in for cleanup. I straightened, because surely that meant that Freya was still alive. And if she was, why had she left me to fend off Ragnarök all by myself?

Tyler spoke to my unanswered questions, showing no shame that he could read my mind. "Your parents love you more than you know," he said, his fingers wrapping around my chin and pulling me up to him. "Please don't hurt, Aerie."

Tears sizzled in my eyes and I was so grateful that Tyler could withstand my heat as a Valkyrie renewed. I couldn't bear to be without his touch just now. "Are they dead?"

A slow nod and my stomach dropped. "When Baldr sent you to earth… Odin activated the Mojinir."

My vision blurred, my tears coming too fast for my heat to wipe them out.

Muspelheim was gone. That's why Mojinir had come to earth. Odin had activated his last resort, destroying the planet so Ragnarök couldn't get any stronger. If he hadn't, I might never have been able to subdue it.

"But, I'm a Valkyrie," I said, the words not making logical sense. All I could think of was that I had nowhere to call home anymore. I was orphaned, alone. "Where will I go?"

He leaned in closer until our breaths mingled. "Aerie, my love. You are the Queen of Asgard."

The shock that came with that statement didn't prepare me for the full force of his kiss that he was no longer able to keep at bay. He crushed his mouth to mine and wound his arms around me to squeeze me close. His fingers tangled with my feathers, the sensitive nerves lighting up under his touch.

I returned his kiss with every ounce of fervor I'd denied myself before. Tyler had always been the one. He'd always been there for me and always held my heart.

"Ragnarök has been vanquished!" shouted Billy, who'd become my new overseer for matters concerning Asgardian management.

The crowds loved him. The Surtr had enough charm to go along with his wit and most importantly, his voice carried with undiluted adoration of his new queen.

It felt weird to be a queen, but as I sat on the throne with a wide back to accommodate my wings, Tyler slipped his fingers through mine, a stolen touch to help me feel grounded and in control.

Whenever we touched, our shadows mingled and his dark runes quivered over his body. Our love wouldn't bring about the end of the world… it would save it.

He grinned, and even though an entire city cheered and a purple sky danced above us, it felt like we were on our own little planet in our own rotating solar system, where he was the moon and I was the sun, forever revolving around one another in an endless cycle.

"Are you happy?" he asked as his fingers ran up my arm and he gave my wing a strong caress.

I shivered at the possessive touch. Tyler was mine, and I was his. I didn't care if everyone knew it. His internal glow radiated. He was free of Odin's bond and his dark runes gleamed on his bare skin covered only by a sheer, parted shirt. He preferred it this way, even if his corded muscles and rough lines running into a tight waistband made my cheeks permanently red. This was him, son of the Heimdall line and survivor of Ragnarök, his scars and suffering proudly on display. The sharp angles of his face as he gave me a wry smile broke any resolve I might have had, and I gravitated to him until our lips met and I answered his question the only way I knew how. I kissed him, wrapping my wings around us to give us a shield of privacy.

When I came up for breath, he laughed and his hands roamed my face. "Aerie. I'm happy too."

*Asgard had its new queen and Will eventually revealed to me what power it was he'd gained after accepting Yggdrasil's fruit.

The power to read hearts.

It wasn't like Paul who read literal thoughts. Will's power went so much deeper, reading intent and truth that even people couldn't admit to themselves.

A truth such as a certain Valkyrie having always loved Tyler.

Will and I had been bonded by a supernatural magic designed to bring Valkyrie and Soul together, a trusting relationship that was necessary for the reaping. I'd seen that bond turn into love with the outcasts, but as much as Will and I cared for one another, he'd been right. Our bond was a mixture of friendship and duty. He'd never deserved the curse placed on him, and I hadn't deserved the responsibility put on my shoulders. We'd managed to undo the hardships bound to us, but not without sacrifice and pain. He knew that my heart belonged to Tyr, and that it always would, which was why his sacrifice to push me away was the greatest one of all.

I watched him through one of Dalia's telescopes from time to time. Perhaps that's a bit creepy, but I wanted to make sure he was okay. I watched him grow; becoming a leader to the gifted men he'd saved with Yggdrasil's fruit. Dalia's Huldra also bonded with him, listened to him, and the vacuum left behind by the end of the Norse gods quickly filled with his charisma and candor.

Tonight he slipped away into Central Park as I'd seen him do a thousand times. There was a particular Huldra he'd been courting for some time now. It didn't surprise me that the carefree creatures were the only ones who could get him to come out of his shell. When his lips lowered onto a girl with frosted green leaves forming a crown at her brow, I smiled, glad he could find happiness, and lowered my telescope as I returned to my own life on Asgard where we built our family—and a new army.

Baldr had disappeared that night Ragnarök had been vanquished. There'd been no sign of Dalia either, and I wondered if they'd been sucked in by the massive sink Ragnarök had created during its departure, or if something more sinister was at play.

For Tyler's sake, I hoped his mother had survived.

For now, I stood out on my balcony and spread my wings, allowing my feathers to catch the warm sun's rays. Tyler's hands wrapped around my waist and his lips went to my neck, sending new shivers down my spine.

"Is everything all right?" he asked, his voice low and scratchy from sleep.

I wrapped my arms over his and indulged in the mixture of heat and ice he always stirred inside of me. Separated, we were just two broken souls. Together, we were healed, our rough edges sealing together until we became one.

"Everything is absolutely perfect."

THE END

Thank you for reading Valkyrie Allegiance! Please enjoy book 2: Valkyrie Rebellion.

Please take a moment to leave a review and help A.J. to reach more readership. It doesn't have to be much! "Loved it!" will do!

YA Fantasy Romance

Valkyrie Allegiance (A Complete Series)

Valkyrie Landing (Book 1)

Valkyrie Rebellion (Book 2)

Valkyrie Uprising (Book 3)

The Magical Realms Universe

Daughter of Dragons (Standalone)

Dragonrider Academy (Episode 1)

Dragonrider Academy (Episode 2)

Dragonrider Academy (Episode 3)

Dragonrider Academy (Episode 4)

Dragonrider Academy (Episode 5)

Dragonrider Academy (Episode 6)

Dragonrider Academy (Episode 7)

Season 2

Dragonrider Academy (Episode 8)

Crown Princess Academy (Book 1)

Crown Princess Academy (Book 2)

Celestial Downfall: Twisted Angelic Realms (Complete Series)

Fallen to Grace (Book 1)

Rise to Hope (Book 2)

Stand for Justice (Book 3)

Manor Saffron (Book 4)

Epic Fantasy

Soul Legacy: The Dweller Saga Duet

Soul Bound (Book 1)

Soul Child (Book 2)

The Ancient Realms Collection: Books 1-6

Grimdark Fantasy

GameLit

Reborn Online Book 1: Dungeon Worlds

Reborn Online Book 2: Dungeon Seeker

Reborn Online Book 3: Dungeon Master

Post Apocalypse

40 Days: Book 1 in the Atomic Fall Series

40 Weeks: Book 2 in the Atomic Fall Series